Duplicity

Also by Doris Davidson

Duplicity

and other stories

Doris Davidson

BIRLINN

First published in 2009 by
Birlinn Limited
West Newington House
10 Newington Road
Edinburgh
EH9 1QS

www.birlinn.co.uk

ISBN: 978 1 84158 824 7

British Library Cataloguing-in-Publication Data
A catalogue record for this book is available from the British Library

Typeset by Hewer Text (UK) Ltd, Edinburgh
Printed and bound by CPI Cox & Wyman, Reading

Dedicated to Doreen, my No. 1 fan right from the beginning, who died just before Christmas 2008.

Contents

Foreword

These short stories have been included in order to show my progress as a writer (if any). I had been a scribbler since my schooldays in the mid thirties, jotting down little tales for my own and my pals' amusement, although none of those were worth keeping. It was not until the late sixties that I had the urge to write for publication, and as you will see, very few of these stories were accepted, but I never threw any away. An apparent influx of aspiring authors cropping up then, it grew harder and harder to have anything accepted, and I gave up, promising myself that I would try again once I retired.

It was around 1985, aged sixty-three, before I got round to making another attempt, by which time I was set on writing a novel. It was 1989 before I was successful, when the fourth book I had written, *The Brow of the Gallowgate*, was accepted, and was published in 1990. Luckily, I had stored the other three, in order of writing *Time Shall Reap, The Road to Rowanbrae, Jam and Jeopardy*, which have all been published since then.

If any aspiring authors are reading this, take heart. Do not give up if no publishers seem to be interested. Make some improvements and try again, but – one piece of advice: – DO NOT OVERWORK ANYTHING. This leads to lacklustre prose, as does having too many long, unfamiliar words, which break into the actual plot.

Feel free to make your own judgement as to whether or not my writing has improved over the nineteen years since I wrote the first of my fifteen novels. Does practice really make perfect?

Never Marry A Policeman

Dorothy turned a page of the book she was reading and stretched lazily for her packet of cigarettes. As she pressed her lighter, she thought, this is the worst bit of being married to a policeman.

When David was on the two-to-ten shift, she was alone every evening; and he didn't always manage to come home at the proper time. Sometimes it was after midnight before she heard his key in the lock. Tonight seemed to be one of those nights – it was half past eleven now.

She laid down her book and walked across to the window, but could see nothing when she pulled back a corner of the curtain, and wearily let it drop again. She couldn't concentrate properly on what she was reading when David was so late. The thought that something could have happened to him always lurked in her mind. So many policemen were injured or killed nowadays in the course of their duty.

Sitting down in the armchair once again, she picked up the paperback. She had read only about half a page when a faint noise made her lift her head to listen. Was it David putting his key in the lock? After a moment or two without hearing anything else, she bent her head again.

Creak! There *was* someone there, and it couldn't be David; he'd have come straight in here. She listened again and there was silence for some time, then creak, creak, creak! Yes, someone was tiptoeing along the hall.

Dorothy didn't move. It might be a burglar. He could be armed and would shoot her if she opened the door. She couldn't even summon help on the telephone, for the telephone was in the hall. Her best plan would be to keep still and whoever was out there would think that she was asleep, or that she had gone out and left the light on for security.

Then she realised that he might come into the room to make sure. She shouldn't have persuaded David to make the house all electric. If they'd still had a coal fire, she could have used the poker to defend herself.

There had been no sound for a few minutes. Could she chance opening the door and using the phone? The man must still be there somewhere, though. He could be standing outside the door right now, listening for any movement. Her scalp prickled at the thought, and she concentrated all her powers of hearing on the door. Yes, she could clearly make out the regular rhythm of someone breathing heavily.

She had often heard people saying that their hair stood on end with fear, and she could understand it now, for she felt as if every strand of hair on her head was standing to attention. But was it with fear? She was really quite calm; calm, but inadequate. She could do nothing without giving away her presence. But – if she could hear his breathing the man out there would surely hear hers. Holding her

2

breath, she was relieved to hear the creak, creak, creak of the floorboards once again.

He was going towards the kitchen, so she exhaled slowly and could hear definite movements. What could he be doing through there? Did he imagine that people kept their valuables in their kitchens? Surely not. A more sinister explanation came to her. He might not be a burglar at all. He could be a KILLER. He could be looking for something to use as a murder weapon. The bread knife? The meat carver? A hammer?

David kept some tools in the bottom drawer of the kitchen cabinet. Yes, murderers usually prefer a blunt instrument. What would her husband do if he came home and found her lying in a pool of blood? Oh, David, please come home before it's too late.

That was a drawer being closed. Had he found a suitable weapon? It dawned on her that she was now sitting erect in her chair, her white knuckles desperately gripping the arms. This was fear! She had turned stone cold, though rivulets of perspiration ran down her face and between her shoulder blades.

She riveted her gaze to the door handle as the footsteps drew nearer and nearer. They stopped right outside the door! In stark terror, she watched the handle slowly turning until it was at its furthest point and the door opened slightly.

A scream dying in her throat before it actually started, she saw the handle being silently returned to its proper position and heard the footsteps retreating to the kitchen. He must have remembered something, something bigger and better for the job he meant to do. At that moment, her eyes caught sight of a lamp on the coffee table near the door. It had been made from a solid brass candlestick David's father had given them when his wife died.

If only she could reach it before the murderer came in, she could use it to defend herself. Easing herself out of the chair, she took three quick steps and positioned herself behind the door. She picked up the lamp, gripping it by the neck, and stood ready to swing it as the intruder came back towards her. Terror gave her unsuspected strength, and as the door swung open, she struck with all her might.

She felt the heavy base of the lamp crunch sickeningly into the man's skull and leaned back against the wall exhausted, but thankful that the body now lying crumpled in the doorway was not hers. She would have to telephone the Police Station now and report what she had done. After all, it had been self-defence – there would be no doubt about that – and David would be very proud of her.

Bracing herself, she stepped carefully over the man's feet and switched on the hall light, but as she dialled the familiar number, she turned and saw, sitting on the hall table, a tray set for two.

Horror dawning, her eyes travelled slowly round and down to David's body lying in a pool of blood on the floor.

***

Word count: 1017

Published in the *Sunday Mail*, 8 August 1971

If I remember correctly, I received the marvellous amount of £16, but since it was the first short story I'd ever had published, I was absolutely delighted. I WAS A PROFESSIONAL AUTHOR!

The Witch

Peter's granny lived in an old tenement in Mill Street. She kept a jar full of lovely sticky sweeties, and she spoilt him outrageously, so he loved going to see her.

'Ach, he's only a bairn, Mary,' she would say when his mother scolded him for doing something he shouldn't.

The only thing he didn't like about Mill Street was Aul' Babbie, who lived on the ground floor of the same tenement as his granny. He was terrified of Aul' Babbie. She was very old – over a hundred, Peter thought – but that wasn't what scared him. She had a hooked nose, a long, pointed chin and straight, straggly hair. She was the personification of all the pictures of witches he had ever seen. Her face wasn't green, of course, but when she opened her mouth you could see her two broken teeth. No more, just the two broken teeth.

The children of Mill Street liked to torment her. When they played hide and seek, they would hide in the dark lobby outside her door, and run away laughing if she came out to see who was making a noise. She usually did.

'Get awa' oot o' here!' she would shout, 'an' leave an aul' body in peace.'

They would shout back, knowing that she was too

crippled to chase them, and she usually went back inside her house and slammed her door. Peter joined in their games when he was visiting his granny, and would shout as loud as the rest of them when Aul' Babbie was on the warpath.

'Ye young hooligans!' she was liable to shout at them. 'Ah'd murder the lot o' ye if Ah got ma han's on ye.'

'Canna catch me, canna catch me, Aul' Babbie canna catch me,' they would chant, and take to their heels.

'Ah ken fine fa ye are,' she would cry and shake her stick at them. 'Ah'll tell yer ma's on ye. An' you, Peter Ritchie, Ah'll tell yer granny.'

The children knew that she never carried out her threats, but Peter had a huge worry of his own. What if Aul' Babbie lay in wait for him in that dark lobby? She could grab him as he passed to go upstairs to his granny's house. She could take him inside and torture him to pay him back for all the times he had annoyed her. She might even murder him and nobody would ever know what had happened to him.

'I wish the old witch was dead,' he whispered to himself. But witches never die.

When Hogmanay came round with all its festivities, Peter was staying with his granny. He wasn't allowed to see in the New Year, but he didn't mind that, because there were always some 'first-fitters' who came later on through New Year's Day.

In the afternoon, there were about five extra people in the house when another knock was heard. Peter rushed to answer the door, ready to shout 'Happy New Year' to whoever might be there. The words froze on his lips when he saw Aul' Babbie standing on the landing. She made her way past him, surely more unsteady on her feet than usual. He closed the door and slowly followed her into his granny's kitchen.

He couldn't believe his eyes. Aul' Babbie was laughing and joking with the other folk. He had never heard her laughing before and noticed that it was more of a cackle than a laugh.

Definitely a witch's laugh. More convinced than ever, he sat down close beside his mother and silently prayed that Aul' Babbie wouldn't stay long.

Surprisingly, his prayer was answered. She stayed only long enough to get a dram and a piece of his granny's home-made black bun, then rose to go. As she passed him, he saw, with horror, her bony hand coming out to touch him. He closed his eyes tightly and gripped the side of his chair.

She merely patted him on the head. 'That's a richt fine laddie ye've got, Mary,' she said to his mother. Peter let his breath out slowly and opened his eyes to see the old woman hobbling to the door.

His granny had just come back from seeing Aul' Babbie out when they heard a great thump and a rumbling noise.

'The drunk aul' fool has fa'en doon the stair,' said Mr Duff, who lived across the landing.

They all ran out to see if she was hurt, leaving Peter by himself. He felt too numb with horror to move. If she was dead, it would be his fault for wishing her dead, he thought. She would know he was to blame and she'd come back to haunt him. By the time they all came back, he had worked himself into a terrible state.

He looked at their faces, trying to read the answer to his unspoken question. 'Is she . . . dead?' he managed to ask, at last.

'Na, na, laddie,' his granny assured him, 'but she fell fae the top step richt doon to the next landin'. Poor aul' sowl. As if ha'in' a wooden leg wasna bad enough, noo she's broke her good ane.'

Peter gaped at her. 'What did you say, Granny? About a wooden leg?'

'Mercy me, bairn. Did ye nae ken she had a wooden leg?'

The boy's spirits lifted as he realised what this information meant to him. Never again need he be scared at Aul' Babbie. She was just an ordinary old woman after all.

Whoever had heard of a witch with a wooden leg?

***

Word count: 929.

Published in the *Kincardineshire Observer*, 14 April 1972

Written at the end of 1971 and sent to at least three magazines. I can't remember which, but it was rejected pretty quickly each time. Then I took a chance and sent it to a weekly newspaper printed out of Aberdeen. It was not a 'freebie' (it cost 2d per week), and published news local to its area, and this being my husband's birthplace, we had it delivered. I had noticed that it always included a very short story, and I felt that *The Witch* was as good as any of them.

I got a phone call saying that they bought all their stories from other publications and could only offer me £1 for it, although it was better than the stories they usually printed. It wasn't what I had expected, but what the heck? At least it was a payment and it would be printed.

A Gift From William

The story which the teacher had told the class that afternoon had made a deep impression on William. Fancy a baby getting all those presents from people who came to see it.

His sister's baby hadn't got any gifts, for nobody had come to see it. There must be something wrong with it, because Mary had been crying ever since she'd brought it home. She hadn't been pleased about her baby like that other Mary in the story. Jesus must really have been a wonderful baby, William thought, to make everyone so happy.

His mother didn't think much of Mary's baby, either, not as far as he could gather. 'I can't understand why Mary won't just have it adopted,' she had said to his father. 'People would soon forget, if the child wasn't here as a constant reminder.'

'Well, she wants to keep it,' his father had answered, 'and there's nothing you can do about it, dear. After all, it's her life.'

'You don't understand either, Bill. It's the disgrace.'

His father had patted his mother's shoulder. 'It'll soon be forgotten, love – a nine days' wonder.'

11

William hadn't understood half of their conversation, but he realised that his mother didn't want the baby in the house. He decided he had better take a close look to see if he could find out what was wrong with the baby to make everyone so unhappy.

He knew that his mother and Mary were in the kitchen, so he went over to the pram standing in the corner and peered down at the little face which was all that was showing above the covers. He had half expected to see something horrible and was pleasantly surprised to find that it looked much the same as any other baby he had seen. In fact, it was quite pretty, like a doll in its pink jacket and its eyes shut.

But, if the baby looked so beautiful, why were his mother and Mary so unhappy about it? He puzzled over it for some time, then suddenly it came to him. It was because nobody had come to see it, or give it gifts, but he could put that right. Yes, he could give the baby a Christmas gift and make it just like the Baby Jesus.

He didn't have any money, though. He wondered if there was anything he could sell, but his train set was broken, so no one would want to buy that. Nothing else he had was worth very much.

Wait – there was the new winter coat his mother had bought him. Anyone would pay a lot of money for such a beautiful coat – lovely and hairy, with five leather buttons to fasten it. He had felt like a prince the only time he had worn it. He didn't want to sell it, the best coat he had ever had, but if it would make his mother and Mary happier about the baby he would willingly give it up. He would get a few pounds for it, he was sure, and he could buy a really good present with money like that. Not gold or myrrh or that other precious stuff, of course, but something worth giving.

But – what would his mother say about him selling the coat? He remembered hearing her tell his father that coats for children were very expensive nowadays. 'I'll just have to make do with my old winter coat,' she had said. 'William has grown out of his and he'll have to get a new one.'

No, it wouldn't be a good idea to sell it; his mother would probably be angry with him. Or else she would start crying, and he didn't want to see her crying any more – she cried too much already. What could he do?

Just then, Mary came in to change the baby, a process that usually made William so embarrassed that he left the room, but today he was so preoccupied that he didn't even notice. Mary took the baby over to him when she was finished. 'Keep an eye on her for me, William, till I wash the nappies, there's a good lad.'

He looked at the baby who gave a little mew and opened her eyes, so he hastily laid her down in the pram and gave it a gentle rock. 'I'm going to bring you a gift,' he announced decisively. 'I don't know how I'm going to manage it, but I promise you I am. I'll let them see that I like you, little . . .'

He stopped, aghast. This baby didn't even have a name. Mary always said, 'the baby', while his mother usually called it 'that child'. So *that's* why they were always crying – no one had remembered to give it a name. *Whoopee!* He would give the baby a name for a Christmas gift; what a wonderful idea. Nobody had thought of it and it wouldn't cost anything. He would pick a really magnificent name and make all the family proud of him – and of the baby.

When Mary came back, he went up to his own room and thought over all the girls' names he knew. What about the girls in his class at school? One of their names might do.

Lynne? No, she had a spotty face.

Susan? She nipped you when you weren't looking.

Lorraine? He liked Lorraine, and thought she was pretty, but lots of girls were called Lorraine, and he wanted something special.

This was much more difficult than he had imagined. He looked at his books to see if he could find a better name there.

Alice in Wonderland? The name Alice didn't seem to fit the baby.

Hansel and Gretel? He quite liked the idea of Gretel, it was unusual, but he didn't think his mother and Mary would like it.

'Tea's ready, William,' called his mother.

After teatime, he went back to his room and lay down on his bed. He wondered how babies ever got names if it was so difficult to choose them. By the time he went to bed, he still hadn't hadn't found a name, and he tossed and turned for what felt like hours before he fell asleep.

He dreamed of that first Christmas, of how the Angel Gabriel appeared to Mary and told her that she would have a son, of how the Angel told the shepherds in the fields when the Baby Jesus was born, of all the gifts the Three Kings brought.

When he woke in the morning, he knew that somewhere in his dream was the name he was seeking, but he couldn't think what it might have been. Then he remembered! The Angel Gabriel! That was it – what a perfect name for the baby! 'Angel Gabriel.' He said it slowly, letting it roll round his tongue and savouring the beauty of the sound. He could bet that no other baby ever had a name like that.

He froze, suddenly. How could he make a proper gift of a name? It wasn't something you could wrap up in Christmassy paper or put in a fancy box, and he did so want to make it a good gift. A gift card! He had seen them in the shops with pretty pictures on them, and they just had to go in an envelope. He couldn't buy one, of course, but he could try to make one. He could write the name on a piece of paper in his best, joined-up writing, the kind they were learning at school.

He rummaged about in his toy box, looking for his drawing book, and at last he found it – luckily with a few empty pages. Tearing them out carefully, he searched for his packet of felt pens. A red one was all he could find, but it would do. Red was a nice, cheerful colour. He went down on his knees and laid the book on his bed, putting one of the blank pages on top.

He made a mistake on the first page, and it wasn't until his third attempt – on the last page – that he was satisfied that he had done his best writing. He studied it critically. It didn't seem much for a gift of such importance, but he could draw something on it to brighten it up. What would a baby like? He drew a little butterfly for a start and it looked quite good, so he drew a few more. Then he decided it needed a fancy pattern around the edge, so he spent the next half-hour making little squiggles all the way around. He propped the card against the mirror on his dressing table, and stood back to admire the effect. It looked really good, he thought, and all he needed now was an envelope.

He took the strongest white envelope he could find in his father's bureau, slipped the card inside and licked the flap. Thumping it vigorously to make it stick down properly, he let out a long sigh of satisfaction. All that remained to be done was to write on the front, and it didn't matter so much about that. The card was the real gift, the special gift.

With love from William, he wrote, laboriously, then placed the envelope with its precious contents inside the drawing book. He would give it to the baby tomorrow; that was Christmas Day, the proper day.

William went about for the rest of that day with a secretive smile on his face, making his mother wonder what mischief he was hatching, but as he was behaving rather well otherwise, she didn't upset him by asking any questions.

Once, when no one else was in the room for a few moments, he moved over to the pram. 'Angel Gabriel,' he said, experimentally. The infant hiccoughed and opened her eyes, then to William's delight, a smile passed across the tiny face. This convinced him that she liked the name and he gave a whoop of joy, causing his mother to pause in her preparations for the next day to listen for the crash which inevitably followed the familiar noise. Nothing happened, however, so she shrugged her shoulders and carried on.

When he was hanging up his stocking that night, a disturbing thought bothered William. 'Mum,' he said, 'will Santa know about the baby?'

She didn't answer immediately, and he looked anxiously into her face. She looked as if she might cry again, so he put his arm round her neck. 'Mum,' he repeated, 'will you hang up a stocking for . . . it?' He had nearly given his secret away.

She gave him an unexpected hug. 'Yes, darling, I will. Santa won't forget her, I promise.'

William rose before anyone else was up and ran downstairs to see what Santa had brought him. He enjoyed opening the packages, but he knew his greatest thrill would come when the baby's envelope was opened. Making sure that indeed there were other gifts for the infant, he took the envelope out of his pyjama-top pocket and pushed it well down into the other stocking – like his, one of his father's large golfing socks. It was going to be a happy Christmas after all.

He could scarcely contain his excitement until the rest of the family came down, and when at last Mary starting taking the things out of the baby's stocking, he held his breath in glorious anticipation.

'Oh, thank you, Mum. Thank you very much.' Mary's

voice was choked as she shook out a lovely lemon pram cover. 'Dad. This is gorgeous.' She held up a furry teddy bear for William to see.

He was wondering why she was thanking them for the things that Santa had brought when he heard her say, 'What's this?'

He lifted his head and saw that she was looking at the envelope – his envelope. His heart began to beat faster, but with studied nonchalance, he murmured, 'It's my gift to . . .' He stopped. He had nearly given the game away, again, 'To . . . to . . . it,' he finished, lamely, pointing to the pram.

His sister opened the envelope, read the card and passed it over to her mother and William felt a great weight descending on him They didn't like the name – they would have said something if they did.

Then his mother said, 'What does it mean, William?'

He looked down at his slippers,, his face scarlet. 'It's my gift to the baby,'he said, doggedly. 'It's a name for it.'

'But why?' Mary was obviously puzzled.

This was when the boy decided to tell the whole truth, so he stood up and looked her straight in the eyes. 'Well, Mum and you don't seem to like it, and nobody ever gave it any presents, not until Santa came last night. Babies should get gifts, like the Baby Jesus. And it didn't even have a name.'

Mary ran out of the room at that, but before he could say anything, his mother followed her. He looked across at his father, who signed to him to sit down and eat his breakfast. Each mouthful of cereal tasted like sawdust to him, and he was just about to excuse himself from the table when the two women came back. He stared at them in surprise; they had their arms round each other and were laughing and crying at the same time.

Mary stretched out her free arm and pulled him to her. 'Oh, William, it's a lovely gift, and you don't know how much it means to me.'

'It wasn't for you,' he objected. 'It was for Angel Gabriel.'

His mother patted his cheek. 'I'm afraid we can't call her Angel Gabriel, darling, because that was a man, but it was a really good idea, just the same.'

He swallowed to get rid of the lump in his throat, but couldn't trust himself to speak. His mind was a jumble of confused thoughts. They didn't like the name he had so carefully chosen. There couldn't be a man angel, he'd never heard of that before. All angels were beautiful girls, he had always believed. But his mum knew everything, and she was always right. That meant that his gift to the baby was useless.

Mary saw the bitter disappointment in his face and wished she could comfort him. He had gone to a lot of trouble to try to make the family happy. 'I know, William!' she cried suddenly, as an idea occurred to her. 'We'll call her Gabrielle for short. But we'll always know she was named after an angel, and that it was your idea.' She watched him anxiously as a teardrop spilled over and trickled down his cheek.

After a moment or two, however, his face cleared. 'Gabrielle?' he whispered.

Oh, yes, he thought, it sounded nearly as good as the name he had chosen. 'Gabrielle,' he repeated. It sounded better the more he said it. His gift was a success after all.

***

Word count 2506

Published in *Woman's Way*, December 1973

This magazine stopped being published not long after this story was printed, and I sincerely hope that I wasn't the cause of its demise . . .

The Night Before Christmas

Whooo-ooo-ooo! The whistling of the wind coming in round the window frame was annoying rather than frightening, and the two slight figures huddled by the fireplace were suitably annoyed.

'Why has somebody not done something about the window before this, Archie?' the younger one said mournfully.

'How would I know? It's a damned disgrace after all this time. I remember when I was a laddie . . .'

'Ach, not again man. I'm tired of hearing about when you were a laddie. It's the same every winter, like the cold did something to your brains.'

'Oh, well I'm very sorry.' Archie, the elder by a good number of years, sounded quite offended. 'I was only saying . . .'

'I know what you were only saying, but I'm saying . . .'

Whooooosh!! They both jumped back as a fluff of soot came spewing down the chimney.

'Ach, the wind's changing.' Archie shook his head in disgust. 'I suppose you'll be saying next that somebody should block up the lum.'

'There's no need for you to be sarcastic.' Fergus was

21

offended now. 'We shouldna have to freeze like this every winter.'

Archie was silent, his white head hunched into his shoulders, his arms clasped round his middle, while Fergus regarded him sadly. 'It's bad enough the rest of the winter, but to be as cold as this on the night before Christmas . . . it doesna seem right.'

'Whisht, man.' Archie lifted his head as a distant clanking came to his ears.

'What is it, Archie? Are you hearing something?'

'I would be hearing something if you didna keep speaking.'

They both strained their ears for a few moments, but the noise was not repeated. 'What was it you thought you heard?' Fergus persisted.

'I didna *think* I heard something, I *did* hear something,' Archie snapped.

Realising that he was getting nowhere, Fergus changed his tactics. 'If you would tell me what you *did* hear, seeing your hearing's apparently better than mine, we might be able to settle down again.'

Archie was only slightly mollified by the back-handed compliment. 'It was chains rattling,' he volunteered.

'Ch . . . chains? Ghosts, d'you mean?' The younger man was very agitated now.

'Huh!' Archie snorted. 'There's been nothing like that in this place for as long as I've been here.'

'That doesna mean to say . . .' Fergus was stopped by a malevolent glare.

'I thought I could hear something else, man. Would

you just keep your big mouth shut for a while? You never stop blethering.'

Fergus grimaced and said no more, but he looked even more alarmed at the sound of approaching footsteps in the corridor outside. His head jerked up, but Archie motioned to him to be still. The footsteps drew nearer.

'We'd better get out of sight,' Archie whispered. 'We don't want anybody to know we're here. We'll just have to wait and see who they are and what they do.'

They stood up noiselessly, and went to crouch behind the dilapidated sofa by the far wall. In a few seconds, the door creaked slowly open.

'I canna see a thing in here,' a deep voice said, peevishly. 'Hold up the lantern, Sandy.'

An arc of pale light swept round the room, growing brighter as the bearer advanced, and Archie had to hold Fergus back from poking up his head to have a look.

'It's an awful big room, Donald,' said another voice with less resonance.

'It is that, and just look at that fireplace. It's big enough to roast an ox.'

'You'd never want to roast an ox, surely?'

'It's just a saying.' Donald sounded rather exasperated. 'And that couch. It could seat six, I wouldna be surprised.'

The lantern now illuminating the area around their hiding place, Archie and Fergus remained absolutely motionless until the beam swung away again. They had been unable to look before, but with the light not focused in their direction any longer, they took the chance to peep over the low back of their shield. At first, all they could see was the lantern, because everything behind it was in darkness, but as the light moved round, they could see two shadowy shapes. One was round and small, but the other was huge.

They looked at each other in dismay, and with his mouth against Fergus's ear, Archie whispered, 'We'll have to scare them away.'

Fergus turned his head and put out his hand to find the other man's olfactory organ. 'You canna scare them away, if they're ghosts,' he muttered into it.

Archie gave him a push, and started to moan softly.

'What was that, Donald?' One of the newcomers stood still to listen. 'Did you say something?'

'I thought it was you, Sandy.'

Both voices held a deep note of apprehension, so Archie moaned again, a little louder this time and Fergus joined in, an octave higher, more a screech than a groan.

There was dead silence when they stopped. The two figures in the middle of the room stood as though transfixed. 'It sounds like g . . . ghosts,' Donald said at last, his voice low and quivering.

'You never said nothing to me about the place having ghosts,' Sandy said, nervously.

'Nobody never said nothing about it to me, either, and I'm not paying good money for a haunted castle, even if it is cheap. Come on, let's get out of here.'

To convince them, Archie moaned again. He didn't fancy strangers moving in and upsetting their placid existence.

'I thought it was cheap because it was needing a lot of

repairs,' Sandy observed slightly unsteadily, as they moved towards the door, 'and I was quite willing to give you a hand to fix things up and get rid of the draught there would likely be, but . . .'

The door closed behind them with a loud click, their footsteps echoed along the corridor and died away, then the heavy portal clanged and there was the sound of chains and lock being secured.

'You see what you did?' Archie exclaimed, accusingly. 'If you hadna been so sure they were ghosts, they'd have bought the castle and fixed things up, and we'd have been warm every winter instead of near freezing into snowmen.'

'It was your idea to scare them away,' Fergus said, child-ishly, 'for I thought the little one might be Santy Claus, and I've aye wanted to see him, ever since I was . . .'

'For any sake, man! It's your brains that get touched wi' the cold, I'm thinking.'

'You're as bad!' Fergus retorted, trying to have the last word for a change. 'If they *had* been ghosts, they wouldna have been frightened of other ghosts, now would they?'

'You were,' said Archie dryly, and walked through the wall.

***

Word count: 1138

This ghost story was written in February 1977 for a school puppet show and was very well received. Because of its theme, and also because I had no idea where to send it, I did not attempt to have it published.

Monte Meets The Conquistadores

Monte watched his grandmother expertly turning the cakes which she was baking on the flat stone in the heart of the fire outside the house.

'No one in all Mexico can make such tortillas as my grandmother,' he boasted.

Marilia, his friend ever since they could crawl, was sitting beside him, marvelling at the deft way the old lady used her hands to flatten and shape the cakes. The girl wanted to see everything, to learn how to be as quick as Monte's grandmother. She was to marry Monte in two years, when they both reached the age of twelve, and she wanted to be a good wife to him.

In a few minutes, the old lady piled the tortillas on to a flat wooden platter. 'That will be enough,' she said smiling, as she handed the plate to Monte, who took two, giving one to Marilia and biting hungrily into the other.

'Grandmother, tell us about Montezuma, King of all the Aztecs,' he begged. He loved to hear about their king, the greatest king who had ever lived, after whom he had been named.

'I have told you many times,' the old woman said. She

was now sitting cross-legged, like the children, on the ground.

But the boy knew that she liked to tell about the journey she had made as a young woman – over the mountains to see Montezuma's Palace in the lake city of Tenochtitlan. 'Please, my grandmother, tell us again.'

'We Aztecs are blessed by our gods to have such a good king,' she began. 'His palace is within the city's walls, next to the Temple of the Humming Bird. It is large, very large.' Her brown wrinkled face had a faraway look as she recalled the wonder she had felt when she had seen it, so majestic in the waters of the lake.

'How many bedrooms did it have, Grandmother?' prompted Monte, although he already knew the answer. He never tired of listening to her tale.

'Over a hundred, each one with a stone bath and running water.' Her tone was hushed in reverence.

Overcome by the thought of such magnificence, Marilia asked, 'Was the palace the only large building, Old One?'

'Oh, no. There were many temples, each to a different god, and another palace that had belonged to Montezuma's father. There were streets, and canals, and fountains, and many, many wonderful houses. There were other buildings also, where young ones like you could learn how to read, and write, and count. All those things were started by the great Montezuma himself, and the houses he built for his lords were all made of stone.'

The grandmother rose and brushed the dust from her long black skirt. 'Go now, Monte, my boy, and gather some wood for the fire, before your father comes back from the fields.' She pulled her embroidered shawl back off her head, bent down and passed through the low open doorway of the mud house which was their home.

Marilia accompanied her friend to help him gather the wood, and they made their way down the steep mountain path. 'What a great king Montezuma must be,' she whispered as they stepped carefully through the stones. 'Building all those beautiful places and caring so much for his people.'

'My father says that he is not always so good,' Monte told her. 'He says that the gods the king worships are cruel and they have to be fed with human hearts. He sends out his tax-gatherers and any person who cannot pay his taxes is taken back to Tenochtitlan and given to the gods as a sacrifice.'

Marilia shivered. 'He does not sound so good after all, this Montezuma.'

'He is good in all other things. It is only his religion that is cruel. Father says the king lives in fear of the god Quetzalcoatl – the feathered serpent – who was driven out of the kingdom by the other gods hundreds of years ago. The sacred books foretell that he will come back to claim the city in the year of One Reed.'

Turning pale, Marilia grabbed his arm. 'But this is the year of One Reed. I heard my father say so.'

Monte nodded. 'That is why the king is so afraid. The traders and the men at the market have told my father that there is news of a great army coming to capture Tenochtitlan.'

She looked at him with pride. He knew everything that

went on in the world, but she did hope that what his father had heard was not true.

They were alarmed at that moment by the sound of someone shouting, although it was difficult to judge how far off the person was because of the echoes from the surrounding mountains. To their relief, a moment later a man came running round the bend in the path.

'Father!' cried the boy, but the terror in the man's eyes made him add, 'What is wrong?'

It was some time before his father could find enough breath to tell them, and Marilia felt herself starting to shake in fear at the thought of what he might be going to say.

'The great army is coming,' he managed to gasp at last. 'I was finishing my work in the main field when I saw clouds of dust in the distance. I waited until I could see what was causing this – sometimes the llamas stampede if they are frightened by a rattlesnake or a puma – then I saw them. Many, many men are on their way with banners and flags. The god Quetzalcoatl must have sent them to destroy Montezuma's kingdom.'

'But what are we to do, Father?' The boy asked as the man started to run again.

'I do not know, my son, but we must go home at once.'

The grandmother was not so easily alarmed. 'The army will not harm us if we do not put up a fight,' she said when her son had breathlessly given her the news. 'If Quetzalcoatl sent them, they will want only to capture Montezuma's city. He must be warned.'

'I will go,' offered Monte. 'I will take the mule and ride over the mountain. The great city lies at the foot of the other side, does it not?' He knew that from his grandmother's stories.

She spent no time in arguing, but cut some tortilla, laid out some fruit and a flask of goat's milk on one of her shawls, tied them up and handed over the bundle. 'Take this to eat. It is a long, long journey to Tenochtitlan.'

As he passed other mud huts like his own, Monte pointed back and shouted, 'The army is coming! They have come to destroy the king's city.'

It took some hours for the boy and the mule to clamber up the rocky mountain, and when they reached the top, Monte halted the sturdy little animal and stared down in surprise. He had always known that the city of Tenochtitlan was beautiful, but even from his grandmother's descriptions of it he had never imagined anything as large as the panorama spread out in the valley below.

It was not until he was much nearer that he could see the white buildings and giant temples reflected in the waters of the lake – the fabulous Halls of Montezuma. As he tore his eyes away from the glorious sight and looked around him, he saw smoke rising from another mountain not very far off. The Mountain of Fire. He had heard his grandmother speak of it, and she had said its real name was Popocatépetl.

Gaining renewed strength, Monte urged the mule onwards. He could not bear the thought of the beautiful city being invaded by enemies. His father had told him that the Sacred Book foretold this, and that the invaders were to be led by a tall, white-skinned, black-bearded man, whose followers would unleash thunder and lightning on Tenochtitlan.

After another hour or so, he heard what sounded like the hooves of many mules, but coming much faster than mules could travel. Looking over his shoulder, he saw about fifteen men riding strange animals, larger than mules and much more impressive. This was no great army, so he relaxed and waited for the men to catch up with him.

As they passed, they shouted to him in words which he could not understand, and carried on down the path. He urged his sturdy steed forward again, but the beast was exhausted from the long hours they had been travelling, and could go at only a very slow pace.

Some time later, he again heard sounds behind him and turned round. This time, it was indeed an army, descending on Montezuma's city, now only a few miles off. Dismounting, he led his mule to some nearby bushes; from this hiding place he watched while hundreds of men rode past. Leading them, on an animal like those which had passed before, was a tall man, white-skinned and black-bearded, just as the Sacred Book said. After him came men with crossbows, men with chained hounds and last of all came men with strange rods in their hands.

He watched while they entered a small village farther down the mountain, with mud houses like his own. Some of the Aztec men tried to stop the army from going on, but suddenly the men at the rear of the line took up their strange rods and made thunder and lightning spit past the local men, making them jump back in alarm. He waited until the army had moved on, and then rode into the village.

'Who are they?' he asked one of the wailing women, who had come out in curiosity.

'He said his name is Hernando Cortez,' she answered. 'He has come to capture Montezuma's wonderful city. He comes from a land called Spain, far across the ocean, and they have conquered the rest of Mexico – the Maya, the Toltecs and all the smaller tribes – and now he wants to claim Tenochtitlan and all of Montezuma's gold and treasures for his own king. He called his men conquistadors, and they mean to capture the city with their crossbows and rifles. The rifles are what made the thunder and lightning. Fifteen men on horses – the strange animals are called horses – have gone on before. Cortez said there will be no bloodshed if our king gives up peacefully.'

It was too late now for Monte to warn the king, but he carried on down the mountain path, anxious to find out what was happening. When he neared the city, he saw that Montezuma himself had come to the gates, and was waiting at the end of the broad causeway which had been built across the lake as an entrance. His golden throne was carried by eight lords in silken robes, and his jewelled crown was also decorated with green plumes. Even the soles of his sandals – visible from the way he was sitting – looked to be made of pure gold.

The boy lay down behind a group of bushes to watch and to listen. Surely the great king would be able to stop this army from plundering the city?

When Cortez and the conquistadors came closer to

him, Montezuma looked scared, but ordered his bearers to lower him to the ground so that he could speak to the strangers. Monte wished that he could hear better, so he crept as close as he dared. Cortez had dismounted from his horse and faced the king boldly.

'If the god Quetzalcotl has sent you to destroy my city,' Montezuma said, 'I beg you to listen. I will give you all my gold and jewels and any other riches you want, if you will leave all the buildings I have worked so long to have erected.'

Monte's eye was caught by a man in plain clothes who appeared then. The face was familiar but it was a moment or so before the boy recognised him to be the Wise One, who travelled amongst the villages on the mountain, and who was said to have visited many foreign lands. He went fearlessly up to the leader of the army and was translating what the king had said. Cortez listened carefully, then turned and spoke to two of his men, who stepped up to the king and took hold of his arms.

Monte held his breath. Were they going to kill Montezuma? But the king smiled, and they all went inside the city gates – the king and the two men holding him, Cortez and the Wise One.

The rest of the Spanish army were standing outside the walls, so Monte plucked up his courage and walked past them, into the city where the Aztecs were murmuring together. 'They have taken our king a prisoner,' said one man.

'We must fight the enemy,' said another. 'They must not destroy our lovely city.'

One of the lords stepped forward now. 'They will kill Montezuma. Without a king we will be lost, and they will kill us all.'

'I will be your king.' A tall, cruel-faced man pushed himself forward. 'Montezuma is a coward and will put up no fight, but I will lead you to victory.'

Some of the other men cheered, but Monte heard one woman whisper to her husband, 'He is wicked, that one. Many men will die before he, too, is killed.'

The husband nodded. 'He could never be as good a king as Montezuma.'

Cortez, who had been talking with the king and trying to reach an agreement, suddenly brought him out to the city walls to tell his people what had been decided. Most of the Aztecs went down on their knees to show their king that they believed in him, but the self-appointed ruler issued orders to the slingers to let loose their ammunition on the invaders. With the first volley, Montezuma himself was struck on the head by a stone and fell to the ground.

An eerie silence fell now, then the slingers were again told to fire, and Cortez and his conquistadors turned and retreated. They joined the rest of their army and left Tenochtitlan.

Running up to the Wise One, Monte asked, 'What will happen now? What are they going to do?'

The man shook his head sadly. 'Hernando Cortez intends to gather a larger army and come back to destroy the city. Montezuma had said that they could have all his gold and treasures, and Cortez had promised that there would be no fighting, that they would leave the city as it is. Now this new king has ruined everything, and there will be much bloodshed. It will be the end of the Aztecs.'

'Would you have liked our city to fall into the hands of the conquistadors?' Monte asked.

'They are not wicked men, although their religion is different from ours, my son. They worship only one god, a good god, who asks for no human sacrifices. He even sent his son, Jesus Christ, to earth to show the people how he loved them. Their religion is called Christianity.'

When he went home a few days later, Monte told his friend some of what had happened.

'So Montezuma joined their Christianity?' Marilia said, happily, 'and all ended in peace?'

'It did not end like that. The people of the city chose another king to lead them, a cruel man. Montezuma went out on to the walls to speak to them, and when they saw him they knew they still loved him, and went down on their knees before him. The other man was angry and ordered our slingers to let loose a volley of stones at Cortez and his men, and Montezuma was accidentally struck on the head. He died just a few hours afterwards.'

'Then Cortez won the city for Spain?' Marilia's eyes had filled with tears of sorrow.

'No, our people defended bravely and the Spaniards had to withdraw, but Cortez vowed that he would collect a larger army and come back to win all Mexico for his emperor – Charles the Fifth, of Spain.' His face assumed a determined expression. 'I hope that I will be old enough to fight when he comes back. I would not like to see

Tenochtitlan fall into the hands of the Spaniards . . . and yet . . . their Christianity sounds better than Montezuma's religion, and Cortez did not mean to fight.'

After briefly thinking this over, Marilia said, 'Yes, with Montezuma gone, it would be better if Cortez and his men were to rule over us instead of this cruel new king.'

'We must live in hope that the conquistadors do return.'

***

NOTE:

Hernando Cortez went on to gather a much bigger army, and built a huge fleet of ships to cross the lakes. He and his conquistadors destroyed the city of Tenochtitlan in November 1519, and it was in this place that Mexico City was built.

The Aztecs were a Mexican tribe ruled by Montezuma. They were good at building stone houses and making tools, but they had no wheel, nor any form of transport except boats and mules. They were dark-skinned and black-haired, and the men had no beards.

***

Word count 2878

This story was written in 1981 for a competition run for the Writers' Conference, held once a year in Pitlochry. Most of us who attended were only would-be writers but enjoyed listening to REAL authors talking about their work. I was disqualified, because the story had to be written for reading to children, and the age had to be stipulated. I put the age as 10–12 and the judge maintained that children of that age did not want to be read to. I pointed out that I had been teaching this age group for some time, and they loved having stories read to them. I did not send it anywhere else, and it is only included here because it is different from anything I wrote later.

The Bobbydazzler

'But Mam, a' the ither loons've got bikes, an' they mak' a richt fool o' me 'cos I havena gotten ane.'

'I've tell't ye afore, Jeemsie. We jist canna afford to buy a bike for ye wi' yer faither laid up like he is. There's naethin' comin' in, an' the little I'd laid past has to buy food for the six o' us an' mixters for yer Da. I'm hard put to manage as it is.' Lizzie Wilson wished with all her heart that her eldest son would be reasonable. He should have more sense, him being ten years old. Why couldn't he take no for an answer?

'But I've been thinkin', Mam. I've often seen auld bits o' bikes lyin' on the dumps, an' if only I could get the right bits, I could mak' ane for masel'.'

His mother sighed. It was bad enough trying to make ends meet since her Jeems had been taken ill again, without having Willie pestering her like this. He was more bother than the other three put together. 'Weel, weel,' she muttered at last, considering it easier than arguing any more. 'Jist you cairry on an' try to mak' a bike, loon.' At least it would keep him occupied for a while and give her some peace, though she doubted if he would ever produce a roadworthy vehicle.

* * *

Every day now, after school and after he'd had his supper, Lizzie could see him pottering about in the backyard with the things he'd found on the rubbish tips, a lantern illuminating his labours. He was utterly engrossed in his self-appointed task, having shooed his young brothers away when they showed an interest in what he was doing.'Ye should jist see Jeemsie,' she told her husband one evening when she went to take away his supper tray. 'He's up till his elbows in grease a' the time, an' he leaves muck on a' the doors. I dinna ken fit I'm gan to dae wi' him, for he tak's nae notice o' me tellin' him to wash his hands at the pump afore he comes inside.'

'Ach, jist let him be, lass. Ye should be gled the bike's keepin' him oot o' yer road.'

Jeems Wilson knew that their eldest son was Lizzie's favourite, although she was forever complaining about him. If only this bronchitis would stop bothering him every winter – that's what really upset his wife and made her take it out on the boy, but it seemed to get worse every year. He'd been off work for three weeks so far this time, with no sign of him being fit for a while yet, and he was worried that Geordie Milne, the farmer at Mains of Mucklefour, wouldn't keep his job as first horseman open for him much longer.

It was just as well that there wasn't so much to do at the farm, it being the middle of winter, but there were still certain jobs that had to be done. Sandy Fraser, the cattleman, had told him last week that it was taking them all their time to manage without him, and that old Doddie Morrison had offered to help out with the horses at nights.

Jeemsie was feeling quite excited. He'd been cleaning and oiling all the bicycle parts he'd managed to pick up, and he only needed a fork to fit the handlebars to the frame. 'Tam Fernie says his dad's got some aul' bikes a the back o' the smiddy,' he confided to his mother one night before he went to bed. 'I've to gan roon' the morrow straight fae the school to see if there's onything there that would work.'

'That's fine,' she said absentmindedly, too busy drying the stack of dishes to take much heed of her son, but it suddenly penetrated her mind what he had said, and she looked at him sternly. 'Dinna be late hame for your tea, then. For I'm needin' you to gan to the Mains for me. I hear they're to be killin' a pig the day, an' I want some o' the bleed to mak' black puddens. Your dad hasna been feelin' like eatin' much lately, an' that might kittle him up a bit, for he just loves black puddens.'

'I'll be hame as quick as I can, Mam, I sweir. An' if I get a fork at the smith's I'll be able to finish the bike an' use it to gan to the fairm. I'd be back in time for you to mak' the puddens after suppertime.'

His round freckled face was turned to hers earnestly, and his smile revealed the gap where he'd knocked out two teeth jumping the paling to catch a sheet that had blown off the washing line a few weeks earlier. Then she remembered that the sheet had been torn when he caught his foot in it, but it wasn't his fault that things went wrong every time he did anything for her.

What lay in the blacksmith's outhouse proved a treasure trove for Jeemsie the next day.

He found the required fork, and two wheels with better tyres than the ones he'd pulled out of the dump. He ran all the way home to assemble the last pieces, then stood back to admire his handiwork. It looked perfect, and with a lick of paint on it, nobody would ever know he'd made it himself – except Tam Fernie, the smith's son, of course, but he was Jeemsie's best friend, so he wouldn't tell.

Washing his filthy hands at the outside standpipe, he went into the kitchen, leaving his masterpiece propped against the wall of the coalshed. 'My bike's ready noo, Mam. You can get a'thing ready for makin' your puddens, for I'll be back afore ye ken I'm awa'.'

'Change your claes then, an' I'll ha'e the bucket ready for you fan ye come doon.'

He sauntered out a few minutes later with the pail slung over his arm, lifted his creation reverently, then put his foot on the pedal and swung his leg over an imaginary bar. The seat, even at its lowest, was too high for him, but he'd manage fine without having to sit on it. As he wobbled on to the rough track, his mother called, 'Watch yersel' noo, Jeemsie.' It was a wonderful feeling, to be going along at such a speed with the wind blowing in his face, on his own bicycle, though the pedals were a bit stiff and he'd have to oil the chain again. But he reached the farm in record time and was soon on the homeward way with the pail slopping full.

It was much harder to keep his balance now, weighed down on one side, and he couldn't see all that well in the darkening late afternoon. He had forgotten that he would need a lamp, but he knew every step of the way and he could look for one the morrow. Coming to the beginning of the track up to the cottar houses, he swung round carefully and made a perfect right turn. Sadly, however, he soon found himself wobbling uncontrollably and, in trying to control his steed, he forgot to watch out for the hole in the track. THUMP! Crack!

Picking himself off the stony round, dripping with blood, he wondered fleetingly if he had been mortally wounded, but when he got his breath back and felt himself gingerly all over, all he could find were skinned hands and knees. Then he realised, with a sinking heart, that it was pig's blood that was oozing from his clothes. His mother would be angry about that, and doubly angry at not being able to make the puddings, and he turned cold at the thought of what she might say – or do – to him.

He rose slowly to his feet and picked up the empty pail before noticing that his beautiful bicycle was lying in two parts – the fork had snapped. He could never wheel it as it was, so he'd have to leave it and come back in daylight with some tools to see if he could fix it. Laying down the pail, he threw first one piece of his construction and then the other over the dyke into a field.

His mother's first reaction, on seeing the small bloodied figure appearing at the kitchen door, was concern for her son. 'Jeemsie! Michty me! What happened? Are you bad hurt?'

He was quick to take advantage of the situation. 'I've cut my knees an' I feel real queer.' He limped with great exaggeration into the room and placed the empty pail on the table.

'I'm sorry aboot the puddens, Mam, bit I scaled the bleed an' my bike's broke.' He looked up at her pathetically.

Lizzie was aware by now that it was not her son's life-blood that had so shocked her and, in her relief, couldn't summon up the anger that she should have felt at the loss of the main ingredient of her delicacy. She contented herself by snapping, 'Get yoursel' cleaned up. It's a good job you hadna on your school breeks.' But she felt like giving him a good shake for the scare he'd given her.

In the school playground the following morning, a large knot of boys had gathered in one corner by the time Jeemsie arrived, so he ambled over to find out what was going on. His bosom pal, Tam Fernie grabbed his arm in great excitement. 'Hiv you heard aboot the murder, Jeemsie?'

'Murder? Fa's been murdered?' He could feel the morbid interest of the uninvolved rearing in his breast.

'Naebody kens, but it wasna that far fae your hoose, an' aul' Doddie Morrison saw the bleed in the licht o' his lamp fan he wis comin' back fae the Mains last nicht. He says the track wis fair covered wi' it, an' the bobby's gan roon askin' if onybody's missin'. There wis a broken bike in the tattie park as weel, so the murderer must've knocked the victim aff his bike afore he killed him.'

Tam was almost jumping off the ground with the thrill of the vile crime that had been committed in their midst, but it had slowly dawned on Jeemsie how the story had originated. He couldn't tell a soul the truth, not even Tam, not if the bobby was asking questions. There would be a real murder – his – if his mother connected him to this.

He couldn't concentrate on his lessons that morning, and received several raps over the knuckles from the dominie's round black ruler.

At a quarter to one, the two friends were standing behind the lavatories eating their dinner pieces – Tam's contained butter and beef, while Jeemsie's just had a scrape of dripping – when Tam asked, 'Did you get yer bike finished last nicht? I thocht you'd be bikin' to school the day.'

'It's nae quite ready yet. 'Twis mair fikey than I thocht, an' I havena got a lamp yet.' Jeemsie mixed fact and prevarication and felt pleased at his ingenuity.

'You ken, I wondered at first if it was you that got murdered,' Tam was saying. 'It wis the broken bike, you see, and I wis richt glad to see you this mornin'.'

Willie laughed half-heartedly. 'Na, na, I havena been murdered . . . yet,' he added, thinking of his mother's wrath, still to come. They munched on companionably, each busy with his own thoughts about the event that had taken place the previous day.

'I jist minded!' Tam's hand stopped halfway to his mouth. 'You wisna here in time to hear aboot the ither crime that happened. The Mains's hoose was broke into last nicht, as weel, an' the bobbies think the buggular must've murdered the man 'cos he saw something – maybe him comin' oot o' the farmhoose – an' could indentify him.'

'Oh!' It was all Jeemsie could say. He was thinking that he'd been lucky not to have been the victim after all, although never a soul had he seen on the road.

When he arrived home that afternoon, he tried to sneak up to the attic bedroom without his mother hearing him, but she came out of the kitchen with the rolling pin in her hand. 'Come ben here this minute, Jeemsie!'

Her tone warned him that he'd better do as he was told, so he followed her on trembling legs and stood studying the American cloth on the table as though his life depended on him knowing every inch of its pattern.

Lizzie was making oatcakes, and the lump of dough was ready to be flattened into a circle. She attacked it savagely as she fired her question. 'Where's yer bike, Jeemsie?'

The unexpectedness of it floored him. He hadn't taken time to prepare a plausible story, and he couldn't tell his mother a barefaced lie. She always found him out. The rolling pin was still. 'I asked you a question, Jeemsie.'

'I threw it in ower the tattie park.' He waited with bowed head for the explosion.

'Mmmmmm.' Lizzie drew out the sound in a satisfied manner. 'That's what I tell't the bo . . . em . . . Constable Taylor you must've done, after you fell an' lost a' the pig's bleed I sent you for. He wis here in the forenoon but he's comin' back at suppertime to speak to you.'

The game well and truly up, Jeemsie supped his brose automatically at suppertime, dreading the coming interview. Constable Taylor would be anything but pleased about the trouble caused by the spilled blood – the murder that had never taken place.

As soon as his bowl was empty, he rushed upstairs. In no time at all, there came a loud knock at the door, but he remained sitting on his bed, waiting for the summons. It came almost immediately.

'Jeemsie! Here's the b . . . Constable Taylor to speak to you.'

He went down, squaring his shoulders to meet his fate, and was astonished, and very much relieved, to find the policeman sitting in the kitchen with a smiling face.

'Come awa' in, Jeemsie. Well, we've sorted things oot and you've naething to be feared aboot. In fact, loon, you're a bit o' a hero.'

The boy's spirits lifted – but what had he done to be a hero?

Harry Taylor began in his official voice. 'When we were lookin' for the body in the tat . . . potato field, we found something else aside the broken bike.' Pausing, he looked around his three listeners to make sure they were taking everything in, before continuing, 'We found a sack wi' a' the articles stolen fae the Mains. The thief must've heard you comin' on your bike an' been feared you would see him.'

Jeemsie decided that he may as well give the story a helping hand. 'I did think I heard something afore I fell aff my bike, but I thocht it was a futteret. It must've been the buggular.'

'Aye, that's mair nor likely.' Gratified that his supposition had proved correct, the constable nodded his head so vigorously that the boy had to make a great effort not to laugh at the sight of the hat wobbling precariously.

'He'd thrown the bag in ower the park wi' the intention o' comin' back for it later, nae doot, but wi' me an' Davey

– the ither bob . . . policeman – bein' alerted, an' the two o's searchin' for him, he was seen an' apprehended at eleven hundred hours. So you see, Jeemsie, we wis lookin' for a body an' if your ma hadna tell't me aboot the bleed you scaled, the thief would likely have gotten clean awa' wi'his ill-gotten gains.'

The boy chanced a quick glance at his mother, and was pleased that she was smiling and looking proud of him, and his father, usually pale and weak, was looking brighter than he had been for a long time.

'But there's even better news than that for you, Jeemsie,' the policeman continued. 'Fan we gaed to the Mains to tell Geordie Milne the case was solved, he tell't us he'd been meanin' to offer a reward for the recovery of his property. He thinks, in the circumstances, it should come to you, laddie, an' he says yer faither's job's there for him as lang as he wants it. You're to get the £25, enough to replace your bike and ha'e a bit left ower.'

Looking just as stupefied as he felt, Jeemsie soon recovered his equilibrium and laughed importantly. 'Na, I'm nae buyin' a bike, for it's mair fun makin' ane for masel'. I'm gan to gi'e a' the money to Mam to buy food for us, an' mixters for my Dad till he's better o' the brownkatis.'

He looked round at his mother, and was disappointed to see tears rolling down her cheeks, when he'd thought she'd be pleased with him, grateful to him. But Lizzie, deeply affected by everything that had happened, soon showed her gratitude. 'Oh, Jeemsie,' she sobbed, throwing her arms about him, 'you're a right bobbydazzler, so you are.'

***

Word count: 2863.

Written 27 January 1986.

Sent to *New Writing Scotland* – rejected 7.5.86

Sent to Scottish Arts Council – rejected 25.8.86

Sent to *Scots Magazine* – rejected 11.10.86

This story was never published. It was actually based on a true story, an incident in the life of a man I knew, and graphically described by him. It appealed to my sense of humour, which is why it remained in my mind for so long. I had not looked at these short stories until after I had written my novel *The Nickum*, and didn't realise until too late that I had used the same anecdote – but to better effect second time around.

Paul, First and Foremost

The kettle spilled out its tears in streaming rivulets and Anne MacIntosh watched it dispassionately. If only she could relieve her turbulent feelings like that, she wouldn't be eaten up by this sick gnawing at her heart.

Poor Paul. Once again, she felt pity for him struggling to master the intense anger she felt at Debbie. When Paul had told her about the poor girl in his office whose home life was so tragic, Anne had said involuntarily, 'Ask her to tea some time.'

She had glowed with the inner satisfaction of a philanthropist when Paul phoned the next day to tell her that he was bringing Debbie home with him that night. 'She was so grateful, there were tears in her eyes,' he had added. 'She's really a pathetic little thing.'

She had replaced the receiver and glanced at the hall mirror. There had been tears in her own eyes, but she was looking forward to meeting someone who worked with Paul. She might find out more about his work – not that he was secretive, as if he had anything to hide, but he just wouldn't discuss it with her.

The girl had seemed such a nice person at first, her brown spaniel's eyes serious between their dark fringes. Anne had felt sorry for the teenager whose father had married a young woman not much older than his daughter. It would have been bad enough that her mother died when she was only ten, but having a stepmother in the same age bracket as herself must be awful.

Anne wished fervently now that she had never encouraged the friendship. If Debbie hadn't become a regular visitor to the house, Paul would probably never have fallen in love with her. He had never looked at any of the other girls, as far as she was aware. He was normally shy and rather unsure of himself in strange feminine company.

Debbie was a lovely girl, much shorter than Paul's five feet ten, and so willowy slim that Anne had felt lumpy and gauche beside her. Her silky black tresses, long and swinging round her face, were in direct contrast to Paul's fair curls, and Anne had been conscious of her own mousey hair, lank and neglected. She must have been blind not to notice the tell-tale signs of Paul's attraction to the girl.

Debbie had made herself at home straight away, hadn't been in the least shy when she sat down to that first meal with them. 'It's great to have something decent to eat,' she had laughed. 'Kate, my father's wife, can't even boil an egg properly.'

In the comfortable fullness following the good square meal, they had leaned back in their chairs for a few moments, and then Debbie had jumped to her feet. 'I'll help with the washing-up, Mrs MacIntosh.'

'No, no. I'm accustomed to doing it myself, and please call me Anne,' she had insisted.

But the girl had been determined, and unusually for

him, Paul had helped, too, laying past each dish as Debbie handed it to him. They relaxed in the sitting room afterwards, and the other two had laughed together about some of the actions of their colleagues, giggling over little in-jokes, until Anne felt completely excluded and leaned across to pat Paul's hand. 'What about pouring us a drink, dear?'

'Oh, sorry!' He had leapt to his feet at once. 'Sherry for you as usual, but what do you drink, Debbie?'

'Sherry'll be fine, Paul.'

The remainder of that first evening had passed in companionable near-arguments on a variety of topics until Debbie got up to leave. 'Look at the time. Dad'll be creating.'

'Why don't you run Debbie home?' Anne had suggested, and that's when it must have started. 'Feel free to come round at any time,' she had foolishly added, while Paul held Debbie's coat up for her.

'Thanks, Anne; I'll keep you at your word.'

And she had. At least once a week she had come to tea and Paul had driven her home each time. He had even stopped phoning to warn her, as it became a recognised thing for the girl to be there every Thursday evening.

It had gone on like that for over three months, until the Thursday that Paul came home alone. 'Where's Debbie?' she had asked.

'She sent her apologies, but said she couldn't manage tonight.' Paul did look rather disappointed, but Anne thought that it was because she'd had everything prepared for supper, and he was upset for her.

51

The following week, he had rung her in the forenoon to let her know that they would be dining alone that night again, and she felt a stab of disappointment herself.

'What's Debbie up to that's she's stopped coming?' she teased when he came home.

Paul had shrugged his shoulders, so she never mentioned it again, and life went on as it had done before they'd ever had their weekly visitor.

Some eight weeks later, she went into the kitchen one morning with the post to find him staring white-faced at the local newspaper. 'What's wrong, Paul?' she asked, anxiously.

Silently, he handed her the page. There, smiling in a frothy white creation, was Debbie, under the headline 'Beautiful secretary weds American banker from Carson City Nevada, USA. After honeymooning in the Bahamas, the couple intend to make their home in Carson City.'

'Well,' she exclaimed indignantly, 'and she never said anything about him. Did you know, Paul? Did she tell you?'

When he didn't answer, she looked searchingly at him, and realised with a sinking heart what she should have tumbled to months earlier. 'You're in love with her!' It was a bald statement of fact, not a question, not an accusation.

He had risen blindly from the table, and she heard the front door close quietly as he went out. She had been left alone to wonder. Why had Debbie done such a such an under-hand thing? Why had she allowed Paul to fall in love with her? She must have known – a woman always knows when a man feels that way about her, an inner sense, the magazines called it, woman's intuition. But what about the other woman in the man's life? She didn't always recognise the signs.

Anne's attention returned at last to the long-neglected kettle, which had been switched on to make coffee. The pseudo-pine Formica worktop was awash with water now, and she hastily flicked the switch up with her thumb. She would have to buy an automatic one if she was going to be as absentminded as this. As she wearily mopped up the puddle, all she could think of was poor Paul. It was hardly his fault that he had succumbed to Debbie's charms; she was such a lovely girl.

Pouring the water on to the granules in her mug, she suddenly thought of something else. Perhaps she was judging Debbie too harshly. Perhaps the girl hadn't wanted to take Paul away from her. Perhaps she had never realised that he loved her. Or . . . had she known and not wanted Paul to commit himself? She'd been committed already, of course, to her Carson City banker.

Anne laid down the mug without being conscious of drinking the contents. She wouldn't have stopped Paul from falling in love with Debbie, if she'd known about it. His happiness had always come first with her before anything else. She carried out her usual tasks in the house automatically all day, not having to worry about them. She had never been fanatical about cleaning and Paul always said he liked coming home to a homely house, not a showpiece.

What would happen when he came home tonight, though? What would he say? More important, what would she say? She would have to wait and take the lead from him – that would be best.

Paul was very late. Anne had switched off the oven hours before and had been agonising over whether he would come home at all, when he walked in, tired and haggard.

'Before you say anything, I don't want anything to eat. I've been walking around since I came out of the office, and I had a sandwich at a snack bar.' He went off without further explanation, leaving Anne to clear the table and set it for breakfast before she followed him upstairs.

Paul never referred to Debbie again, or to his love for her, and life carried on in a state of limbo until, after nearly a month of emotional strain, Anne plucked up courage to broach the subject. 'Has anyone been taken on to replace Debbie?' She watched for his reaction.

His flat voice was the only sign that the name disturbed him. 'They found a young girl through an employment agency. She's very popular with all the bachelors, and leads a full social life, I believe.'

Was this his way of telling her that he wouldn't get involved again, Anne wondered? She felt relieved, yet upset in a way because it proved that he still hadn't recovered.

Their relationship slowly reverted to almost pre-Debbie; almost, but not quite. In fact, Anne felt the need of something new to occupy her mind. She took to studying the Situations Vacant columns and came across one which read: 'Are you bored being merely a housewife? Would you like to earn money while you occupy your spare time? Ladies required for Market Research work.'

She dialled the telephone number that followed, and her application was successful. She enjoyed her afternoons interviewing women passers-by, but always made sure that she was home in time to prepare a proper meal for Paul.

'I should have done something like this before,' she told him one evening. 'I feel more human, not like a cabbage any longer. It's refreshing, meeting other people again.'

Paul's smile was a little strained. 'I'm glad you're not stagnating anymore. You won't feel so lonely when I leave.'

Anne's face blanched. 'When you leave,' she repeated in bewilderment. 'What do you mean, leave?'

'I put in for a transfer to Edinburgh. I felt I must get away, have a change, but I'll be home every weekend.'

Her drowning senses clutched at a straw. At least he wasn't leaving for good. She took a deep breath to steady her voice. 'When do you have to go?'

'I start a week today, so I'll be leaving on Sunday.'

Only a few more days left! Oh, Paul, she cried silently, why did you spring this on me when I thought I was coping again? But she was determined not to make a scene. 'I'll get everything ready for you to pack,' she said brightly. 'Thank goodness I put your grey suit in to be cleaned on Saturday. I've to collect it on Thursday.'

'It wouldn't have mattered. You fuss too much.'

By the time Sunday morning came round, and with it Paul's departure, Anne had made herself believe that it was probably a good thing, after all. He would meet different people and, hopefully, would forget Debbie. If this transfer achieved nothing else, that would be a move in the right direction. She hadn't been sorrowing for herself, only for Paul. He had always come first and foremost for her. If he could regain his peace of mind, he'd come to realise that he shouldn't be working so far away from home, and everything would be back to normal.

He phoned on Monday night to let her know how his first day had gone. 'It's all a bit strange, but I expected that, to begin with. There's one thing you won't have to worry about, anyway. The digs the firm arranged for me are clean and really comfortable. Plus, Mrs Martin seems determined to fatten me up a bit. Well, I'll see you Friday night, so keep your pecker up, tweetie-pie.'

Anne was overcome by happy tears when he rang off. It sounded as though he were coming back to normal again, getting over Debbie. 'Keep your pecker up, tweetie-pie.' That had always been his tagline when he rang to say he'd been kept late at the office, or couldn't get home on time for some reason or other.

Paul had looked after her and comforted her ever since that dreadful day just over two years ago, when her whole world had crashed around her. She had thought she would never get over her husband's death in that horrible, senseless crash. To think that an uncaring, drunken apology for a man could have . . . Ah, it was still too painful to think about, but now that she had picked up the threads of life again, she would be able to cope without him; even make new friends again.

They had both survived his first unhappy love affair, but there would be other girls for her nineteen-year-old son.

***

Word count: 2119

Sent to *Woman's Realm* 21.1.86 – rejected 2.3.86
Sent to *My Weekly* 4.4.86 – rejected 3.5.86
Sent to *Annabel* 9.6.86 – rejected 25.7.86
Sent to *People's Friend* 9.10.86 – rejected 29.11.86

Four rejections? Always hopeful, I did not bin this story, but never had the nerve to send it out again. Probably just as well.

The Peak Of Happiness

'But Grandad, I'm tired. Why can't we sleep in a bedroom?'

'I told you, Sean, Grandad hasn't paid for a bedroom, just two seats.' Arthur Rowse sighed and wished that British Rail employees wouldn't leave the sleeping compartments with their doors sitting open – the boy would never have known about them if he hadn't seen them for himself. 'We'll easily manage to sleep in here. It'll be great fun, won't it – not sleeping in a bed?'

He slung his duffel bag up on to the luggage rack and sat down, his heart sinking at the sight of the little boy's disappointed face. Stretching out a gnarled, weather-beaten hand, he patted the fair, curly head. 'It'll be easy. Put your feet up and lie down with your head on Grandad's knees and you'll be asleep in no time.' He hoped fervently that no other travellers would want to come in.

'When I waken up, will we be in Scotland?'

'Like enough, Sean.'

'Will I see the mountains, Grandad?'

'Once we're in Scotland, you'll see them, I promise.'

It was 11.15 p.m., and their train was still standing in King's Cross station. They had left Yarmouth at 3 o'clock that afternoon, so it was little wonder that the boy was tired. Plus, he'd been up at six to wave goodbye to his father and mother, on their way to Aberdeen where his father had taken a job as an engineer with an oil company. As most of their belongings had gone on ahead of them, it was just the odds and sods which had been loaded into the boot and back seats of their Capri.

The two adults and baby Susan had taken up all the space in the front of the car, so Arthur had volunteered to take Sean by train, trying to postpone the evil hour of parting. It was going to be a long, lonely journey back to Yarmouth by himself.

The six-year-old settled himself down and was very quiet, and Arthur wasn't surprised to see that he had fallen asleep already, his long, surprisingly dark eyelashes resting on his flushed cheeks.

With a shudder, the train drew slowly out of the station, and Arthur shifted his hip slightly to take his pipe out of his pocket. Puffing contentedly, he wondered how Nell and he would fill their lives now that the young folk had left. His wife was probably lying awake right now, going over their John's life from the time he'd made his first squawking appearance.

Nell was going to miss John and Marge, his wife, but it was he, Arthur admitted to himself, who was going to miss young Sean most. He'd been the boy's slave since the day the small dimpled hand had first clutched his finger and taken over his heart. How proudly he had taken out the pram to show off his grandson to his fisherman friends, and when at last the boy was old enough to walk with him, it had always been the harbour they had headed for.

Since Sean had started school, of course, they'd only been able to go out together on Saturdays and Sundays, except during the holidays, when they had set off early every day, rain or shine. 'Was that the boat you used to go on, Grandad?' Sean would ask a dozen times. 'When I grow up I'm going to be a trawlerman just like you and go out to sea in my boat.'

Arthur had been pleased about that. It had gone some way to make up for the disappointment he'd felt when John had refused to follow in his father's footsteps. Sean loved to hear stories of his grandfather's experiences in the Royal Navy during the war, and, especially just lately, of the time he'd been in Aberdeen. Arthur remembered that time, taken off a minesweeper and spending four weeks in Foresterhill Hospital after having his appendix removed. He hadn't really seen much of the place, but had told the boy that it was a beautiful city, clean but cold.

'Will I like it in Aberdeen?' Sean had asked. 'Maybe I'd better stay here with you and Gran.'

He had felt his heart lift then, but said, 'What about your mum and dad, though? They'd miss you, and you'd soon be wanting to see them again, and Susan. No, son, you'll like Aberdeen and you'll forget all about Yarmouth in a short time.' And about your grandad, had come the sobering thought.

He watched Sean shifting his position in his sleep. He was now lying with his feet against his grandfather's leg, his head against the side of the carriage, one hand dangling over the edge of the seat and the other flung across his forehead. He looked so sweet and defenceless that Arthur had to restrain himself from grasping him up in his arms, and had to swallow several times to get rid of the lump in his throat. Knocking his pipe out in the ashtray, he put his feet up on the seat opposite.

No one else had come into the carriage – probably worried that the boy would be noisy when he woke up; but his Sean was never noisy. Well, not all that much. He fell asleep himself eventually, vaguely aware of the station noise at York, but the next time he surfaced was in Newcastle.

It was daylight now and he took a newspaper from his pocket. It was yesterday's news, bought before they'd boarded the train in London. But it would occupy his mind and turn his thoughts away from the parting that had to come. He dozed again after a while, and in no time, it seemed, they were in Edinburgh, the milk churns clanking and a magazine trolley rattling alongside the window.

Sean sat straight up, wide awake at once. That was the best of being so young, there was no land of in-between, when the worries and anxieties of the day, forgotten in sleep, came crowding back to haunt you. 'Is it Scotland yet, Grandad?'

'Yes, son, this is Edinburgh, the capital of Scotland.'

'I'll soon be seeing the mountains, then, and that's two capitals I've seen, because when we were in London, you said that was the capital of England.'

'That's right. You're a clever one, fancy remembering that. You'll get on just great at your new school, I'm sure.'

Sean looked thoughtful. 'I wonder what my new school will be like? Do the people in Aberdeen speak a different language, Grandad?'

'You'll think so until you get used to them.'

'Will they laugh at me for the way I speak?'

'I don't think they'll laugh, but they'll likely find it difficult to understand what you're saying.'

'Why will they? I don't speak funny.'

'It'll sound funny to them, though, Sean.'

The small lips pouted for a second. 'I don't think I'm going to like it in Aberdeen, Grandad. Can't I go home to Yarmouth with you to live?'

Arthur was secretly pleased – there was nothing he'd like more – but shook his head. 'You can't do that, son. Anyway, you're not going to be living right in Aberdeen. Your new house is more than twenty miles north of that.'

The guard blew his whistle, the train left Waverley Station and, after the scary journey through the tunnel, they could see the scenery again. With the quicksilver change of childhood, Sean forgot his qualms about the new life ahead of him.

'Is that a mountain, Grandad?' he asked in great excitement. He was pointing to the Castle, on its pedestal of volcanic rock.

'Not really, but we'll see one soon.' Arthur stood up and took the duffel bag from the luggage rack. 'Your Gran put something in here for us to eat. What say we have some breakfast?'

'Ooh, yes, please, Grandad, but I'll have to go to the toilet first.'

How could he have forgotten the most important of the boy's needs, Arthur chided himself, recognising the same need in himself now. 'Right, then, off we go.' He hoped that the toilet would be free, or if it wasn't, that they wouldn't have long to wait until it was. Thankfully, most of the passengers had been up and about earlier, and they just had to wait a few minutes. Luckily, the Forth Bridge caused a diversion, as Arthur had told Sean just the week before that when he had travelled home from Aberdeen during the war, all the passengers had thrown pennies over the bridge for luck. So he dipped into his trouser pocket, took out a handful of small change and selected a penny for the boy to throw from the open window of the nearest carriage. 'It only brings good luck,' he instructed, 'if it goes into the water.' Unfortunately, the coin landed at the edge of the bridge, but bounced over the side and splashed into the river far below. Arthur wondered if Sean would worry about it not going straight into the water, but he seemed to be quite happy with his throw.

Back in their seats, Sean eagerly opened the duffel bag and pulled out a plastic container. 'What's in here?'

Soon they were munching sandwiches and drinking Coke out of tins. 'It's like a picnic, isn't it. Grandad?' Sean looked up into his grandfather's craggy face, but the excitement on his own small countenance vanished as a shadow passed over it.

He's thinking there'll be no more picnics for the two of us, Arthur mused. It was going to be a heartbreaking business for both of them to say goodbye when he had to leave the boy. But even before they had finished eating, he was keeping constant his vigil.

'That's a mountain this time, isn't it? Say yes, Grandad.' He pointed to a mound in the distance.

'No, no, that's only a slag heap. Coal, you know.'

Mountains seemed to hold a deep fascination for the boy, but the old man realised that he'd been born and brought up in East Anglia, flat as a pancake, so he had probably never seen anything higher than a small hill.

They continued their journey, with Sean jumping up at intervals to say, 'I don't see any mountains yet, Grandad.'

When Arthur did at last point out the ranges that could be seen in the distance, his grandson was rather disappointed. 'They're too far away. I can't see them properly.'

At Montrose, he was interested to see all the equipment lying around in the oil complexes. 'Will my daddy be working with things like that?'

'Like enough, lad, and he'll be out on the oil rigs as well, I believe. Remember, I showed you a photo of one the other day?'

When the train passed Stonehaven, with less than half an hour to go before it reached Aberdeen, Arthur started to dread their arrival. 'I hope your mum and dad'll be there in time to meet us.'

'What'll we do if they're not there, Grandad?'

A note of alarm sounded in the piping voice, and the old man regretted speaking his fears out loud. He had only succeeded in transmitting them to the boy. 'No problem, son. We'll just go in for a cup of char. There's sure to be a tearoom there somewhere.'

The problem was pushed to the back of the boy's mind when they passed a range of low hills. 'Are they mountains, Grandad?'

'Only little ones, lad. They're likely the foothills of the

Grampian Mountains. I'll show you on the map when your dad unpacks it.'

They fastened up the duffel bag, took their coats off the rack and were standing at the door of the carriage as the train drew into the platform at Aberdeen Joint Station. It was a long walk to the ticket barrier and Sean was still tired. Even as he walked steadily forward, he surreptitiously wiped his eyes with the back of his hand. 'Is it much farther, Grandad? I wish I could see Mummy.'

'Come here, son, till I clean your face. It's all sooty from poking your head out of the window on the Forth Bridge.' The deep voice held a gruff note as Arthur took out his handkerchief, wet it at the boy's tongue and scrubbed the greyish rivulets on the tear-stained face. 'Your mum wouldn't want to see you dirty, now, would she?'

It wasn't long until they could see the ticket collector, and just behind him were a smiling Marge and John Rouse. 'Mummy! Daddy!'

It was all Arthur could do to restrain Sean until they went through the gates. As they settled into the thankfully empty Capri, Marge took her son on her lap for the last stage of his daunting journey.

'Mummy, where's Susan?'

'We left her with the lady next door. She was still very tired after yesterday. Did you enjoy being on the train, darling?'

'Oh, yes! Me and Grandad saw all of Scotland.' Then, rather wistfully, the boy added, 'But we didn't see any mountains near us. Grandad said there weren't any near the railway line.'

Marge Rouse winked at her husband. 'Wait till you see our new house, Sean.' She gave an odd laugh as if she were hiding a secret joke.

The boy looked at his father, who was also laughing. 'D'you understand what the Scotch people are saying, Daddy?'

'We haven't had time to speak to many of them,' John began, but was interrupted by his father.

'Scots people, Sean, not Scotch;' Arthur felt obliged to correct him, because all the Scotsmen he had ever met during the war had always objected to anybody making the same mistake. 'Scotch is either whisky or broth,' they would say He didn't give his grandson this explanation, however, and waited for him to ask, but Sean's face had turned bright red with excitement.

Arthur looked in the direction where the boy's eyes were turned and nodded happily. 'Yes, lad, that's a mountain.'

They had left the city well behind them and there was no mistaking the massive shape towering into the sky. 'It's called Benachie,' John informed them, 'and it's not one of the highest mountains. Our home is just along this road.' He turned off to the left, and in a few minutes drew the car to a halt in front of a modern villa.

'That Bena-whatever-you-called-it looks like it's right at the bottom of our garden,' Sean observed, reverently, as they walked up the garden path.

His father shrugged. 'It's not really, though. It's a good few miles away, but the estate agent said that lots of people climb to the top to see the wonderful view.'

'Will you climb up to the top with me, Grandad, before you go home?'

'Oh, well . . . I'm not able to climb mountains nowadays, son. I'm too old.' And he hadn't felt inclined to climb any when he was younger, either, came the thought.

'Will you, then, Daddy? Please?'

John laughed. 'One of these days, maybe.'

'Tomorrow?'

'No, I've a lot of things to do tomorrow. We'll wait until some time after Grandad goes home.'

'Must we wait, Daddy? I want to climb it tomorrow. I'm going to love the mountains, especially Ben-thingummy.' He rushed through to the kitchen where his mother was setting the table for a meal, and discovered that the window there commanded a panoramic view of the huge mass.

'We're going to have a lot of good times up there, me and Daddy.'

Looking at the boy's radiant face when he went back to the lounge, Arthur realised with a sinking heart that this mountain was to be the love in Sean's life now – a love to replace even his grandad.

They spent the rest of the day helping to unpack the tea chests and arranging the furniture to suit Marge, who couldn't always make up her mind where she wanted things to go. From time to time Arthur noticed Sean going to the back door, or looking out of one of the windows, to see the impressive Benachie.

'Wait till I tell the boys at school I've got my very own mountain at the end of my garden,' the boy said, his voice quivering with the thrill of it, then his face fell. 'I forgot. The boys at this school won't be the boys I used to know.

The ones here will know Ben-a-whatever better than I do.'
Disconsolately, he went to his grandfather and pushed his
small hand into the large one, and Arthur ruffled his hair
in sympathy.

By 7 p.m. they were all exhausted. Marge put Susan
to bed first, then gave Sean a bath before he went to his.
John poured out a couple of drinks and handed one to his
father. 'I think we deserve this, Dad, don't you?'

They sat in companionable silence for a while, then
John asked hopefully, 'Have you changed your mind
about coming here to live? There's plenty of room for you
and Mum, you know.'

Arthur shook his head. 'You don't want us old folk
living in your pockets, son, and the sea has always been
my life. It's in my blood.'

John gave up. 'I know that, but remember there'll
always be a room waiting for you if you ever change your
mind – or you could come for a holiday any time you like.'

When Marge returned to the large airy lounge, she said,
'They're both sound asleep. Sean was absolutely shattered
and was off as soon as his head touched the pillow.' She
collapsed on to the settee and held out her hand for the
glass John had risen to fill for her.

It wasn't very long before the three adults realised that
they, too, were shattered, so the whole household was
asleep by ten o'clock.

The daylight streaming in through the uncurtained
window woke Arthur. He listened to the unaccustomed
country sounds – birds twittering, a cow lowing nearby

– then swung his legs stiffly out of bed. As he dressed, he looked out at the dark outline of the mountain Benachie, with white mists swirling round its top – not a peak, more a plateau. There was something about a sight like this that grabbed you, he thought. No wonder some men go mountaineering. It had never appealed to him, though, and he was too old now even to consider it.

He walked into the kitchen and made himself a cup of tea, then decided to take a walk before breakfast. Putting on his coat, he noticed by the clock in the hall that it was only five past five.

'Where are you going, Grandad?' came an anxious little voice. 'It's not time for you to go home already, is it?' Sean was also fully dressed. 'I heard you getting up, so I got up, too.'

'I'm just going for a little walk, lad. If you want to come with me, you'll need a coat.'

The boy disappeared, to come back struggling into his bright red anorak. He took his grandfather's hand and the two crept out like conspirators on some unlawful mission.

The keen wind whipped colour into their faces as they stepped briskly past the cluster of houses and turned, naturally, into the road leading towards the mountain, Arthur all the while listening to Sean's chatter. 'Mummy and Daddy'll get a shock when they know what we got up to, won't they Grandad?'

'You're right, son. Maybe we should have left a note.'

A young woman passed them on a bicycle. 'Aye,' she called, 'fine mornin'. You'll be fae the new hooses?'

'Yes,' Arthur shouted to the retreating figure.

'She did speak funny, Grandad. "You'll be fae the new hooses".' The boy giggled as he mimicked the girl's broad accent.

They had been walking for half an hour when they came to a road branching off, with a sign 'Private Road. Home Farm'.

'Well, we can't go that way if it's private,' Arthur said.

A little farther along, another sign pointed the way to the 'Mither Tap'.

'What's a Mither Tap, Grandad?' Sean asked when Arthur told him what it said.

'I don't know, son, but we could go along and find out, I suppose. It didn't say it was private, and it's probably some king of drinking well.'

As they went along the narrow road, not much more than a stony track, Sean hopped and skipped happily in front, looking for the myserious mither tap. Suddenly the road widened out into a large car park, at the far side of which the path continued, but now winding upwards. 'This must be where people leave their cars when they want to climb up Benachie,' Arthur announced.

'And that's the path to the top.' Sean raced across the grassy surface towards it.

'It doesn't really look high enough to be Benachie,' Arthur puffed, as he hastened to catch up.

They scrambled over the rough stones, and when they had almost reached the top, they found that it wasn't the top after all. The path carried on over the brow of this part and went on and on up to the summit. Arthur had no doubts now about it being Benachie, and no doubts either that he wanted to climb to the very top now that they had come this far.

He noticed with relief that the mists were lifting and the sun was beginning to shine, but remembered that it might take some time to reach the highest point, and that he had taken nothing for them to eat.

'What are those bushes, Grandad? I've never seen that kind before.'

'That's heather, son. Later on in the year it'll come out in beautiful purple flowers. That's why people speak about the purple hills of Scotland. About August or September it'll look like one solid mass of colour from a distance.'

There were no trees now, and realising they had passed the tree line – the height above which trees will not grow – he explained this to the interested boy. The path had become more and more uneven, and they found the walking quite laborious.

'It's a long way, Grandad, but I still want to go to the very top. Mummy and Daddy'll get a real surprise when we tell them we've been right up the mountain. And you said you were too old. You're not really old, are you?'

'I'm beginning to feel my age,' Arthur laughed. 'I'm getting short of puff.'

'We can sit down and have a rest. We've plenty of time.'

The old man glanced at his wrist watch as he sat down thankfully on a grassy knoll. 'It's after eight o'clock, Sean. Your Mum and Dad'll be up by now, and wondering where we are. We'd better turn back.'

He was surprisingly glad when the boy protested. 'No, Grandad, we must nearly be at the top now. You said we'd passed the tree line ages ago, so it can't be far. Please can't we go on?'

'In a minute, then.' Arthur suddenly remembered that he had bought two bars of chocolate in King's Cross, and they hadn't needed to eat them; not with the load of sandwiches Nell had packed for them, and the fact that Sean had been asleep for a big part of the journey. He took them from his pocket and gave one to Sean, who sat down beside him. The foil was stuck to the chocolate, but they still tasted wonderful to the two hungry climbers.

'Are you ready now, Grandad?'

Arthur hoisted himself to his feet and set off after the boy. After a while, the path deteriorated gradually until there was no path any longer. A wall of rock rose out of the earth in front of them, which Sean was madly trying to clamber up. 'Come back, son, it's maybe dangerous there.'

His grandson paid no attention and in a few seconds was out of Arthur's sight, but his excited voice floated back. 'Grandad! I'm at the top! Come on up!'

'Eh, son, I don't think I can make it.'

'I'll give you a hand up.' The small hand dangled into view, but the man, shamed into action, forced himself upwards. He succeeded with no mishaps, although one step had been dodgy as he had dislodged the rock he'd been using as a toehold.

Shakily, he stood up and looked around him. On the flat plateau stood a plaque, showing the surrounding landmarks and naming the distant mountains on the skyline. He tried to place them all for the child, and a wonderful feeling of peace engulfed him; a peace he'd only thought to savour while he was at sea. This was very different from being aboard a ship, though it was still a marvellous, moving experience.

'Masters of all we survey,' he laughed, 'and I can see for miles.'

'There's my new house, Grandad.' Sean was pointing to a row of tiny doll's houses far below them. 'I'm going to like it here after all . . . except . . . I wish you could stay, Grandad.'

Arthur recalled the day John had told him that he'd taken a job wih an oil firm in Aberdeen, such a distance away. 'Why don't you and Mum sell your house and come and live with us? There's nothing to keep you here, is there?'

Nothing, except that Yarmouth's always been my home, Arthur had thought. 'Sea's in my blood and I don't like mountains', was what he had said.

Nell had been quite keen on the idea of moving to be with John and Marge, he knew, but he had held his ground. But now, up here in the sky, his love for the sea was struggling to conquer his love for the boy – and losing. Aberdeen and the sea weren't that far away, and he couldn't honestly say now that he didn't like mountains. This feeling of peace and intoxication, this bracing air, could grow on him. Yes, this place could be the El Dorado he'd been searching for ever since he'd had to give up the trawling.

'Grandad, are you OK?' Sean was rather alarmed by his silence.

'Aye, lad. I'm OK. Definitely OK. Come on, then, we'd better be getting back. I bet your mum and dad won't believe we've climbed Benachie.'

'Ben-a-heeeee!' shouted the boy, and with a leap, he turned and ran down the proper path, the path they had somehow managed to stray from on the way up and had been forced into a bit of actual mountaineering. With youthful footsteps, Arthur went after his grandson, and broke into song as they marched, ever downwards.

'One man went to mow, went to mow a meadow,

'One man and his dog, went to mow a meadow.'

When they reached the car park, they found John and Marge waiting for them, along with the girl they had seen on her bicycle when they had been on their way to find Benachie.

'Mummy! Daddy! I've been right to the top with Grandad, and it's beautiful, really beautiful. And we saw heather, and rabbits, and after a while there's no trees because they don't grow if it's too high up, and . . .'

'Steady on, son,' laughed his father. 'We were worried about you, wondering where the two of you had gone. By good luck, we met this lady and asked if she had seen you. She told us you were heading in the direction of the Mither Tap, and showed us the way.'

'We didn't see the tap, Daddy, and we could have been doing with a drink at the top, I can tell you. But we did climb the mountain.'

The girl laughed loudly. 'The Mither Tap is our way of saying the Mother Top. It's the main peak of the range.' Marge was to find out much later that the name had originated because of its shape – the outline of a woman's breast.

They returned to the car, and Arthur settled gladly back against the cushions. He wasn't really tired though they had been on the go for hours, but he was glad of the seat. 'What was your estate agent's name and address?' he asked, casually.

John cast a quick, questioning glance at his father, who nodded happily and patted the curly head now resting against Marge. 'I've changed my mind, son. Even an old man can be wrong – not often, mind, just once now and again. I think we'll buy a house here after all. The mountain has cast its spell on me and I know your mother wanted to come, anyway.'

Sean snuggled deeper into his mother's arms. This was all too much for the exhausted little boy's emotions to cope with. 'It's like a fairy story, Grandad, and we can all live happily ever after.'

***

Word count: 4796

Written February 1986 before I had a computer, so the words were counted individually, as I also had to do for my first three novels. The computer was a marvellous invention.

Sent to *Annabel* 12.2.86 – rejected 19.4.86
Sent to *Woman's Realm* 22.4.86 – rejected 1.6.86

Search For A Prince

Roselle lazily shifted the slice of lemon with her tongue to get the last drops of sangria out of the glass.

If only the girls could see her now – sitting drinking by the blue Mediterranean, while the rest of the world passed by. But that was the whole trouble; they kept on passing by. She had hoped, dreamed, when she made up her mind to go to Spain on this Singles trip, that she would at last meet her Prince Charming, and find Romance (with a capital R) – no, True Love (also with capital letters) that would last for ever. But every likely lad seemed to have a girl glued to his side, and there were no unattached males to be seen.

As though to prove the point she was making to herself, a young couple sauntered past, arms linked. Roselle heard them talking softly to each other, in German she thought, but as she watched them stop and kiss tenderly, she reflected that it didn't matter what nationality you were. Love was the same in any language. If you could find it, that is.

She hadn't been able to find it back home in South Norwood. Not that she hadn't had boyfriends. There had been quite a few, but she hadn't once felt THIS IS LOVE!

She'd been quite fond of them at the time, but when they moved on, dropped her for another girl, her heart hadn't been broken or anything like that. Rather, she'd found herself looking expectantly for somebody else, in the hope that this time it would be the real thing. But it had never been.

The last time had been the nearest. She probably could have fallen in love with Derek, given time. It hadn't been the love-at-first-sight, legs-turning-to-jelly, fluttering-heart sort of business, but she *had* dreamt about him at nights, and thought tenderly of him when she should have been concentrating on her word processor, so there must have been a spark of something there. All it would have needed to fan it into a flame was . . . what? That was what she didn't know.

She remembered how surprised and disappointed she'd been when Derek had stood outside her door that Saturday night. 'No, Roselle, I'm not coming in. I'm not even going to kiss you. I thought I'd be able to make you love me, but I've tried everything.' He had ignored her spluttering protests. 'No, it seems to me you're waiting for somebody to sweep you off your feet and carry you off to an enchanted castle, or something along that line. Well, it doesn't happen like that in real life, Roselle, and I'm no fairy prince. I've got very human emotions, so it had better be goodbye. I really hope you meet your Prince Charming some time, somewhere.'

She had cried after he left. Had she been expecting too much? Was he right? Was it only in fairy tales that love was instantaneous and all-consuming? Later on, she had remembered that he had said 'some time, somewhere', and her heart, not broken, just slightly bruised, had made a miraculous recovery.

Why should she expect love to come to her? Why shouldn't she go and search for it herself? That was why, three weeks later, she was here on the Costa del Sol. Her parents had been horrified when she told them what she intended doing. She recalled the conversation as if it had been the dialogue in a play.

ROSELLE: I was lucky there was a last-minute cancellation.

MOTHER: You can't go off to the south of Spain on your own.

FATHER: You know the kind of things that could happen – a young vulnerable girl on her own in a foreign country.

MOTHER: What'll the neighbours think?

FATHER: Never mind what the neighbours think, woman. Think of your daughter, alone over there, a prey to any disreputable Casanova.

MOTHER: I am thinking of her. What if . . .

Et cetera, et cetera, et cetera.

Surprisingly, she had felt quite stimulated as their argument reached a crescendo, and waited for a lull to make her solo contribution. 'I'm unattached, I'm over eighteen and I can look after myself. No wolf in sheep's clothing can pull the wool over my eyes. Besides, it's all paid for.'

That had clinched it, as she had known it would.

Neither of them liked to waste money under any circumstances. She'd been here nearly a week now, though, and was no nearer to realising her dreams. She toyed with the empty glass and looked around her. The French family at the next table were chattering and gesticulating violently to each other, while two small Italian girls in their dainty frilly sun-suits were pestering their mother for money to go to the amusement arcade. At least, that's what it looked like. This was the first time she had come to the open air lounge bar, and it was like sitting in the stalls watching a drama unfold before her eyes.

'*Pardone me, señorita.*'

A waiter hovered anxiously. Roselle shook her head, then decided in favour of another drink after all. 'Sangria, por favor.'

Her knowledge of Spanish was very limited, but she had managed to get by so far. She watched him as he walked towards the bar. His rear view was rather nice, in a Spanish sort of way, with the dark curly hair and the short white jacket trimmed with blue. Could this be *him*? She hadn't noticed him before and found herself waiting impatiently for him to return.

He was back in a few minutes and she looked up into his face as he set the glass in front of her. 'Gracias,' she murmured, meeting the full force of his dark brown eyes. Her heart fluttered manically, her legs turned to jelly – *it was love*! Love at first sight, as she had always hoped for. Her shy smile was rewarded by a toothpaste commercial.

'Ramon!' The summons came from the bartender, competently shaking cocktails.

'Si.' He gave her a sketchy salute and hurried off.

So his name was Ramon. It suited him. She watched him covertly as he glided between the tables. Like all Spaniards, his movements held no sense of urgency. Mañana, mañana. It was a good maxim, one to which she could quite easily be converted.

Once or twice, he caught her watching him and smiled a sweet, secret smile for her alone. Wait till she told the girls back home about this! She could fabricate a bit and tell them he had kissed her hand before introducing himself. He would have to be the son of a rich, visiting Spanish family, though, not a poor waiter. They wouldn't think that was so romantic. His family could be from Madrid, down here on holiday from the overpowering heat of central Spain. He had fallen in love with her and swept her off her feet. He had taken her to Torremolinos and Marbella, wined and dined her and then made love to her.

'Ramon's so passionate,' she would tell them. 'A true Spaniard, but so gentle and tender.' They would be sick with envy.

'Say, Ramon, d'ya speak any English – Inglasia?' It was the massive American at the corner table with his wife, a striking blonde in a green kaftan with gold embroidery round the low neck and down the front.

'Si, señor, I spik English good.'

Roselle couldn't help smiling. She wouldn't have much of a language barrier with him after all. The conversation in the corner went on, while she spun more romantic fantasies with which to regale her friends at home. 'Ramon said he first noticed me at the swimming pool, as I was so bronzed and radiant,' she would tell them. She'd go straight on to explain that, although she wanted to stay on with him in the hotel, she'd said she must go home to tell her parents. He could make the wedding arrangements and she would join him later. She was quite sure within herself that before her holiday was over he would propose to her, and the question of parental opposition never entered her mind. No technicalities were ever allowed to interfere in her daydreams.

Ramon was still talking to the Americans. 'I – student – here for summer only.'

Ah now, that bit would be all right. She wouldn't need to tell fibs about that. He went out of sight for a few moments and came back with pots of coffee for the Americans. When he left them, heading in her direction, she decided to jump in. After all, what better place than Spain to take the bull by the horns?

'By the way, I'm English.' She spoke very slowly and deliberately so that he could understand her. 'I'd like to find out about the entertainments in town, for young people, you know? Could I talk to you after you finish work?'

His eyes lit up. 'I finish . . . er . . .' He held up three fingers.

'Three o'clock? That's great. Where can we talk?'

He made as if to say something, but obviously changed his mind and said instead, 'Kiosko on beach?'

She barely had time to nod eagerly before he turned and walked off, and Roselle picked up her canvas bag and floated up to her room to shower before lunch.

Prince Charming Ramon, she laughed to herself as she stepped on to the bath mat. It was worth travelling all this distance to find him . . . to find *real love*.

She settled on her white seersucker sundress to show off her tan. She was very proud of her bronzed skin. She had spent most of her first week lying on a sunbed by the pool, looking, she had hoped, beautiful and exciting, but nobody had noticed. No brown-skinned Adonis had stopped to chat her up, not even a callow, pimply-faced youth, and there were plenty of them about, too. Still, her trip abroad was about to pay its dividend, in the shape of a six-foot tall Spanish student-waiter. Her heart accelerated at the thought of what the afternoon might hold for her.

In the huge dining room, at her little table set for one, Roselle craned her neck to see into the bar where Ramon was working. Occasionally she caught sight of him, laughing with some of the world's most beautiful girls. Now it was a tall black-haired Amazon in the briefest of brief bikinis; now he was talking to the French brunette with the poodle; now a ravishing redhead with a cleavage that would have made Roselle's mother hurriedly avert her eyes. Where were all the husbands or boyfriends? She gave herself over to the old green-eyed monster and made a poor show of eating her lunch.

Five minutes before the appointed time, she went along the beach to the small wooden café called The Kiosko, imagining while she walked that Ramon had been making dates with all the girls he'd been flirting with. He's just a philanderer, she thought, and probably never intended turning up.

She fumed silently until half past three, then decided to call it a day and go for a walk. There was no point in waiting any longer; she would just make herself look ridiculous. It wasn't very pleasant being left in the lurch like this in public. But just as she stood up, she saw him hurrying over the sand.

'*Perdoneme, por favor, señorita.* The people and more people they come.' He gave an apologetic shrug.

'That's all right. I didn't even notice that you were late. I've only been here a few minutes myself.' She made light of the past thirty minutes of agonizing uncertainty.

'Come.' He took her hand. 'Quiet place – over there.'

Roselle's spirits took a high jump. He wanted to take her away from the crowds, to get her in an isolated spot, to pour out his love for her, the love he had kept secret for a few days in case she spurned him.

They walked slowly, it was too hot to hurry, away from the little tables clustering under their thatched umbrellas – past the mini-golf course, the tennis courts, the beautiful gardens with their giant cacti and palm trees; past all the hordes of campers from the site on the hill. Very few locals were about. They had the sense to take a siesta during the hottest part of the day.

They took off their sandals and splashed through the sea, gently lapping at the sand, and clambered over the rocks. Beyond this point, as Ramon had said, quietness reigned in a small secluded beach, hidden from the view of any 'peeping toms'. They found a flat stone and squatted down. 'What is your name, please?' Ramon asked now, looking at her in a way that made her heart lurch.

She always enjoyed telling people her name, grateful that her parents had chosen it so thoughtfully. 'It's Roselle. Roselle Harrison.'

'Is good. Perfect for English rose. When I see you by the pool, I think you so pale and sad. I think to make you happy. The hair – like silk. The lovely eyes – blue like the sky.'

The soft voice carried on, the words caressing her soaring spirits. This was *it*! Her prince really was charming. Then her thoughts stopped roller-coasting as he made a grab for her, but his kisses were too demanding, altogether too passionate.

'Stop, Ramon.' She pushed him away, but he pulled her to him roughly again.

'Come to my room tonight,' he whispered against her hair.

No, no, she thought. This isn't Prince Charming. This is the Big Bad Wolf in person, and she laughed aloud as he was about to kiss her again.

Looking astonished, Ramon stopped in mid pout. 'Why you laugh, please?'

'Nothing. Nothing at all,' she managed to say, struggling out of his embrace. 'It's just that you're exactly the kind of man my father warned me about.' She ran back along the beach, leaving her perplexed Casanova standing forlornly on the rocks, his mouth gaping.

When she reached the hotel, she locked herself in her room and flopped down on the bed. She didn't care for that kind of behaviour at all. She longed to be back home with good, safe Derek. At least she could depend on him, predictable, protective and loving. Yes, that was really love. She'd been wrong all along, always reaching out for something more. She hoped that Derek hadn't found someone else while she was away.

In the tiny en suite bathroom, she splashed her face with cold water, then sat down to write a letter to her mother. Maybe, if she was lucky, it would reach home before she did.

By the time she went down for dinner, she had composed her thoughts and was glad that Ramon kept his eyes away from the dining room. She needn't speak to him again. She would never go back to the lounge bar, that was for sure. She must have given him the wrong impression by asking to meet him in his off-duty time, and she'd certainly been too trusting – naïve.

She spent the rest of her second week lying near the pool, reading and trying to deepen her tan. Pale and sad, Ramon had called her, when she had thought she was bronzed and radiant. That hurt!

While she was packing on Friday night, Roselle found that she was just as excited at the thought of seeing Derek again as she had been about coming here to look for a Prince Charming. How could she have been so immature?

In Heathrow, waiting for her luggage to come on the roundabout, she decided to take a taxi home. She still had enough money left; she hadn't spent all that much in Fuengirola. In a few moments, she spotted her suitcase at the far side of the conveyor belt, but before she could move an inch, she was spun round and there was

Derek. All five foot ten of him, laughing and hugging her.

'Your mum phoned to tell me when you were arriving and asked if I'd come to meet you.' He didn't say that her mother had added, 'I don't know what happened there, but I think she realises how she feels about you, so now's your chance. Good luck!'

'Oh, Derek, I'm so glad to see you,' Roselle sighed blissfully.

'No more running off in search of a Prince Charming?'

'I don't want any princes, only you.'

'Not very flattering,' he grinned.

'You know what I mean. Dash! My case must have gone round again. I saw it just before you arrived.'

'And you forgot everything in the joy of having me here?'

Roselle had never seen him like this before, so self-assured and happy. 'Yes, darling,' she told him. 'You see, I really do love you.'

And so she did, her wobbly legs and fluttering heart confirmed it, with a deep new meaning to Love, with a capital L.

Who needed a Prince Charming, anyway?

***

Word count: 2850
   Sent to *My Weekly* 13.2.86 – rejected 28.2.86
   Sent to *Woman's Story* 4.4.86 – rejected 30.4.86

Sent to *Blue Jeans* 22.5.86 – rejected 1.6.86
Sent to *Romance* 3.6.86 – never returned

Four rejections? I think I gathered that this story was an F-L-O-P.

The Arches

Archie Murchie opened his *Observer* with no premonition of what it contained. He had gone out with the dog to collect the local 'rag' before breakfast, but liked to leave the reading of it until Alice was clearing up. He may have been retired, but washing dishes was woman's work.

He had filled his pipe, taken his glasses down off the mantelpiece, before he settled back in his armchair to find out if anything interesting had happened in Kilstrath since last week. The news was sometimes days old, but it was a change from all the strikes and disasters that filled the national dailies and blasted out at him from the television and radio.

'I see the Flower Show's to be on the 23rd of next month,' he called through to his wife. 'I hope my dahlias winna be past.'

'They'll be fine.' Alice knew that he hoped to lift the prize one year, but so far he had been unsuccessful.

'I see young Billy Williamson's got promotion again,' he remarked in a few minutes. 'He's fairly got on in that bank in Inverness. Manager now, would you believe? And he was a real scallywag when he was a lad, mind?'

Alice laughed. 'Aye, he used to chase the hens and put them off laying. I was forever raging at him.'

'Och, he was a likeable enough laddie though.' Archie had always had a soft spot for their neighbour's youngest son. He smiled as he turned the page. He would have liked a son like Billy Williamson. His mind suddenly stopped wandering, as a heavily outlined item caught his eye. He sat up, took the pipe from his mouth and read the two paragraphs under their heading 'KILSTRATH TO BE SOLD?' When he came to the end, his eyes went back to the beginning and he read it through again, hardly able to believe what he saw.

He was still staring at the page when Alice came through, pulling down the sleeves of her old cardigan. 'What is it, Archie?' she asked anxiously, noticing the set expression on his lined face. Silently, he handed her the paper and pointed to the place. Alice read it aloud, slowly. 'Lord Kilstrath died at his London home early on Monday morning. The estate and the title are inherited by his nephew, who lives in Montreal.' She looked up, in surprise. 'But this winna affect us, surely?'

Archie looked grim. 'Read what else it says.' His voice was hoarse and he bit his lower lip. His wife searched for the place again. 'The new Lord Kilstrath has put the whole estate up for sale, and an offer has already been made by an American electronics company. They intend to convert Kilstrath House into a factory . . . Oh no.'

'It doesna bear thinking about,' Archie said sadly, 'but carry on. That's nae the worst o' it.'

'They intend to convert Kilstrath House into a factory,' his wife repeated, 'and say that some of the village houses will be required for their key workers, but employment will be given to many of the local men. The company promises to provide new, terraced houses in Strathdene for all those forced to leave their homes.' Alice handed the newspaper back to her husband and sat down heavily. 'What does it mean, Archie?'

'It means we'll ha'e to get out, woman, for I'm well past the age for employment. The Americans love old cottages, so our wee house'll be snapped up for one of their "key workers" as they call them.' Archie ran his hand through his wiry grey hair. 'We'll be put away to one of their new, terraced hooses in Strathdene, though what we would need wi' a terrace in a hoose beats me.'

'They'll maybe leave us,' Alice said hopefully. 'We could offer to pay them a rent and . . .'

'No, no. They're not wanting old folks here, just young men. We'll be put out, there's no two ways about it, and the whole place'll change. What a thing to happen, and me aye thinking I'd be able to draw my last breath in the house I first saw the light o' day in.'

Alice frowned. 'I wish you wouldna say such things, Archie, you're just tempting fate.'

'I tell you this, I'd rather go to sleep under yon arches than move from this cottage.'

His wife snorted. 'Och, you and your arches. You never think on anything else.'

They sat in silence, one on each side of the fire, wondering what was to become of them, until Archie stood up. 'I'm away out.' He walked into the small square porch, lifted his coat from the peg and whistled to the dog. Belle, the spaniel, lifted her head off the hearthrug, but did not rise – it wasn't the usual time for their walk. When she heard the door being opened, however, she got slowly to her feet and followed Archie out.

Alice knew, without being told, where they were going. Her husband always went down to the old railway bridge if he was troubled about anything. He said the arches were his friends and had helped him make decisions and to face up to life's problems. She hadn't found out until after they were married that this was an obsession he'd had ever since he was a boy, and had often resented it, but had complained only once . . . a long, long time ago.

She couldn't see what comfort or direction a dozen stone arches would be to anyone, though Archie did usually come home calmer and more settled in his mind after being there.

Belle ran on ahead, checking every now and then that her master was following, but Archie was paying little attention to her. His thoughts were fully occupied, his stomach had a weird sickness in it. After a lifetime of service to the laird, himself and his father before him, to think it would come to this – thrown out of the house he'd been born in. There must be a law against it.

'Aye, aye, Archie.'

He looked up, scowling, not in the mood to make idle chit chat with anybody, even an old friend, but the postie was standing smiling, obviously waiting for an answer, and he wasn't the kind you could brush off easily; he'd a hide like a rhinoceros. 'Aye, aye, Geordie,' Archie mumbled and would have walked on.

The postman, however, was curious to know what Archie thought of the news that had been going round, startling news. 'A terrible sad thing, the laird dying in London sudden like that.'

'Aye.'

Geordie raised his eyebrows, but carried on, 'It's a richt shame aboot this American buying the whole village lock, stock and barrel, isn't it?'

Archie didn't want to discuss it, but was well aware that his old friend was desperate to take it through hand. 'It is that,' he said bitterly, 'after the hundreds of years this place has belonged to the laird's family.'

'If he'd married again after his wife died,' remarked the postman, 'and had a son, things would've been different, but this nephew in Montreal fell heir to the whole caboodle, and he'd only be interested in the money side o' it. He wouldna be bothered to come and see things for himsel'. He's nae worried about Kilstrath or his uncle's folk.'

'Aye.' Archie agreed wholeheartedly with this.

'I'm due to retire in six months, so I'll be like you, Archie, nae use to them. Still, there's one good thing, they're going to set us up in better houses.'

Geordie didn't sound all that concerned about it, and Archie remembered that he was an incomer to Kilstrath, taking over as postman when old Willie Thomson retired, about fifteen years ago, so he'd be accustomed to flitting. 'Aye, I suppose that's a good thing,' he said grudgingly, not feeling like arguing.

He carried on along the street, past the wee Johnnie-a'

-thing shop, where a group of customers were deep in talk, speculating about the proposed changes, more than likely. The changes were actually only proposed, nothing really settled, he reminded himself, but he knew in his heart they must be pretty near settled before the *Observer* would print such a bombshell. Pat Wilson had always stayed on the safe side, terrified he'd be taken up for misrepresentation of facts.

After leaving the village behind, Geordie stopped, as he always did, to savour the shape of the huge railway viaduct ahead, looking, this grey overcast morning, uncannily forbidding. The spaniel raced on, through the arches and into the field beyond, where she usually spent her time chasing rabbits while her master was communing with the granite stones.

Archie was alone, alone with his beloved arches to whom, all his life, he had poured his heart out over everything that had ever troubled him. Not only troubles, he remembered, smiling to himself. He had asked their advice and blessing before he married Alice, and had told them proudly about the birth of their son. His eyes clouded as he recalled the comfort he had drawn from them when the boy died of a fever only three years later. That was the only time Alice had ever really complained about him coming here, though he knew it was because he had left her alone at a time when she needed him to be strong for her.

When he left the house that terrible day, she had called after him 'You think more of that arches than you do of me.'

It wasn't true, of course, yet he had walked out blindly,

unable to cope with the emotions that were tearing him apart, let alone deal with hers. Only when he reached the towering viaduct had he found blessed relief in tears, and he'd gone home prepared to be the tower of strength she needed.

Dragging his mind back from the past, he realised that there was no relief for him this time. He felt nothing except that ever-present, excruciating gnawing at his heart. 'What'll I do?' he asked the silent arch nearest him. 'If this new laird sells the village, what'll happen to Alice and me? We're too old to make a fresh start in another place. We're not easy at making new friends.'

Nothing! No feeling of peace. No serenity. No sign of anything. After almost seventy years, from the first time he had run to them to escape his mother's anger, the arches had let him down – forsaken him. In a few minutes, he lifted his head and whistled to the dog, who came running up, tail wagging twenty to the dozen. Touched by her affectionate dependence on him, he patted her head and they set off.

'You haven't been long,' Alice smiled when they went in, but did not ask if his pilgrimage had been successful. She could see by his whole dejected attitude that it hadn't.

He pottered about in his garden for the rest of the day, a horrible sense of doom closing in around him, and he sat picking at his supper until his wife said, in some irritation, 'If it's to be, Archie, it's to be. If it's God's will that we have to move from here, we'll just have to move. It's nae as bad as you're making out, in any case; you're worrying for nothing. They'll leave us here in peace, I'm sure.'

It was all right for her, he thought resentfully. She hadn't been born here like him, nor spent the whole of her life loving every stone of the four walls surrounding them, nor tenderly caring for their great skelp of a garden. The new terraced house would be absolutely gardenless, or if it wasn't, there would be a wee bit the size of a postage stamp, for the young folk today hadn't the slightest interest in growing things. They likely believed that the only place to get flowers and vegetables was in a shop; one of them supermarket places. What was more, builders wouldn't waste their precious land for folk to make gardens. It was money, money, money all the time for everybody these days.

Having finished clearing up, Alice sat down with her knitting to watch her favourite TV programme – Archie could never understand how she managed to concentrate on both things at once – he just stared into the fire. Once or twice, she was about to say something to cheer him, but thought better of it. Nothing she could say or do would lift him out of this depression.

Lying beside him in bed that night, she longed to put her arms round him and tell him it didn't matter where they lived as long as they were together, but fear of being rebuffed held her back.

Archie also spent long wakeful hours until daylight, pondering over what he could do, and it was rising time before he came to a decision, a decision he definitely could not pass on to his wife. It was something he would have to do by himself.

He set off after breakfast, with Belle, as usual, padding in front of him down the street, and as he neared the one and only shop, a familiar figure came out. Jimmy Masson, a year or two younger than he was, was already bent and walking with a stick.

'Aye, aye, Archie, grand morning, for a change.' The man stood up, ready for a chat to pass the time.

'Aye, aye, Jimmy.' Archie gave the expected response and walked on, eyes straight ahead.

The other man looked after him in bewilderment. Archie Murchie always stopped for a blether, and they would speak about matters of interest in the world or just in their own small community. With all this speculation going on about the future of Kilstrath, he'd have thought Archie would have plenty to say. He'd always been different, of course, forever sitting under the railway arches, even when he was just a wee laddie. That's why his schoolmates had tormented him.

'Archie loves the arches!' they had shouted, and he was blowed now if he could remember what Murchie's real first name was. Even Alice called him Archie. Reminding himself that nothing was as queer as folk, Jimmy went home to see if *his* wife could refresh his memory.

Belle was obviously pleased that her master hadn't stopped to talk, leading the way to the viaduct, and running back several times to hurry him on. They were within twenty yards of it when Archie stopped to admire the magnificence of the old structure. He had always been impressed by it and loved standing underneath to hear a train rattling past over his head. There were no trains now, though – the line had been closed with the Beeching cuts, years ago, and the village itself would soon be as good as dead; with nobody there but noisy Americans swaggering about as though they'd owned the place since the year dot.

Alice was drying the breakfast dishes when she heard the postman's knock, and hastily laid down the towel. Geordie Forbes didn't believe in simply pushing letters through letterboxes, for he liked to pick up any gossip available at each house on his round.

'Well, well, then, Mrs Murchie,' he observed as she opened the door, making her smile, because he'd called her by her Christian name for years. 'It's a grand day – in more ways than one.' He held up a long, brown, official-looking envelope. 'Is Archie about?'

'He's out with the dog.' Alice didn't mention their destination in case he laughed, for most folk knew it was a sore point with her.

'Oh, well. I'd have liked to see how he took it, but never mind. It's good news I'm delivering this day. It's from a firm of solicitors in Edinburgh, telling all the laird's tenants their houses are safe.' Since he had discussed the contents several times with earlier recipients, he was well informed. 'He's not selling unless the buyer agrees we're left where we are. I'm telling you, that's a load off a lot o' folks' minds, for they were worried sick at reading that bit in yesterday's *Observer*.'

'Oh. Geordie,' Alice breathed as soon as she could get a word in. 'I'm right pleased to hear this. I was that sorry for Archie. He never got a wink o' sleep last night for worrying what would happen to us.'

'I noticed he was terrible upset when I saw him yesterday morning. If I was you, I'd give him this as quick as I could . . .'

Grabbing her coat from its peg and the envelope from the man's hand, she pushed past him and set off as fast as her rheumaticky legs would carry her to pass on the good news.

Once again, Archie had the awful feeling that, far from giving him guidance, the arches were unfriendly, even menacing, although the sun was shining on them. There would be no peace for him here; no solution to clear his agonised mind. He'd have to do what he'd made up his mind to do.

Walking under the bridge, he carried on along the road until he came to a gate in the field, then lifted the bar and walked back across the grassy incline up to the railway tracks. The steep embankment was quite a struggle for him, and when he reached the top he had to stand a few minutes to get his breath back before he bent to go under the wire fence.

After waiting a few more seconds until the pain in his lungs eased, he walked on to the viaduct. He hadn't been up here since he was a youth, coming for the sheer excitement of facing the danger his mother had always warned him about, and had forgotten that this high vantage point afforded such a beautiful view of the village and surrounding countryside. In spite of everything, he felt more at ease; there was something about this wonder of Victorian engineering that gave him strength and courage . . . courage to do what, though? He couldn't remember now what he had planned in the early hours of the morning.

He couldn't face leaving his cottage, though Alice didn't seem to mind. If it wasn't for him, she wouldn't need a new house at all. She could go and live with her widowed sister in Aberdeen; they'd be company for each other. His thoughts paused there. Yes, that was what he had decided to do.

He clambered up on the parapet to look down at the road below. It was quite a distance, but if he closed his eyes he could forget all his worries. Holding up his head, he felt the keen wind in his face – for the last time. It was better this way, far better, and it would be all over in no time at all.

He suddenly became aware of a calling voice that was invading his consciousness and tried to shut it out. But no matter how hard he fought against it, it kept on. 'Archie! Archie! It's all right! It's going to be all right!' Opening his eyes reluctantly, he saw Alice looking up at him from the road beneath, terror showing clearly on her face. What did she mean? Why was she here? She'd no business coming to the arches. She never came. She said they gave her the creeps.

He closed his eyes – that would shut her out. She wasn't really there, anyway. It was all in his imagination. But his confused brain couldn't recapture his previous train of thought. What had he been going to do? It was somehow connected with Alice, that was all he could remember.

The sound of a dog barking made his eyes jerk open again, and there was his spaniel at his feet, looking up at him with her head on one side. What was she doing up here on top of the viaduct? He couldn't even remember having climbed up himself, but he crossed over and ducked under the wire fence again. Stumbling down the embankment, he saw Alice coming up to meet him. She said nothing as she turned with him down on to the road, but that was when he noticed the envelope in her hand. A long, business envelope. Here was the news he didn't want.

'It's for you, Archie.'

He opened it with trembling fingers and drew out the single sheet of paper, but the typed words blurred before his eyes and he handed it back. 'Read it out for me, lass. I haven't got my glasses.'

She had to read it through twice before its full significance dawned on him, and he was silent so long that his wife felt anxious. 'Archie?' As he lifted his head she was relieved to see him smiling, his eyes clearer and brighter than they had been a moment before.

'I'll be able to die in the house I was born in,' he said, happily. 'It's what I've aye hoped for, and not many have the good fortune to do that.' The worry and conflict of the past long hours were gone from his face, and his shoulders lifted as they turned towards the village. 'We'll just get back home now, lass.'

A lump in her throat and tears in her eyes, Alice painfully

matched her steps to his, but in a couple of minutes, he stopped and looked back at the arches. 'They didna help me,' he said, simply.

'I ken, Archie, I ken. Just forget about it.'

He put his arm round her ample waist, for the first time in many years. 'It's you that never lets me down, lass.'

Alice smiled at him fondly. 'Ach, you're just a great, soft lump.'

***

Word count 3647

Written in July 1986 and rejected by *People's Friend*.

The Christmas Baby

'Why's your tummy so fat, Mummy?'

Three-year-old Iain poked his podgy finger into his mother's pregnant body and looked up into her face, his eyes demanding an instant, truthful answer.

Fiona Angus sighed. She had known it would come but, coward that she was, she'd put it off as long as she could. Gently, she lifted him on to her knee, her brain searching wildly for the proper words.

Her son snuggled against her, his question already forgotten. 'A story, Mummy?'

She relaxed against the cushions of the wide armchair, relieved that the awkward moment had passed, then made up her mind that it would be best to get it over after all. She couldn't face having to go through this panic another time. 'No story just now, Iain,' she smiled, shifting her position slightly to be more comfortable. She dreaded his reception of what she meant to tell him, but took the plunge. 'Mummy's going to tell you why her tummy's so fat.'

She got a flash of inspiration when his hand rested on her 'bump'. 'Can you feel something moving inside there?'

After frowning in concentration for a few seconds, he smiled broadly. 'Ooh, yes, it's a frog jumping about.'

Fiona had to laugh. 'It's not a frog, it's a baby, a little brother or sister for you. I'm sure you'll like that, won't you?'

He nodded absentmindedly, still engrossed in feeling the movements under his hand.

'Mummy and Daddy thought it would be a good idea for you to have somebody to play with. Once it's grown, of course,' she added hastily, 'and we'll still love you just as much as ever when the new baby arrives.'

He lifted his head now and studied her face earnestly, making her apprehensive of what was going through his mind. 'Did I grow in there, too?' he asked slowly.

'Yes, darling. All babies grow in their mummy's tummies.'

'How does it come out?' His eyes were wide open, but very interested.

This was the tricky bit. This was where the difficulty lay. 'It can't come out by itself,' she said, carefully. 'Mummy has to go to hospital to have it taken out.'

'Oh.' He fell silent, obviously trying to picture the hospital staff making a door for the infant to pass through.

Fiona held her breath, waiting for an avalanche of further questions about this strange phenomenon, but Iain seemed to accept it with no thoughts as to why or where. 'When will I have my new brother?' he asked eagerly, taking it for granted that it would be a boy, because his little friend next door had recently acquired a baby brother.

'It should be around Christmas time,' Fiona said, very glad that her son was showing no signs of jealousy. 'It'll be like the story about Baby Jesus that Gran told you, remember? Won't that be fun?'

'I bet it'll be better than Mark's brother,' Iain boasted, jumping off his mother's knee. 'And I bet it'll have more hair.'

She gave a relieved giggle, recalling the tiny bald head that had both fascinated and disgusted Iain when they had gone to see the new arrival next door. He ran off now, full of excitement, to let Mark into the secret, while she lumbered to her feet to prepare the evening meal.

After Iain had been put to bed, she told her husband how their son had received the announcement. 'He wasn't a bit jealous. He's just sure our baby'll be better than Mark's.'

Gavin Angus chuckled. 'I told you not to worry about it. Iain's not spoiled even if he's an only child – but not for much longer.' Picking up the newspaper, he asked solicitously, 'How have you been today, darling?'

'Fine, really, but I wish it was all over. The last few weeks are always the worst.' She lifted her knitting from the workbag at the side of her chair, and held up the tiny white matinee jacket for him to admire. 'Iain's sure it's going to be a boy, but I've played safe by not using blue or pink.'

'Mmmm.' Gavin was already engrossed in the sports page.

'You're not listening!' she said, sharply.

'What? Oh, yes, it's very nice, but isn't it a bit small?'

Grinning, she shook her head. 'It's not meant for a monster. Remember how small Iain was when he was born?'

'You're right there. I was terrified to hold him at first, in case he slipped through my fingers. He soon grew, though. He's a real boy now, and I'll be taking him along with me to football matches in no time at all.'

'Oh, you and your football! It's all you think about nowadays.' She sat down heavily, to crochet the strings for the tiny jacket.

'Not exactly all,' Gavin teased with a twinkle in his eyes.

The days passed slowly for Fiona until, at long last, on the afternoon of Christmas Eve, she felt the unmistakable signs of her baby's imminent arrival. 'Mum,' she told her mother, who was to be staying in the house until Fiona was back on her feet, 'you'd better phone for a taxi, while I tell Iain.'

Mrs Simpson went out to the hall, saying over her shoulder, 'I'll tell Mrs Baxter next door to be ready, as well.'

Fiona grabbed her son as he rushed past shouting to an imaginary playmate. He'd be much better with a brother or sister to keep him company on rainy days like this, she assured herself. 'Mummy's going to the hospital now, darling, to have the baby,' she told him. 'You'll be a good boy to Granny, won't you?'

'Yes, Mummy. When are you going away?'

'Quite soon, dear.' She fully expected a flood of tears, but Iain seemed to be anxious for her to be gone.

It only took the taxi little more than five minutes to arrive and Fiona asked the driver to carry out the travelling bag that had been sitting ready in the hall for the past four weeks. Then she went back to her son. 'I'm going now, but don't come outside. It's absolutely pouring with rain.' She kissed him quickly, but he wriggled out of her grasp.

'I'll hold him up so he can wave from the window,' her mother consoled. 'Now, you're sure you'll be all right? Is Mrs Baxter there?'

'Yes, Mum, she's waiting in the taxi. She'd been looking out for it. And don't worry about me – I've done it all before.' Fiona turned to Iain again. 'Bye, darling, and look after Daddy and Gran until I come home. We're lucky it's going to be a real Christmas baby, aren't we?'

'Yes, Mummy, but hurry.' He didn't appear to care that she was leaving, and it was a rather downhearted Fiona who joined her neighbour in the taxi.

His grandmother held the small boy up to the window, but felt his little body suddenly stiffen. He's just realised his Mummy's away, she thought, keeping a firm grip on him as he turned and buried his face in her shoulder. 'It's all right, my wee lamb, she'll be back in just a few days,' she comforted. 'Wait till you see the bonny new baby she'll be taking home with her.'

'Don't want any silly baby,' came the muffled reply.

Mrs Simpson was puzzled by this sudden change of heart. Fiona had told her how Iain had been delighted with the idea of a new baby, so why should he be in tears about it now?

Was he beginning to be jealous? Was he scared they

wouldn't love him if there was a new baby? Depositing him on the floor because he was growing a bit heavy for her to carry, she tried to take his mind off himself. 'Come on, my dearie, we'll have to phone Daddy to let him know.'

He withdrew his chubby little hand from hers but held his head down, so she went into the hall by herself. 'I'll go straight to the hospital when I'm finished here,' Gavin told her when he heard the news. 'I wish I could have gone with her, though. Was she all right?'

'She was fine, and Mrs Baxter went with her in the taxi.' She hoped that she wasn't going to be saddled with two disconsolate males while her daughter was away.

At teatime, Iain ate his scrambled eggs in silence, this new sulkiness worrying his grandmother. She had never seen him like this before. After she had washed the dishes and tidied up, she took his hand and led him upstairs. 'Come away, my dearie, and Gran'll tell you a nice wee story when you're tucked up in bed.'

She ran the water for his bath and watched him as he undressed, spurning the help she offered. By the time she was rubbing his hair with the huge striped towel, she had come to the conclusion that it wasn't just pique that was troubling Iain. He was really a sad little boy, she mused, as the fair curls sprang to life from the head that had, a few minuted before, been wet and bedraggled. 'What's wrong. my pet? Tell Gran.'

But he just shook his head and ran through to his bedroom. She decided to tell him the Christmas story again. It might help him to accept the coming child without feeling neglected and resentful. He listened, unmoving, as she began the tale, but his wide blue eyes never left her face.

'And so Mary and Joseph had to go to Bethlehem. Joseph knew that Mary couldn't walk all that way when she was going to have a baby, so he got an ass, that's just like a donkey, for her to sit on, and they started . . . '

'It's not true!' Iain shouted suddenly. 'It wasn't an ass, or a donkey. It wasn't!' He burst into tears, deep, racking sobs that shook his whole small frame.

Mrs Simpson was utterly perplexed as she held him close and patted his back. What on earth could be upsetting him like this? 'Aye, my dearie, Mary did ride into Bethlehem on a donkey, and the Baby Jesus was born in a stable because they couldn't find anywhere else to stay.'

He cried until he was exhausted, while she sat, at a loss how to deal with him, until she was sure that he was sound asleep. His face looked so peaceful now, still wet with tears, so she tiptoed out, leaving the door open.

It was almost one o'clock before Gavin came home. 'It's a boy,' he announced joyfully, 'and they're both doing well. Seven pounds four ounces, and lovely with it. He was born at twelve minutes past midnight, so Iain'll be glad it's a real Christmas baby.'

'Poor wee Iain,' said his mother-in-law, and told him what had happened.

Gavin was just as perturbed as she was, and went upstairs to make sure that his elder son was sleeping. The sight of the small face, so angelic in repose, brought a lump to his throat. Small children were so vulnerable. He pulled the quilt up gently, and vowed that he would never give Iain cause to resent the new arrival.

At that moment, the boy opened his eyes. 'Daddy,' he whispered, 'is that you?'

'Yes, son.' Gavin gathered up the pathetic little figure, quilt and all, and carried him downstairs. He sat down in an easy chair by the fire and cradled his first-born in his arms. 'Mummy's got our baby now – a real Christmas baby.' He was quite unprepared for Iain's reaction, as the boy jumped off his knee on to the floor, tears steaming down his cheeks.

'It's not a real Christmas baby! It's not! Mummy didn't go on a donkey! She went in a silly old taxi!'

Gavion sat, mystified, as his mother-in-law, enlightened by the boy's outburst, knelt down beside her grandson and her arms round the sleepy, pyjama-clad figure. 'Mary and Joseph lived a long, long time ago, my wee lamb. Long before there were any motor cars. If there had been, Mary would have gone in a taxi just like Mummy. So you see, it *is* a real Christmas baby, after all.'

'Really and truly, Gran?' Iain hiccupped, his face breaking out in a huge smile.

'Really and truly.' She brushed a tear from the corner or her eye. 'Now, you'd better go back to bed quickly, because Santa won't come if you're not sleeping.'

She held up the old football sock of Gavin's that Fiona had explained was to be used for this purpose. 'Look, your Christmas stocking's all ready and waiting.'

Using the sleeve of his pyjama jacket to dry his own eyes, the astonished boy said, 'I forgot all about Santa.'

He took his father's hand to go upstairs, then anxious again, looked into the man's still bewildered face. 'Is our baby better than Mark's baby?'

'Of course he is,' Gavin grinned. 'He's absolutely beautiful, with fair hair just like ours.'

'Wheeeee!' Iain jumped up abnd down with excitement. 'Just wait till I tell Mark that our baby's got hair. Can we call him Jesus?'

***

Word count 2197

Written July 1986 – rejected by *People's Friend* and the *Sunday Post*

The Christmas Spirit

Leila Paul hurried through the milling crowds, all last-minute shoppers like herself. This is ridiculous, she thought. Why do so many people leave their gift-buying until Christmas Eve? Every person she looked at seemed to be under pressure of some kind – no happy faces at all. What a horrible time Christmas was.

She struggled through the entrance of a large store, against the tide of customers coming out laden with parcels and large shopping bags, and stood inside the shop to get her breath back. A young woman with a worried expression was making her way towards the doors, carrying a bulky parcel. Its shape was easily recognisable even if its wrappings hadn't come adrift to reveal the contents. A pedal car for her young son, Leila thought, pityingly. No wonder she's worried; probably can't afford it, but the boy would have made it quite clear that it was what he expected Santa to bring. Modern children expected, and got, so much.

A harassed old lady appeared now, with two plastic carrier bags filled to overflowing. As she passed Leila, she had to bend to pick up a small parcel that had fallen out, and as she did so other packages slid and dropped to the floor.

'Oh, thank you.' She said breathlessly, as Leila helped her to gather these together. 'Isn't this a terrible crush, and everything's so dear. Christmas is so commercialised nowadays, isn't it?'

Leila nodded and smiled as the woman passed out of sight. Yes, she mused, there's none of the old-fashioned Christmas spirit about any more. Each of the faces she could see was set and strained due, no doubt, to money worries and the nagging doubt that someone special had been forgotten in the rush; or the what-on-earth-can-I-buy-her-she-has-everything problem.

It was then that she spotted the young couple. Very young, they looked, surely not old enough to be married. But, of course, boys and girls did everything together now, even their Christmas shopping. As they came nearer, she heard the girl say, 'Isn't it fun, darling? Our baby's first Christmas. I can hardly wait to see his face when he opens his stocking.'

The boy's look of sheer adoration as he smiled back at his young wife made a lump come into Leila's throat. A Christmas stocking; how many memories that brought back.

First of all, had been the filling. Down into the toe had gone an apple, then a packet of sweets, a little colouring book, a square of the Swiss milk toffee she always used to make, some crayons, perhaps, then a tangerine and lastly, the present. It was usually a large parcel and was laid on the floor – always opened first. She could recall dolls, a doll's house, a cot and a nurse's outfit for Helen over the years, and a tricycle, a cowboy outfit, a fire engine and a football at different times for Michael.

Money had always been in short supply when the children were small, but Alan and she had always managed to fill the stockings, buying little items throughout the year when they could afford them. There was one year, though, when they had bought, at a jumble sale in September, the space suit that Michael wanted, but hadn't been able to get the desk that Helen had asked Santa to bring.

Alan had said, 'Don't worry, dear, I'll make one for her', and had put together a beautifully sturdy desk with spaces for pens and paper and things like that, working at it every night after Helen went to bed. Leila smiled at the memory of what came next. Alan had painted it white, and had to varnish it on Christmas Eve, but he'd had to use the cheapest brand, which hadn't been dry by the time they were acting Santa.

They had carried the desk from their bedroom, where it had been hidden from prying eyes, and stood it in front of the coal fire in the living room to dry more quickly. They had been sitting there, talking quietly when they heard Helen coming downstairs. Leila laughed out loud as she recalled how they had jumped up in confusion and placed themselves in front of the desk to screen it from its owner.

'Mummy, I just wondered if Santa had been yet,' she had murmured sleepily.

'No, darling, he doesn't come until well after midnight. I told you, remember?'

'Remember to lay out the Christmas pies you bought for him – and a glass of milk,' and the six-year-old had gone back to bed, quite unaware that her shattered parents had collapsed on the settee in hysterics.

Christmas mornings had been fun, too; noisy fun, with two drowsy adults being shocked into consciousness by an avalanche that descended on them about five or six a.m.

The stockings were always carried up and emptied in the main bedroom, wrappings and boxes being strewn all over the floor; it kept the living room free from rubbish. Oh, the excitement, the laughter, the love!

The house had been full of love in those days, Leila reflected, and excitement and laughter. Now, though, with Helen married and living so far away, and Michael a rather difficult eighteen-year-old, the atmosphere was different. There was little excitement, except when Michael argued with his father, and she could do without that; laughter only now and then, and certainly no show of love. She supposed that it still must be there, somewhere, under their veneer of middle age.

Sighing deeply, she raised her head and met the anxious gaze of the young couple who had started her thoughts wandering. 'Are you all right?' asked the girl. 'You were standing there as if you were miles away. There's nothing wrong, I hope?'

'No, there's nothing wrong, thank you,' Leila smiled. 'I was years away, not miles.'

She turned, to move off but the girl came after her. 'You don't look all right, you know. Come round to our flat, it's just round the corner, and I'll give you a cup of tea to revive you. I always think tea's the best medicine in the world.'

'Oh, I couldn't,' Leila protested.

'It's no bother, really. We'll be needing one ourselves

114

and my mum'll likely have the kettle boiling. She's looking after our baby.'

Leila looked at the girl's lovely face, and at the boy smiling in agreement with her. How deeply in love they were; she wished that Helen and Harry were as happy as that. Her daughter and son-in-law had no time for enjoyment; they were too busy making money. Helen was a dedicated career girl and had said, more than once, 'We don't want to start a family until we have everything we need for our home.'

Leila often thought that they'd be less self-centred if they did have a baby; it would make them content with what they had, but she couldn't tell Helen that. Realising that the young couple were still regarding her with some concern, she smiled at the girl. 'Thank you, my dear, but I must finish my shopping, and my husband is expecting me home.'

'You look tired, dear,' Alan said, taking her shopping bags from her. 'Sit down and I'll bring you a cup of coffee. I switched on the percolator a few minutes ago.'

Leila sank down thankfully into her armchair and kicked off her shoes. Her feet were throbbing. She would have to reduce her weight a bit.

'There's a Christmas service at eleven forty-five tonight,' Alan remarked when he returned with two steaming mugs. 'I was remembering how we always used to go when the kids were younger.'

She looked at him, his dear curly hair almost white, but his eyes still deeply twinkling blue. 'I've been remembering those times past, as well.' The thought of having to go out again was not a pleasant one, but she said, quickly, 'Would you like to go, Alan? It would be like the old days again, wouldn't it?' It would be a pity to disappoint him and she could put her feet up until nearer the time.

He looked surprised that she had suggested it. 'Yes, Leila, I would like to go, as a matter of fact, but are you sure you're feeling up to it?'

'Of course I am, and I want to go. We always used to come home from the midnight service feeling at peace with the world, remember?'

They returned to the house at five minutes to one and, as he closed the door behind him, Alan took his wife in his arms and kissed her. 'Happy Christmas, darling.'

It was a long time since he'd kissed her like that – it was generally just a quick peck on the cheek nowadays, if that. She sighed happily. 'It *is* like old times, isn't it? At any minute I'll be shouting to the children to stop making a noise and get to bed at once.'

At that moment, the door burst open, almost sending them flying. 'Ha! Caught you, you two old lovebirds.' Michael wagged a finger at them. 'What's this, then? Snogging behind the door at your age?'

'Don't be daft,' Alan laughed. 'We just got home from the Christmas Eve service and I felt like kissing your mother. There's nothing wrong in that, is there? What have you been up to tonight?'

'You're not going to believe this, Dad, but I've met a girl I'm sure you'll approve of – for a change.'

The weird girlfriends he brought home had long been a bone of contention with his parents, and were often the cause of heated arguments with his father. 'She's a medical student but she lives in the nurses' home because she can't travel in and out from her own home every day. I've invited her here for Christmas dinner . . . if that's OK, Mum?'

Leila pulled a face, then grinned. 'That's OK, Michael.' The peace she had found in the church made her feel happily contented. The hall telephone shrilled at that moment and she turned to lift the receiver.

'Hi, Mum, I'm just phoning to give you our news.' Helen's excited voice came over the line, bubbling with happiness.

'But . . . aren't you coming home tomorrow – I mean today?' Disappointment clutched at the pit of Leila's stomach.

'Yes, of course we are, but I couldn't keep this to myself any longer. We're going to have a baby, Mum. What do you think of that?'

'Oh, Helen, I'm so pleased. That's the best Christmas present you could have given me.' Tears were streaming down Leila's cheeks, and she turned to explain hem to her husband. 'Helen's going to have a baby.'

Her daughter was still speaking. 'I found out for sure this afternoon, but we'd been invited out to dinner and we've just arrived home, so this is the first chance I've had to phone. We'll be leaving shortly, Harry thinks it's best to drive overnight when there's less traffic. See you when we arrive, Grandma. Bye.'

Grandma! Leila laid down the receiver and held her hands out to her husband and son. 'What a wonderful time Christmas always is.'

***

Word count 1863
Sent to *People's Friend* 31.7.86 – rejected 10.9.86
Sent to the *Sunday Post* 6.10.86 – rejected 17.10.86

From Paula's Journal

This journal belongs to:

Paula Inglis,
14 Jamaica Close,
Forest Hill,
Aberfithie,
Scotland,
Great Britain,
Europe,
The World.

Date of Birth: 12 June 1969
Colour of Hair: Reddish brown
Colour of Eyes: Blue
Height: 5 feet 2 inches
(in bare feet)

MONDAY 27th

I swear to keep this journal written up every day, in the hope that it will give future generations an insight into the life of a teenager in 1986. Not that anything exciting ever happens to me, but I keep hoping.

At the moment, I'm absolutely cheesed off with never getting out at nights, and that's why I started writing this – to give me something to do. Mum hates being in the house by herself, and invents all kinds of excuses to make me stay at home.

For instance: 'Why don't you stay in tonight, Paula, and

we can have a dressmaking session? There's still that length of blue polyester we got at Milligan's sale, remember?'

Or another for instance: 'I'd be grateful for a hand to clean out some of the kitchen units. Would you mind . . . ?'

Or another for instance. 'Could you sort out your wardrobe tonight, dear? The scouts are having a jumble sale and they're collecting tomorrow.'

That's the kind of thing, multiplied by dozens. I got so guilty about leaving her on her own that I started putting my friends off, and now they never ask me to go out with them, not even Tim. He's my boyfriend, at least he was until he lost interest because I never knew if I'd be able to meet him or not. Mostly not. My social life has ground to a dismal halt.

If only Mum would start to go out again. But she won't. She just says, 'When I went to other people's houses, it was always couples, and I felt the odd man out.'

I sympathise with her in a way. I can understand how she must feel, because Dad was a great one for socialising, and they went everywhere together. He was always there when Mike's pals dropped in, or when my friends came round. He was young at heart and great fun, so they all used to enjoy an evening at our house.

I don't know what went wrong between him and Mum. I was only fourteen when they were divorced, and Mum never speaks about it, but over the past three years I've watched her retreating further and further inside herself. It's very sad, really.

My brother – that's Mike, full name Michael – comes round every week with his wife, and they try to shake

Mum out of her seclusion by asking her to their house to meet their friends, but she always says, 'You don't want an old fogey like me putting a damper on things.' And she's not that old – only just over forty.

Mike even brought Mr Dunne, his boss, round a few months ago. He's an eligible bachelor; eligible because he's in his forties, too, but she suspected Mike of match-making, and was quite offhand with the poor man. I'm pretty sure he likes her, though, because he comes round occasionally, and phones to ask her out, but she always refuses.

Back to my own life. I met Tim Reynolds this afternoon as I was coming home from work, and he told me there's a former pupils' disco on Friday. He asked if I would like to be his partner, though he must know I can't. Mum would hate being left alone for so long. But it would have been fab dancing with Tim again.

I thought of asking someone to 'Mum-sit', but Mike and Lorraine have a dinner dance the same night, and they're the only people who come here these days – except Mr Dunne, of course. When he calls, to cheer Mum up he says, I take the chance to slip along to Kerry's for a chat, but she's often out and I end up sitting with *her* mum. Not much of a change, is it?

TUESDAY 28th

Tried to talk to Mum last night about the disco, but she changed the subject before I got round to asking if I could go, just as if she knew what I was going to say. If I could only stand up for myself and make the break, she might accept it and untie the apron strings, or sever her lifeline, or whatever it is that makes her depend on me the way she does. The trouble is, it feels more like a heavy chain to me.

Every time I've ever suggested having a night out with Kerry, Mum looks at me with that pitiful, hurt expression that makes me feel like a monster, so I give up. I suppose I'm a coward, but I can't cause her any more unhappiness than she's had already.

I had a look at some gorgeous outfits in Milligan's at lunchtime. If I walk to work the rest of the month, and take sandwiches instead of going to the little café next door to the office, I might just manage to afford the green seersucker pants and top. Kerry said that it would really suit me with my creamy skin and reddish hair. She's my best friend, but I must admit I feel slightly jealous of her at times, out nearly every other night with one boy or another. She can't really understand my problem.

'Just go out, Paula,' she says. 'Your mother's had plenty of time to learn to adjust, and she's not all that old, is she?'

WEDNESDAY 29th

Went back to Milligan's with Kerry at lunchtime. She was right, as usual. The green pants suit is perfect for me, and shows up my colouring. I let her persuade me to buy it, though I don't know when, if ever, I'll get the chance to wear it. It'll likely be out of fashion by the time Mum's able to stand on her own two feet, and it's left me flat broke for the rest of the month. That's not just a couple of days, either. Our salaries go into the bank on the 15th of each month, worse luck.

Tried the suit on at home after teatime. It's really dreamy, and with the right make-up and a new hair style, I could be the belle of the ball, well the school hall, if only I could go.

Must have that talk with Mum, but I don't suppose it'll make any difference. Mr Dunne has just called in . . . I wonder?

THURSDAY 30th

Took the chance last night when Mum was making coffee, and Mr Dunne was very understanding. He's going to insist on taking Mum out tomorrow to let me be free.

'I'll buy two tickets for that new show at the Palace,' he said, 'and I'll tell your mother they were given to me. She won't like to refuse. Rest assured, Paula, it will be OK. You'll get to your disco and enjoy every minute of it.'

I dyed my white sandals before I went to bed, because I can't afford to buy new ones, and I only hope they'll turn out the right shade of green.

Mr Dunne rang at teatime to ask Mum to go to the Palace with him. I could just hear her side of the conversation of course, and my heart sank deeper and deeper into my old fluffy mules with each word she spoke.

'Oh, hello, John . . . That was kind of him. It'll be nice for you to see a show . . . What? Oh, no, I couldn't . . . No,

I haven't been out for . . . No, honestly, I mean it. Thanks for asking me, but it's no use. I can't go. Goodbye, John, and I hope you find someone for company.'

She came back into the living room. 'That was John asking me to go to a show with tomorrow night, but I said I couldn't.'

I said, 'Mum, you'll have to start going out again some time. This sitting cooped up in the house every night's not good for you.' Nor for me, I thought.

'I can't leave you on your own, dear.'

'That's rubbish and you know it. It's just an excuse. Anyway, I'm seventeen now and there's a former pupils' dance I'd like to go to.'

'You haven't anything suitable to wear to a dance, have you?'

'I bought a new outfit yesterday.'

She looked at me suspiciously, but made no comment, so I pressed on. 'Why don't you ring back and tell him you'll go?'

'I can't go, Paula. I haven't been out for so long I can't face meeting people again. They only pity me and introduce me as a divorced woman.'

So that was it! And for years I'd been thinking she was suffering from some form of new agoraphobia that only affected women in the evenings. 'Nobody thinks anything about divorce nowadays, Mum. A lot of my school friends had divorced parents, and a few of the girls in the office, too. In fact, there are at least three of the older women there that are divorcees. Anyway, it was three years ago, and it's past history.'

She looked dubious, but seemed a little more cheerful. 'Do you really think so?'

'Yes, I do really think so. Stop carrying on like a long lost soul and phone him back right now. You know he likes you, a blind man could even see that, and maybe . . .'

'No, no. Don't go reading anything into it. There's a huge gap between liking somebody and loving them. I'll tell him I'll go with him this time, since he was given the tickets, but that'll be the end of it.'

I should have known it was useless, but it was worth a try. She's a really stubborn woman, my mother, and I don't seem to have any more success as a matchmaker than Mike did. But at least it's all right for tomorrow night . . . and the disco. Whoopee!!

FRIDAY 31st

Haven't time to write much tonight. Kerry'll be round shortly to do my hair. She's got a special mousse she wants me to try, and she's going to put it in a new style, and we're going to the disco together. I wouldn't bank on us coming home together, though.

The sandals turned out fine, a shade darker than the green seersucker, but toning in perfectly. I wonder if Tim is taking somebody else? A new girlfriend? I hope not.

SATURDAY 1st

Well, that's that! What an anticlimax! I didn't enjoy the disco all that much. The only good thing I can say is that it was a change from sitting in the house. All the boys I used to know are going steady and there wasn't one unattached male there. I see now what Mum felt about being the odd man out.

Tim Reynolds had taken that stuck-up Angie Davis, and she looked like a cat that had got at the cream – tickled pink with herself. At one point, she sidled up to me when I was standing trying to look as though I was having a super time, but failing miserably. 'I was just saying to Tim,' she purred, 'that I hadn't seen you for ages.' She was absolutely gloating that she was his partner, I could tell that. It wasn't difficult.

He did ask me up once, though, but he hardly spoke a word while we were on the floor, and I danced with some other boys, but I came home by myself. Eric Morton saw Kerry home, so I bet she's pleased with herself. She's fancied him for months.

Mum's night out didn't go any better than mine, unfortunately. 'The show wasn't all that good,' she confessed over breakfast, 'so John took me to Pelham's afterwards for a few drinks to make up for it.'

That sounded quite hopeful, but her next words sent me down in the doldrums again. 'I told him I'm no good at socialising these days, and he didn't argue. I'm sure he found me dull – no scintillating repartee – so it's no good you hoping something will come out of it. ;

I wouldn't have minded my own fiasco so much if Mum had enjoyed her evening out – but here we are. Back to Square One.

SUNDAY 2nd

With all the excitement of going to the disco on Friday, and yesterday's depression, I forgot all about it being Mum's birthday today, until Mike and Lorraine came in with a huge box of chocolates for her, so I'd to phone Kerry to borrow some cash.

Of course, being Sunday, the shops were closed and I couldn't buy the kind of present she'd want, so I decided to take her out for a celebration meal. Not that either of us had much to celebrate, Mum being a whole year older and me well on the way to being a dried-up old maid, but I had to make an effort of some kind. I mean, you can't just let your mother's birthday pass unmarked, can you?

Kerry came round after lunch with £12, all she could spare, and I told Mum what I had planned. She wasn't keen on going out, not even with me, and it took a lot of persuasion to make her change her mind. 'Slap on some warpaint and wear something really nice,' I urged. 'You'll feel better, I promise.'

We went to the Carvery on the Ring Road and had a lovely meal – I don't know how they can do it for £5.60 each – but it didn't make either of us feel any better. Then just before the coffee came – I couldn't afford a sweet but Mum said she wasn't able for one anyway – I noticed her smiling to someone behind me and blushing a deep rosy red. It actually comes as quite a shock when you discover your mother's still a beautiful woman.

Her hair's dark brown with just enough silver in it to make it interesting, and her blue eyes matched her dress

127

exactly. Someone else evidently thought she was beautiful, because, while we were still waiting for our coffee this tall, handsome man with short grizzled hair came to our table. The recipient of her smile, presumably.

'Sylvia!' He beamed at Mum as if he thought she was the best invention since TV dinners. 'I thought it was you when you came in, but I wasn't absolutely sure till you smiled at me. It must be twenty-five years since I saw you and you don't look a day older.'

It was a cheesy thing to say, but she giggled like a young thing. She'd have been eighteen when they'd seen each other last, of course. But she wasn't fooled.

'You were always good at paying compliments, Martin, but don't overdo it. Today is my forty-third birthday, and I feel every year of them.'

'I meant every word I said. May I join you? I've just ordered my coffee.'

'So have we. Please sit down. This is my daughter, Paula. Martin's an old friend, dear.'

He shook my hand but his eyes scarcely left Mum's face. 'I can't believe you have a daughter as old as this.'

How old did I look, for heaven's sake?

'I've a married son, too, Martin. He's twenty-three. Have you any children?'

'Two daughters, both married.'

'Is your wife not with you tonight?'

'She died five ears ago.'

'Oh, I'm sorry!' Mum looked confused. 'I'd never have said anything if I'd . . .'

128

'It's all right, Sylvia. I've got over the shock, now, but I suppose a person never really gets over the loss.'

'No, it's a dreadful wrench when you're left on your own. I know all about that.'

'Oh, is your husband . . . ?'

'We were divorced three years ago.'

Were my ears deceiving me? Was this my mother speaking so matter-of-factly about something she was usually so uptight about?

It was Martin's turn to be confused. 'I'm sorry. Trust me to say the wrong thing. I'm well known for always putting my foot in it.'

Mum laid her hand over his where it rested on the table. 'Don't worry about it, Martin. I'm just beginning to see things in perspective – it's past history now.'

My very words. Sitting there listening to their conversation I felt like the proverbial gooseberry, but my spirits were soaring. Could this Martin be the answer to all my problems? Or would Mum retreat further into her shell if I tried matchmaking again? I'd have to watch my step.

The coffees arrived and I closed one ear when they began to talk about their respective homes and families, and allowed my thoughts to wander in the direction of Tim Reynolds. He couldn't be serious about Angie Davis, she was such a creep. He must have taken her to the disco because . . . he thought I was unavailable? And he might have been off-hand with me because he felt embarrassed at being there with her?

I could make myself believe anything, as long as it was in my favour, that's the effect Tim had on me, and if Mum started going out with Martin, I'd be free to start again with Tim where I'd left off. If. A small word to have such an important meaning. I'd have to give my full attention to the talk across the table to find out whether there could be any likelihood of my dreams coming true. Stranger things have happened.

Mum was looking quite animated, as if she'd found a new lease of life. 'What brought you back to Aberfithie? Are you on holiday?'

Martin smiled. 'As a matter of fact, I'm being transferred back to Aberdeen, after all these years in Newcastle, so I thought it over and decided I'd rather commute again than live in a city any longer. I'm staying in my sister's house for a couple of weeks, but she was called away to look after her mother-in-law, and Bill, her husband, had to go to some meeting in London. That's why I came out for dinner tonight, and I'm very glad I did, otherwise I'd never have met you again.'

'What a coincidence that we were eating here, too.'

A potential miracle, that's what it was. And it wasn't over yet. Martin was still talking.

'My nephew has been looking after me so far, but his cooking's a bit unimaginative and that's being euphemistic. His mind's not on it, of course. He's mooning over some girl he met at a disco on Friday night. It seems they used to go out together, but she broke it off because her neurotic mother didn't like being left on her own. Poor Tim.'

Once my heart stopped roller-coasting and settled back into its own position, I found my tongue. 'Is your nephew Tim Reynolds, by any chance?'

Martin looked as if he'd forgotten I was there. He probably had. 'That's right. Do you know him? No! Don't tell
me you're the girl?' He turned to Mum with a stricken
face. 'And you're the neurotic . . . Oh, oh, I've done it
again.'

Mum's face was pale. 'He was quite right, though,
Martin. I *have* been neurotic, but not any more. I've seen
sense at last.'

He looked at me. 'Your mother and I were very much
in love once, but we had a senseless quarrel and I asked for
a transfer. That's when I was sent to Newcastle.'

'It was all my fault,' Mum said sadly. 'I fell for David's
charm and it took me nearly twenty years to see through
him, though I'd been suspecting for a while that his nights
away weren't really on business.'

'Well, that's all behind you, Sylvie, and we're both older
and wiser now. Do you think we could make a fresh start?'

The way she looked at him was enough. I knew she was
out of my hair at long last. Mind you, I was rather upset
at learning the truth about Dad. But it made me understand the strain Mum had been under and why she'd been
acting like she had. Anyway, I'd succeeded in bringing her
to her senses. Well, it *was* me who'd made her go to the
Carvery in the first place, wasn't it?

She's downstairs with Martin right now, and things
seem to be very quiet, but I don't intend being a spoil-
sport. Let them recapture their old romance. I'm very
happy for both of them.

This has been some week. I wonder that the next seven
days will bring? Me and Tim back together as well, I hope.

***

Word count 3468
   Sent to *Just 17* 29.5.86 – rejected 5.6.86
   Sent to *Woman's Realm* 10.8.86 – rejected 17.11.86
   Sent to *Woman's Story* – not returned, but never printed

Beginnings

It wasn't fair! Janey Martin pouted at her reflection in the mirror of her dressing table. Why should she always be the one to take the dog out? After all, she'd only been fourteen, a mere child, when she asked for a puppy for Christmas two years ago.

Her mother hadn't been keen on the idea. 'I know who'll be left to look after it. The same as I was left to clean out the gerbils and the guinea pig, when you were tired of them. It won't always be a cute little puppy, remember.'

Janey had appealed to her father then. 'Please Dad?' He never refused her anything, within reason, and, of course, he had given in again. 'Only on condition that you promise to look after it,' he had added.

She *had* looked after it – most of the time anyway – but she'd promised to go up to the Record Market today with her two best friends. Now Jacquie and Tish would be there without her, and this would likely be the day one of the boys would speak to her.

She sighed, skimmed her comb lightly through her long, fair ponytail, then slid the wardrobe door open with more force than was necessary to take out her new yellow leather-look coat. She may as well look her best in case she ran into somebody exciting, though there was little hope of that.

She stamped noisily down the stairs and lifted the dog's lead from the hallstand, making Dactyl, her Yorkie, go into such a frenzy of anticipation that she had to hold him between her knees before she could hook it on to his collar. She tried one last desperate protest when her mother came out of the kitchen. 'Why can't Mike take him out?'

'He's gone out to play football; and it's your dog.'

Janey knew the real reason for her own bad temper – no one had asked her to the school disco that night – so she closed the door quietly instead of slamming it – and switched her mind to deciding a possible career she might take up when she left school.

She walked down the path slowly and gracefully, and by the time she reached the gate, she was already a top model drifting across a raised walkway, showing off gorgeous outfits to an admiring group of wealthy buyers. There may even be a film producer among them, who would take one look at her slinky movements and then offer her a contract to star in his next musical opposite . . . ?

Before she could decide who would be her leading man, she was jolted back to reality by her dog. Dactyl was in great form, sniffing at a gatepost then bounding on to the next one, and Janey found it impossible to keep up her measured glide. She even began to enjoy his antics and let him pull her along towards the park. She didn't often go there, it was a bit far, but Dactyl seemed to be enjoying himself, too.

Beginnings

The sun was shining though there was a nip in the air, and Janey's spirits lifted, her feet almost dancing as she kept pace with the dog. It might be fun to be a ballet dancer instead of a model or a film star. She pirouetted daintily on her toes and could hear the thunderous applause from her phantom audience.

When Dactyl stopped to inspect a stone, she picked up a stick and let him off the lead. He ran off, not even waiting for her to throw the stick for him to fetch, and she laughed as he chased a cheeky little sparrow and then stood looking puzzled when it flew off. Leaving him to entertain himself, she sat down on a bench and drew pictures in the sandy soil of the path with the stick. The dog was racing about on the grass now with a Jack Russell, so she kept a wary eye on them until it was clear that they were quite friendly.

'They're having a whale of a time.'

The voice behind her made her jump; she hadn't heard anyone coming. Turning, her eyes widened when she saw that it was Neil Wallace, the head boy from school. 'Yes . . . yes they are,' she stammered, aware that he didn't recognise her. Why should he, when all the girls at Mountford ran after him?

He sat down beside her, rather belatedly asking, 'OK?' She nodded and swallowed nervously. 'D'you live round here?' he was obviously just making conversation.

Wishing that she could be as self-confident in real life as she was in her daydreams, she murmured, 'Yes, well . . . er . . . not really all that near. Mayfield Terrace, actually.'

'I'm quite near you, then – Mayfield Avenue. I haven't seen you in the park before, though. What's your name?'

135

'Janey Martin.'

'I'm Neil Wallace.'

As if she needed to be told! She could see his eyes taking in every detail about her, and was glad she had worn her yellow coat. She felt absolutely tongue-tied. Why couldn't she laugh and joke with him like the other girls did?

'D'you go to Mountford, Janey?'

She nodded again. 'Fifth year.'

'Only fifth?' he sounded genuinely surprised. 'I'd have said you were older than that.'

Pleased about this, she relaxed a little. 'It's the coat, I expect. It's more flattering than the school blazer.'

'It sure is! I get out of mine whenever I can, as well.'

She glanced at him quickly. She hadn't noticed that he wore a black leather jerkin, and found that it made him more handsome than ever, with his blond curly hair showing up well against the dark collar.

'I'll likely be seeing you at the disco tonight.' It was a statement, not a question.

'Well . . . no . . . not really.' She felt shy again.

'Why not? It's for fifth as well as sixth years.'

'Nobody asked me,' she admitted, trying to look as if she hadn't wanted to go, anyway.

'What? No boyfriend just now?'

'No, not at the moment.' She was grateful to him for handing her the face-saver.

'That's my good luck, then,' he laughed. 'You can be my partner. I was supposed to be taking Pat Connon, the head girl, but she broke her leg last night playing badminton.'

'Oh, I'm sorry, but surely there's another sixth-year girl you could take?' Janey was thrilled at being asked to her first disco by Neil Wallace, of all people, even if it was just a matter of convenience, but she didn't want to appear too eager.

'I don't fancy any of them,' he smiled. 'Great puddings, always flirting and giggling. You're different, more sensible.' He looked at her anxiously. 'I'd really like you to be my partner, Janey, if you've nothing else on?'

The open admiration in his brown eyes, surprisingly dark for his blond colouring, went to her head, but she said, cautiously, 'I'll think about it.' She brushed a stray strand of hair off her forehead and turned away from him. She could see that her apparent lack of intrest was making him more determined, but, just then, the two dogs came running up, jumping boisterously on their owners.

'That's enough, Dactyl,' she told him, pushing him down. 'It's time we were going home.' She took the lead from her pocket and Neil held the dog until she fixed it on.

'What did you call him?' he asked, bending to attend to his own dog.

'Dactyl. It's short for pterodactyl – the flying dinosaur, you know. My young brother was mad about them at the time I got him as puppy, so I called him Dactyl. It seemed to suit him, somehow.'

As she stood up, Neil rose and put his hand on her shoulder. 'Say you'll come tonight, Janey. Please?'

Laughing, she twisted from his grasp and ran back along the path. She was almost certain that he would follow, but was beginning to doubt it by the time she reached the park gates. She stopped, waiting for Dactyl to come away from the lamp post, and stole a quick glance behind. Neil *was* running towards her.

'Janey,' he puffed, when he caught up with her, 'Terry wouldn't let me fix on his lead and I thought you weren't going to wait. I don't know the number of your house.'

'Terry? That's a nice name for a dog.'

'Short for pterodactyl, would you believe? I was mad about dinosaurs, too, a few years back.'

'No! Not really?' She was astonished at the coincidence.

'So you see, we've a lot in common, great minds thinking alike and all that. Now, will you say you'll come tonight?'

'I haven't anything to wear.'

'You'd look smashing in anything.'

Janey learned then the age-old truth that boys don't have the least understanding of the importance the right clothes have for a girl.

'Please, Janey?' he pleaded again.

Frantically, she went over her wardrobe in her mind, and decided that the pink leggings and matching baggy top might just do. 'OK,' she smiled.

'Great! I'll come round for you at quarter past seven.'

When they reached her house, he took her hand and squeezed it. 'Boy! Am I looking forward to tonight! Wait till the other boys see you!'

Janey watched the tall, slim figure striding away from her, every now and then taking a hop-skip-and-jump, with the small terrier running joyously round his heels. For once, she wasn't imagining something impossible. This date was for real. She had a vague feeling that his dog was called Terry because he was a terrier, but it was sweet of Neil to say it was short for pterodactyl, like hers.

She sighed contentedly and burst into the house to tell her mother.

***

Word count 1641
    Sent to *Just 17* 7.9.86 – rejected 5.10.86
    Sent to *Patches:* 9.10.86 – rejected 30.10.86

The Tomato Plant

Elizabeth Miller had never wanted the plant to begin with.

'Tomatoes aren't meant to be grown inside houses,' she said when Henry had first mentioned it, 'and we certainly can't afford a greenhouse. I've enough to do in the garden, anyway, since you've had angina.'

'The man at the Garden Centre assured me that' – here he laughingly imitated the man's sales talk – '"Tomatoes are very successful in the house."'

He'd tell you anything,' she said, scathingly. 'There's no room on any of the window sills for anything else. I've eleven plants already.'

She had seen by his set mouth and steely eyes that he had made his mind up, and sure enough, he came home next day with a small green shoot in a huge pot and upset her tasteful arrangement of cacti in the lounge to make room for it.

As the days passed, however, she had found herself taking an interest in the tomato plant's progress. She even marked its height on the supporting stick each day, and was amazed to see the marks rising more than an inch at a time. The plant kept growing rapidly, and by the time the small yellow flowers appeared, it was filling the window.

She'd had to remove all her cacti because she couldn't get near enough to water them, also to give the huge mass of foliage space to expand.

'That thing makes the room too dark,' she complained to her husband. 'You'll have to shift it from the window.'

'I can't shift it now. Not while it's in flower.' He tickled one blossom with a piece of wool and transferred the clinging pollen to another yellow trumpet. He performed this sacred rite every evening, another reason for his wife's annoyance.

Elizabeth's dislike for the plant changed to outright resentment. She wasn't allowed to draw the curtains or close the window, in case she damaged it, and while she was sitting knitting one afternoon, she had the strange sensation that she was not alone in the house. Laying down her needles, she walked all through the downstairs area to make sure that no one had broken in, but saw nothing. She had the same unsettling feeling the following day, and came to the conclusion that it had something to do with the hated tomato plant.

When her husband arrived home that night, she ran to him in great relief. 'Oh. Henry, I'm glad you're back! There's something really fishy about that thing.'

'Fishy? What thing?'

'That blasted tomato plant. It gives me the creeps.'

'For heaven's sake, Liz, you must be joking.'

He laughed her to shame and carried out his pollination routine reverently, but next day, she was sure that the plant was watching her. Everywhere she went in that room she could sense eyes following her. She couldn't tell

Henry, not after the way he'd laughed at her before, he'd only make a fool of her again. She began to dread going into the lounge where the enormous leafy excrescence overshadowed everything, and started going out by the back door, walking round the house and in by the front door to reach the bathroom and bedrooms.

Every evening, Henry came home and crossed to the window to admire and tickle his plant before going into the kitchen to fill the old plastic container with water and plant food to quench his protégé's insatiable thirst. Only after attending to all its needs, did he deign to speak to his wife, but he did, at last, notice that she was extremely edgy and irritable. 'What's up, Liz? You look a bit under the weather.'

'Nothing's up!' she snapped, avoiding his eyes.

'Oh, come on! I know perfectly well something's bothering you. What is it?'

'It's your damned tomato plant!'

'Oh, for any sake! I thought you'd got over that silly idea.'

'It's not a silly idea. I told you before there was something fishy about it. It's been watching my every move for days, and . . .'

'Oh, Liz!.' He raised his eyes to the ceiling in exasperation.

'It has, Henry! And I'm sure it's evil. It's planning to do me some harm, I can feel it. It's – oh, it's really sinister, just sitting there plotting all day.'

He was astonished at her vehemence. 'Look darling,' he began in a soothing tone, 'you must have been overdoing things lately. You're run down and beginning to imagine things. I'd better phone the doctor.'

'I have not been imagining things!' Elizabeth shouted hysterically. 'That monster's just biding its time, then it's going to do something terrible to me, I know. You don't understand! It's different when you're in the house. That plant's very clever. It can hide things from you, but I can see right through it. It can't fool me!'

She buried her face in her hands but allowed her husband to lead her upstairs. She undressed automatically and sank thankfully on to the bed, while Henry went to the telephone in the hall.

Dr Sim rang the doorbell in a little over five minutes. 'You just caught me,' he said when Henry let him in. 'I'd a call to make in Graham Street, but I came here first since it's on my way. Now, what's all this about Elizabeth?'

When he heard the whole story, the old doctor shook his head. 'I've never known her to behave like that and I brought her into the world – forty-something years ago, would you believe? She sounds as if she's bordering on a nervous breakdown, I'm afraid, but I'll have to check her to find out more.'

In the bedroom, he checked her pulse rate, her heart beat and even under her eyelids, then asked her what was worrying her. Remembering Henry's reception of her suspicions – more than suspicions – she wouldn't tell him anything. He could easily cart her off to an asylum. Unwilling to admit that he hadn't a clue about what was wrong, Dr Sim gave Henry a prescription for tablets, along with instructions to keep her in bed for a week or so.

'She's probably been overdoing things, over-tiring herself, so a few days in bed may do the trick. The brain's a fragile, unfathomable piece of mechanism, but rest quite often works wonders.'

'Thanks Doctor, I'll get these made up straight away.'

Henry did wonder if he should ask old Mrs Will next door to sit with his wife while he was out, but Elizabeth would probably be even more upset if he allowed a neighbour to see her in her present state. In any case, the chemist was only a few minutes' walk away, and was one of those who remained open until doctors' surgeries were closed.

While he waited for the prescription to be filled, his thoughts were on his wife. It was most unusual for her to be so irrational. Surely she couldn't have been jealous of the tomato plant? Had he been lavishing all his attention on it to the exclusion of her feelings? But she couldn't be so . . . childish, surely? He'd have to make it up to her, let her see how much she meant to him.

He hurried home with the small pillbox, took the stairs two at a time and then stood looking at the empty bed, prickles creeping all over his scalp. Liz was definitely not in the bedroom, nor the spare room nor the bathroom. Blind panic setting in now, he shouted 'Liz!' as he leapt down the stairs.

She was not in the louinge, either, and he stood in the doorway looking at the tomato plant, an icy horror deadening all his senses.

*   *   *

144

Mrs Will poured Elizabeth a second cup of strong, sweet tea. 'I'm glad you told me about it, dear. How do you feel now?'

Elizabeth gave a wan smile. 'Exhausted, but much more sensible. How on earth could I have been so mad as to believe a plant could harm me? Just talking about it has made me realise how ridiculous that was.'

The old woman patted her hand. 'You're too much alone in the house, that's the trouble. It's enough to make anybody imagine things . . . especially at your age. I used to think daft things, and do even dafter things, when I was going on fifty.'

'If only Henry would have discussed it with me, but he wouldn't listen.'

Mrs Will silently resolved to have a quiet word with the man later.

Elizabeth stood up and pulled her neighbour's coat closer round her shoulders. 'Thanks for everything, Mrs Will. I don't know what you must have thought of me running here in my nightie.'

'Don't worry about it, my dear. I'd better come round with you in case your husband's been held up at the chemist's.'

They were quite unprepared for the sight that met them when they went through the open front door of the Millers' home. Amid the wreckage of broken furniture and ornaments lay the tomato plant, chopped off in its prime by the axe on the floor near Henry's lifeless hand.

Some of the foliage had fallen across him, tiny green clusters showing vividly against his death-white face.

***

Word count 1533 words

Written July 1986 for *Writer's Monthly* competition. Returned 24.10.86 with no comment. Because it wasn't the sort of thing I usually wrote, I didn't know where else to send it.

Committed

Margaret Donaldson looked sadly around the room; cold and forbidding now, yet she didn't want to leave it. It hadn't always been so unfriendly. She had liked the whole house when she came here as a bride, fifty years ago, this room in particular. It seemed to stretch out a hand of welcome to her and she had always loved it far more than any of the others. What a host of memories was contained within its walls. When she left it for ever, in so short a time, would she lose this link with the past?

When she voiced her fears last night, Kate had said, 'Don't be silly, Mother!' but then Kate had never been in the least sentimental.

Adam had always been mystified by his daughter's cynicism. 'Hard-boiled,' he had described her years ago, 'and she doesn't take that from you – you silly old romantic,' he had added, with the usual twinkle in his eyes as he patted her hand affectionately.

Dear Adam. How she had missed him over the five years since he passed away. He'd lain for many months in this room, yet his spirits had never flagged, and he had cheered her up when she felt depressed. Not that she often got depressed when she was sitting here with him.

'Come on, Maggie,' he used to say, even after he knew his life was ebbing away. 'Let me see your smiling face again. If I'm not worried about it, why should you go about with your chin touching the floor? It's such a bonnie chin.'

She recalled how happy he'd been when Kate made her first squawking appearance, although she'd been disappointed for his sake that the baby wasn't a boy. 'Are you sure you don't mind it being a girl?' she had asked him.

'I'm delighted with her,' Adam had smiled, 'and I'll be even more pleased if she turns out half as good as her mother.'

The following year, when John was born, their joy had been unbounded. Kate had always been her father's girl, while she had doted on her son. Her heart jolted as her thoughts jumped forward twenty-five years to the day John had announced he was emigrating to Australia. It had felt like only the next week that she was waving tearfully to a fast-disappearing train and turning to her husband for comfort.

Later, he had taken her in his arms in the big double bed and whispered, 'We can't live their lives for them, Maggie. If that's what he wants, we'll have to try to accept it.'

She had cried silently far into the night, long after Adam had fallen asleep. She had fully believed that she would never get over the parting, but almost fifteen years on, she could recall it rationally. John had never come home, but he wrote regularly and sent snapshots of his wife and their twins. Her only grandchildren, Margaret mused sadly, and she had never met them.

Then there was the night before Kate's wedding. Her daughter had come into her bedroom and cried on her shoulder. 'I can't get married,' she had sobbed.

Margaret had questioned her gently. "What's wrong, Kate? I thought you loved Robert, but don't tie yourself to him if you're not sure. It's not too late to cancel the wedding.'

'I do love him,' Kate had gulped. 'It's just . . . oh, I don't know. I can't explain it.'

'It's pre-wedding nerves, dear. Most girls go through that.' And sure enough, Kate had walked down the aisle the next day on her father's arm, her delicate, floaty, white dress making her look like an angel.

She had been happy and content then, not at all like the aloof person she had become. Perhaps, if she and Robert had adopted a child, she wouldn't have developed the hardness that seemed to encase her like armour. But it was foolish to think of the might-have-been.

When Kate and John were small, they had loved this room as much as she did. They had played in the huge bed when the weather prevented them from going outdoors, making it do duty as a circus ring, a classroom, a battlefield or whatever their busy young imaginations commanded. When they had measles and chickenpox, they had lain in this bed during the days, rather than in their own single ones, until she nursed them back to health. Funny, they had always taken all the childish complaints at the same time – except when John got mumps. Poor soul, he didn't know what to do with himself lying there on his own and she had had to spend a lot of time amusing him.

Sighing, she walked over to the door and went down the stairs to the kitchen. Kate called it the sitting room, but to Margaret, born and brought up in a tenement, it had always been the kitchen. Here, again, the bareness struck chill into her bones. Had she made the right decision? Was she being rash in giving up her home? If only Adam were here to advise her. But then, if Adam were still alive, she wouldn't be in this position.

There were only about fifteen minutes until she would be entering the tall gaunt building, grey and hostile, in that dingy side street. All the arrangements had been finalised a few months ago, she had signed the necessary forms with some misgivings. The wheels had been set in motion and there was no way to stop them. She wasn't even sure that she wanted to stop them.

If only she could make herself a cup of tea, but everything was packed away ready for disposal. Kate had arranged for the removal van to call tomorrow to take her belongings to a sale room. All her lovely things, which it had taken her a lifetime to collect. She could hardly bear to think about it, though she had put her foot down and was taking some of her more personal mementos, like photographs and jewellery, with her. She didn't suppose she would ever wear the jewellery again, but you never knew.

Margaret blew her nose on her way to the bathroom to comb her hair, and then studied her reflection in the glass. She didn't think she looked her age, and sixty-nine wasn't really old nowadays. Her hair was white – pure white without that yellowish tinge so often seen in white hair – and Adam used to say it made her even prettier. He would never let her have it cut, even when bobbing the hair was the height of fashion. She pinned it in place, then fetched her new hat from the hallstand because, although Adam had never liked to see her wearing a hat, she thought that this occasion called for some degree of respectability.

'Don't cover up your bonnie hair,' he used to say, in the Scottish burr she'd loved from the first time they met.

There, she was ready for Kate to collect her in the taxi. She hoped that her daughter wouldn't think the hat was too frivolous, but she needed a little colour to give her the courage to take this momentous step.

Ah, that was the taxi now. 'Goodbye, dear house. Goodbye, Adam, I'll never forget you,' she whispered, wiping away a tear as Kate opened the front door.

'You're looking very nice, Mother, but you haven't been crying, for goodness' sake, have you? Come on now, it's a lovely, sunny day, and you don't want to be late today of all days, do you?'

'No, dear,' Margaret said quietly, and the sadness dropped from her as she walked down the path to the car which was to take her to marry Walter Munro, Adam's closest friend, at the Registry Office.

***

Word count 1299

Written in September 1986 and refused by *Woman's Story*.

The Intruder

Mrs Repper opened her eyes and listened. There was a noise somewhere in the house, an alien noise she was unable to place.

She knew every creak and whisper of this house –she should do, after living in it for over sixty-five years – but she had never heard that particular sound before . . . and she didn't like it. Everything seemed silent now, but she held her breath and strained her ears in case the sound came again.

Yes! There it was! She lay motionless, frantically wondering what it could be and what she could do about it. It would be absolute madness to go downstairs and confront a burglar at her age. An eighty-five-year-old woman would stand no chance against one of those young hoodlums she had read about, who took a delight in preying on old people. She had seen some of the results of their handiwork on the television, and had shuddered at the sight of the poor, battered faces looking at her pathetically from the square box, but she had never imagined that it could happen to her. The newsreader had even said that some of the victims had died from their injuries. Murder, really, when you came to think about it.

Her heart was pounding like an express train, but, if she

lay quietly enough, the intruder might think there was no one in the house and go away. The trouble was, if it really was a burglar and he was looking for something to steal, he'd come upstairs. All her money and jewellery were in the bedroom, not that the jewellery was worth very much, apart from the beautiful cameo brooch that had belonged to her grandmother.

She wished now that she had listened to her daughter. Catherine was always going on at her. 'You're just asking for trouble keeping that money in the house, Mum. Get it into a bank, or a building society, or somewhere safe.'

Mrs Repper had just laughed, she recalled. 'Nobody'll suspect an old woman like me has any money worth stealing. I'll be all right.'

She didn't trust banks. Well, it wasn't exactly that she didn't trust them, but some of her friends had told her that they had to pay income tax on what they had in the bank. That was the main reason for her keeping hers under the mattress. The tax man would never find out about her hoard, and nobody would ever take her four hundred pounds away from her without her knowing.

That was the noise again. Keeping perfectly still she prayed that the thief would give up if he found nothing of value downstairs. Then she remembered something else that Catherine had said. 'You should have a phone put in, Mum. If you were ill, or in trouble, you could phone the doctor or Mrs Haley next door. They would help you, or let me know and I'd come as quickly as I could.'

She had sniffed, she recalled. 'I can't be bothered with those new-fangled things.'

'Oh, Mum!' Catherine had sounded exasperated. 'The telephone isn't new-fangled. You're so stubborn.'

Mrs Repper smiled at the memory. She supposed she was stubborn. Frank had always said so, too. How long was it since Frank died? 1956? No, definitely 1955. Goodness, it was over thirty years ago. Time certainly did fly. He was such a tall, well-built man, afraid of nothing, and if he'd been here now he'd have made short work of any housebreaker.

But . . . he'd been two years older than she was – the fact had nearly escaped her – so he would have been eighty-seven by this time. She couldn't imagine her husband as an old man, but her own legs were giving out on her nowadays, and she got a wee bit muddled now and then, so Frank would probably be showing his age, as well. He wouldn't have been much use as a defender, but he'd have done his best. Oh yes, he'd have done his best.

If only she had agreed to get a telephone, she could have called her neighbour. Young Mrs Haley was strong and athletic, going jogging, as she called it, every morning. She'd have come round immediately, even if it was the middle of the night. Mr Haley would have come to her assistance, too, and he was over six feet and played rugby every Wednesday. Tackling a burglar would be child's play to him.

They were a nice couple, always willing to help her. Mr Haley had even fixed a chain to her front door a few weeks ago. 'There's a lot of unscrupulous characters going around these days, Mrs Repper,' he had said. 'When anyone rings your bell, you only have to open the door as far as the chain will go, and if it's a stranger don't let him in. And nobody can force their way in, either.'

She was very proud of the chain, but it hadn't kept this intruder out. She gasped as her mind returned to her present predicament. The man couldn't get in. The noises she'd heard were from outside the house, that's why she hadn't recognised what they were. It was all right, then . . . but it had given her a proper turn and her heart was still palpitating madly.

One thing was sure, though. When she rose in the morning, she would go and ask Mrs Haley to arrange for someone to install a telephone for her. Catherine was right about that; it would certainly be a boon in an emergency.

She would even ask Mrs Haley to accompany her to the bank, so she could put all her money away safely . . . but maybe that was going a bit too far. Her imagination was playing tricks on her and if she carried on like this every time she heard a funny noise, she would soon be afraid of her own shadow. That was what came of watching the Haleys' television set occasionally. All those programmes about thugs – that's what they called them – beating up old ladies for their money. It couldn't happen in real life . . . could it?

Mrs Martin was not altogether sure in her mind now what could happen and what couldn't. She had a vague recollection of reading some terrible things in the newspapers. It would really be best not to have anything of value in the house, she supposed, but she had saved that four hundred pounds to cover her funeral expenses when she was gone.

CRASH!

That was definitely glass being broken. Of course! The only way an intruder could get in would be through a window. Clutching her flannelette nightgown up round her neck, she admitted the truth. This was not her imagination. This was really happening!

Why hadn't she listened to Catherine? Please God, she prayed, don't let this intruder come up here, but if You can't stop him, make it quick. Murder, not a beating. She felt as if she were choking. She had always thought that authors were exaggerating when they wrote about people having their hearts in their mouths, but it described exactly how she was feeling right this minute.

She could hear voices now. Voices? More than one! A gang? They were inside – coming up the stairs. She must shout for help. She jumped out of bed, the panicky terror giving strength to her arthritic legs, and turned the key in the lock before she ran to the window.

Sam had tried the back door, found it locked and placed his shoulder against it. He knew from experience that these old houses had stout doors inside as well as out, and gave up after the fourth attempt to break it down. 'Hang on a mo, Pat. I'll have to get something heavy from the car to try to prise it open.'

He came back in a few moments with a tyre lever, but was just as unsuccessful as before. 'It'll have to be a window,' he said, his mouth gripping with frustration. 'It's the only way we'll get in, Pat,' he added noticing his companion's worried expression.

The crash of splintered glass echoed shrilly, but he led the way in and straight up the stairs. They found the old lady in a crumpled heap on the floor.

Sam felt for a pulse. There was nothing, and he looked up in dismay. 'She's dead.'

Patricia Haley shook her head sadly. 'I knew something had happened to her when I saw her milk still on the door-step in the middle of the day. That's why I phoned you. She's still in her nightie – she must have had a heart attack when she got up this morning, poor soul! If only she had given me a key, I might have been able to do something, but I don't think she liked the idea of us being able to get in at any time.'

'Don't upset yourself, Pat. Even if it was a heart attack, you wouldn't have been able to get in if she'd had the chain on. At least she went peacefully.'

His wife sighed deeply. 'Yes, that's one consolation.'

***

Word count 1533

Written for *Writers' Monthly* Competition. Sent: 25.8.86 – returned (with no comment) 1.12.86

Teddy Bare

'We've stopped! Oh God, Phil, something's wrong with the ferry!' Tessa's blue eyes were fixed anxiously on her husband.

Philip Martin tried to appear calm. 'The engines hadn't been properly started, I expect. Nothing's wrong.'

She leaned against him, briefly. 'I'm scared, though . . . after Zeebrugge.'

'They've doubled their safety precautions, Tess. A disaster like that couldn't happen again.'

'I suppose not . . . it's just . . .'

'We'll be all right, I tell you!'

Tessa summoned up a tight smile although she had never felt less like smiling. There were so many people milling about in the saloon, they would all be trapped if anything happened. A wild stampede to nowhere . . . except destruction.

She grabbed her husband's arm for support. 'It's suffocating in here. Can we go on deck, please? It would be better for Christopher as well.'

'Sure! Why not?'

They unwittingly caused much amusement as they made their way to the exit – the leggy man and the slim, blonde girl, in matching navy shorts and red striped T-shirts, and, strung between them, it seemed, a small boy in blue and an enormous teddy bear wearing a yellow tracksuit – but at last they were outside in the fresh, gentle breeze.

When one of the Belgian crew began setting out chairs, Philip asked him, 'Can you tell me why we're being held up?'

The sailor just shrugged his shoulders brusquely, and Philip turned to his wife. 'Damn! Why can't any of these ruddy foreigners speak English?'

His vehemence made Tessa suspect that he was more apprehensive about the situation than he cared to admit, so she said, tentatively, 'What d'you really think's happening, Phil?'

'How should I know?' His childish anger evaporated when the ferry's engines suddenly sprang into life and the vessel began to move. 'Whatever it was, it's been fixed. I told you not to worry. Grab a couple of seats before they're all filled up, too.'

After almost half an hour of silently watching the tall buildings of Ostend seafront gradually dwindle in size and disappear, Philip leaned over, solicitously. 'Are you feeling any better now, darling?'

'Not much,' Tessa replied, truthfully. 'And I'll tell you one thing – I'm never going to do this again, Phil.'

A flurry of movement at their feet made them both look down. 'Christopher's taken the tracksuit top off his Teddy.' Tessa gave a brittle laugh. 'That's quite clever for a two-year-old.'

'I bet he's not clever enough to put it back on, though,' her husband remarked, drily.

Sure enough, after a few minutes spent wrestling unsuccessfully, the boy looked up. 'Mummy put it on?'

While his mother performed the operation, she said, 'We had a lovely weekend, hadn't we?'

'I told you we would,' Philip smiled, 'and we'd never have been able to afford a hotel like that, if it hadn't been . . .'

'I know, but . . .' She paused, and handed the dressed toy back to the child. 'Whole streets and streets of shops, with no traffic allowed, it was heaven, and Christopher really enjoyed that park, with the lake and the pedal boats. I only wish . . .'

'We'll come back some day,' Philip interrupted. 'When you've forgotten.'

'Not to Belgium,' she said quickly. 'I don't want to be reminded, ever, and the strain's telling on you, too, isn't it?'

'A bit,' he admitted. 'But it'll be over soon.' His voice became sharp. 'No, Christopher. Leave Teddy's tracksuit on. He'll catch cold if you take it off.'

'He's too hot with clothes on. I'm not cold, Daddy.' The piping voice carried to a chair a little distance away, where a stout, middle-aged woman was smiling at the little episode.

'Yes, but you've got clothes on, darling.' Tessa yanked the interlock trousers up the bear's legs. 'It was lucky your old tracksuit fitted him, wasn't it?'

'I'm thirsty.' Christopher had lost interest.

'So am I, son.' Philip stood up. 'Let's go and get something.'

In the cafeteria, another worrying thought struck Tessa. 'Are you sure about the arrangements, Phil? I don't fancy hanging about in Dover, if that man meant he'd meet us off the boat train.'

'For God's sake, Tess! I'm one hundred per cent sure, but read his bloody letter for yourself.' Pulling an envelope from the money belt round his waist, he almost threw it at her.

Hurt by his harsh words, she unfolded the single sheet of paper with tears in her eyes. 'Will pick you up at Dover 5.45 Sunday. Have a good trip,' she read out and passed the letter back.

'Satisfied?' He laughed to take the sting out of his sarcasm. 'If Parker says he'll be there, you can bet your bottom dollar he'll be there. Okay? We're due to dock at 5.15, so we should be through customs and out in plenty of time.'

They lapsed into a somewhat awkward silence, broken only when the small boy muttered fretfully, 'I'm tired.'

Philip pushed back his chair. 'Find somewhere comfy for him to have a nap, Tess. I don't want him whingeing in Parker's car. I'll go and get our duty-frees.'

Fortunately, several other passengers had also taken advantage of the privilege, so Tessa commandeered a long padded seat in the saloon and let her son stretch out with his head in her lap. But he refused to give up his 'friend'.

'No, Mummy, Teddy with me.' He snuggled against the bear and was soon fast asleep.

Looking idly around her, his mother nodded to the stout woman who had been sitting near them on deck, and who had obviously also felt the need to relax more comfortably, then she lay back and closed her eyes, glad of the peace and quiet.

She came to with a start some time later and, realising that she had dozed off, she checked that the two ruck-sacks were still at her feet, then her eyes flew anxiously to the clock. God! It was almost five and Phil hadn't come back yet. The second hand whizzed round madly and her agitation grew with each passing minute. Why was he taking so long? Had anything happened to him? What if he didn't come back before they arrived at Dover? She couldn't possibly manage by herself – not with two bags and Christopher and his teddy bear.

A tide of movement to the exits had already begun by the time her husband appeared, carrying a white plastic bag bulging with his purchases. 'Sorry I've been so long, darling,' he said breathlessly. 'It was a proper shambles through there, but I got whisky, brandy and four hundred Rothman's. That should keep us going for a while.'

'Keep you going, you mean.' Her smile was broad with relief. 'We're nearly there, Phil, and I was really worried.'

'No sweat, darling, there's loads of time.' But he bent down and scooped up the sleeping child and his furry companion.

Christopher's voice came weakly. 'What is it, Daddy?'

'We're getting off the boat now, son.' Philip turned in some concern to his wife. 'Can you manage the two bags if I carry Christopher and the bag of booze?'

'I think so. They're not all that heavy.'

In the crush to disembark, Tessa felt a wave of nausea

wash over her, and was thankful when her feet were on terra firma, her apprehensive glance confirming that Phil was close behind her.

'Last leg now, sweetheart,' he soothed. 'We'll be safe at home in less than an hour.'

Her sudden sense of security was shattered in seconds as they were swept along by the pressing crowd into the Customs area.

Philip's answer to a brisk 'Anything to declare?' was equally as brisk. 'Two bottles of spirits and two cartons of fags.'

'Would you open your bags, please, Madam?' The official was addressing Tessa, but her husband saw with some dismay that she was deathly white.

'I'll do it, dear,' he muttered hastily. 'You come and stand beside Christopher.'

Her gaze never left the man as she moved unsteadily to where her son was standing, still clasping his beloved teddy.

'What are looking for – drugs?'

Philip's tone was too flippant, too edgy, his wife thought. She had heard that they pounced on anyone showing signs of nerves, and there were stories of suspects actually being body-searched if nothing was found in their luggage.

'Drugs amongst other things, sir.' The officer's voice was cold as he began his search.

'You won't find anything in there except dirty laundry,' Philip grinned.

He was right, Tessa reflected. The rucksacks held only

the clothes they had been wearing over the weekend. There was nothing of any interest to Customs, but she couldn't help wishing this was all over. She flushed suddenly with embarrassment as her bras and panties were held up and shaken out, in full view of dozens of tittering travellers, but she caught the sympathetic eyes of the stout woman she had noticed before and felt better. She even smiled when the grubby underwear of her husband and son was also put on display.

The man was only doing his duty, after all, but she experienced a rush of relief when he cleared the two bags and said, 'Sorry for the inconvenience, sir', before turning to the stout woman.

Once outside, Philip lowered his son with a grimace. 'We'd better wait here so Parker can see us.' He sounded calm but his hands trembled as he lit a cigarette.

'You've been just as scared as me all along,' Tessa cried triumphantly. 'That's why you were so nervous in there.'

He was stung by the accusation. 'It's better to look nervous. Most people do, not panic-stricken like you.'

'Well, Martin. How did things go?'

A small, dapper man had come up behind them, and Philip turned to him thankfully. 'Perfect, though Tess was worried sick.'

'I'm pleased to make your acquaintance, Mrs Martin.' Parker held her hand for rather longer than was necessary. 'And now I'd like to meet your son.'

They all turned round to the little boy, their expressions changing drastically as they met the grim stares of four unmistakable plain-clothed detectives, who had positioned themselves behind him.

Then their eyes were drawn downwards, hypnotised, horrified and hopeless, to the matted yellow tracksuit on the ground where Christopher had tossed it, and to the polythene-covered package emerging from the gaping slit in the teddy bear's groin. It landed silently to land on top of dozens of others already there, then slid slowly, as if guided by the hand of Fate, to land at the feet of the stout middle-aged woman.

Her expression, when she stooped to pick it up, was no longer amused . . . or in the least sympathetic.

***

Word count 1799
 Has never been tried out.

Decision at Gowanbank

Catherine Walker wrestled with the road map, her annoyance fuelled by her frustration at being lost.

She had thought she could find Gowanbank with her eyes closed, but obviously she couldn't – not even with them open. Surely the place hadn't changed all that much in twenty years? She'd been depending on the peace and quiet of her childhood holidays – a trip down Memory Lane – to help her to make up her mind about Donald Robson, but . . .

'Can I be of any help?' The voice came through the half open window, and she looked up into the smiling face of a man with a bicycle.

'I was looking for Gowanbank,' she explained, 'but I must have taken a wrong turning somewhere. I remembered there was a church and a manse at the foot of quite a steep hill, and from the top I'd see the farm at the other side. But I can't even find the hill.'

'You haven't gone wrong,' the man grinned, pointing straight ahead. 'There's your church and the manse, and there's your hill.'

'No, it can't be – that hill's not steep enough, and the church is too small . . . and the house.'

He laughed loudly at this. 'Your memory's playing tricks on you, Katie.'

Katie? It was years since anyone had called her that, so she looked up into his face, trying to place him. The unruly red hair and the deep dimple in his chin told her instantly who he was. 'It's Billy Raffan, isn't it?' she smiled. 'You haven't changed much.'

'You didn't recognise me at first, though.'

'I wasn't expecting to see you,' she defended herself. 'I thought I was in the wrong district.'

'You've changed quite a bit, Katie.' His smile was slightly rueful now. 'You look really smart and sophisticated, like a successful career woman . . . or a model?'

Pleased though she was by the compliment, she hastened to put him right. 'Not a model, but yes a successful career woman. I'm head buyer in the gown department of Bannerman's in Edinburgh.'

He gave no sign of being pleased for her, but maybe he hadn't done so well with his life. It would be best not to ask him what he did. 'It's been great seeing you again, Billy, but I'll have to be getting on.'

She made to switch on the ignition, but his hand didn't move from the window.

'Is somebody expecting you?'

'No, I just wanted to see Gowanbank again – and have some peace and quiet.'

'I'm sorry.' He withdrew his hand at once. 'I've been disturbing your solitude.'

'Oh no, I didn't mean that. It's . . . um . . . I've a most

important decision to make, and I can't seem to find the time in Edinburgh to think things through properly.'

'I understand. Off you go, then, and good luck, whatever you decide.'

'Thanks, Billy.'

She drove on, past the little country church with its manse tucked by it side, both of which she had remembered as much larger and more imposing, over the small hill that she had thought so high and so steep when she was a young girl. From the top, however, just as she remembered, she could see the farm of Gowanbank, and went slowly down towards it, savouring the memories.

What happy times she'd had here, all those years ago; helping Uncle Jamie, watching the animals and being able to know each horse and cow by name. Happy, carefree days, until Dad died of pneumonia when she was fourteen, and there was no car and no money for her to have holidays.

Almost at the farm, where Uncle Jamie had been grieve, she turned left, to see where he and Auntie Aggie had lived, but the row of cottar houses seemed to have shrunk, too. She was bitterly disappointed. It hadn't been a good idea, trying to recapture the past. Things were never the same when you went back. Her aunt and uncle were both gone, years ago, and she wouldn't know any of the present farm workers – except Billy Raffan, of course.

She continued her journey along the rough road she remembered so well, at least it hadn't changed, until she reached the haven she had subconsciously been seeking. This was where she had come in the old days when she had wanted to be alone to sit and dream. There was a sort of entrance through the trees, just a gap between them really, and she drew the car to a halt on the mossy grass verge. Walking over the springy turf, sprinkled with cones as it had always been, her heart was uplifted by the old familiar smell of firs. She soon found the cluster of tree stumps fashioning a sort of chair in the clearing, and sat down to decide her future.

Her mind refused to be harnessed for quite a long time, however, recalling the games she used to play with the other children, including Billy, who had lived two houses along from her aunt and uncle. Billy had always defended her when the others laughed at her strange city way of talking. They had run barefoot – 'barfit' they called it – for the whole of the school holidays, the entire length of her stay there, and she could still remember how upset she'd been when her parents came to take her back to Edinburgh. Catherine abruptly reined in her wandering thoughts. This was not why she had come here. The burning issue still had to be decided. Was it only last night that Donald Robson had given her the ultimatum?

'I can't allow you to carry on working after we're married, of course,' Donald announced.

'But I need my work. I need the excitement of travelling, and meeting other people.' Catherine looked earnestly at her fiancé across the restaurant table.

'If you really loved me, you wouldn't need any other excitement.' His tone was firm, but cold. 'Being the wife of a professor should be enough, and we certainly won't need the money.'

'It's not the money, David. I can't see myself acting the little woman waiting for her man to come home every evening.'

'It wouldn't be like that. You'll have plenty to keep you occupied – organising and entertaining – and being invited out in return. There are several other wives who would be delighted to be your friends. They have bridge mornings and . . .'

Catherine interrupted angrily. 'I don't want to twiddle my thumbs and play at being a wife, Donald. Other married woman have their own careers, and they manage to cope.'

'They don't have luxury holidays in New York and Paris twice a year on their own.' His lips were compressed in a thin line now. His eyes were icy.

'They're not holiday trips, and you know it,' she said, calmly although she could feel her temper rising. 'I go to fashion shows because I have to know the current styles if I'm to do my job properly. You are being totally unreasonable.'

His handsome face softened suddenly. 'Darling, I love you, but I really can't have my wife working. If you think about it objectively, you'll see that I'm not being unreasonable.'

Biting back a hasty retort, she sat back in her seat to study him. His brown eyes were begging her to give in, his dark wavy hair was just that little bit ruffled, one of the things she loved about him. She knew that, in spite of his position, he was insecure, that he needed her backing to give him confidence in himself. She'd been bolstering his ego every since she first met him at a party, two years ago. There had been instant attraction between them, but she had been the one to invite him to a concert when her girlfriend let her down. She had been the one to suggest that they made it a weekly arrangement. She had found it really difficult to convince Donald that she loved him. She sighed now. 'I'll think it over.'

'Catherine.' His voice had softened. 'You will have to decide one way or the other. Your career or . . . me. You can't have both.'

Irritation with him was setting in, but she held herself in check. 'I said I'll think it over.'

'I want to know as soon as possible, Catherine.' His tone was icy. 'We can't go on like this any longer.'

She took a deep breath. 'We were stocktaking all last week, so I'm due a day off. I'll take it tomorrow, and I'll go to a little place I know where I can think this out properly, with no distractions.'

'If you really loved me, you wouldn't have to think,' he muttered.

'I do love you, Donald, but I had to sacrifice quite a lot to be where I am today, and it seems ridiculous to throw it all away now. Maybe I'll see things in perspective once I'm away from Edinburgh, though I can't promise what my answer will be. I do promise to think it over really carefully, and I'll phone you in the evening.'

* * *

Slowly, with the silence around her being broken only by the occasional chirping of a bird, she came to the conclusion that Donald had been right. She couldn't love him as deeply as she had thought, otherwise she'd have given up her career willingly and been proud to spend the rest of her life looking after him. Giving in to him; was that more like it?

Her decision made, her heart wasn't broken at the prospect of never seeing him again. It was Donald who would have to face up to being on his own. Her heart was much lighter as she made her way back to the road, and she was pleasantly surprised to see Billy Raffan sitting on the grass beside her car, his bicycle propped against a tree.

He jumped up when he saw her. 'I thought this was where you'd be, and I knew I was right when I saw the car. My mother sent me to invite you to have some dinner with us – though I suppose you call it lunch nowadays?'

'I still call it dinner,' she grinned, recalling many arguments with Donald Robson about her sticking so stubbornly to her own vocabulary, lower middle class he called it, 'and it's very thoughtful of her. I hope you haven't been waiting here long.'

'Not long.' His smile was still as boyish as it had always been. 'I allowed you an hour to do your thinking in peace and quiet. I hope that was enough?'

'Yes, I've done all the thinking I need.'

'Right then, follow me.' He lifted his bicycle and set it upright.

'Don't you still live in the same house?'

'No.' His laugh was teasing. 'Just follow me.'

They passed the cottar houses, passed Gowanbank Farm, up the hill and down the other side, and then he turned left along the narrow track leading to the church.

When he stopped outside the manse, Catherine came out of her car and said, accusingly, 'Why didn't you tell me you worked here?'

'You never asked.'

'What do you do? Gardener?'

'Gardener, odd job man, whatever.'

His twinkling eyes made her suddenly suspicious. 'You're not a gardener at all, are you?'

He burst out laughing. 'You'd never have expected me to be a minister, would you, Katie?'

'You're the minister?' she gasped. 'No, I'd never have dreamt of that. You were one of the liveliest, funniest boys amongst the whole lot, Billy.' She hesitated. 'I can't call you Billy now, though. It would be disrespectful.'

'Oh, don't worry about that. Mother still calls me Billy, and half my congregation. And I'll keep calling you Katie, even if you're probably known as Catherine now.'

She nodded her agreement to that. 'But I feel Katie here.'

'Good. Come on then, Mum's waiting.'

'Mind and put your bike in the shed, Billy,' was Mrs Raffan's first remark, 'and bring in some coal.'

'She orders me about like a skivvy,' he laughed, joking, but went out to do as he'd been told.

'It's good to see you again,' the small white-haired woman went on. 'I didna believe Billy when he said he'd

173

seen you. You were only a bairn when you were last at Gowanbank.'

'I was only fourteen,' Catherine said, pulling a face as she added, 'twenty years ago. I'll be thirty-four in a couple of weeks.'

'Still just a bairn. You'd been surprised to ken Billy was a minister now?'

'I could hardly believe it. He was always the wild one, the one playing tricks on everybody else. I thought he'd have gone in for farm work, like his dad.' She hoped that Billy's mother wouldn't think she was belittling him.

'He was never keen on that. He aye said he wanted to be a minister, from the time he was about fifteen. He was real clever, and got through the Divinity degree with no bother. His first charge was in Ayrshire.'

The woman smiled sadly. 'I was pleased his father lived to see him ordained, for he died just a month after.'

'Oh, I'm so sorry.' Catherine had liked Will Raffan, a big, bluff man, with reddish hair like his son.

'Aye.' Mrs Raffan was silent for a moment, then said brightly, 'Billy had been in his first kirk five year when old Mr McIntyre died. You'll mind on him, Katie? He'd been minister here for near forty year.'

'Oh, yes, I remember him bellowing out his sermons when I was a kid. I was absolutely terrified of him.'

'But he was a good man, for a' that, a kind man, obliging. He went out of his way to do things for his parishioners, and the kirk session didna fancy the idea of a stranger coming upsetting a'body. The upshot was, they sent two men to hear my Billy preaching and they liked him, but they asked him up here so the congregation could judge for theirselves. And he got the call to this kirk.'

'That must have been a very proud day for you.'

'It was that, and I was even prouder when Billy asked me asked me to come and keep house for him. I'd been stopping with my sister since my man died and I'd to get out o' the cottar house.'

'She keeps me in order as well as the house.' Billy had come in with the filled coal scuttle.

Mrs Raffan laughed with delight. 'You need it, lad. Go and wash your hands afore your dinner.'

He made a face but disappeared again, and his mother turned to Catherine. 'I'd have been fine pleased if he'd taken a wife,' she confided, 'but he never seemed to bother much with the lassies.'

'As long as he's got you, he'll be well looked after.'

'But he'll no aye have me, and I'd like to see him settled. You ken, Katie, I used to think he'd a soft spot for you, when you used to come here for your holidays.'

Catherine's face flushed. She'd had quite a soft spot for Billy Raffan when she was fourteen, but circumstances had nipped that in the bud. She hadn't even given him a thought over the years.

'Right, Mum,' the minister said, when he came back. 'I'm sure Katie's hungry by this time.'

'I was waiting for you afore I dished up. If you want to wash your hands as well, lass, the bathroom's through there, second door on your left.' Mrs Raffan stood up, and Catherine obediently followed the pointing finger.

While she ran the water, she studied herself critically in

the mirror. Most of her hair had escaped from its elegant chignon; her face was practically free of make-up now although her cheeks were quite rosy from her spell in the bracing country air. This was not Catherine Walker, head buyer, this was Katie, who could never be a professor's wife; nor a minister's, came the unbidden thought. Drying her hands, she took out the remainder of her hairpins, letting her long hair fall in waves to her shoulders. She looked much younger when she returned to the kitchen, and couldn't help noticing that Billy's eyes had lit up in admiration.

Mrs Raffan was laying steaming plates on the table. 'Sit doon, lass. I hope you dinna mind eating in the kitchen?'

'Oh, no.' Catherine's eyes went round the old-fashioned room, and lingered happily on the huge range where a fire was crackling merrily. 'It brings back memories of my Uncle Jimmy and Auntie Aggie, and it's so nice and cosy.'

The elderly woman didn't talk much during the meal, smiling at the two animated faces as her son and Catherine reminisced about the escapades they had shared in their childhood, but when the conversation tailed off, she took her chance. 'Are you married, Katie?'

'No, I'm not.' She paused, then decided to tell the whole story. 'At first, when I was working my way up, I went out with a few boys, but I never had serious feelings about any of them.'

'Same as Billy,' remarked his mother.

'Then, when I finally made it, and got my present position, I was too engrossed in my work to bother . . . until I met Donald.' Aware that Billy had lowered his eyes, she hurried on, 'We've been engaged for a year and he wants us to get married.'

'And you're not sure about it?' the woman asked, kindly.

'I thought I was,' Catherine said, frankly, 'but he told me last night he expected me to give up my job. He said it was either my career or him. That's what I came here to decide.'

Billy leaned forward when she fell silent. 'When you came out of the wood, you said you'd done your thinking?'

Her nod came slowly. 'Yes, I've decided to break it off with him. I don't want to marry him if it means giving up all I've worked for over the years.'

Mrs Raffan laid her hand over Catherine's. 'If you'd come all the way up here to think about it, you couldna have loved him enough.'

There was great relief in Catherine's smile. 'That's the conclusion I came to, as well.'

'You'll find somebody else, lass, somebody you'll not think twice about giving up your job for.' The elderly woman sat back and looked meaningfully at her son. Catherine caught Billy's eye, and her heart missed a beat at the unconcealed hope she saw there. Her hand went up automatically to brush back a curl that had fallen over her eyes, a gesture she remembered from the past, a gesture she hadn't made for some time because her hair had been in the same severe style since she'd been promoted eight years ago.

Billy had also remembered. 'You used to do that when you were a kid. Now you're really Katie again – the sweet-faced, toffee-nosed kid who spoke with a tattie in her mouth.'

She joined in the laughter. 'You punched the other boys for saying things like that about me. Fancy you remembering.'

'He's still the same old Billy, as you can see,' his mother said fondly, 'still full o' fun. He can mind near everything about everybody, and his congregation love him for it.'

'Oh, Mum,' he mumbled, sheepishly, his face scarlet with embarrassment. 'Katie doesn't want to hear about me.'

But Katie did. This new, old Katie, who had just discovered that she would love to be the wife of a minister – if she were asked.

***

Word count 3280
Written in May 1987 and refused by *People's Friend*.

Duplicity

Chapter One

Having just carried their last case in from the car, Brian Lewis whipped round angrily when the doorbell rang. 'Who the devil can that be? Can't they at least give us a chance to settle in before they start poking their noses in?'

'I'll go.' Roselle stepped carefully over the luggage scattered haphazardly over the hall carpet and inched the door open. She hadn't given a thought to who might be on the doorstep. In fact, she hadn't really been capable of any rational thinking for some time.

The middle-aged woman smiled apologetically. 'I'm sorry to bother you, lass, but I thought you'd be glad of a wee something to keep the wolf from the door.' She took a vacuum flask from the basket over her arm. 'I know you've rented the house furnished and won't know where to find anything, so I took what I thought you'd need. Let me come in, and you and your husband can sit down. The two of you look absolutely whacked.'

She walked into the lounge as if accustomed to having her orders obeyed, smiling at the man, who seemed somewhat suspicious. 'I live next door and I like to be a good neighbour, so put your feet up. I'll just pour out and you can have a wee rest and I'll take the babies with me so you can get on with your unpacking.' She stopped speaking, probably to regain her breath, and soon had the small coffee table set neatly with two china mugs, two small jars – one with tea and one with milk – a plate of sandwiches and another with biscuits and an assortment of dainty little cakes, all of which were clearly home-made.

Having poured the tea, she stated firmly, 'Now, get on with it. I'll take the wee pets and give you peace to get things organised. And you've likely been too anxious to get here to stop and feed them, so give me what it is they get and I'll do the needful.'

With Brian seemingly struck dumb by this chattering avalanche, Roselle had to make an effort. 'It's very kind of you, Mrs . . . um . . .'

'Milne.'

'We're really grateful to you, Mrs Milne, for all this, but we can't expect you to look after the twins as well.'

'No arguments, I'm looking forward to it.' Waiting until the younger woman had handed her a shoulder bag that obviously held the necessities for the babies, she raised her eyebrows at Brian. 'If you'd be as good as carry one of the little cots, I'll take the other one.'

For a moment, it was as if he would refuse, but he got to his feet reluctantly and lifted both cots. 'Lead the way, Mrs Milne.'

He returned in less than five minutes and plonked

down wearily on one of the well-worn armchairs. 'Nosey old bitch!'

'Oh, she wasn't being nosey. She was being neighbourly and I'm glad she came. I was starving.' She grabbed another sandwich as he reached for the plate. 'And we'll get so much more work done with the twins out of the way.'

He nodded. 'I suppose you're right, darling.' He studied her as he ate. Her cheeks, so pale for days, had a little tinge of pink in them; her deep blue eyes were brighter. She even held her head higher, although tresses of her usually well-coiffed blonde hair were straggling round her face. His heart went out to her. She'd come through so much, and he was glad that she couldn't remember what had happened. It had all been so sudden, although he'd planned the move for over a year with no definite date in mind, but fate had played into his hands. It was as if it had all been arranged, and it had gone so smoothly, he could hardly believe it. As long as she didn't regain her memory, everything would be hunky-dory, though he'd have to make sure she'd didn't get too friendly with Mrs Milne. That woman would probably keep asking things until she winkled the whole sorry business out . . .

'They seem a nice young couple,' Mrs Milne was telling her husband. 'Mind you, Frank, I think he's the boss – I wouldn't like to get up his wrong side. I don't think he trusted me, but she's a quiet wee thing, wouldn't say boo to a goose, so we'll get along fine.'

Frank took off his glasses and laid them on the low mantelpiece. 'Give her a bit of space, though. You can be overpowering at times, Helen.'

'She's hiding something, I can tell that, and he's scared she'll give the game away.'

'Och, woman, it's love stories you should be reading instead of all that crime stuff.'

'Maybe, but I know I'm right, and I bet I'll manage to get round her.' She turned to look down at the twin carry-cots by her feet. 'They're little darlings, aren't they, and they don't look like twins, which is likely a good thing for them.'

'Why? What's wrong with twins looking like twins?'

'People would get them muddled, of course.'

'Only if they were dressed the same, and from what I can see, there's a pink one and a blue one. A girl and a boy, I'd say.'

'Clever dick! You think you know everything, Frank Milne.'

'I stop and think before I open my mouth, that's why.'

They looked at each other now and laughed softly. Thirty-odd years of marriage had taught them never to let a small tiff develop into a full-blown row. 'I'm just glad they're a young couple, though, and we'll see the babies grow up. They should keep us young, too.'

Lifting his newspaper and reaching for his spectacles, her husband just said, 'They've rented the house furnished, remember. They likely don't mean to stay very long.'

* * *

In the next-door cottage, two exhausted people were enjoying the last of the food and tea they had been given. 'Thank goodness that's everything put away,' sighed the man. 'I'll just have ten minutes, before I collect our wee demons.'

'They're not demons. They've been really good.'

'I'm only teasing. To be honest, I'm astonished at how well they've behaved. They've been moved about from pillar to post, different places, and so many strangers speaking to them and fussing over them. Still, from tomorrow, it should be plain sailing, and they'll get used to a steady routine.'

Roselle watched him as he lay back and closed his eyes. He seemed oddly unfamiliar, she couldn't understand it. His dark hair was not as tidy as it usually was, his eyes had seemed to be a lighter shade of blue, his face was leaner, but, of course, they'd been on the move for what seemed like forever. But it did worry her that her memory wasn't to be depended on. She couldn't remember anything of her life until she was in that small hotel in London with the babies, waiting for her husband to come back from whatever he'd nipped out to do. Any time she mentioned this, he held her closely and assured her that it was nothing to worry about. She had come through a terrible ordeal and memory loss was how that kind of thing affected some people.

'Don't try to remember,' he had urged her. 'It'll all come back to you some day, but only if you give it time.'

'But I want to know what happened,' she had persisted. 'It's awful being like this. I couldn't even remember my

183

own name, or yours, or the babies'. But you told me all that, so why can't you tell me the rest?'

'All the doctors we saw told us the same thing. Your condition is a fairly normal reaction to trauma, and it will improve as time goes by.'

Why could no one tell her what the trauma had been? It was the not knowing that worried her. Surely doctors should have known that? Not that she could recall ever having been seen by doctors. Her life seemed to have started on the day she woke up in that hotel, with someone at the door shouting, 'Open up, darling. It's me, Brian.'

Remembering, she had the same feeling of bewilderment at a name that was familiar, but at the same time strangely unfamiliar.

'Yes, your husband. Come on, Roselle, don't play silly beggars with me.'

She had risen and opened the door, but hadn't recognised the man who came in and took her in his arms. 'Oh darling, you had me worried. Are you all right?'

It had taken him some time to understand what she told him, and even then, he didn't seem to be convinced that it wasn't a joke. Maybe he had taken her to see a doctor after that, or more than one doctor, but that was a blank to her as well. That was little more than a week ago, of course, so maybe she hadn't let enough time pass. Maybe she was expecting too much of herself. But at least Brian couldn't have been more considerate and caring, helping with the babies. There wasn't much she could recall of the journey here, though; only that it had taken two days.

Jerking up suddenly, Brian said, 'I'd better collect the

last of our luggage from the old dears next door – only joking.'

She smiled as he went out. Yes, they were part of the luggage, the little darlings – the most important part.

Chapter Two

Roselle knew better than to remind Brian that this was the afternoon she took the twins round to see Helen. She was aware that, even after four years, he was still inclined to be unhappy about the friendship, but he'd never ordered her to stop it. In any case, she wasn't doing anything wrong, and the Milnes treated the kids like grandchildren; and she sometimes felt as close to them as if they were her parents. It crossed her mind then that perhaps that was what she was doing wrong. Maybe Brian was jealous. Well, too bad if he was. He'd just have to lump it.

Her conscience gave a twinge. He was a good husband and a good father, and she really had no reason to complain. If only he would help her to remember.

'Come away in, my lovies,' Helen beamed. 'Frank's out in the garden . . .' She broke off with a laugh as the small boy and girl scrambled past her, heading for the back door. 'You can give me a hand, if you like, Roselle, but we'll have a wee drop sherry first.'

The little tipple had become a habit, a welcome habit, during which Roselle very occasionally – and unwittingly – gave the older woman slight hints of her troubled mind, although no matter how hard Helen tried, she couldn't get her to talk about herself. As she had often remarked to Frank, 'Something bad must have happened to her, but she won't speak about it. I could maybe help her, but . . .'

'I'd a letter from my sister in Chicago yesterday,' she observed now. 'Georgina, Georgie we always called her.'

'Yes, I remember you telling me before. She's younger than you, isn't she?'

'She was the baby – an afterthought, my father used to tease her. I'm nearly fifteen years older, and Lavinia's two years older than me. It's funny. I hardly ever see her, though she's only twenty miles away.' She took a breath before asking, 'Do you have any brothers or sisters?' It was something that she brought up occasionally, hopefully, but always in vain.

'I wish I knew, Helen.' Her eyes were moist. 'I keep trying to remember. You'd think nobody could forget a thing like that, but it's hopeless.'

Giving up, Helen got to her feet. 'We'd better go and join the warriors, or they'll be wondering what we're doing.'

The afternoon sped past, with Frank playing all kinds of games with the children and the two women looking on fondly. It was a few minutes after five when Roselle looked at her watch. 'Oh, gosh! We'll have to be going home, kids. It's time I was getting your tea ready.'

'Oh, not already.' The words came in unison, like everything they did, although they were not identical twins. Blue-eyed Dyllis – usually known as Dilly – had golden hair that hung to her shoulders in lovely, soft waves, while Roderick – Roddy – had deep brown eyes to match his tight curls. Their personalities were also very different. Roddy was quick to anger, and thankfully, equally quick to simmer down.

Frank flopped down on the grass. 'You know, lass, I *have* felt a lot younger since those two kids came to live next door. I just hope they stay around for a long time yet.'

'I'm sure they will. Roselle looks much better than she did when we saw her first, and so does Brian. And the twins have grown even bonnier than they were. I think they're settled. They'll maybe think of buying that house.'

'I hope so. Now, are you thinking of making something for us to eat, or are you cemented to that chair?'

'Ach, you.' Helen couldn't help smiling as she stood up. He, too, was so much happier nowadays, and long may it continue.

The twins were in bed when Brian came home from the job he had found in Edinburgh only a few days after they'd arrived here. It was a long day, but he didn't mind that as long as his family were happy. At least he'd been able to provide them with a good life without having to dip into his 'emergency' money. In fact, he'd almost forgotten that there had ever been a need for such a fund. 'What have you three been up to today?' he asked, after going up to kiss the children goodnight.

Roselle smiled. 'Just the usual, really. Frank took us to the beach at Portobello for a while, but it was too hot, so we just came back and took it easy in their garden. He's very good with the kids, you know.' She looked at him to see if he was jealous, but he was smilingly nodding agreement, so she added, 'We're lucky having him and Helen next door.'

'You're right. I wasn't too sure about Helen at first, I thought she was too nosey, but she was just being friendly. I realise that now.'

'I told you that long ago, but I'm glad you've seen sense at last.'

Roselle and Brian soon had more reason to be grateful for having the Milnes as neighbours. It all happened on the afternoon of the twins' fifth birthday. Because they were to be starting school in less than a week, Helen had prepared a large amount of their favourite foods, savoury as well as sweet, and had also invited several of the children who lived nearby. Frank had hired a bouncy castle and engaged a magician to entertain the young ones after their meal. It was another glorious day, Brian had managed to wangle a day off and everything had gone according to plan.

The bouncy castle had been a huge success, backed with several children's games that Frank had also organised for them. There were no tears, no nasty moments; the selection of food and drinks was so big that no one had to go hungry or thirsty. A few of the mothers, including Roselle, had begun by watching their offspring carefully in case they overate and made themselves sick, but everything had sailed along so perfectly that they soon gave up.

The magician enthralled young and old alike, most of the parents taking some snaps of the happy and amazed faces of his audience. Then, as a last item, and to get the excited children calmed down a little before they had to go to bed, Frank had driven Helen mad for days before by practising a medley of nursery rhymes on his accordion. The entire company joined in now, and would have raised the roof if they had been inside. As it was, several passers-by stopped to join in and even neighbours who had no small children hurried round to take part. All in all, the day could not have gone better, and the visitors dispersed with many thanks and congratulations to the hosts.

Most of the women had helped to tidy up after the meal, so there was very little mess for the Milnes to clear, and Helen refused Roselle's offer to lend a hand. 'No, no, off you go and get the twins to bed. Dilly looks done in.'

'She hasn't looked really well all day.' It was Brian, least involved in the preparations and amusements, who was the only one to have noticed the little girl's lack of energy.

Ashamed of themselves for being so remiss, the other three adults looked at each other in dismay and Helen said, hastily, 'He's right, Roselle. Maybe you should phone the doctor in the morning and get him to have a look at her.'

'Maybe she's just eaten too much,' Frank suggested.

'I don't think so,' his wife said now, 'but you should still phone, dear, just to make sure. I'll come round first thing and see how she is. Off you go, now.'

So the two children were hustled away, Brian even sweeping the little girl up in his arms and carrying her home. Then he handed her over to her mother and busied himself putting his son to bed.

'What's wrong with Dilly?' Having lost a pet canary a few weeks ago, the boy couldn't get the idea of death out of his head. 'Is she going to die?'

'Of course she's not going to die! It'll be an upset tummy, that's all. Now lie down and sleep, like a good boy, and let her get a good night's rest. She'll be OK in the morning.'

He was to be proved very wrong, however. Dyllis wouldn't settle, crying now, and looking so flushed that Roselle decided to stay with her. Roddy was carried through to the parental bed to sleep beside his father, and they were the only two who did get any peace. Dilly's sobs became moans and she grew so hot and flushed that Roselle phoned for the doctor just after midnight. She hated the idea of making the man lose his precious sleep, but she was really worried about her daughter. Doctor Alexander obviously recognised the panic in her voice and told her he'd be right there. Good as his word, he arrived in a few minutes.

After only a brief examination, he murmured, 'I'm afraid it's serious, Mrs Lewis. I'm not absolutely sure, but it could be meningitis and she needs to be in hospital, the sooner the better. We don't want to wait for an ambulance, so I'll take her myself.'

Brian, who had run through when he heard the car stopping, said now, 'Do you want me to go with them, Ros?'

She shook her head. 'No, I'll go. You stay here with Roddy.'

Having wrapped his patient in her duvet, Doctor

Alexander carried her downstairs, standing aside until Brian opened the door for him. Roselle came last, pulling on a coat she had lifted from the hallstand before going into the back seat beside her daughter. At that moment, the Milnes came running out of their front door, and without asking any questions, the woman said to Brian, 'If you want to go with them, I'll go in and be with Roddy. And don't worry how long you stay, I'll manage fine. Anyway, Frank'll likely help out, as well.'

Dilly was whipped away as soon as they arrived in the hospital, and her parents were shown into a small room to await the results of the doctors' examination. It was almost an hour before anyone came near them to give them any news. Sadly, when an elderly man came in, his face was extremely grave. 'I'm Doctor Fielding,' he said. 'I'm afraid the news is not good. Your little girl is suffering from meningitis and the next few hours are critical. However, she is young, and has been well nourished, so she should be able to fight this, and indeed to overcome it. However, I cannot promise a miracle cure, and can only advise you not to lose hope. Keep praying for her recovery.' He turned away as Brian voiced his heartfelt thanks for him being so honest, and left the young parents to face up to what may lie ahead.

Hour after hour they huddled together, not speaking, just holding each other, the close contact helping them to keep a tight rein on the fluctuating levels of their anxiety. At one point, what Brian had been thinking for some time came to the surface, and without realising he was doing so, he muttered, 'Please God, if you are punishing me for the crimes I've committed, you've succeeded a hundred-fold, but please don't take your anger at me out on this innocent child. Please don't take her from us. Please God. It would kill her mother. Look, if I promise never to go off the rails again, will that satisfy you?'

Realising that he was saying this aloud, he glanced apprehensively at Roselle, but she didn't appear to be paying any attention. She hadn't heard, thank God.

At four o'clock, a young nurse brought in a tray with tea and biscuits, saying as she laid it on the small table beside them, 'I know you won't feel like eating, but it'll help you.'

'Do you know how our daughter is?' Brian asked, hoping against hope that she had at last heard something of the little girl's condition.

'I don't really know anything definite,' she replied apologetically, 'but I did hear she was holding her own. That's a good sign, you know.'

'Thanks.' Brian did not look at all convinced although he squeezed Roselle's arm to encourage her to think positively.

And so they sat, for another four hours, hearing doors closing, footsteps coming and going in the corridor outside, hushed conversations as nurses or doctors hurried by, but eventually the door opened and the same tall, balding man came in, evidence of hours of strain clearly on his thin face.

'I'm very pleased to tell you that your daughter has turned the corner, and is now on the road to recovery.'

'Thank heaven!' Brian said, while Roselle burst into tears of joy.

'She has a long way to go yet, Mr Lewis, but I feel positive in saying that she will be as good as new in a few weeks. She is a fighter, your little girl. Now, if you want to see her, just stay a few minutes and then I'd advise you both to go home to get some sleep. You want to be bright-eyed and bushy-tailed when you come in tomorrow, don't you?' He gave Roselle's shoulder a reassuring pat, and Brian murmured, 'Thank you for what you've done for our daughter, Doctor Fielding.'

Despite longing to hug the little girl, both parents stood silently at the side of the cot, looking down on the still figure whose pale face was now peaceful in sleep, thanking God that she had not been taken from them, and after the allotted few minutes, they turned away reluctantly and left.

The evening meal was past before they reached home in a taxi, but a relieved Frank Milne took Roddy out for a little walk while Helen prepared something for the younger couple to eat, and although they told her they didn't want anything, they did not leave much of what she set in front of them. Then she packed them off to bed, with the order not to come downstairs again until next morning. She didn't really think that either of them would sleep after the ordeal they had gone through, but, surprisingly, she had to call them twice before they came down at nine thirty for breakfast.

This meal was one that everyone enjoyed, laughing and joking most of the time, but letting slip the odd remark that showed how grateful they were that things had turned out well. Roddy, not old enough to understand what the adults were feeling, was aware that this was a kind of celebration, and was glad that a cloud had been lifted from the household.

Dilly was awake when Roselle and Brian visited that afternoon, but they were warned by the sister not to expect much of her, and not to stay for more than ten minutes. They were also told that no other visitors would be allowed in until the following day.

The next day being Sunday, Roselle asked Helen if she and Frank would watch Roddy in the forenoon to let them go to church to give thanks.

'I'm glad you thought of that,' Helen beamed. 'We'll be here any time you want.'

'Oh, thanks, I don't know what we'd have done without you. You'll want to see Dilly some time, as well, of course?'

'Of course we do, but you and Brian have first claim.'

'How would it be if you and Frank come with us this afternoon? We'll take Roddy, too.'

Helen turned to Brian now. 'If that's all right with you?'

He nodded, smiling. 'Of course it is, Helen. We owe you and Frank big time.'

Dyllis looked a good bit better that afternoon, but was only allowed two visitors at a time. The first, naturally, were her parents, then Brian went out to let Roddy in. A few minutes later, Helen replaced Roselle, and Frank replaced the boy in another few minutes, and then the two parents had the last few minutes alone again with their daughter. All in all, the time covered was less than half an hour, which was what the sister had advised them would be long enough.

On Monday morning, Roselle gave her son all her attention. This was his first day at school, and he would be on his own – no Dyllis for company. Not for a while yet. Brian went off to work as usual, but Helen, ever on the lookout for some good deed to do, accompanied the new pupil and his mum to school. 'It'll be a nice walk for me,' she smiled, when her young neighbour protested. 'And it'll let Frank have the house to himself for a wee while.'

Roddy wasn't at all upset when they had to leave him, although Roselle was glad that Helen was with her on the way home. She refused the offered 'cuppa' when they arrived at the Milnes' gate. She had something to think about; something she had pushed to the back of her mind for a couple of days, but was aware that she would have to come to terms with some time. She didn't want to discuss it with Helen, although that good lady might well be able to lull the suspicions that had arisen in her mind.

They hadn't surfaced at the time Brian said the fateful words, not until the following night in bed, when her thoughts were not so involved in worrying about Dyllis. That's when they had come back to her. Back to torment her. What had he meant? Crimes? What crimes had he

196

committed? Had he done something really bad? Was that why he didn't want her to regain her memory?

Carrying out her usual routine of housework, she puzzled over it, thinking up several things that could be described as crimes. Murder, of course, was the first, but she couldn't believe for one second that Brian had murdered anybody. Grievous bodily harm came next, but the same applied there. Vandalism? Not Brian. No way. He was as gentle as a lamb, never lost his temper. In any case, if it had been any of these, the police would have been after him long before now. Wouldn't they?

It was while she was having a cup of tea – she couldn't face any lunch – that it dawned on her. Of course. The police must have *been* after him. That was why they'd had to move from – damn it! If only she could remember where they had lived before. Rising, she swilled out the cup, gave her face a splash with cold water and put on her coat and shoes. She was going to visit Dilly first, but wouldn't have to stay long, otherwise she would be late in collecting Roddy from school.

On her way to the hospital, she was praying that her daughter had improved at least a little, and was most relieved when the little girl smiled at her as soon as she entered the ward. 'Mummy.' The word was little more than a whisper, but it gave Roselle the boost she needed.

'Oh, Dilly, darling, I'm so glad you're able to speak to me. You were still very ill when Daddy and I came to see you yesterday, and we were so worried about you.'

The ten minutes she sat holding the small girl's hand, seemed to be enough. Dilly's eyes had closed, her face had lost what little colour it had before, so she eased her grip slowly and left. On her way along the corridor, the sister came out of her little sanctum and said, 'I'm sure you must be delighted with Dyllis's progress, Mrs Lewis. She is doing well, but is very easily tired.'

'Yes, she fell asleep a few minutes after I saw her, but she did know I was there.'

'It may take some time, but we're sure she will make a full recovery.'

Her mind easier now, Roselle's thoughts returned to the strange utterance her husband had made during those first terrible few hours, but no matter how hard she tried, she had found no explanation by the time she arrived at the school. Almost immediately, Roddy came bounding out amongst a horde of other children. Only the Primary Ones, of course, because they didn't have to stay a whole day until after Christmas. The boy didn't stop chattering all the way home, describing all that he had done in the classroom, all the toys he had played with, what his teacher had said, and in spite of herself, she felt her spirits lifting.

Home once again, she kept Roddy up until Brian came in, knowing that his father would want to hear about this first, important, day at school, but at last, their son safely asleep upstairs, their evening meal over, she decided to beard the lion in his den – not that that was an apt description of the situation, but nevertheless . . .

'I've been thinking about that awful time we spent in the hospital,' she began, 'waiting to learn what was wrong with Dilly. Remember?'

'How could I ever forget? They were the worst few hours I've ever lived through.'

'I know, I prayed silently, but I heard you . . .'

'You heard me? You never said.'

'I didn't really take it in, not then, but I've had time to think about it. Brian, what crimes did you commit?'

'I don't know what you're on about.'

'You said God was punishing you for the crimes you committed, and you promised never to go off the rails again if He let Dilly recover.'

'It was nothing really. Honest, Roselle. I stole some money from the bank, but nobody knew. It wasn't much, just . . . a hundred or two.'

She could scarcely believe this. 'You stole . . . how many hundreds?'

'I don't know, exactly. A little here, a little there. I didn't count it and I didn't really worry about it until the auditors were due.'

'And that's when you moved us out? In case they discovered what you'd done?'

'You make it sound so bad, Roselle, but I was doing it for us. Truly. I had banked it in a London bank, so we could have a better life. You, me and the kids.'

'Did you never intend to pay it back?' Her voice was quite chilly.

'I don't know what I thought. Something happened, something I had nothing to do with. I know you don't remember, and I don't want to remind you, but it meant that everything was destroyed. All the computer systems. All the records. It was an ideal opportunity and I took it.

Nobody can ever find out. Please, Roselle, don't misjudge me. It wasn't for myself, I swear. It was for you and the kids and nobody's been hurt by it. I'm sure the bank's insurance companies would have reimbursed all those people involved – I only took from those with high balances, nobody who would suffer because of what I was doing. You're not thinking of reporting me, are you?'

'I should. I know I should, but . . . oh, I don't know.'

He grabbed her hand now. 'Please, darling, I did it because I love you; because I wanted to give you a better life. And nobody's been hurt, I guarantee that.'

'You're sure it wasn't a huge amount of money?'

'Absolutely sure. It was less than two hundred, anyway. Nothing at all, nowadays.'

'And you promise never to do anything like that again?'

'I promise. Oh, Roselle, you'd break the family up if you . . .'

'I realise that, and it's the only reason I'm going to say nothing. I feel awful about it, especially now Dilly's beginning to get better, but surely God will understand.'

'I'm sure He will.'

'I hope so. Well, that's it. I'll never mention it again.'

In bed that night, Brian went over their conversation in his mind, hardly able to believe that he had got off so lightly. The money he had embezzled had amounted to much more than one or two hundred pounds – not even one or two thousands, more like tens of thousands, maybe hundreds of thousands, he hadn't kept a note of it all – but he had told the truth about his motive. It had been for her and the kids, though he might never have had the courage to make the break if Fate hadn't stepped in to give him a hand. The opportunity had been handed to him on a plate and he had just taken it. No time to think, no time for doubts. It had been a case of Now or Never. He hadn't once regretted it, and as long as Roselle kept her promise to say nothing, he never would.

Thankfully, Dyllis's recovery progressed steadily, even Roddy observing after one visit, 'She's like my Dilly again.'

Roselle had a good weep at that, and Helen, on the verge of tears herself, took the young woman in her arms. 'You know this, Frank?' she observed to her husband afterwards. 'I don't know how you feel about them, but I love those kids like they were our grandchildren, and Roselle – well, she's the daughter we never had.'

'I know what you mean.' The obstruction in his throat made his voice husky. 'But Helen, don't forget, they won't always be living next door. Brian's an ambitious man, and they're still only renting that house, so he's intending to move on.'

'Ach, you,' his wife sniffed. 'You had to go and spoil it, hadn't you?'

Frank was well aware that she wasn't really angry at him; she had never been really angry in all the years they'd been married – it must be nearly twenty-five. She'd been cross with him at times, had said things she didn't mean in the heat of the moment, but they had both been devastated when their girl baby was stillborn. They had been so close then, each finding consolation through the other, but

201

even the son they had three years later had not compensated for the loss.

Oh, they'd loved Andrew, had made sure that he had a good education, let him make his own choice of career and hadn't stopped him from joining the police, and what did he do? He went on holiday to Ireland one year and decided to stay there. He wasn't a good correspondent, and the letters he sent had dwindled over the years until the only communication he sent was a Christmas card. Helen had been heartbroken about that, and he'd had one hell of a job getting her to understand that parents shouldn't expect their children to return the love that had been bestowed on them, that she should be thankful that Andrew at least kept in touch. As a loving husband, he would have to keep a strict eye on her if, when, the Lewises moved away.

Chapter Three

Although Roselle had been worried that Dyllis's illness would affect her education, the little girl surprised them all when she was released from hospital by begging Roddy every afternoon to tell her what he had been taught that day. She even did all the little exercises that he had been set, learning all her letters and studying the reading books he brought home, and she was never happy until she could read the few words below the picture on each page. By the time she was allowed to go to school, she was as fluent as he was.

'Miss Adams says Dilly's really bright,' Roselle had told Helen Milne, proudly. 'She says she can't get over how well she can read and write.'

'They're both clever,' Helen smiled. 'I've known that since they began to talk.'

As the years passed, it became more and more evident that there was a degree of competition between the two children; not a rivalry exactly, more a friendly desire to keep up with each other.

By the time they were nine, they were both avid readers, forsaking comics for such books as *Black Beauty*, *Heidi*, *Swallows and Amazons*, *Alice in Wonderland* and other well-known titles available in the school library, as well as those they received as gifts.

'Of course, you and Brian are bookworms, too,' Helen pointed out one day. 'It makes a difference if the parents are readers.'

'I suppose it does,' Roselle nodded.

'Well, you don't think it's a waste to buy good books for their birthday and Christmas. Some people would never dream of doing that.'

'I always think you can learn so much from books. They give a far wider view of things.'

The two women were sitting, as they often did in an afternoon, Helen knitting jumpers for the twins, Roselle doing some intricate embroidery. They generally talked about current affairs, or, failing that, any titbits of local gossip that interested them. Today, however, Helen had received a letter from her son, which, because it was quite an unusual event, was to be the topic for that day.

'Andrew's never been one for writing,' she began now. 'He's thirty now, but we've never really been close. We usually just send Christmas cards, so when I saw his writing on the envelope, I knew there must be something he needed to tell me.'

'And was there?'

'Oh yes. We all thought he was a confirmed bachelor, but he's actually getting married.'

'So that's good news?'

'Yes, it is. I'm happy for him. He's a hard worker – in the police force in Northern Ireland, so he hasn't had it easy.' Noticing that her friend's expression had changed, Helen asked, 'Is something wrong, Roselle? Are you feeling sick or something?'

'I'm all right. It's just – a queer feeling came over me when you mentioned Northern Ireland.'

Helen had given up some time ago in trying to find out about Roselle's past, but this could be a breakthrough. 'You know something about Northern Ireland? Belfast? That's where Andrew is.'

'Belfast? No, I'm wrong.' How could she admit that she couldn't remember?

Her worried face smote at the older woman's conscience. It wasn't fair to keep on at her. Whatever had happened to her, she didn't want to talk about it, and that was her right, wasn't it? It might do more harm than good. 'Never mind just now, dear. I'm sure it'll come to you when you're least expecting it.'

'I wish I knew what had happened to her,' she observed to Frank later.

'Maybe she's lost her memory,' Frank suggested.

'But it's been such a long time,' she countered. 'It must be wearing on for ten years now.'

He smiled. 'That's nothing. My mother used to tell us about a soldier who went missing in the First World War and everybody thought he'd been killed, but he turned up nearly thirty years later. He'd lost his memory and had started a new life from the day a French farmer found him wandering about and took pity on him. After a while, he married the man's daughter and had been very happy until he started remembering things about his old life.'

Intrigued, Helen asked, 'What happened then? After he went home again, I mean. Was there a happy ending?'

Hesitating, Frank said, doubtfully, 'I don't know. Mother thought he'd split up with his wife – his French wife – and was reunited with his real wife, but whether that was a happy ending or not, she never told us.'

'It couldn't have been happy for his French wife.'

'No, it couldn't have been.' He regretted having repeated the story and went back to the previous topic. 'I wish you would just let her be. Don't say anything. Let it all come from her. If she wants you to know, she'll tell you. Brian never speaks about their early life, either, not even to me, so we'll have to respect their privacy.'

'Yes, I suppose you're right.'

When Brian was told, he, too, frowned. 'I always knew Helen was desperate to know more about us, but I'm telling you, darling, it's better that you don't remember. It was so long ago – and we're happy the way we are . . . aren't we? We don't want bad old memories interfering with that.'

'Yes, I suppose you're right, but it's just . . . well, I sometimes feel I would like to know. I'm not . . . um . . . comfortable thinking there's something hanging over my head that might crash down on me any minute.'

'Oh, my darling, darling.' He took her in his arms and held her close. 'Nothing's going to crash down on you. Everything's all right. What happened will never happen again – can't ever happen again.'

His assurances did seem to satisfy his wife, but the

episode had unsettled him. He had believed that Helen Milne had stopped prying, but she obviously hadn't. If she mentioned any of this to her son, the policeman in Belfast, the shit would hit the fan with a vengeance. Even after nine long years. Yes, he would have to do something to prevent it.

After puzzling over it – agonising over it – all night, he had only come up with one solution. They would have to move away from the Milnes; and leave no clue as to where they were going. It would take some arranging, and it would have to be done asap if not sooner.

From the extensive list he received from an estate agent, it didn't take Brian long to find alternative accommodation. It was a case of taking his pick, and he settled on a rented house in Cruden Bay, almost two hundred miles farther north. He was truly thankful that he had never bought the house in Grangemouth. They would have no furniture to pack, only their personal gear and that was it. Even better, he had managed to wangle a transfer to one of the bank's branches in Aberdeen. That would be just twenty-odd miles to travel every day – no distance at all nowadays.

Roselle, of course, couldn't understand why he wanted to move, even when he said it would lead to promotion, probably as branch manger, and, hopefully, eventually to manager of the main Aberdeen branch. When she saw the house, however, she was much happier about it, a larger, airier, more modern villa in the quaint seaside village, where the children loved their new school and there were several neighbours of her own age.

Dilly and Roddy, soon settled down, making friends in the easy manner of ten-year-olds, and, although for the first few weeks, they sometimes mentioned their 'Auntie Helen and Uncle Frank', the gaps between lengthened until it seemed that the Milnes were completely forgotten. Their mother felt saddened by this, but being aware that her husband had never taken to Helen, had always regarded her as nosey and wanting to pry into their private lives, she said nothing.

When it came nearer to Christmas, she decided to send a card to Helen, to let her know that she still thought fondly of them. She wouldn't give any address, so there couldn't be a card sent in return, and Brian would never know.

The greeting duly sent, Roselle felt quite guilty for deceiving her husband, but glad that she had made the effort. At least Helen would know she was thinking of them.

'Roselle's surely forgotten to give us her address,' Helen observed plaintively, having thoroughly examined the front, inside and back of the communication which had been delivered with some other Christmas mail. 'I can't send a card, and she'll think I don't want to keep in touch.'

Realising how upset his wife was, Frank Milne laid down the morning paper. 'She won't want Brian to know she's written. You knew he wasn't happy about you always asking her questions.'

'I didn't mean any harm . . . I was only trying to help her.'

'That's what's wrong, as far as I can see. He doesn't want her to remember.'

'I'm sure he's got something to hide. He's done something he shouldn't, or committed some kind of crime.'

'Ach, woman, your imagination's running away with you. What kind of crime could a man like him have committed, I ask you? He's an honest, hard-working, family-orientated man who wouldn't hurt a fly. It's just . . . well, you got up his wrong side the very first day you met him. He thought you were just a nosey old woman.'

'I was only being friendly.'

'You know that, and I know that, but he didn't. Whatever happened to Roselle to make her lose her memory must have been really bad, and he's only trying to protect her. He thinks she'll lose her mind altogether if she ever does remember.'

'But remembering it might help her to get over it.'

He heaved an exasperated sigh, but his voice was tender as he said, 'All those doctors had been trained to deal with disturbed minds, Helen, so just leave things alone.'

'I can't do anything, anyway', she sniffed. 'All I know is the envelope is postmarked Peterhead.' After a moment's silence, she added hopefully, 'Peterhead's not that big . . .'

'Don't even think about it, madam. You don't know what you might stir up if you start making inquiries. It could be like opening Pandora's Box. If Roselle had wanted you to know where she is, she'd have given you the address. At least you know they're all right.'

Her lips gripped angrily, his wife said no more. Knowing

they were all right just now, didn't mean that they'd always be all right. But like Frank pointed out, she could do nothing – except hope that a Christmas card would arrive every year.

Chapter Four

Despite missing the first few months of her schooling, Dyllis had caught up very well, and was now on a level peg with her twin. They were not at the top of the class, neither were they at the foot, but floating around the best quarter. They were very popular, still only interested in their own sex, and enjoying all their seasonal interests – football and marbles mainly for the boys and, for the girls, skipping, playing houses or hospitals, and in mixed groups, playing tick and tack, hide and seek, leapfrog and so on. Of course, out of school, the harbour was often where the play landed, or the sandy beach. Although her children often came home with pockets full of seashells or small rounded pebbles that had been washed up, and worse still, left small heaps of sand all over her floors, Roselle didn't mind. She was glad that they were happy, glad that Brian was happy, glad that she, herself, was happy, talking to her neighbours, exchanging recipes and knitting patterns. Only when the other young women talked about their own schooldays and teens did she feel out of it. Give them their due, not one of them had quizzed her, or tried to get her to speak about her own early life. She had told them that she had lost her memory because of something

211

that had happened, so it was quite surprising that they didn't push her for answers. She was almost sure that, being an incomer, they regarded her as an outsider, yet they did not treat her in any way differently from the way they treated each other. She had, however, found out that most of them were not natives of Cruden Bay either, their husbands, like hers, commuting to Aberdeen.

She was closest to her immediate neighbour on the left, Jacqui Donald, and over the five years they had known each other, they had all become very friendly. Brian had been more reserved at first, and had clearly not been at ease when they were invited to visit one evening. Since then, he had accepted that she, at least, did need some time away from the children, and seemed to be quite happy to leave them in the charge of the sixteen-year-old daughter of another neighbour.

Instead of only the two couples, their circle had soon included another two who lived in the same street and developed into one evening a week of playing bridge in each house in turn. Roselle now looked forward to her 'nights out' and even to the nights when it was her turn to be hostess, and was glad that Brian got on so well with all of them, entering into the light-hearted 'criticisms' of partners and taking any directed at him with a genuine laugh.

This happily contented existence could not carry on. Roselle recognised this fact one stormy night in December. It was too easy, too comfortable.

'What's wrong, Ros? Is the wind bothering you?'

'Yes, Bri, it's the worst I've ever heard.' How could she admit to what was actually bothering her? 'I'm sure the roof's going to be blown off.'

'Don't be daft. These houses are really substantial, the builders knew the kind of gales there are here in the winters.'

'Nothing like this, though. This isn't just a gale, it's a . . . hurricane!'

'Snuggle up to me, darling. We should be doing something a lot more pleasurable than listening to the wind.'

As his arms pulled her towards him, she tried to give herself up to the joy of his loving, but it was almost impossible, and as his lips met hers hungrily, a deafeningly loud crash made them both jerk up.

'What the hell's that?' He flung back the duvet and jumped to the floor.

Panic tearing at her innards, she screamed, 'Don't leave me, Brian! Don't leave me! I don't want to die on my own!'

'You're not going to die.' Realising at that moment exactly why she was panicking, his voice lost its anger. 'It's likely just been somebody's garage roof blown off. I hope it's not ours.' Although he was desperate to find out what had actually happened, he gathered her into his arms again. 'It's OK, darling. It's OK.'

Another loud gust caused her to shiver even more but the door burst open and Roddy rushed in and jumped on the bed between them. 'What was that? It woke me up.'

'It must have wakened the whole street, I think.' Brian managed to smile as his daughter ran in. 'It's all right, it's all right. Just somebody's old shed blown to bits, I expect. Come on, jump up and we'll play some guessing games, until the storm stops.'

The next forty minutes were occupied in 'I spy' and 'The minister's cat is an A cat.' and going right through the alphabet to '. . . is a zippo cat', by which time they were all sore with laughing, although Roselle was still worrying about the amount of damage done by the gale, and to what part of their home? It was a full hour later – with the two children fast asleep in their parents' arms – before Brian was able to extricate himself and venture outside.

He returned in little more than five minutes, his white face pinched with the cold. 'My God,' he muttered. 'Our garage roof's been blown away, and so have most of the others in the street, but there's dozens of slates lying all over the place so I suppose we're lucky to still have a roof over our heads.'

'Do you know if anybody's been hurt?' Roselle asked, anxiously.

'There was no word of it, but a lot of house roofs will need to be repaired. I don't know about ours yet,' he added. 'We'll have to wait until daylight to find out.'

The wind and the damage it had done was the main topic of conversation for residents of Cruden Bay for several long weeks, until all the repair works had been carried out, although some of the payments – insurance as well as private – took much longer than that.

It also took Roselle much longer than that to recover from the terror she had felt. It had been childish, she scolded herself. It was only the wind, the houses were solidly built, so why had she felt as if her insides were being riven apart? As if the end of the world had come? She had been absolutely blind with panic as though she was reliving a terrible experience where her world had almost actually come to an end. Was that what had happened to her years ago? Was that why she had lost her memory?

She decided many times to demand that Brian tell her what had happened all those years ago, if it had been a hurricane or what, but her courage deserted her when it came to the point. But she should know, shouldn't she? She was a mature woman. She could face up to anything . . . couldn't she? On the other hand, maybe her husband suspected that she couldn't, that learning the truth might unhinge her for good. That would be why he kept the truth from her.

She got over her fears gradually, time, as it always did, healing even open sores that had once seemed incurable. Only very occasionally in the still of the night, with the spaces between them lengthening considerably, did fear stir within her, this fear that she could never explain to herself, and certainly dared not mention to anyone.

Having removed his wristwatch in case he got dirt in it, Frank Milne suddenly realised that time was marching on. He loved his garden so much that he forgot everything else once he got started, but something was niggling at him today. Helen had said she was just going to the post office and then popping in to see old Mrs Rattray, who was always glad of a visitor, but she surely wouldn't have stayed all this time. His stomach told him it was nearly teatime, and his wife was always home in time to make him a good meal. Of course, he didn't eat as much as he used to do, but she made sure that he never went hungry.

After laying past the trowel and rake, he washed his hands in the kitchen sink, then looked at the clock in the sitting room. My God! Half past six! What on earth had happened to her?

Or maybe something had happened to the old woman? She must be ninety, if she was a day – a tiny rickle of bones, as Helen said – but his wife would surely have let him know. Well, he would just have a seat for a few minutes, maybe take a quick look at the evening paper and then he'd set the table. He had no idea what Helen had planned for tea, and anyway, maybe she would bring in chips, seeing she was so late.

Almost twenty minutes later, he was startled by the loud ring of the doorbell. He must have dozed off and Helen had surely forgotten her key. What a pair they were, he smiled to himself, as he hoisted himself out of his old easy chair. 'I was beginning to think you'd . . .' he began, but halted in dismay at the sight of the young policeman on the doorstep.

'Mr Milne? May I come in, please?'

Frank stood aside to let him pass. 'It's my wife, isn't it? What's happened?'

'She is in hospital, I'm afraid. She was knocked down by a car as she crossed Rose Street.'

'Is she badly hurt?'

'I can't say, but I'm here to take you there. You'd better put on a jacket, though.'

Forgetting his grubby face, his old baggy trousers, Frank grabbed the first jacket off the hallstand and followed the young PC out. His heart was beating twenty to the dozen with fear for his wife. He and Helen had celebrated their ruby wedding some years ago – it must be wearing on for the golden – and he didn't know what he'd do if she wasn't there. She had always been there for him.

He had to wait for over an hour before she was taken back from the operating theatre – an hour in which he imagined the very worst and was sitting chilled with sorrow. It was not as bad as he had feared, thank heaven, but bad enough. The nurse told him that his wife's left leg was broken in two places, her right knee was smashed and her face was badly bruised, which he could see for himself. She was still under the effects of the anaesthetic so he held her hand until she stirred.

At her first movement, he leaned forward. 'Helen, pet, it's me. How are you feeling?'

Her voice was weak, but held the usual humour. 'How d'you think I'm feeling? Bloody awful, that's how. But at least I'm still here to nag you.'

'Oh, God, I'm so glad!'

The nurse made a sign for him not to make her talk, and he sat there for another two hours before he was convinced that she was had fallen into a natural night's sleep. 'You'd best go home,' the young nurse advised him, 'or else you'll be our next patient. She'll be able to talk more at visiting time tomorrow.'

Just wearing his gardening clothes, he had no money on him at all, so there was nothing for it but to walk home.

He was glad in a way, because he knew he wouldn't sleep anyway.

The walk did help. By the time he reached his house, it was beginning to get light, and he wasn't in the least surprised to see that it was almost six o'clock in the morning. Too exhausted even to make himself a cup of tea, he tumbled into bed and was asleep almost as soon as his head touched the pillow.

The sun was as its highest when he awoke, and, his stomach now desperately needing some nourishment, he boiled himself a couple of eggs and made two slices of toast, keeping an eye on the clock as he ate. He didn't want to miss a minute of the visiting time that a large notice had told him before he left was from two till five in the afternoon, and from seven to eight at night.

Refreshed after the food and the shower he took, he found some clean clothes – his wife usually saw to that for him – and got the car out of the garage. At least he wouldn't have to make any more journeys on foot.

Helen looked much better now, although still quite pale and shaken, which was only natural. 'It was my own fault,' she said, in answer to his question as to what happened. 'I'd stayed too long with Mrs Rattray – she loves having somebody to speak to – and I was hurrying to catch a bus, and I didn't stop to look if anything was coming when I stepped off the pavement. I'm getting to be a silly old woman.'

'No, you're not,' Frank protested. 'You're still as young and lovely as the day I first saw you setting that display in the hairdresser's window.'

'And you're still as big a flatterer,' she grinned. 'No, we're both growing old, and I won't be able to do anything for weeks now. How on earth are you going to manage?'

'Don't worry about me, lass. I'll manage. I'd a decent breakfast this morning, you know. Couple of eggs and two slices of toast. You've plenty of cookery books lying around, and I'll soon learn. Anyway, you'll likely get home in a week or two, so you can keep me right.'

It was quite a few weeks before Helen was allowed home, however. Her broken leg was healing satisfactorily, but her smashed knee was causing quite a problem, and once she was discharged, she had to attend once every week to have it examined. In spite of this, or perhaps because of it, they became even closer to each other than they had been for many a long year, Frank taking pride in being the cook/housekeeper and his wife enjoying an easier life than she had ever done.

'You know something?' she remarked one afternoon when they were sitting together after lunch, 'I'm wondering what happened to Roselle and Brian and the twins.'

'I thought she'd have kept in touch.'

'So did I, and I'm sure it was because of Brian. He never liked me, you know, and there was something about him that I . . .'

'No, you were wrong about him, pet. He's a good lad.'

'Did you never wonder why they moved out so quickly?'

'The bank shifted him to one of their Aberdeen branches.'

'Yes, that's what he told Roselle, but I'm not so sure. It was just after she told me they'd been in Belfast before they came here. That's why he got her away from me.'

'Ach no, you're imagining things.'

'I'm telling you. He's got something to hide, and I'm telling you, he was scared I was trying to make her remember things.'

'So you were, but what was wrong with that?'

'He doesn't want her to remember, that's what. He must have done something wrong, committed some kind of crime or . . .'

'Oh, for any sake! Listen to yourself, lass. Who d'you think you are? Miss Marple? The doctors told him not to force her, and her memory would likely come back by itself.'

'Well, it never did, did it?' Helen looked triumphant. 'I wish I knew where they were. We could have driven up to see them.'

'They don't want to see us.' Frank lifted his newspaper. 'Now that's it. I'm not going to discuss it again.'

Knowing that she had no way of finding out where the Lewises had gone, Helen closed her mouth, but she was still convinced that Brian was hiding something. Maybe he wasn't a criminal, he didn't look like a criminal, but he had something to hide. Something he didn't want her, especially, to find out. She heaved a sigh. And she never would find out, not when Frank wouldn't listen to her.

Chapter Five

Both now attending Peterhead Academy, a ten-minute run in the bus from their home, Roddy and Dilly had both stretched, although the girl was not as tall as the boy's almost six foot. They were still very close, and although their classmates were at the age of trying to attract the attention of the opposite sex, they were only interested in each other. This did not escape notice, and Roddy especially was the butt of many barbed remarks, but he didn't respond, even when another boy accused him of being a 'poofter'. He knew that wasn't true, he did have feelings for a girl, although, unfortunately, that girl was his sister.

It was not until they were both almost sixteen that Dyllis tumbled to this fact. She was teased by the other girls because she didn't have a boyfriend, but not one of them had had the nerve to say it wasn't healthy for any girl to be so attached to her brother.

Dilly had been flattered by the attention paid to her by the tallest boy in her year. Malcolm Finnie was even taller than Roddy, broader and more athletic, and a big hit with the other girls. One after the other, they did their best to hook him, but after a couple of 'dates' he moved on to someone else. When he picked on Dyllis, she did not have the experience to recognise him for the philanderer he was, so she believed every word of his sweet talk. Of course, she was aware that he'd taken a few of her friends out, but assumed that they had greatly exaggerated what they said had happened. He would never have told any of them that they were the prettiest girl in school, nor that their eyes were deeper than the blue of the sky, nor that their mouths were the cutest, their lips the sweetest – which he whispered in her ear.

She was completely swept out of her senses by him, not knowing that he had slowed down his usual rapid methods of getting to the 'nitty-gritty', which was all that really interested him. He had recognised that she was different from the other girls, that his usual tactics would scare her off, and he found that it was even more fun prolonging the build-up than the actual seduction itself.

Roddy couldn't understand his feelings when he saw Dilly with Malcolm Finnie. It felt as if he was jealous, but he wasn't. He couldn't be jealous of somebody getting friendly with his sister? Could he? No, it couldn't be that. Maybe it was because Finnie was the most popular boy in their year.

Even having more or less convinced himself of this, Roddy couldn't stop himself from keeping a close eye on them, so much so that the other boys started teasing him.

'What's up with you, Lewis? You can't keep your eyes off your sister when Finnie's anywhere near her – are you in love with her, or something?'

'D'you wish it was you she was smooching with?'

When he was in bed at nights, he found himself imagining that he was the one with his arms around Dilly, was pressed against her, had her looking at him with that soppy look. What was wrong with him? He must be going off his head, thinking of his sister like that, even though there was no doubt that she was the prettiest girl in the whole school. There was only one girl who came anywhere near her for looks, Tracy Little. She was a tiny doll-like thing, blonde hair done up in two plaits, quite nice blue eyes and quite a cute little nose. Yes, the more he thought about Tracy, the more he could see her good features. As for other good points about her, her figure was blossoming, her waist was so small he would surely be able to span it . . . if he tried; if he wanted to. Which he didn't.

Dyllis was quite sure that what she felt for Malcolm Finnie was love; the speeding up of her heart when he looked at her, the misery that swamped her if he so much as looked at another girl. It was stupid really . . . unless it was love. Love excused everything, even this ever-growing need for him to kiss her properly, instead of the peck he gave her on the cheek when they parted. Probably he didn't want anyone to see. His pals would likely tease him if he showed how much he loved her. Of course, that was it. That was why he actually stopped his lips from coming in contact with hers. If she could only bring herself to move her head a little at the crucial moment, and put her mouth in the firing line, so to speak. Once the first time was past, everything else would fall into place.

The lovesick girl had no idea of what could follow the

passionate kisses that she longed for. Her mind did not touch on the sexual complications that would arise, the arousal of a boy who was well experienced in the art of seduction. She believed that she was aware of all aspects of the making of another life and was confident that she could stop any boy from going that far, but she was, in fact, quite ignorant of the dangers of allowing passions to have their full rein.

Thus assured, she let Malcolm persuade her to skip school one afternoon, each hiding in the appropriate toilet block until all the other pupils were gone. When she heard his soft call that it was safe to come out, she opened the cubicle door to be violently shoved back inside.

His hands were everywhere, and no matter how she tried to stop him when he lifted her skirt, he had touched her most intimate parts. He stopped her screams by covering her mouth with his, and had almost succeeded in pushing himself inside her when, in sheer desperation, she bit his tongue.

He jumped back in agony. 'You little bitch!'

Whipping out his handkerchief and holding it with his left hand to staunch the blood running down his chin, he gave her a hard slap across the face. 'You stupid, ignorant bitch! You must've known what I was going to do. You were kissing me hard enough. You were wanting it just as much as me.'

He turned on his heel, yanked up his zip and stamped out angrily, leaving her to sink down on the toilet seat with a hand to her hot cheek. He was wrong! She hadn't known what he was going to do. She would have stopped him long before this if she had. He hadn't loved her at all. He had only wanted sex with her. He would likely tell everybody what a baby she was, frightened to go 'all the way', as they euphemistically called it. The searing tears came then, as she realised what a trusting fool she had been. All the other girls would laugh at her – they already knew what kind of boy he was; just out for one thing.

Having cried herself calmer, she decided that she couldn't go back inside, where everyone would see how upset she was. She had better sit here until lessons came to an end, and then walk out as if she had just been to the toilet. She would make straight for Roddy. He'd see that she was upset and would take care of her. He wouldn't let Malcolm Finnie touch her.

Just over an hour later, the noise of the exodus began and Dilly walked as steadily as she could on her still trembling legs out into the playground, keeping her eyes straight ahead while she turned towards the gates. When the hand touched her shoulder, she knew it was Roddy, but kept on walking.

'Hey, Dill, what's up?' he asked, stepping alongside her. Her silence told him more than she knew, and he said no more, guessing that she wouldn't want to talk about it. The only thing was, he really wanted to know what Finnie had done to her.

Not a word was said while they waited for the bus, and they were practically home before he asked, 'Finnie, I suppose?' Her nod made him go on, 'What did he do to you? You'd better tell me the truth. Did you let him . . . ?'

'He tried, but . . . I bit his tongue.' Quite put out when Roddy burst out laughing, she snapped, 'It wasn't funny.'

'I'm sorry, it was just picturing the great Romeo not getting his own way.'

What he was picturing made her smile herself, recalling the utter shock on the injured face. 'I suppose he wasn't expecting that.'

'I bet he wasn't. I can't wait to tell the boys.'

'No, no, you mustn't tell anybody,' she pleaded. 'I'd be too ashamed.'

'You've nothing to be ashamed of.'

'Promise you won't say anything.'

'OK, I promise . . . but I'd really have enjoyed it.'

Nearing their stop, they both stood up, and by silent consent the matter was not brought up again, but the incident had also made Roddy realise something. It was far too painful for him to think of what could have happened in that school toilet, and shuddered at where it had almost taken place. If he hadn't promised not to say anything to anybody, he'd have sought out Finnie next day and battered the living daylights out of him, but then everyone would have wanted to know why – although most of their classmates would have a good idea.

The thing was, would he have felt so badly about it if it had been anyone other than Finnie? Or anyone other than Dilly? That was the worrying point. He felt almost as if she had betrayed him, when it wasn't her fault. It was the simple fact that she had felt safe enough and even wanted the sod enough to go with him into the toilets. There was only one explanation for his own aching heart, and he had to admit it. He did love her, but it was clear that she didn't feel the same way about him, and his only consolation was that she didn't love Malcolm Finnie now, either.

Dyllis was very self-conscious when she went to school the following morning. If word of what had happened had got round, she wouldn't know what to do with herself. But not a word was said, not a knowing glance was shot her way, not a hint that anything was different today from any other day. It was well into the forenoon before it came to her that Finnie himself would have said nothing. He wouldn't want a soul to know how she had rejected him. He had probably got his eye on one of the other girls already, and was planning her seduction.

Roddy had been doing some really serious considering about his innermost feelings, and had come to the conclusion that he should get to know Tracy Little. Concentrating on her should take his mind off what he felt for his twin; perhaps even banish it altogether. His mind made up, he hung around the school gate one morning until he saw her coming, and made a bee-line for her before any one else spotted her. Unfortunately, Malcolm Finnie, of all people, must have had the same idea, stepping close to her and pipping Roddy at the post. He, however, was goaded into action by the Lothario and, determined not to give him the chance to speak, he grabbed Tracy's arm and pulled her aside.

'Are you doing anything after school?' he asked, diffidently.

Being something of a flirt, and accustomed to boys demanding her for a date, his shyness intrigued her, plus the fact that Finnie was listening with a sneer on his face, she switched on her sweetest smile. 'No, I'm not. Why?'

'I thought maybe you'd like to come for a walk with me.'

'We'd likely miss the bus home,' she pointed out softly, 'and my mum'd be worried.'

Finnie's curled top lip gave Roddy courage to give an instant solution to this. 'I'll ask Dilly to go and tell your mum you'll be on the next bus. Would that be OK?'

'I suppose so.'

'So I'll see you here at the gate at twenty to four?'

'OK.' She pulled away, but tossed her head defiantly as she passed Malcolm Finnie.

Roddy carefully turned the other way. There was no need to raise friction by crowing about his little victory, and he still had to ask his sister to tell Mrs Little.

His mind was not on his lessons that day. The very act of making an actual date had made him feel better about it, and Tracy was a lovely girl. He certainly wouldn't try to do anything he shouldn't; maybe on some future date, though.

The more Roselle thought about it, the stronger grew her conviction that an unhealthy relationship had grown between the twins. It had just been on Roddy's side at first, but it had developed more noticeably on Dilly's side during the last week or two. She couldn't let it go on, perhaps even now it was too late to stop it, and what could she do anyway?

Hopefully, once they left school, the jobs they found would keep them apart during the day – although Brian was trying to talk them into carrying on their schooling and following on to a university, or some kind of further education. She came to a sudden decision. Let fate take its way. If there was going to be trouble – incest or whatever they called it – well, hers couldn't be the first family it had happened to, but she needed to talk about it. She'd been putting off mentioning anything to her husband, but it had reached the point where she was almost sick with worry over what she suspected. As soon as the twins had gone up to their rooms one night to study for their exams, she tackled him. 'Brian, I know you won't like what I'm going to say, but I've got to say it.'

'Say what? It sounds really serious.'

'It is, and I'm surprised you haven't noticed for yourself.'

Her husband frowned slightly. 'Noticed what, for goodness' sake?'

'Haven't you seen how Roddy and Dilly look at each other? I'm sure they're in love.'

His scowl deepened. 'Are you off your trolley, woman? They're twins – off course they love each other.'

'No, I don't mean that kind of love. I mean proper love – between an ordinary boy and girl who aren't related.'

She had his full attention now. 'But they're . . .' He hesitated for a moment before saying, decisively, 'You're talking rubbish, Ros. They do love each other, the same way we love them, but it's not the same kind of love as a man feels for a woman – not like I feel for you.'

He could see that even this made no impression on her and went on, 'There's always a special bond between twins; what one thinks, the other one thinks as well, and so on. I've heard of twins living in different places – one takes ill, the other one feels the same pains.'

'You honestly think that's what it is?'

'Of course it is. I've even read of twins buying the same clothes although they're living hundreds of miles apart. It's a kind of built-in bond between them that nobody understands, that they don't really understand themselves.'

'You're sure that's all it is?'

'One hundred per cent. Now can we watch this programme in peace?'

She lay obediently back in her armchair, but she couldn't concentrate on the events in *Coronation Street*. Maybe Brian was right, but she couldn't believe him – not one hundred per cent.

'You know, Frank, I've been thinking a lot about Roselle and the twins lately. I'm sure something's not right with them.' Helen Milne had ample time to think these days, still unable to get around, except to the hospital for check-ups, where her husband took her every two weeks in the people-carrier he'd bought to accommodate the wheelchair.

He was regarding her now with the expression he always

wore when she mentioned the Lewises. 'I'd forget about that family if I were you,' he told her, firmly. 'If Roselle had wanted to keep in touch, she'd have given you their new address.'

'I'm sure Brian must have told her not to.'

'She's not scared of him. She's got more spunk than that. No, make up your mind that she wasn't as fond of us as we were of her.'

'I loved them all, and I'm positive that she and the kids were fond of us.'

'They can't be kids now, they must be wearing on for thirteen or fourteen.'

Helen gave a loud sniff. 'Shows how much you notice. They'll be seventeen on the twenty-fourth.'

His eyes opening in disbelief, her husband shook his head. 'No, they can't be.'

'They will, I tell you, and it's them I'm really worried about, though I suppose Roselle will be even more worried. There's something far wrong, I know it.'

'Look, lass, even if that's true, there's nothing you can do about it.' His tone was much more sympathetic, however. 'Concentrate on getting your legs strong, and forget about everything else.'

She told herself that she was a stupid old woman for worrying. There was nothing she could do for the Lewis family anyway, and Frank was right – they had made it clear that they didn't want to stay friends.

Dilly was amazed at how much she minded seeing Roddy setting off for walks with Tracy Little. They looked so right for each other, but they weren't really, were they? Everybody knew that the girl went out with any boy who asked her, and he deserved better than that. She tried to pick out a girl who might be more acceptable, but gave up in disgust after five minutes. Not one of the girls she knew fitted the bill. They were either not pretty enough, or too pretty; either too smart for their own good, or so dumb they didn't know right from left; either too rowdy and laddish or quiet wee mice. Roddy wouldn't be happy with any of them.

Her wandering thoughts turned to picking a suitable boy for herself. Not Malcolm Finnie, that was sure. This search proved as useless as her first. She didn't fancy any of them. Some were bullies, some were really good-looking but knew it; the ones who had no claim to good looks knew that, and were too self-conscious to be any fun. The only one she would feel comfortable with was . . . her own brother, and that was taboo.

Determined to banish her jealousy of Tracy Little – she had to admit that it *was* jealousy – she started to ask Roddy where they went on their walks and what they talked about. His bored expression soon told her that he wasn't as smitten as she'd feared, that he was actually rather bored with the girl.

'You know, Dill,' he said at last, 'All she thinks about is how she looks. "Does my hair look all right, does it suit me? Is my lipstick smudged?" Yeuch!' He dropped the affected high imitation. 'I'm beginning to hate the sight of her.'

'Why don't you dump her, then?'

'I don't like to be nasty. How can I say I don't fancy her any longer?'

'Break a few dates, then. That should tell her.'

As it happened, it was Tracy who did the dumping, by doing exactly what Roddy had been told to do – not turning up for a couple of dates.

'I don't care,' he declared to his sister, but she knew his pride had been hurt.

The next few weeks were taken up by revising their various subjects, then came the exams themselves, so it was not until all the stress was off them that they had time to relax and think of other things. On the first day of their freedom, it was unfortunate that their parents had been invited out for the evening, leaving them at a loose end in the empty house. For the first hour, they sat on the settee together as they always did when watching television. Roddy had opened a large packet of crisps which they were sharing until she twitched them away from him. He didn't know how it happened, but he leaned across her to retrieve them, she laughed up at him, and before they realised it, they were kissing – like lovers.

It was a long kiss that neither of them wanted to end, but at last Roddy pulled himself away. 'Oh, Lord, Dill, I'm sorry,' he muttered, shamefacedly. 'I shouldn't have done that.'

'It was my fault as much as yours,' she whispered, 'and to be honest . . . I liked it.'

'Did you? Really?' He could scarcely believe it.

She gave a naughty little giggle. 'Would you mind doing it again, so I can be sure?'

It was half an hour later, if not longer, before the kissing stopped, and they looked at each other in dismay. 'We shouldn't.' His whisper was throbbing with emotion. 'I'm sorry.'

Taking in a deep breath to help her to answer, she murmured, 'I'm not sorry.'

'Aren't you?' He looked at her face, flushed with passion, and at long last admitted what he should have known some time ago. 'I love you, Dilly. D'you know that? I really and truly love you with all my heart.'

'Oh, I'm glad. I thought it was only me.'

'You mean . . .'

'Yes, I love you, too, really and truly with all my heart.'

About to kiss her again, Roddy drew back. 'We can't, though. We can't love each other. It's against the law for a brother and sister to . . .'

They regarded each other silently, sadly, shaken by the force of their passion, yet knowing that it could not go on. After a few moments, he stood up. 'I'm going to bed. So should you.'

Her eyes shot open. 'To your bed?'

'My God, no! That would be asking for trouble. If Mum and Dad came in and even saw us like this, they'd know what was going on, but in bed together, God! They'd go ballistic.'

Her gaze held his. 'I wish we could, though.'

He wisely said nothing else and went out, while Dilly

gathered up all the scattered crisps and put them in the kitchen bin before she, too, went upstairs.

Both youngsters got little sleep that night, each thinking of what might have been, but knowing only too well that it could never be.

Chapter Six

Although, like most men, Brian had never been quick to pick up the signs of increasing attraction between two people of the opposite sex – the meaningful glances exchanged, the accidentally-on-purpose touching of hands in the passing – it had not taken long for him to become aware of what was blossoming between his children. The realisation clobbered him like a kick in the gut from a mule as they were getting into his car one morning to go to work. They weren't even sitting together, Roddy in front with him, Dilly in the back seat, but it was almost as if there was a banner attached to them announcing, 'We are in love.'

He had tried telling himself that it was pure imagination, but it was even more noticeable on the return journey. His stomach doing all sorts of impossible gymnastics, he did little justice to his meal, and excused his lack of appetite by pleading an excruciating headache.

'I'll be better if I get some fresh air,' he told Roselle rather sharply when she fussed.

His favourite walk was down to the sea, where he often sat and watched the young lads with their little motor boats, but tonight he wanted to be alone to think, so he walked out of the village altogether until he came to the ruins of Slains Castle, practically on the edge of the cliff, an eerie spot even in broad daylight, but ringed at this time of evening by shadowy shapes. Sitting down on a large stone, he wondered what he should do.

Maybe he'd been imagining it; maybe he'd been seeing things – but it wasn't that. He was sure it wasn't. The point was, should he tell Roselle or not? It would likely upset her as much as it had upset him, and that was something he didn't want to do. Should he have a word with Roddy? Sort of warn him about the dangers of getting too fond of his twin? Or would that make things worse? Teenagers didn't like to be told, and it might make him more determined than ever.

Bending over, holding his head in his hands, Brian knew that something had to be done, but he couldn't face being the one to do it. Surely, though, the boy must know without being told that it was against the law for a brother and sister to marry, and twins were even more closely related than that . . . weren't they?

If only he had noticed before, but it was too late now. If they ran away together, the resulting scandal in the village would be too much for Roselle – she had gone through so much before. It would turn her brain altogether and he couldn't bear to think of her being hurt any more. He couldn't take this himself, come to think of it. His carefully planned family, the lovely house, he would lose everything He tinkered now with the idea of jumping off the cliff, ending it. His wouldn't be the first suicide in this place, and after all, it was his fault, wasn't it?

*   *   *

Roddy had been working with an internationally important oil firm in Aberdeen for almost a year before a solution to his problem occurred to him. With Dilly also travelling in the car every morning and evening, it was getting more and more difficult for them to keep their feelings for each other in check, and it was growing more obvious that their father was regarding them in a curious way. Their mother, too, seemed to be in a constant state of apprehension, and he decided that it would be better if he moved away from home altogether – pushed temptation well out of his reach. He put out a few feelers in the office to the effect that he wouldn't mind a transfer to another branch, but said nothing to anyone else, not even his sister.

The daily routine went on as usual for the next few months, and he was thinking of just answering adverts in the press when he was called into the Under Manager's office – the holy-of-holies, the inside of which was a mystery to most of the staff. At the barked 'Enter' to his timid knock, he turned the handle and walked in, trying to recall the opening words he meant to say. He need not have worried about it.

The VIP looked up from the papers before him and said, quite kindly, 'You'll be the young fella who wants some promotion?'

'It's not that, sir,' Roddy answered. 'It's because I'd like to see a bit more of . . . Britain.'

'So it's not because you hoped to see the world at our expense?'

'Oh, no, Mr Petersen. I want to learn a bit more about the company and how it's run.'

'You're anxious to take over the running of it, are you?'

But the twinkle in the man's eyes let the youth know that he was joking. 'I don't seem to be doing much here except running errands, sir, and I know I'm capable of more than that.'

'You think that it's beneath you?'

'No, sir . . .'

Petersen took pity on him at this point. 'It's all right. I admire someone with the guts to get on. I grant you that being an office boy is the lowest form of life here and that you must wonder how a firm of this size works. I take it that you feel rather young to go overseas – maybe some time in the future? – but as it happens a vacancy has arisen in our Liverpool office for an assistant in their financial department. You will be given training in all aspects of the job – and will have to satisfy the Head Cashier before you are given the position permanently – so you will have a lot to learn. I trust you are not afraid of hard work?'

'No, sir, I'll be glad of the challenge.'

'That's what I like to hear. The only other thing which needs to be tackled is – I see that you are not quite eighteen, so what will your parents say about you leaving home so young?'

About to assure him that his parents would not object, Roddy decided to tell the truth. 'I don't suppose my mother'll be very happy about it, but at eighteen I won't be a minor any more. I'm able to look after myself .'

'Lodgings will be arranged for you. Apparently, there is a very decent widow woman who has looked after several of their younger employees. No one has ever complained about her, and she has never complained about any of our staff.'

He rubbed his forefinger reflectively against his nose. 'It would probably be best if you ask your mother to come to see me, so that I can set her mind at ease about your welfare.'

'Yes, sir. She could come in Dad's car with my sister and me in the morning.' It dawned on the boy that the man may not start work so early, so he added, apologetically, 'If that would suit you?'

Mr Petersen laughed heartily at this. 'You think that I start work in the middle of the day? No, my boy, a sluggard gets nowhere in this world. I keep the same hours as all the staff – with, perhaps, a little leeway where lunch is concerned. I do, however, make up for any time lost by working late on many occasions. I do not take advantage of my position.'

'I'm s-sorry, I didn't m-mean . . .' Roddy stuttered, acutely embarrassed by his *faux pas*.

'No, I am well aware of that. It was a natural assumption to make. Well, you had better get back to work, and I will expect to see your mother tomorrow morning, so that I may set the transfer in motion.'

Once again, the boy's mind was not on his work that day, but he got through without making any further gaffes, and he decided to keep his excitement to himself until he went home and the whole family was together.

It had been Roselle's day for playing hostess at the Coffee Morning. The Mothers' Club met fortnightly, organised some two years ago by three other mothers in the street. They took it in turn to supply the venue and the refreshments, and used the rest of their two hours together by knitting and sewing articles to despatch in boxes to various charities at home and abroad. Brian had not been very keen on the idea at first, saying that it was only a way of gathering gossip, but she had stuck to her guns. Of course, a lot of gossiping did take place while their fingers were busy, but nothing really out of place – none of them had malicious tongues, just a healthy interest in what was going on in the village, with events in the rest of the world coming a trailing second.

That afternoon had produced two unexpected pregnancies, with much discussion on looking out infants' clothes and other items that were offered to the women concerned, both nearing forty and having passed on years ago all the baby clothes they had had for their older children. As she prepared supper for her own brood, Roselle recalled Laura's and Cheryl's differing reactions and hoped that she wouldn't fall victim to the 'Baby Boom'. She had had enough bringing up twins, and now that they were more or less grown up, she didn't want to be lumbered again. That was exactly Laura's attitude, but Cheryl, with only one child, a boy of seven, was delighted to be expecting another.

'I can hardly believe it,' she had crowed. 'I love the smell of babies, the talcum power, the fresh nappies . . .'

'The *shitty* nappies,' Laura had corrected, to nods of agreement, 'and sick all over your T-shirts and jeans.'

Cheryl had shaken her head in pity at this outlook. 'The

thrill of tiny fingers gripping yours, and the look of love in the tiny eyes.'

'Ah, yes,' Judy had sneered, 'but don't forget the months you can't get into any decent clothes, and folk smirk when they see you in the street with your belly sticking a mile out in front of you. I used to get really embarrassed by that. What about you, Roselle? What was it like having two at once? Your stomach must have been ginormous.'

Knowing that her husband would be angry if she admitted that she couldn't even remember giving birth to the twins, she said, 'It was awful. I was like the side of a house, and waddled about like a misshapen duck.' She had read about, and seen several programmes on television about twins, their births, their similarities, their differences, and this was what had intrigued her about the mothers.

The others laughed at this, and the conversation moved on, but now her visitors had gone she tried to remember at least a tiny something, but no matter how hard she tried, nothing would come to her. Could their birth have been the trauma responsible? She shook her head at her stupidity; her memory only went back to when they were almost a year old. That was when it had happened, that terrible event that had robbed her of all the memories she should be able to treasure – the highs and lows of the first few months of her babies' lives. Well, she wasn't going to take Brian's refusals any more. She would make him tell her everything this very night, even if it took until tomorrow morning. She had let him bully her into acceptance of something she couldn't possibly accept until she found out every last detail of it. Her mind made up, she checked the progress of the steak pie she had put into the oven almost an hour ago and, satisfied that it would not be overcooked, she poured herself a small glass of sherry to give her added strength. The gang shouldn't be home for half an hour yet, so she might even have a second one.

They were ten minutes later than usual – 'Another snarl-up on the A90,' Brian moaned – and Roselle was kept busy dishing up and making sure that they all had enough. She could see that Roddy seemed to be a bit excited about something, but her own mind was churning with the dread of what she meant to do when she and her husband went to bed. She did not mean to say anything in front of the twins. They knew nothing of what had happened.

Mother and daughter were gathering the dirty dessert plates when Roddy said, rather hesitantly, 'Sit down, you two. I've something to tell you.'

Dilly clapped her hands. 'Oh good, you've got a promotion?'

'Not exactly, but I think it *is* good news. I'm being sent to Liverpool, to be in the finance department of the office there. I'll have to serve a kind of apprenticeship, I suppose, but—'

'Liverpool?' His mother was horrified. 'They can't send a young boy like you away from home like that. Brian, you'll have to tell them.'

To hide his relief, her husband pulled a face. 'If they think he's fit for this job . . .'

'Oh, you! He can't be fit for a job like that at his age.'

'Mum,' Roddy said, quietly. 'Mr Petersen wants to speak to you, and I said you'd come to Aberdeen with us tomorrow morning. He'll tell you all about it.'

'You see?' Brian said, triumphantly. 'They'll make sure he'll be all right.'

Her son's news devastated her, however, so her own planned confrontation with her husband went completely out of her head. All she could think of was poor Roddy, torn out of the bosom of his family and having to fend for himself in an alien world. He had no idea of the kind of people he could meet, the rogues, the velvet-tongued villains, the predators who might . . . Oh, it was too horrible even to think about.

'There's no need to worry, Ros.' It seemed her husband knew how worried she was. 'He's got his head screwed on the right way.'

'He's still just a kid.' She couldn't chance admitting what she had been thinking. He would only laugh at her.

'He has to learn to stand on his own two feet, dear. We all had to.'

It would have been an ideal opening for her to remind him of her ignorance of her own early life, to demand that he told her everything, but she couldn't face any more revelations at this moment. She was about to lose the son she loved; her family was soon to be halved.

Brian slid his arms round her. 'Stop worrying, darling. He's looking forward to it, and his boss must think he's capable enough, otherwise he wouldn't have suggested it.

Besides, he's not going to the other side of the world. He'll be able to have weekends at home sometimes.'

'I suppose so.' About to point out that Roddy wouldn't be able to afford the fare from Liverpool very often, she decided to make sure that he always had enough money to come home. She accepted her husband's kiss, and was glad that he turned away to sleep. He didn't understand how she felt and if she kept on about it, he'd soon get annoyed. Men were all the same, and she didn't suppose that this Mr Petersen would be any different when she saw him in the morning. He'd likely regard her as a neurotic mother who was scared of letting her son off her apron strings.

Neither Roselle nor Brian noticed that Dilly had fallen silent since Roddy had dropped his bombshell – which is how the girl considered his news. She couldn't speak, he had wounded her to her very core. It was as if she had been turned to stone; only her heart was still beating, beating out a series of agonising pains in a fluctuating rhythm that threatened to overcome her altogether.

It was not until she was in bed, having had no chance for any discussion with him, that she could think about it. How could he do this to her, when they had only lately discovered their love for each other? They both knew that nothing could come of it, of course, although it had crossed her mind several times during the previous few weeks that they could run away together, go to a place where no one knew that they were actually twins – she'd have been willing to go anywhere in the world with him – and live happily ever after. Why couldn't Roddy have thought of that? Why was he taking the coward's way out?

She let her mind slip to an imaginary scenario, where she was a happy housewife, cooking and cleaning for the man who had vowed to love her for ever, having his babies and watching them grow up.

Her thoughts came to an abrupt halt, a searing stop that shook her. Was it true, as she had heard or read somewhere, that children made by close relatives would be born insane? If not altogether mad, they would probably be born malformed in some way. No, no! That couldn't be true! It couldn't!

Her heart had almost stopped at the very idea, so she pushed it away vehemently. She and Roddy would have been different. Their children would have been perfect in every way – healthy, wealthy and wise, as the old saying went. But the old beliefs refused to go away. It was against the law for brothers and sisters to marry, and, presumably, it was far worse if they were twins, born from the same seed.

Roddy was right to leave, to put all temptation behind them, and she'd have to steel herself to abide by his decision. But how she wished that it had been different.

The whole family had been dreading this day, the day of Roddy's departure. Roselle's fears had been a little allayed by what his boss had told her, but she knew that she was still going to be extremely upset. She just hoped that

246

she'd be able to hide her fears from her son. He would be putting on a brave face, no doubt, but his mother's anxiety could undermine him.

As it happened, she was the most composed of them all. She had her feelings well under control, while Brian's eyes filled with moisture as Roddy, biting his lip to keep back his tears, closed the carriage door, and Dilly was sobbing loudly. Saying goodbye like this was a harrowing experience, even knowing that it was not for ever. The three sad figures stood waving until the train was out of sight, and it was Roselle who shepherded them off the platform. The journey home was made more or less in silence, with only Dilly saying, as they left the city behind, 'He'll be all right, Mum, won't he?'

'Of course he will.' Her mother's confident reply soothed the girl, who leaned back in the back seat and closed her eyes, while the woman fought back the tears that were threatening to break through at last. She had to keep calm. If she let down her defences for a single moment, she would be lost.

She had been assured by Mr Petersen that her son would be well looked after, that the woman who would be his landlady had proved her worth over and over with his young employees, but this, instead of helping Roselle, had raised a new fear in her: would this Mrs O'Shaughnessy turn into a surrogate mother, take over the role that should be hers, Roselle's, alone?

No matter how much she scolded herself for this thought, she couldn't shake it off.

* * *

'Today's the twins' eighteenth birthday.'

His wife's remark took Frank Milne by surprise. He had believed that she had forgotten about the Lewis family ages ago, or if not entirely forgotten, had surely given up on worrying about them. 'So they've reached the age of majority,' he remarked.

A frown crossed her face. 'What d'you mean by that?'

'Nothing, I was only saying. I hadn't forgotten how old they are.'

A little mollified, she gave a sigh. 'I just wish I knew if they stayed on at school to take higher education. I think they'd both have been clever enough.'

'Aye, I agree there. They were bright wee things, the pair of them.'

'They were that, but they knew their own minds, even at that age, especially Roddy, and I can see him wanting to leave school, to earn some money.'

'He'll get on, whatever he's doing.'

After a brief silence, Helen said, reflectively, 'I can't understand why Roselle never wrote. I thought she liked us, and she must have known we'd want to hear about the twins.'

'You used to think it was Brian's fault. You thought he didn't want her to keep in touch.'

'A girl can change her mind, can't she?'

Her husband wasn't convinced. 'So you've stopped blaming him, then?'

'I don't know what to think, and that's a fact. Mind you, I hope she would write to me if she ever needed help. She has nobody else to turn to, as far as I know.'

'She's likely made a lot of friends wherever they are. She was a friendly soul.'

His wife nodded her agreement, and then changed the subject abruptly. 'Well, do you want to watch the football or not?'

Deciding to be diplomatic, and aware that Helen preferred *The Bill*, Frank shook his head. It was better than telling a deliberate lie.

Chapter Seven

For his first few weeks in Liverpool, Roddy did feel home-sick, although Mrs O'Shaughnessy did all she could to make him feel at home. He missed his parents, he missed his old school pals, but most of all, he missed his sister. When he awoke each morning, he felt this acute pain nagging at his heart, and it grew worse at night. It was as if part of him had disappeared, had been lost for ever, yet he knew that he would always have this same love for her, whether it was right or wrong. Deep down, of course, he knew that it definitely *was* wrong.

As the weeks passed, however slowly, so slowly at first, he got to know his workmates and other young men in his lodgings, and the hollow feeling diminished and almost died, although there were times when, late into the night, he woke up with the same yearning eating at him; the yearning that could never be appeased.

It was another young clerk from the same firm who guided Roddy's feet onto the road to enjoyment. He had, as a result of his mother's nagging letters and enclosed postal order, made the journey home to Cruden Bay after three months, and returned after the weekend in deep depression. It had been agony to see Dilly, to have to talk about mundane things, never to have the slightest chance of touching her, or speaking privately to her. On the Monday morning, he looked so miserable that Tony Riley, at twenty just over a year and a half older than him, asked if he would like to go to a café with him for lunch. Roddy agreed listlessly, lunch wasn't a priority for him just then, and he was pleasantly surprised by how well they got on. Over their soup and sandwiches, Tony had him smiling, then giggling, then laughing out loud, and lunch together became a regular thing, followed by the weekends.

The invitation to spend Saturdays and Sundays at the Rileys' home was issued on only the third week of their acquaintance, although Roddy was reluctant to accept at first – he didn't feel up to mixing with other people, nor intruding on a family's weekend – but when he arrived there it was obvious by their welcome that they enjoyed extra company.

Indicating each one with a wave of his hand, Tony made the introductions, 'Mum, Dad, Boppy – my pest of a baby sister – and my faithful companion Google. After my favourite website,' he added with a grin.

His mother shook her head at his casual manner. 'You'll have to excuse my son, Roddy. He's got no finesse. I'm Tess, my husband's called Wilf, my daughter was christened Barbara but called herself Boppy when she was just a wee tot, and it sort of stuck. Google's a mixed breed . . .'

'He doesn't like being called a m-o-n-g-r-e-l,' Tony interrupted in a loud whisper, stroking the dog's head affectionately.

Noticing the adoring way the dog's eyes regarded Tony, Roddy knew that the dog felt the same way about his master. 'Thank you very much for inviting me for the weekend, Mrs . . .'

'It's Tess, and we're delighted you agreed to come.'

Wilf came forward with his hand out, giving the boy a brief, but extremely firm, handshake. 'Now you've met my unruly brood, you'll maybe have reservations about coming again, but we'll always be pleased to see you.' He turned to his wife. 'And now the introductions are over, perhaps we can have our meal, Tess?'

Still feeling slightly ill at ease, Roddy sat down in the chair Wilf pulled out for him, while Tess and Boppy went through to the kitchen to dish up and the other two took their seats. The meal passed in a flurry of light, teasing talk, especially between the brother and sister, with their parents smilingly putting in an occasional few words to settle a difference of opinion. Roddy was soon drawn into the discussions and mock arguments about anything and everything.

The evening was spent in playing Monopoly, which lasted until Tess said, 'I think we should call a halt now. I don't know about the rest of you, but I need my beauty sleep.'

Roddy was surprised to see that the large clock on the wall was showing five past twelve, and realised that he actually felt quite tired. Of course, the scores had to be totted up before the table was cleared – Boppy having most of the cash and only Roddy left with some property. He had never played the game before and thoroughly enjoyed the pseudo-serious bargaining that went on, and when he went to bed – a cup of cocoa and a digestive biscuit later – it dawned on him somewhat belatedly that he had laughed more over the past few hours than he had done for months. The Rileys had been a proper tonic. They were a very close-knit family although they pretended to bicker about this and that. Brother and sister were not in the least alike physically, Tony taking after his mother with his almost black hair and startlingly blue eyes, while Boppy and her father had light brown hair and dark, nearly black eyes.

It was the opposite from his own family, he reflected, sleepily; he with the same colouring as their father and Dilly with their mother's. He fell asleep thinking of her, as he had done ever since he had realised that he loved her, but this time it did not keep him awake as it usually did.

He awoke in the morning feeling refreshed He still loved her, he always would, but he was only too aware that they had to lead separate lives now, find new friends, new happiness. Boppy Riley was the only girl he had come to know in Liverpool and it was too early to tell if she would be his eventual Fate, though he was almost sure that she wouldn't. She could be good company, though, and that was what he needed now.

'He's writing a lot about this Tony Riley who works with him.' Roselle Lewis handed the letter to her husband, but couldn't stop speaking her thoughts out loud. 'He's been going there for whole weekends and . . .'

'I can read, thank you.'

Brian's quiet comment made Dilly smile a little. Her parents often argued but not for real, and she knew they loved each other as much as she loved Roddy. She was not quite so sure now, though, that he still loved her. How could he when he was for ever going to see Tony Riley's family? There was a sister there, too, so it was on the cards that she and Roddy would get together . . . wasn't it? Not that he ever hinted at anything like that, but if she was a pretty girl, he must be tempted. He'd been seeing her every weekend for months now; it was too awful to imagine what they could be doing together. They did go to the pictures, and her brother surely wouldn't want to play gooseberry, so they'd be sitting together, walking home together, maybe even sitting in the sitting room or lounge or whatever after everyone else had gone to bed.

Her father cut into this agonising thought. 'What d'you think about it, Dilly? Your mother seems to think he'll hit it off with the daughter of the house.'

'He could do worse, I suppose,' she said, forcing herself to make a joke.

Roselle shook her head. 'He could, and she seems to be a nice girl, but he's still a bit young to be thinking of settling down.'

The knife turning in her daughter's heart stilled at this. Of course he was too young to get serious, with this Boppy – stupid name – or any other girl. She was worrying for nothing. Once he'd had his fill of Liverpool, he'd come back to her, even though he'd said they could never be *really* together. They could, if he loved her as much as she loved him. She would go away with him tomorrow, if he asked her to. Nobody would know they were twins if they went to a strange place. He said that was impossible, of course, because any children they might have would be insane, or misshapen, but they wouldn't need to have any children. There were all sorts of contraceptives available. She felt the blood rushing to her face, wave after wave, at the thought of having sex with Roddy.

'Are you all right, dear?' Her mother was eyeing her in concern. 'You're very flushed.'

'I feel a bit queasy,' she lied, 'but I'll be all right when I get outside in the cool air.'

'You should have a lie-down.'

'I'm all right, I tell you. I promised to meet Janice Burns at eight. She wants to go for a walk in the hope of seeing Jeff Dawson and his pals.'

'So are you after one of his pals?'

'Don't be silly! They're a bunch of dopes. Well, I'd better be going, or I'll be late.'

She was barely out of the door when her mother said, 'You know, Brian, I'm getting really worried about her. She hasn't been well for . . .' she paused, then ended, '. . . for a long time.'

'You mean, since Roddy went to Liverpool?'

'Well, yes, but it surely couldn't be that? He's her brother – her twin brother.'

Pulling on his jacket, her husband pulled a face, and then said, quietly, 'I've read somewhere that if one twin goes away, the other pines, and I've heard people saying it's true.' He turned as he went out, adding, 'It's only natural, Ros.'

Knowing that there was no sense in arguing further, she wisely said no more, but she was still convinced that there was something far wrong going on in her family.

Although Roddy enjoyed Boppy's company, it did not take him long to realise that she felt more for him than he felt for her, and he was always relieved when there were other people present. Then, to his horror, over lunch one day, Tony said, with mock drama, 'Thou art not the only one with an admirer, Roderico. I, too, am being pursued by a tasty wench. Which of us, prithee, will get his leg over first, I wonder?'

'Stop clowning,' Roddy snapped, angry at his own embarrassment. 'I don't know what you're on about. I don't have a girlfriend.'

Tony shook his index finger at him reprimandingly. 'Cruel, cruel. Thou cannot pullst the wool over mine eyes, however. Canst thou not see that the fair Boppy is ready for the plucking?'

'Don't be daft, man! She's your sister! How can you say anything like that?'

'It be the truth, Roderico. Hast thou not got eyes in thy head?'

Deciding that changing the subject was the only way out, Roddy said, 'So you've found a girlfriend, have you? Come on then, out with it. Who is she?'

'Nice try, my friend, but thou willst soon find out the truth for thyself, so I willst answer thy question. See, here she cometh, the delectable Desdemona.'

'Cut it out, Tone,' said the tall blonde girl now taking a seat beside them. 'Hi, Roddy.'

He blinked in amazement. 'Samantha?'

'Didn't you know about Tony and me? Everybody else in Finance does.'

Guffawing at his friend's blank look, Tony said, 'Blind as a bat, this one, Sam. Never mind, m'laddo, it'll be your turn next.'

Roddy gave his head a vehement shake. 'I don't think so, Tony. I'm not ready for a girlfriend.'

'Hast got a wench waiting for thee in Aberdeen – or that Godforsaken place you call home? Is that it?'

'If you mean Cruden Bay, it's a lovely village, and there might be somebody there.' As far as he could see, it was the only way to stop the teasing.

His ploy certainly worked. Tony's face turned a deep red, and his brows shot down. 'My God! So you've been leading my sister up the garden path all this time. Well I tell you this, you low-life, you'll never be welcome in our house again.' He jumped to his feet. 'Come on, Sam! I can't stand to look at his two-timing, lying face!'

The girl did as she was told, but before following Tony out, she turned and shrugged apologetically. Roddy, however, was left with a horrible sinking feeling in the pit of his stomach. He hadn't told Boppy any lies, he hadn't let her believe he was serious about her. He hadn't wanted to hurt her, but he would never get the chance now to tell her so. Unless . . .? Should he write and explain? How could he, though? He could never tell her, or anyone else, for that matter, that the girl he loved was his twin sister. That would set alarm bells going with a vengeance. It would be blazoned from the rooftops and soon everybody he knew would believe he was some sort of pervert. His name would be in all the papers, with a photo, no doubt. Maybe he'd land in prison for – whatever the crime was called, because it *was* a crime, he was well aware of that.

He had to force himself to return to work, and was thankful that Tony Riley was on another floor, but no doubt he'd be telling all and sundry what had happened. He did not see his ex-friend during the rest of the week, but knew by the embarrassment of the other members of staff he encountered that news of his 'girlfriend' had got out. He purposely avoided the little café where he and Tony had always gone for lunch. Going hungry was better than being ridiculed by the people who had witnessed the incident.

On finishing work that Friday afternoon, he made for the railway station. He had to go home, to be with people who wouldn't turn their backs on him.

Roselle had been delighted by the phone call from her son a couple of days ago. It was time he put in an appearance. It must be at least four months since she'd seen him, and she was beginning to think that he was serious about this Boppy girl he'd got to know. She wasn't sure how she felt about it. As his mother, she thought he was far too young to be serious about any girl, but, on the other hand, it would mean that he'd got over his feelings for Dyllis, which would be the best news she'd had for ages.

As soon as she saw him, she could tell from his manner that something had happened, and made signs to her husband and daughter when they returned from their usual

Saturday morning walk. Sometimes they went to Slains Castle, the eerie ruins standing on the edge of the cliff, where, the story went, Bram Stoker had got his setting for *Dracula*. Today, however, they had gone a little farther, to the Bullers of Buchan, the fearsome natural formation where, over hundreds, thousands, of years, the sea had eaten deeply into the cliffs, leaving only a tiny footpath between two bottomless pits in which the sea constantly churned in a massive vortex. Both places were known to be extremely dangerous – several accidents, even suicides, had taken place there – and Roselle was never happy until they came home again.

Fortunately, each gave Roddy a loud and boisterous welcome now, and conscious of what Roselle was trying to convey to them, asked him no questions. It was not until after lunch, when the ladies were washing up, that he took the chance of speaking to his father.

'I suppose you're wondering why I'm not with the Rileys this weekend?'

'It did cross my mind,' Brian said, quietly, 'but don't tell me if you'd rather not.'

'It was Boppy, you see, the daughter. She . . . she . . .'

'You didn't . . . ? For God's sake, man, you haven't made her pregnant, have you?'

The young man hastened to dispel the gathering anger in his father's face. 'No, no, nothing like that. It was just, um, well, she got the wrong impression. I didn't feel the same way she did.'

Brian nodded wisely. 'A woman scorned, was she?'

'I didn't give her any reason to think I was interested in

her. I did like her, she was good company, but I think her family must have been expecting a romance.'

'What's this about a romance?' Roselle asked as she came in. 'Have you found a girlfriend at last?'

Stricken with guilt at seeing Dilly's stunned expression as she followed her mother, Roddy said, 'No, no, it's not me.'

Roselle saved the situation by adding, 'It's your friend, then? Tony?'

Unwittingly, his mother had given him a way out. 'Yes,' he nodded. 'Tony's got a girl, and I'd just be odd man out.'

'Never mind, dear,' she consoled, 'your turn'll come.'

Dyllis's face had brightened as she sat down. 'You're still quite happy working in Liverpool, are you?'

He turned to her. 'Oh yes. Of course, it's much bigger than Aberdeen, and Cruden Bay would fit in dozens of times, so there's a lot to do – lots of things to see.'

'I was going to suggest a walk,' Roselle said now, 'but I suppose you and your dad have done enough walking for one day, Dilly, so what about a wee run out in the car? It'll be like old times again, the four of us.'

Sitting close beside his sister in the back seat, as he had always done, was a heavenly torture for both of them, as Roddy could tell when she turned her wistful eyes on him. He took hold of her hand with the intention of comforting her, but instantly wished that he hadn't. This was worse than torture, it was absolute purgatory, but he couldn't break away now. And so they sat for the rest of the journey, through the rural countryside, the small villages, and back along the shore road, past Boddam, which had been home to an important aerodrome during World War Two and had remained as RAF Buchan until its closure in 2005, but which was better known now for the huge chimney that had been built for its role as an oil terminal.

Five minutes later, they were home again, the back-seat passengers having to untangle legs as well as fingers before spilling out of the car, relieved that neither of their parents had noticed. Both Roselle and Brian, however, although they had their own separate reasons for not mentioning it, had been acutely conscious of what had been going on.

That night, after an evening of watching television, each of the Lewis family spent a wakeful night. For hours, Roddy's thoughts veered between love, lust and guilt, but just as dawn was coming up, he made the great decision. He couldn't go on like this. He couldn't expect Dilly to keep loving him when there wasn't the vaguest chance of a future for them. He would have to put an end to his visits home . . . but how could he explain that to his parents? He agonised over this for some time before the answer hit him like a kick in the stomach. When he went back to work on Monday, he would ask for a transfer. He'd been in Liverpool for just over a year now, and the Head Cashier seemed to be pleased with his progress, so there shouldn't be any problems. It would also take him away from the uncomfortable situation he was in because of Tony Riley. The move would need to be out of Britain altogether, though; somewhere far enough away so that he couldn't afford to come home very often . . . if ever.

The idea of never seeing Dilly again was unbearable, but it would be the only way to give her a chance to meet and, hopefully, fall in love with somebody else and start a family of her own. This was another unpalatable thought, but he did wish for her to be happy, and – who knows? – he might fall in love with somebody, too. Stranger things could happen, although he couldn't believe that at the moment. Having jumped the hurdle, almost, he dozed off only to be awakened in what seemed like minutes by his mother calling, 'Breakfast's ready, you two sleepyheads. Come and get it!'

Dilly was reliving the ecstasy of Roddy's fingers twining through hers, of his hip against hers as they sat in the car. Why couldn't he see that she didn't care how closely they were related? What had that to do with being in love? Even if they had a child together, it would be all right. They were both healthy – she'd only had that silly meningitis when she was newly five – what was that? It wasn't catching! It didn't run in families – not that she'd ever heard of, anyway. She would never – could never – love anyone else, and Roddy said the same, so why wouldn't he throw convention, or whatever, to the wind and take her away somewhere. They could be really happy without this constant worry that somebody who knew them would spill the beans. Nobody would know them if they went far enough away. It would be heart-wrenching to leave Mum and Dad, but they had each other, and they'd been in love once – maybe still were – so they shouldn't begrudge their children the same happiness.

Her imagination lingered over the loving life she and Roddy could lead, maybe somewhere in the Caribbean, their kiddie-winks turning as brown as berries in the sun, and she and Roddy would sit holding hands on the beach to watch them. It would be absolute heaven . . . wouldn't it? Common sense edged in now. Was Roddy right? Would their children be born disfigured, or have something far wrong with them. If that happened, people would know, or at least suspect, that they weren't an ordinary couple at all – they were criminals living a life of lies, that they had committed a sin and were being punished for it.

Restlessly, she turned over. It could never happen. She could see that now. Even if Roddy did swallow his principles and take her away, their parents would never rest until they were caught. It was all a pipe dream and she had better try to get some sleep or else she would be like a washed-out dishcloth in the morning, when she wanted to look her best for Roddy. She had barely closed her eyes, it seemed, when her mother's voice penetrated her dulled senses. 'Breakfast's ready, you two sleepyheads. Come and get it!'

He couldn't let it happen, Brian thought. It wouldn't be so bad for him now that he was thinking more rationally, but Roselle would go out of her mind if she knew that their son and daughter had really fallen in love and wanted to go off and live together. It was a confounded, difficult situation, but there was surely some way out of it. The trouble was that Dyllis, vulnerably romantic, was probably, at that very moment, spinning some airy-fairy dream of them running away together and setting up home somewhere exotic. In her mind, Roddy would be her knight in shining armour, taking her away from her humdrum existence. It was going to be a bugger getting that out of her head. The best way to go about it, he supposed, was to speak to Roddy, warn him that he must not let her talk him into doing something stupid. The boy was more wordly-wise, however, so maybe he had the sense himself to steer clear of it. It was Roselle who was the real problem for him, Brian concluded, and he would do anything, within reason, to save her from being hurt. He had overcome the panicky fear of this same situation that had almost led to him taking his own life before.

'You awake?' The soft question came as he had nodded off, but what did that matter? She likely hadn't been sleeping either.

Roselle's mind was a welter of ifs and buts, it's not trues and it *is* trues. It couldn't be possible, she told herself, over and over again, but the reflection she had seen in the front-seat mirror of the car told a different story. It *was* true, there was no getting away from that. Not only had her twins been holding hands, they'd been gazing into each other's eyes as if they couldn't see enough of each other. It had given her a right shock, but she didn't intend to say anything to Brian. Relationships don't last at that age. In another few months, they'll have moved on to someone else and she'd be left wondering why she'd been so upset today.

But she couldn't stop thinking about it. She needed to

confide in somebody, talk it over with somebody, but she didn't want to drag Brian into it. It was better that he was left in ignorance. She lifted her head to look at the clock, the hands capable of being seen even in the dark. Ten to six – there was no point in trying to get some sleep now. 'You awake, Bri?' she said softly.

'Mmm, what is it?'

'I was thinking we could go for a picnic today. The forecast's good.'

'We'll have to be back in time to drive Roddy to Aberdeen to get his train.'

'Oh yes. Well we can still have a wee run around. It'll be good for all of us to get away from the house.'

'I suppose so. We'd better get up, then, and get breakfast going. We can have lunch somewhere on the road.'

When Brian took the Fiat out of the garage Dilly was excitedly looking forward to being close to her brother in the back seat again, but Roselle said brightly, 'I'll go in the back with you, Dyllis, and Roddy can go in the front. He'll get a better view.'

The girl was obviously disappointed, but the thought that she was still in company with him soon cheered her. Brian took the coast road, all of them marvelling at how lovely the sea was with the sun shining overhead.

'It reminds me of pictures I've seen of the Meditteranean,' Roddy said, which started a discussion on holiday resorts they would like to see some day.

Cruden Bay and Peterhead were well behind them when Brian decided to stop for some ice cream in Cullen.

They all got out when they got round to the Seatown part of the town, and sat on the sands to enjoy the treat.

'Look at the three rocks over there,' Dilly said. 'They look like a family, as well. The one farther up the beach is the father, the middle one is the mother, and the smaller one just coming out of the sea is the child.'

'I'd say they were probably all standing in the sea at high tide,' Brian observed. 'They're quite a height, anyway. Look how small those people look beside them. Do you want to go and see them properly?'

The boy and girl were quite keen, but Roselle said, 'No, I'd rather not. I don't like the idea of stones being human. They give me the creeps.'

Brian grinned at Roddy. 'Your mum's got some peculiar ideas.'

But he didn't try to force her, and took them a walk round the harbour before going back to the car. 'This is great,' he smiled as he turned on the ignition. 'The whole family out for a jaunt. I'm glad you thought of it, Roselle.'

The other three nodded their agreement and off they set again, through all the quaint fishing villages, until they reached the signpost to Pennan, the setting for the film *Local Hero*. Brian had to carefully negotiate the extremely steep road down to the inn, where they went in for lunch. An hour later, their stomachs pleasantly full, they left the seaside and made for the main road to Aberdeen. The A90 was, as usual, very busy, but they all enjoyed this part of their trip as much as the first part. This route, of course, took them through agricultural land, fields of corn almost ready for harvesting, large areas of vegetable crops, and villages and towns completely different from those in the coastal areas.

They had taken Roddy's haversack with them so it was straight to the Joint Station in Aberdeen, with some manoeuvring to get a parking place before going to the tea room for a quick snack. Roddy had been worrying over his departure all day. His family didn't usually come to the station with him, and he feared an emotional fare-well, and when his father pointed out that he wasn't going to the other side of the world, it struck him that that was what he might be doing – should be doing.

His mother's eyes were moist when he said, 'Well, this is it,' and without thinking he gave her a kiss on the cheek. This could be the last time he would see her. With this painful thought in his mind, he had to hold himself from kissing Dyllis too, knowing that he would have difficulty in breaking away from her. His father came forward to shake his hand, and luckily the guard blew his whistle, so he had only time to touch his sister's hand briefly. Even the tears on her cheeks did not stop him from jumping aboard and by the time he found his seat, he was too far away for his family to see the tears trickling down his face. Having waved from the window until he could no longer see them, he sat down. He felt as if his heart had been torn from his body by some alien force and lashed with a whip until it bled.

Three very despondent people made the journey back to Cruden Bay, Roselle being the first to speak, her voice husky. 'I don't think we're ever going to see him again.'

'Don't be so daft!' her husband reprimanded, although the pressure of his son's hand on his had made him suspicious. It *had* seemed as if the boy was bidding him a final farewell, but his wife couldn't have thought that, too? Glancing in his mirror, he saw that his daughter was also wiping tears away, and his resolve to be strong for them wavered a little – but he had to reassure them. After all, he couldn't be sure. He had probably imagined it. 'He's a bit upset with the misunderstanding over the Riley girl, and you can't blame him, can you? Anyway, he won't be going there for his weekends any longer, will he, so he'll be home a lot more.'

Roselle's sigh was long and deep. 'Oh, I hope so. It's just there was something about him, I can't tell you . . .' she broke off to look round at her daughter. 'Did you not feel it as well, Dilly?'

'I know he was upset,' the girl said, carefully, 'but he'll get over it, won't he?'

Her forlorn tone, her uncertainty, was almost Brian's undoing, yet somehow he managed to save himself from giving way. Gulping, he said firmly, 'What a pair of worriers you are. He'd be ashamed of you if he knew.'

It was the right approach. For a few moments there was silence, and then Dyllis said, 'Of course he'll be back Mum. It's just because he hasn't been home for a while that we feel like this. It's stupid, really.'

In bed that night, however, she couldn't convince herself of that. She could swear that what she had seen in his eyes just before he jumped aboard the train meant that they would never see each other again. He *did* love her, she was quite convinced of that, but he was just as sure that there was no future for them. If only he had believed her when she said she would go away with him whenever he wanted, that she didn't care what other folk thought of them. That train of thought came to an abrupt end. Other folk, yes, but their parents would never forgive them. *They* were the ones who would suffer. They would have to face the inevitable scandal it would cause.

Much as she hated to think it, Roddy had done the honourable thing, the only thing, really. He was too decent to change his mind, so she would just have to accept it and get on with her life, though she might live to regret it when she was a lonely old maid. Upset by the prospect of having nobody to care for her thirty or forty years on, she turned over to sleep, or at least try to sleep, though she knew that she wouldn't.

Roddy Lewis's long journey back to Liverpool was taken up by imagining the poor quality of the life ahead of him, wherever he ended up. He could never love another girl, never have the comfort of a wife waiting at home to give him a welcoming kiss, with his slippers heating by the fire, a substantial meal ready for him. He'd be a decrepit old bachelor, grumpy with his landladies, working for no purpose at all, going to bed by himself with nobody to unburden his troubles to – for there would be troubles, there was no doubt about that.

He took a taxi to the office. It wouldn't do to be late nowadays; not when he was intending to ask for a transfer to somewhere abroad. The firm had offices in Norway,

Canada, head office in New York, and probably lots of other branches he knew nothing about. There were oil companies all over the world. It didn't matter to him where he was sent, of course, as long as it was far enough away to give him the excuse of not returning home. He wouldn't be able to leave Dilly if he was ever in her presence again. It would be absolutely fatal.

All that morning he had quite a problem keeping awake, and dreaded meeting Tony Riley in any of the corridors. Thankfully, as he was on his way out to buy a couple of sandwiches for lunch, it was only Samantha – he didn't know her surname – who ran into the lift as the doors closed, leaving him waiting for it to come back for him. She did say, quite breathlessly, 'I'm sorry, Roddy', whether because she didn't have time to speak to him, or what had happened the previous week, he didn't know. What did it matter, anyway?

He bought his Spartan lunch at the little delicatessen a few doors along the street, and strolled into the small island of green grass which passed as a place of recreation for many of the men and women who worked in the area. As he unwrapped the tuna baguette and unscrewed the top of his Coke, he began to plan what he would say to the Head Cashier; how he would explain his request for a transfer. He would have to wait until he was absolutely sure of his ground, sure that there were no black marks against him. He didn't think there could possibly be anything, but maybe Tony Riley had concocted a revenge of some kind for the imagined rebuff of his sister. He'd been mad enough.

It took almost a week for Roddy to pluck up enough courage to 'beard the lion in his den', and although there had been no accusations or criticisms raised against him, he was so nervous that his stomach was churning as he tapped on the door. At the loud command to enter, he turned the handle and walked in.

The man sitting in the leather executive chair looked over his horn-rimmed glasses.

'It's young Lewis, isn't it?'

'Yes, sir. Can I speak to you for a minute, please?'

The bushy eyebrows went down. 'I presume you *can* speak to me, but the question is – *may* you speak to me?'

His face scarlet, Roddy stammered, 'I-I'm s-sorry, sir – that's what I meant. Please may I speak to you?'

With a twinkle in the tired blue eyes, the brows lifted. 'You may, but remember that I like my staff to talk in perfect English – it is easier for everyone concerned, especially if dealing with clients from foreign climes. Just say whatever it is that you have to say.'

The planned, well-rehearsed speech vanished from the boy's mind, but he went on, doggedly, 'I feel that I have . . . much to offer the company, but my present position . . .'

'You think that you deserve promotion?'

The smile lurking at the corners of the other man's mouth gave Roddy the boost he needed. 'Well, yes sir, I do. I've been here for well over a year now, I'm nineteen and I'm still only a junior.'

'The problem is, Lewis, that there is no vacancy available here at present, or likely to be in the foreseeable future. I do agree, however that you are worthy of promotion. Perhaps—' The chief clerk tapped his desk as if hoping for inspiration, and then smiled. 'Would you be interested if I suggested a transfer to another branch? Or is there a young lady – the real reason for your rebuttal of young Riley's sister – who makes you want to remain in Liverpool?'

'There is nothing to keep me here.' Roddy could scarcely believe that it would be so easy. 'I'll be happy to go wherever you send me . . . sir.'

'Distance no object?'

'Distance no object, sir.' The farther away the better, came the thought.

'I must say I admire your spirit, Lewis, although I am rather inclined to believe that you need to extricate yourself from the situation in which you find yourself. No matter! I will find out if there is a suitable vacancy anywhere in our numerous branches, and let you know as soon as I can.'

'Thank you, sir.'

Turning, Roddy walked out as confidently as his trembling legs would carry him. He had been astonished that the Big Boss knew about Boppy Riley, and guessed that it had got round the whole staff. It was much better that he got away from here. Of course, it could take weeks or even months, but he'd been battling against his only real problem for well over a year now, and he was quite prepared to wait a reasonable amount of time to make the break from it. He would have to be careful to avoid bumping into Tony Riley, of course, and he'd have to spin some story to his mother about why he couldn't come home. Telling her by letter that pressure of work meant that he was having to work every Saturday and Sunday would probably be the most believable, and though he hated having to lie to her, it had to be done.

That evening, after dining with two of Mrs O'Shaughnessy's other boarders, he went back to his second floor room to compose the fatal missive. He tore up several attempts – too long-winded, too abrupt – and over two hours passed before he was satisfied. He longed to tell Dilly the true explanation for his transfer, but she knew how he felt, and would surely understand.

Chapter Eight

Frank Milne was becoming rather worried about his wife. She hadn't been her usual cheery self for weeks, although she flatly denied that anything was wrong with her.

'It's just old age creeping up,' she had said, quite sharply, when he asked her.

'Sixty-two isn't considered old nowadays,' he had pointed out.

'You've always got to get the last word,' she had snapped.

He had been sorely tempted to point out that it was usually the other way round, but she would only have been more annoyed with him. It seemed he could do nothing right.

They were sitting by the fireside one evening a few weeks later when he noticed that the hands holding the knitting needles were shaking, that the stitches were slipping off. His heart in his mouth, he said nothing for a moment, noticing that her lovely hair, silver now, had not been combed, that her mouth was sagging to one side, and remembered reading an article in the newspaper some weeks ago giving the warning signs of a stroke. That had mentioned sagging at the mouth, shaking hands, and extreme tiredness for some days before. It all fitted! And it had also said, it had to be treated as soon as possible.

'I'm off to the loo,' he told her, hoping that his voice hadn't betrayed his fear. He did go upstairs, but instead of going to the bathroom, he went into their bedroom, dialled 999 and asked for the ambulance service. The urgent tone in which he described his wife's condition was enough to convince the telephonist that this was no hoax.

Only fifteen minutes later – fifteen interminable minutes of holding her hand to reassure her – the two paramedics rang the bell, and it seemed to Frank, only five seconds later, he was sitting in the ambulance praying that his wife would still be alive when they reached the hospital.

She was whipped away from him then, while he had to give the desk the details of her date of birth, their GP and answering all the other questions that they asked. Then he was shown to a waiting room where he would have to remain until someone came to tell him all was well . . . or not. But it had to be all was well, Frank told himself. He couldn't go on if Helen died. He'd have nothing left to live for.

After what seemed like hours, but only thirty-five minutes by the clock on the wall, a young nurse came in with a cup of tea. 'Any news?' he asked.

'Sorry, nothing yet. She's your wife, is she? I'm sure she'll be fine. Don't worry.'

She scurried out, leaving him annoyed that he hadn't thanked her for the tea. He was so worried about Helen, everything else went by the board. He couldn't think straight.

There had always been just the two of them. They had both wanted several children, but they hadn't been so blessed – just one son. That was why she liked being around kids, the Lewis twins, for instance. It must be ten years at least since they had lived next door, but she still spoke about them, wondered what they were doing. She had a heart of gold, and although she hadn't said so, he knew she had been hurt that Roselle and Brian had gone without ever telling them they were going. Especially Roselle.

If he only knew where to get hold of her he would let her know about this. If she could come, it would mean the world to Helen. It could even mean the difference between life and death. Oh, God, no! He shouldn't think about death. Helen wasn't going to die.

He studied the clock now. The second hand touched every mark on the little dial at the side, the big hand clicked when it passed every mark, the little hand didn't move, but he would see it moving if he watched long enough. Twenty-four minutes, four seconds, past ten. It had just been about quarter to nine when they left the house.

Frank fully believed that he hadn't fallen asleep, but he was startled when a woman walked in and sat down a few seats along, and the clock showed a quarter to five. He was too confused to notice the seconds.

Pulling himself together, he said, 'Hello, did you come in the ambulance with somebody?'

'Aye, it's my man. Is it your wife that's in?'

'She's had a stroke.'

'So's my Davey. Have you been here long?'

'Since about twenty-five past ten.'

'Oh, my God.'

Thankfully for Frank, the staff nurse came to escort him to the ward, where a white, wild-eyed Helen was lying. 'Can I go over and touch her?' he asked.

'You can go over and speak to her, but just a few words. She's not quite . . .'

An icy band gripped his chest. 'Is she . . . going to recover?'

'She should, but she'll never get back to normal, I'm afraid. She could regain her speech to a certain extent, but she is paralysed down her right side at the moment. That should ease with exercises, but she'll have to persevere with them when she gets home. You'll have to look after her, and do things for her, and be prepared for her to be angry with you. Do you think you can cope with that?'

'I'll cope with anything if it means I'll still have her with me.'

He approached the bed, 'Hi, Helen,' he said, brightly, 'it's me.'

The look in her eyes did not change, and it dawned on him that she didn't know him.

'It's Frank' he said softly. 'You gave me a right scare.'

Still no recognition, and his arm was touched by a young nurse. 'It'll take a while, but she'll be a bit better tomorrow. Go home now and get some sleep.'

'Will she have to be in here for a long time?'

'It depends. Younger people can usually get out much quicker than the elderly, but it's difficult to say.'

He gave his wife's hand a light pat, but there was no

sign that she felt it, and he left the ward with a heavy heart. Walking towards the exit, he realised that once again he had no means of getting home. It was too early for any buses to be running and too far for him to walk now. As he passed the desk, the girl said, kindly, 'Would you like me to phone for a taxi?'

'Yes, please.' A horrific thought struck him. 'Oh, I didn't take any money with me.'

'The driver'll likely wait till you go into your house to get some.'

'OK then.' He was pleased that she hadn't insulted him by asking if he could afford a taxi. That would have been the last straw.

Roselle was rather hurt by the way Roddy seemed to be happy to work overtime when he could be home with his family. 'I think there's more to this than he lets on,' she remarked to her husband when they went to bed. 'He couldn't know that he'd be working weekends for months on end. It seems a poor excuse.'

Brian pulled a face. 'He's maybe got a girlfriend. You should be pleased about that.'

Her face brightened. 'You think that's what it is? Well, that's a good thing, isn't it?'

'I would say so, but we'd better not say that to Dyllis. Just let things drift on the way they are. She's been speaking quite a bit about this new manager they've got.'

His wife nodded. 'Ah, well, fingers crossed. She's nearly twenty and she's never had a boyfriend, but maybe this, um, Mr Richardson I think she said, maybe he'll be the one for her. Love isn't particular when it strikes – nor where.'

With a sinking feeling, she realised that she could recall nothing of how she and Brian had met, or when they had fallen in love. These were the memories that every woman held most precious to her, and she had lost track of them altogether. For ever.

Roselle's views on love returned to Brian as they were watching television later. The lovebug certainly hadn't been particular where or when it had bitten him. His first sighting of her had been the catalyst for events over which he had had no control, culminating in the unenviable, ongoing predicament which still more or less overshadowed his life, and from which he could see no way of extricating himself. To be honest, he was quite relieved that Roselle could remember nothing of it, and if Fate were kind, their children need never know, either.

Dyllis had no idea that her parents were plotting her life for her. She, too, had been hurt that Roddy preferred to work overtime to coming home to see her. Of course, he had once said that he would keep away from her because their love was illegal, but she had never thought he would actually do it. She hadn't seen him for nearly three months now, and why should he punish her like this when she couldn't help falling in love with him? Plus, he had always said he loved her, too, and if that were true, he was punishing himself as well as her. She couldn't understand it.

It was the following morning that the letter arrived for Roselle, devastating all of his family, although Roddy himself seemed to be excited about being sent to New York at a moment's notice.

'It's promotion for me,' she read aloud, 'and I have to leave tomorrow or somebody else will get the chance. It's a step up the ladder, with a raise in salary and the promise of further promotion if I work hard. It's something I've been hoping for, but I never dreamt I'd be as lucky as to get to New York. It breaks my heart that I won't get time to come home before I leave, but, cross my heart and hope to die, I *will* write regularly to let you know how I'm doing. Love to all.'

Love to all? Dyllis thought forlornly, as her father drove her to work. It was a bit offhand, wasn't it? But later, sitting at her computer, it dawned on her that Roddy couldn't really have singled her out as the recipient of his love. Although he knew how she felt about him, he was doing the right thing as far as he was concerned, and it probably was the only thing he could do. He'd had no intention of setting the cat among the pigeons by taking her away with him, and he must have asked for this transfer to America to get away from temptation. It just seemed a bit insensitive.

'Cheer up, Dilly, it'll never happen.'

She looked up in surprise to find one of the other typists regarding her in some concern. 'What'll never happen?' she frowned.

'You sighed just now like you had the worries of the world on your shoulders. If there's anything I can do to help . . .'

'I'm fine, Trace.' Her conscience reminded her that Tracy Little had grown up with them, had been in the same class at school. 'Well, Mum had a letter this morning from Roddy. He's being transferred to New York.'

'But . . .' The girl hesitated, then went on, 'I forgot you were twins, so I suppose you'll feel it more.'

'It was a bit of a shock, but I should be used to him being away from home. He's been in Liverpool for over a year now.'

'I suppose he got home now and then from there, though. I can understand why you're upset about him going so far away. Mind you, I'd be delighted if my pest of a brother was sent as far away as that. At least I'd be able to have a shower without him yelling that he needs a shower as well as me. You know, I sometimes think he'd like to see me in the altogether.'

Dyllis had to laugh at that, too. 'Oh, Trace, you're a real tonic, and you're right. A brother's just a pain in the neck.'

But it wasn't her neck that was aching. It was her heart, and she would have to learn how to control her feelings, otherwise her parents would realise the truth. Then the shit would hit the fan with a vengeance. She shook her head at her stupid thoughts. By this time, Roddy would be thousands of miles away from her, and they would have to get used to a life without each other.

Her sigh of resignation was so loud that the man on his way past her stopped. 'Is something wrong? Miss Lewis, isn't it?'

'Yes, Mr Richardson. Dyllis, and nothing's wrong, really; just me being silly about something that's happened.'

'Something in the office?'

'No, no! Something in my family, and honestly, it's nothing.'

'It's not nothing, I can tell that. Look, I was on my way to have some lunch, and I'd be glad of some company, if you'd care to join me?'

'Oh, I couldn't. What would people think?'

'People always think something. Let them think what they like. Go and get your coat, and I'll meet you downstairs.'

By the end of the next hour, Dyllis felt much better. Mr Richardson had been good company, not snooty or anything like that. Just ordinary, with a sense of humour that appealed to her, and his eyes – striking blue eyes – crinkled at the corners when he laughed. His light brown hair was brushed back immaculately, but halfway through their meal, a wayward tress flopped down on to his forehead. It made him look younger. He must be in his thirties, she guessed, but he could pass for twenty-five now.

He broke into her assessment of his age. 'I suppose it's time we were getting back to the grindstone, Dyllis. You don't mind if I call you Dyllis?'

'No, of course not, Mr Richardson.'

He did not tell her his Christian name, but of course he wouldn't, she told herself. This was a one-off, very enjoyable, lunch together, only because he'd felt sorry for her. That was it. No more. Finis. And so be it!

Despite her reasoning, she did feel a little peeved that he didn't walk back to the office with her. 'I have an appointment at two at the Exhibition Centre at the Bridge of Don,' he said by way of an explanation, as he turned into the car park. 'Thank you for being such an interesting companion.'

'Thank you, Mr Richardson. I usually just have a sandwich.'

'We must do it again sometime.'

Her steps were light as she ran up the stairs instead of waiting for the lift, and the change in her expression made Tracy say, 'Well, what happened to you that brought the stars to your eyes?'

'Don't be silly. I've got rid of my blues, that's all.'

Her thoughts centred on the manager for the rest of the afternoon. She had always liked him, ever since he took over about six months ago, but he was on a different plane from her. She had never dreamt that she would have lunch with him one day, and chat to him as though he were an old friend. His manner had made her think he was interested in everything she said, and that was heartening. She didn't place too much belief in his last few words, though. He was just being polite.

Helen Milne was bored. She had never been one for sitting about doing nothing, and though she liked to read, she didn't like to spend all of her days reading. If only she had some kind of hobby to pass the time. Frank was in his element looking after her, of course, and she shouldn't complain, but that wasn't how things should be. She had always looked after him, and seeing him with an apron round his paunch cheerfully whistling while he did the ironing, or peeled the spuds, or washed the dishes – well it was rubbing the salt into the wound, so to speak. He sometimes bought her a jigsaw puzzle, but the stroke had left her paralysed down her right side, and it was so awkward using her left hand that she often dropped the pieces. Still, practice makes perfect, as the saying went, so maybe she'd get better if she kept at it.

She was lucky she had Frank for a husband; not many wives were so blessed. She could hear him upstairs now. He had made their bed and vacuumed the floor by this time, so what could he still be doing, moving things about like that? Hearing his feet on the stairs, she couldn't help the edge in her voice. 'What have you being doing up there all this time? You don't need to be so fussy. Nobody's ever going to see it.'

He came round within her vision carrying a large box, which he laid down on the table, the first thing he had bought to help her cope with her disability. Its casters made it easy for her to move, and the top could be tilted to whatever position she wanted. He had got the high chair for her next; more comfortable for her to sit on all day than the sagging old armchair she had claimed before. Watching as he opened the box, she snapped, 'Why did you trail that box of old snaps down? It must be covered in dust.'

'I gave it a good brush out of the bedroom window,' Frank said quietly, having learned to keep his temper with her. 'I thought maybe you'd like to have a look through it, and throw out all the duplicates and mistakes.'

'Ah, well.' It was quite a good idea really, but she wasn't going to tell him that. He had taken so many photos over the years, some of them inspired, some passable, but some double takes, or headless groups, or out of focus. Yes, they were the ones she'd need to weed out.

As her husband had known, this project took her over a month of closely inspecting each photograph, remembering where and when it had been taken, and discussing with him the forgotten names of many of the people in them.

She was nearing the end of her task when further inspiration struck him, and the very next day he came home from his shopping trip with, in addition to the usual groceries and toiletries, a large bag that she saw contained some bulky items, their corners poking through the plastic. 'What have you been buying now?' she queried, annoyed at him for apparently wasting money on things that weren't necessities.

Tapping his index finger, knuckles swollen by rheumatism, against his nose, Frank delved inside the bag and took something out with the flourish of a magician producing a rabbit out of a hat. 'What . . . ?' she began, but he shook his balding head and eventually had six of the identical looking volumes spread over her table.

Intrigued in spite of herself, Helen lifted the nearest one and turned it over. 'Oh!' she exclaimed in delight. 'A photograph album. Why didn't I think of that?'

He was pleased by her reaction. Everything he did, he

did for her, and as a rule she gave no indication when she was pleased, although she was quick to let him know when she wasn't. 'I was wondering what to get for you to pass the time, and it just dawned on me you often used to speak about putting the snaps in albums.'

'And I never got round to it,' she nodded. 'But will I manage to . . . ?'

'I'll give you a hand,' he offered, having already considered the problem.

He also bought a handy laptop computer for her the following week so that she could add captions. Even if her fingers couldn't quite cope at times with fixing on the circular 'glue spots' to the corners of the snaps, she found that she could type reasonably well with two fingers. Not only did this project keep her occupied for several further weeks, it also raised her spirits, and Frank thanked God over and over again for the inspiration that had come to him. His old Helen had returned – in spirit if not physically.

Having taught herself a new skill, his wife spent much of her time now diligently picking out the letters of things she wanted to write but couldn't. Correspondence that had been lying unanswered for months was given her undivided attention, then, after having caught up with each and every postcard or letter he could find for her, Frank became intrigued by her suddenly taking to hiding what she was doing each time he went near her. No matter how much he hinted, how often he tried to catch her unawares, she would close the lid of her machine just enough so that he could see nothing.

When she took to sitting staring into space again, his

heart sank. Surely she hadn't lost interest in this hobby as well, this hobby that had kept her busy for so long? He had heard of people whose brain stopped working if they didn't use it and he couldn't bear the thought of her turning into a vegetable. He kept on and on at her, pestering her, actually bullying her to make her snap out of her lethargy, until he noticed that occasionally, after a spell of vegetating as he called it, there was a renewed spurt of activity on the laptop.

He stopped trying to see what she was doing, so it came as a surprise when she handed him several sheets of paper. 'Read that,' she instructed.

Taking his reading glasses from the mantelshelf, he sat down at the dining table and spread the papers out in front of him. 'Don't say anything till you're finished,' she added.

His eyes had sprung open at the sight of the neatly set out poems, one on each page, and his astonishment grew as he read them. There were ten in all, not expertly typed, by any means, the odd letter missed here and there where her finger had not pressed the key quite hard enough, but each one was perfectly centred. More to the point, when he started reading, he discovered that they were fairly good – not Byron or Wordsworth, of course, but outshining many he had read in magazines.

Having gone through them once, he started at the first again, unaware that Helen was watching him apprehensively, waiting for his verdict. At last, removing his spectacles and laying them on the table, he regarded her with pride. 'They're absolutely great. They really are,

Helen, I'm not just saying it. You should send them in somewhere.'

'Nobody would want to print any of my drivel.'

'They're not drivel, Helen – honestly they're not – none of them. My goodness, I didn't know you had ability to describe your emotions like that.'

Her left hand made a small motion of appreciation. 'I just wrote what I was actually feeling at the time. Thank you for not saying I'm off my head writing poetry.'

'I don't think you're off your head. I think you've found a talent that's been hidden all your life. You could make a fortune with it.'

'It's you that's off your head.' But she couldn't hide the pleasure he had given her.

He managed to persuade her to correct the mistakes in one of the poems and print it again. Then, ignoring her protests that it was a waste of time, he posted it to one of the women's magazines he saw at the newsagent. To his surprise as much as hers, an unfamiliar voice on the telephone almost two weeks later, asked to talk to Mrs Helen Milne. Frank watched her face as she listened to the caller, who went on at some length before his wife said, breathlessly, nodding her head, 'Yes, all right. That will be very nice.' Replacing the handset, she turned to him. 'They're going to print it.'

'I knew it!' he cried jubilantly. 'What did I tell you?'

'That's not all, though. They're going to send a photographer to take a picture of me at my laptop. He's coming tomorrow at ten.' Giving a quick glance round the room, she added, 'You'd better clear all these papers and stuff before he comes.'

288

'Yes, Captain.' He stood to attention and saluted. 'Whatever you say, Captain.'

'Och, you,' she giggled. 'I can hardly believe it, you know.'

'I can. I always knew you were special, lass, and I always will.'

Wiping the tear that had edged out, she sniffed, 'I just hope they don't lose all their readers after they print it. Who's going to be interested in something an old wife like me has to say, I ask you?'

'You're asking for another compliment, that's what.' He had to tease her, otherwise he would have been in tears, too.

The photograph turned out very well, even Helen herself was pleased, and it looked even better when it appeared in the magazine a few months later. The poem itself had a marvellous reception from the readers, and Helen was asked to send some more.

'We would like to print one each month for as long as you keep writing them,' she was told on the phone. 'As long as you keep up the standard of this first one.'

In due course, she received a cheque for £20, which became a regular monthly addition to the household income, and although Frank told her she should use the money for things for herself, she wouldn't hear of it. 'The pride I get every time I see my face looking up at me from a printed age under a poem I wrote is more than enough for me.'

His own heart ached with happiness at seeing her

so happy, in spite of her handicap, and even better was to come. The publication sent on all the mail they had received in praise of her works, and as she said herself, 'I'm proud of myself, you know that?'

He kissed the top of her silvery head. 'And so you should be, lass.'

Many of their neighbours, and not so near fellow townspeople, came to congratulate her and tell her how much they enjoyed her poems, and she looked forward to each day now. Only on one occasion, as he got her ready to meet her fans, she murmured sadly, 'I kept hoping Roselle would buy the mag, and write or phone me, but—'

'She would if she knew, I'm sure she would.'

'Aye, I suppose she would.'

But that was the only time she let her spirits down – as far as he knew, though he had the feeling that she had a little weep sometimes while he was out doing the shopping. He wished with all his heart that there was some way of finding where the Lewises had gone. If he knew, he would pocket all his pride and write to Roselle, pleading with her to get in touch. She was a kind-hearted lass, and she wouldn't refuse.

Chapter Nine

Despite having believed that he would be able to cope just as well in New York as he had in Liverpool, Roderick Lewis was finding it hard going. Everybody seemed to be in too much of a hurry to stop and make friends; even the other members of staff in the huge building hardly knew more than one or two of the people on the same floor; even then, not particularly well. The usual acknowledgements made to anyone passing, or met in the lift, were a slight smile or an equally slight nod of the head.

He was beginning to feel depressed. He wanted company, someone to help to fill his evenings. He sometimes went for a walk, a different direction every time, but what thrill was there in sitting on a park bench by himself? Or looking in shop windows? He did venture a smile to anyone who walked past, but New Yorkers all seemed to be too busy to stop and speak. He wished that he had never left Cruden Bay. He wished – oh, how he wished – that he could hold Dilly in his arms again.

He became conscience of someone shouting, a woman's voice, and opened his eyes to see a small child, little older than a toddler, running as fast as his podgy legs would carry him down the grassy slope, and heading straight for the lake. Not even taking time to look to see who was shouting, Roddy threw himself sideways into the path of the avalanche. The impact practically winded him, but he thanked heaven that his effort had not been in vain. The little boy, shocked, terrified, but obviously unhurt, began to yell at full pitch.

'It's OK,' he assured him. 'You're safe now.' Then, seeing the young woman racing towards them, he added, 'Here's your mummy, look.'

'She's . . . not . . . my . . . Mummy.'

Roddy's brain clicked into gear. Not the child's mummy? Had she kidnapped him?

Instinctively, he gripped the boy closer to protect him from this abducter. Just let her try to grab him. Just let her try!

'Oh, God! Thank you! I never noticed he'd walked away. I was talking to my friend you see, and . . . oh, he could have drowned if you hadn't stopped him.'

Her obvious concern made his resolve waver, but he kept his arms round the boy. 'He says you're not his mummy.'

'I'm his nanny. His mother would kill me if she knew I'd been so careless.'

He had read of the violence in the Big Apple, but his mind could hardly get round this statement. 'She'd kill you?'

'Well, no, not really, but she'd fire me. I'd lose my job.'

The lovely, woebegone face won him over. This girl wasn't a criminal. 'I'm glad I managed to stop him.'

'I don't know how to thank you, though. I don't have any money . . .'

'I didn't do it for money.' He felt quite indignant that she could think such a thing. 'I'll have to be getting back to work now, but you'd better remember to take more care in future.' He strode off, leaving her to clasp the boy against her.

He was kept extremely busy that afternoon, and had no time to dwell on what had taken place during his lunch break. The journey back to his lodgings when he finished work for the day was fraught with battling through home-going crowds and standing in a packed subway train. Then, in the dining room of Mrs Flynn's boarding house, there was no peace to think; an argument had arisen between the two Norwegians and the two Irish boys who never seemed to be happy unless they were involved in some sort of confrontation. It wasn't serious, of course, always sounded much worse than it was, but it was useless to try to blot it out.

At long last, however, he went up to his room, and stretched out thankfully on the bed. Now he could think about what had happened earlier. That young nanny had been a really nice girl, and he shouldn't have been so cold towards her. He hadn't even asked her name. She wasn't a New Yorker, though, not with that English accent. He couldn't place it, but she wasn't from Liverpool, he was sure of that. The Scousers had a distinctive tongue that he would recognise straight away. He'd worked there long enough, hadn't he?

She wasn't from the north-east of England, either, not a Geordie nor a Yorkshire Tyke.

He wasn't so sure about Manchester, nor Birmingham,

they each had their own 'speak'. She had a lovely soft voice, though, and he couldn't help noticing the dimple in her left cheek, nor the way her silken fair hair curled on her shoulders, nor her divine blue eyes.

This thought came to an abrupt end as it dawned on him he had never noticed so much about any other girl at their first meeting. It could be their only meeting, came the next, unwelcome barb. Then his spirits lifted again. Perhaps she would come back to the park to look for him – or was that too much to expect?

He could hardly wait for the next morning to pass, making several mistakes because his mind was on planning what he would say to the nanny if she did turn up. It was quite difficult. He'd had no practice in chatting up a girl. The only girl he had really spoken to was Dilly, and that was in the dim and distant past. The untouchable past. The forgotten past. Yes, it had to be forgotten.

At 12.30 he rose and walked out, speaking to no one, as usual. None of the other young men had ever made an effort to let him join in their conversations at break times, and he had always steered clear of any girls. None of them would want to have anything to do with him, anyway; they had made that quite clear. He was a hick from the sticks, as far as they were concerned. A numpty with ideas above himself. A tall, ungainly Scot they couldn't understand. Although he thought he was speaking in perfect English, with no trace of accent, it seemed to be Double Dutch to them, and they had no interest in him. Well, good luck to them, he thought, as he walked out onto the sidewalk.

See? He was already Americanised. He didn't even think 'pavement' any longer.

Roddy would have been astonished, and gratified, to know that several of the girls were thrilled by his broad vowels and the way he rolled his R's. The only reason they had made no advances to the tall, broad-shouldered Scot was his cold manner towards them. They had no wish to be publicly snubbed.

He stopped on the way to the park to buy a filled bagel and a can of Coke, and then headed for the bench he had been sitting on the day before. He didn't normally go there two days running, but this wasn't a normal day. At least, yesterday hadn't been. Finished his snack, he leaned back and closed his eyes. That was when the magic had worked for him before, but twenty minutes later he had to admit defeat. Bundling up his rubbish, he stood up and dropped it in the nearest trash bin. He didn't feel down-hearted – a little disappointed, that was all. He wasn't beaten yet. There were plenty of other days to come.

Roselle was pleased to hear Dyllis mentioning her office manager more and more often. It probably wouldn't lead to anything, but at least Mr Richardson was taking her mind off Roderick, which was a good thing. Roddy, however, although he was keeping his promise to write more often, didn't seem to have any friends, male or female. If only he had stayed in Liverpool she could have kept an eye on him each time he came home, but he was at the other side of the world now and anything could happen to him.

She still couldn't understand why he had agreed to go to New York – nor, come to that, why he'd gone to Liverpool, in the first place. What drove him on to move about like that? If he'd stayed on in Aberdeen, he would eventually have got a promotion, and the same went for Liverpool. He had never given the impression that he had itchy feet, so why? It seemed that both her children were destined to end up as loners, and they had been so friendly to everybody when they were younger. Even Helen Milne used to remark on that.

Roselle's mind transferred to her old neighbour, as it had often done over the fifteen years since they moved to Cruden Bay. She had banished her guilt for not keeping in touch, by secretly sending a Christmas card every year, but she wished she had the guts to defy Brian and send a proper letter with her address in it. She needed someone to talk to, an older person who could help her to understand her children. She needed Helen.

But for some reason Brian had forbidden any correspondence. She couldn't explain why he had taken such a dislike to their old neighbour; no, not a dislike, more a distrust. That was it, a distrust – but why? What had Helen ever done to him? She'd been so good when Dilly had meningitis, and she had helped out in so many other ways.

There was one thing, though. Roselle had considered this several times but it always seemed too far-fetched. Still, it had been immediately after Helen had spoken about her son being a policeman in Northern Ireland that Brian had first mentioned that his firm was transferring him to Aberdeen; almost as if he'd been taking himself (and family) out of harm's way. He had admitted once, of course, to embezzling money, but surely not enough to warrant this apparent panic of being found out. It didn't seem likely, anyway, not after all this time, and especially not for a paltry hundred pounds.

With Roddy in America, a weight had lifted from Brian Lewis's mind. If his son and daughter had still been in constant touch with each other anything could have happened.

From what he had noticed before, Dilly had been the force behind their attraction – she hadn't cared who saw them holding hands or looking at each other in that lovey-dovey manner – whereas Roddy had obviously tried to cover it up. He had accepted the fact that it just wasn't possible, and had taken himself out of harm's way. Good for him. Maybe, with temptation no longer present, Dilly could let herself get involved with some nice young man – maybe even that manager she kept speaking about. He seemed to be quite friendly towards her, by what she said, maybe even attracted to her, and she seemed to be leaning towards him a little. It was a start, wasn't it? If she did fall in love with this Richardson fellow and marry him, the family would be in no danger of landing in the hellish scandal that would erupt otherwise.

He could breathe easier, with no further repetitions of the searing nightmares he had had for so long. His Roselle would lose that haunted look and be a more loving wife to him. Apart from their son being at the other side of the Atlantic, they would be an ordinary, normal family again.

That was his sole reason for doing what he'd done all those years ago. Of course, he hadn't planned everything. One part had just happened!

Dyllis could hardly believe what was happening to her. For months, years, she had dreamt of being with Roddy, of them living together away from all who knew them, having his darling babies, twins like themselves, one boy and one girl. Over the past few weeks, however, she had been thinking quite a lot about Mr Richardson – Neville, though she could never call him that to his face.

The one random lunch date had developed into a weekly event, and today, just before they split to go their separate ways back to the office, he had looked at her quizzically.

'Dyllis, would you care to accompany me to His Majesty's Theatre next Monday night? A friend gave me two complimentary tickets and I am sure you would enjoy it – a new production of *Carousel*.'

Taken utterly by surprise, she said, 'Oh, I'd love to, Mr Richardson, but I can't. You see, I'd miss the last bus home. I live in Cruden Bay.'

'But that's not a problem,' he smiled. 'I'll book you into a hotel for the night.' He must have mistaken her astonishment for doubt, because he hastened to add, 'Nothing nasty, Dyllis. I'll see you to the door of the hotel and leave you, I promise.'

It was too much for her. She couldn't refuse a night in a hotel as well as a visit to the theatre – she had never been to a hotel or a theatre before – but she couldn't tell her mum and dad. They wouldn't believe that any man would arrange a hotel room for a young woman and not take advantage of her. She would need to find a more accept-able way to explain an overnight stay, but she could surely manage that. Giving it no more thought, she said, shyly, 'Thanks, Mr Richardson, I'd love to.'

A huge beam transformed his craggy face. 'Great, I look forward to Monday then. But can't you manage to call me Neville? At least, out of the office.'

Even his last four words rang no alarm bell in her head. She could understand why a man in his position would prefer not to advertise his new liaison with a minor member of staff – very minor.

At breakfast the next morning, she put out a tiny feeler, a kind of preparation for what she intended to say when she got home that night. 'I told you about the girl that started working with us a few weeks ago? Her name's Aimee – spelt A-I-M-E-E – Riddler, and she's kind of chummed up with me. She's a nice girl, a year younger than me, but we get on great. I think Tracy Little's a bit jealous.'

Her mother raised her eyebrows a little. 'I can't think why you and Tracy didn't chum up together. After all, you were in the same class at school.'

'She was always too keen on boys – she's been after one of the lads in the office upstairs since she started. She'd an eye on Roddy at one time, you know.'

Brian pushed back his chair and stood up. 'Well, I'm glad you've made a close friend now, but it's time we were going.'

Quite happy at the way her fib had been received, Dilly

obediently got to her feet and was waiting in the driveway when her father brought the people-carrier out of the garage. She knew that he wouldn't quiz her about her new 'friendship'; his mind was always on his driving. The road from Cruden Bay to where it met the A90 had one awkward curve after another and was always fairly busy, but it was nothing compared to the main road to the city. He needed all his wits about him there so that they wouldn't end up as statistics in the almost daily reports of accidents somewhere along it.

Two days later, after having brought Aimee Riddler into her conversations with her parents at any suitable point, Dilly decided to make her big announcement at the evening meal. 'Aimee's dad had got complimentary tickets for His Majesty's Theatre – he puts their ads in his shop window – but he can't go, so he's given them to her. She wants me to go with her, it's *Carousel*.'

'That's very nice of her,' Roselle smiled. 'The Saturday matinee, is it?'

Dilly hoped that her mother wouldn't hear her heart thumping in apprehension. 'No, it's for Monday night, actually. It's always the first night for the complimentary tickets, apparently.'

'But . . . you'd miss the last bus home.'

'I know, but Aimee's mum says I can go there for the night.'

'But we don't know anything about her—' Roselle began.

'You know her father's got a shop,' Brian broke in.

'A newsagent,' Dilly supplied, hopefully.

'That doesn't prove they're nice people, though.'

'For goodness sake, Ros, she's not a child any longer. You're like a mother hen.'

His wife's lips closed indignantly, so the girl said, 'I'm able to look after myself, Mum, and anyway, I'm sure the Riddlers are a nice family.' She felt quite guilty as she followed her father out, and an old saying sprang into her mind. 'Oh what a tangled web we weave, when first we practise to deceive.' It was true. One lie led to more lies, and it could grow on from that, so she'd need to watch her P's and Q's, remember faithfully what she had said. One slip would be fatal.

During the journey to Aberdeen, not even the near-misses and long queues took her mind off her own problem, but, thankfully, the more she thought about it, the less guilt she felt. Why should she have to tell lies about something like this? She was over eighteen, past the age of minority, she could do what she liked. She didn't have to ask her parents' permission to go out with whoever she liked, and she certainly didn't need to lie about it.

She'd concocted that stupid story now, though, and she had better stick to it this time. If Mr Richardson – Neville – asked her out again, she would definitely come clean. Her mother might be pleased, anyway, seeing he was the manager.

During the 'Mothers' Club' meeting that afternoon, when Roselle mentioned her worries about her daughter, she was completely taken back by the reaction of the other women.

'I thought Dilly was nearly twenty.' Laura Gibbs' plucked eyebrows had shot up. 'My Andrea's only fifteen and she's out with a different boy every night.'

'My Elaine's the same,' Rhona nodded. 'If I say anything, she tells me I'm living in the Middle Ages. They start pleasing themselves as soon as they're out of nappies.'

'My Stella's only twelve,' Pauline put it, 'and she hasn't started with boys yet – I don't think, anyway – but she plasters her face with make-up when she's out with her chums, so I don't suppose it'll be long.'

Roselle felt obliged to justify her own worry. 'But that's different. Dilly's going to be staying out all night.'

'Not with a boy, though,' Pauline reminded her. 'Or so she says.'

'She wouldn't tell me a lie,' Roselle gasped. She had never thought of a boy.

Regretting making light of the matter and hoping that they hadn't upset their friend, Rhona changed the subject. 'I say, have you seen Lena Lornie's new outfit? Skirt nearly up to her waist and neckline down to her navel.'

The ensuing hilarity changed the mood. Mrs Lornie, in her fifties, was well known for dressing like a showgirl and treating her house as if it were a brothel, and although all the women in the street spoke about her in a disparaging way, they all – if they were honest – envied her the young men she was seen with.

*　　*　　*

Later that day, when everything had been cleared up after the evening meal, the three Lewises were sitting by the fire. Brian had been reading the evening paper, but suddenly laid it down in disgust. 'Nothing but doom and gloom, and nothing worth watching on the telly. Why is it that some nights there's good programmes on all the channels at the same time, and other nights it's just rubbish?'

It was Dilly who resurrected an old argument. 'If you'd only agree to be connected to Sky, Dad, we'd have hundreds of programmes to choose from.'

'That's why,' he snapped. 'The blasted set would never be off, would it? Plus, just think of all the arguments there would be – each of us wanting something different.'

Roselle had been paying no attention to them. 'Dilly,' she said now, rather hesitantly, 'Were you telling us the truth about it being Aimee Thingummy you're going to the theatre with on Monday night? You're sure it's not a boy?'

'It's not a boy!' Dilly answered quickly. 'If you don't believe me, phone her and ask.'

'God Almighty, Roselle,' Brian exploded. 'What on earth's got into you? Why would she tell a lie about something like that?'

'I don't know, it's just – it's because she'll be out all night.'

'What difference does that make? In any case, suppose she's going to be spending a night here and there with a dozen different boys, she's old enough. She knows the facts of life, and . . .'

'I've no intention of sleeping with one boy, never mind

303

a dozen,' the girl shouted. 'What do you take me for? Another Mrs Lornie? Give me credit for some sense. But if you don't trust me, I'll tell Aimee I can't go. Will that please you?' She rose and stamped out of the room.

'Now look what you've done,' Brian snapped. 'She needs to be with young people, never mind what sex they are. You can't hang on to her for ever.'

'Oh, I know, I know. I'm sorry, I just can't help it. I don't want to lose her as well as Roddy. Should I go up and—'

'No, leave her alone. She'll get over it, but don't do anything like that again. It's the best way of making her leave home.'

'I didn't think.'

The anguish in his wife's eyes made him wish that he hadn't lost his temper with her. 'Look, Ros, darling, I'm sorry, too. I know how you must feel, but she *will* leave some day, you know. Not for good, of course. With any luck, she'll get married and give us grandchildren. Do you not look forward to that?'

'I suppose so.' She did not appear to be any happier, however, as she picked up the newspaper he had discarded.

Brian lay back and closed his eyes. He wasn't sure that he was looking forward to having grandchildren, but they had to let Dyllis have her head. At least it would take her mind off Roddy. It had been blatantly obvious that the two of them were in love, and the boy had done the right thing by taking himself off, although it would appear that it had broken Dilly's heart. She had never looked at any boys, most unusual for someone her age, and he, for one, would be really pleased if she did find someone else to love. She was a lovely young woman and there must be dozens of men who would jump at the chance of going out with her. He had hoped, for a while, that this Mr Richardson, the manager that she spoke so much about for a while, would step in but maybe it was just as well he hadn't. For all they knew, he could be one of those old Lotharios, biding his time to seduce another young girl.

Upstairs, Dilly was beginning to simmer down. She had been so stupid not to tell her parents the truth before. Like Dad said, she didn't need to ask their permission at her age, but having told the lie, she couldn't back down. She couldn't even tell them if Neville Richardson asked her out again, otherwise they would recognise the original fib. She wished with all her heart that she had never started down this slippery path.

Roddy had been returning again and again to the seat in the park where he had first seen the girl, the nanny – he didn't even know her name – but she had never appeared again. He made up his mind, as he headed for it this lunchtime, that this would be the last time.

She had probably not given him a second thought, and if she happened to go there again and found him sitting in the same place, she might be embarrassed. It was a whole month now, so he really should give up – after today.

He couldn't explain why he had been so sure that she'd come back, and he had no real hope of being lucky this time, so he was completely bowled over when the little boy shouted, 'It's the man, Nanny! It's the man!'

He jumped up and wheeled round to see the girl – *the* girl – beaming all over as she hurried down the path to catch up with her charge.

'Hi,' she said, 'I didn't think there was any chance you'd be here today.'

'I've been here every day,' he admitted, bashfully, 'hoping I'd see you.'

'I'm really sorry about that, but Mr Schueyler was sent to Florida for a month and we all had to go with him.'

The doubt was yanked straight out of his mind. She *had* wanted to see him. 'Mr Schueyler being your employer, I suppose?'

'Yes. They're a very nice family, and I'm very lucky to be with them. No, Harvey, don't go near the water,' she ended sharply. 'I'd better go, he gets bored if we don't keep walking.'

'Tell me your name first. I'm Roderick, Roddy Lewis.'

'Patricia Doran, Pattie.'

'May I walk a bit with you?' he ventured now.

So they walked, quite close together, although not even touching hands, while the little boy, Harvey, ran backwards and forwards in front of them. Roddy told her how he had asked for a transfer abroad and was sent to New York, while she said she had been at a nursing college in Guildford and then decided to see a bit of the world before settling down into her chosen profession. 'I'm glad I did,' she went on. 'Not only have I seen the greatest city in the world, and been to Florida, but I've had an insight into the life of a Jewish family, and I've loved every minute of it.'

'Have you never been lonely?'

'Never. I meet other nannies when we're out, and we compare our jobs, you know. I'm sure I'm the luckiest one. Some girls have very little time off, or the food's not good, or in some cases, the man of the house thinks they should be playthings for him.'

'Not your Mr Schueyler I hope?'

'Oh, no, he's a real gentleman.'

'Do you get any evenings off?'

'Two a week, after eight, but I don't often bother going out. It's no fun wandering about on your own.'

'No,' Roddy sighed. 'I know that, but . . . would you come out with me some night?'

'I'd love to. I'd have to be in by eleven though.'

'That's all right.' Three whole hours with her, he thought. Absolute heaven. 'Is tonight too soon?' He didn't want to sound too eager.

Her eyes twinkled mischievously. 'Tonight's not soon enough.' Giggling, she added, 'Ten past eight at the top gates of the park. That'll give me time to wash my face and make myself pretty.'

He knew it was corny but he had to say it. 'You'll always be pretty to me.' Then, shy at being so personal, he hurried on, 'Ten past eight it is.'

In another ten minutes, back at work, he couldn't get her pretty face out of his mind, nor her soft voice out of his ears. He was definitely attracted to her, he couldn't deny that, yet there was something missing, though he couldn't pinpoint it.

* * *

Their one date per week soon became two. She was good company, she could make him laugh, but the vital spark wasn't there. He couldn't always tell what she was thinking, whereas he and his twin had thought in duplicate, really. He felt ashamed that he wasn't the boyfriend Pattie clearly expected him to be, though they had many likes in common. Although he hadn't been interested in art much before, he accompanied her willingly to any of the art galleries she wanted to visit, large or small, and listened carefully to all she told him. His knowledge of modern and ancient artists thus gradually increased from zero until he could talk fluently about what he saw, and was happy when Pattie looked pleased.

Their evenings were not always confined to the arts, however. They visited Coney Island one Sunday, when she had been given the whole day off. They had fun such as neither of them had ever had before. They went on the rides and howled with excited fear as they were whizzed from one height, down to ground level and up to another terrifying altitude. They tried them all, the Waltzers, the Chair-o-planes, then the Dodgems, which were less hair-raising. They giggled, they grabbed each other without realising what they were doing and then moved away sheepishly. They had hot dogs at one point, ice cream some time later – both of which they rather regretted when their innards protested during a particularly stomach-churning journey through the air.

It was all very strange, and enjoyable, to them, and they talked and laughed about their experiences as they made their way back to the Schueylers' home. They stopped just before they came in sight of the imposing entrance, embarrassed and shy with each other now. Unfamiliar emotions were coursing through Roddy – should he take Pattie in his arms and kiss her properly, or should he give her the usual light peck on the cheek? At least they were past the formal shaking of hands as a farewell.

'I know what you're thinking,' she whispered, 'but stop thinking and just do it.'

He held her gently, he kissed her lips tentatively, but his passion had been kindled during the highly exciting day. It was some time, and many searching kisses, before she drew away. 'It's late, Roddy, I have to go in. See you Tuesday.'

In a way, he was glad. If the kissing had gone on for much longer, he'd have found it impossible not to go further, and if he wasn't mistaken, she wouldn't have stopped him if he had tried. He did care for her, quite deeply, but he didn't love her – or was his body telling him differently? Walking back to his lodgings, he relived their day. So much had happened, exciting, unusual things. Their emotions had been heightened, building up and building up on a day-long journey that could have had a very different ending.

He had showered and was in bed before he thought of Dilly, and that made him feel more ashamed of himself than ever. He had done what he had never believed he would or could do, yet really, reasoning it out properly, it was what he should do. He could have no future with

Dilly, and a future with Pattie was a pleasant thought – most pleasurable, in fact. He settled down to sleep, looking forward to their next date.

Alas for planning ahead. When he reached their meeting place on Tuesday, Pattie was already there, looking so forlorn that he knew something was wrong. She took hold of his arm and led him to the nearest bench.

'What is it, Pattie?' he asked, a horrible feeling of impending doom at the pit of his stomach. 'What's wrong?' She burst into tears, making him more worried than ever. 'Tell me, Pattie, please.'

'We're leaving for Florida in the morning.'

'We? What d'you mean?'

'All of us. Mr Schueyler's been promoted, and he's taking over his firm's head office next Monday. They're taking me with them.' Her tears began again.

'Couldn't you find another job? American women love having English nannies.'

'Oh, you don't understand, Roddy.'

'I'm doing my best.' He felt hurt now. 'If you liked me you'd want to stay here.'

'I do like you, but this is why I took on the nanny's job in the first place; to see more of the world. Mrs Schueyler told me at the interview that there was a strong chance of them being moved around – even as far as Europe.'

The penny had dropped. 'So this is goodbye? For good?'

Her eyes dropped guiltily. 'I'm sorry, Roddy, but I thought you'd understand.'

'All I understand is that you think more of the Schueylers than you do of me.'

'Think what you like, then.' She leapt up and ran off.

As deflated as a burst balloon, Roddy remained sitting for another hour before he rose and made his way out of the park. It served him right. He hadn't been completely honest with her, and he was being punished for that now.

When he arrived back at his lodgings, he ran upstairs and flung himself on his bed. This was a new experience for him. He had never been dumped before and it was not at all pleasant. A vague memory suddenly stirred, making him give a rather lopsided smile. He had been dumped once before, although he had actually planned to do the dumping, so it hadn't bothered him much. What was her name again? Tracy, that was it. Tracy Little. Little madam, she had been, after all the boys in their class, plus some in fourth, even as young as third, years.

This thought dredged up a far more unpleasant recollection. Tracy had thrown him over for that vile Malcolm Finnie – a name he would never forget.- the creep who had tried it on with Dilly in the girls' toilets. Thank God she'd had the sense to bite his tongue.

His thoughts jumped again. Had Dilly fallen in love with somebody by this time? Although it did give him a pang in his heart, he honestly hoped that she had. He knew that she had been as upset as he was when he jumped on the train in Aberdeen, what seemed like a decade ago, but it was the only thing he could have done – for both their sakes.

The trouble was, why was doing the decent thing, the right thing, so bloody difficult to live with?

Chapter Ten

Although *Carousel* was a stage show, it was, as Neville Richardson had assured Dyllis, as good as the film, if not better. He had taken her to a small restaurant for something to eat before they went to the theatre, and had bought her a big box of chocolates, all of which made her feel like a pampered socialite. Despite this, she was rather apprehensive of what would come later. Would he keep his promise and not take advantage of her at the hotel? Would he leave her at the door or see her up to her room?

She need not have worried. At the reception desk, he made sure that she was given the correct key and accompanied her up to the third floor. Finding her room, he waited until she opened the door. 'I really enjoyed your company tonight, Dyllis,' he said, then added, 'I hope you sleep well, my dear,' before kissing her hand and walking back to the lift.

She locked the door and sat down on the bed feeling that something was missing. She had thanked him for everything when he was driving her here, but she had expected him to kiss her properly, though probably it was best that he hadn't. Passion could rise quickly, she knew that, and he was a perfect gentleman, who wouldn't presume to kiss on a first date. A first date? She was the one who had presumed; he had only taken her out to use up a theatre ticket – there wouldn't be a second time.

After undressing and washing off her make-up, she lay down to think about the show she had seen, but the excitement of the whole evening proved too much for her, and within minutes she was fast asleep.

She awoke at her usual time in the morning, delighted that there was an en suite bathroom where she could take as much time over her shower as she wanted, and thirty minutes later she made her way down to the dining room. The elderly lady sitting smoking by the window had obviously finished eating, and rose as Dilly sat down at the other side of the room.

'I didn't realise someone else was here last night,' she said as she passed. 'I don't usually smoke in the dining room. I hope the smell won't put you off your breakfast.'

'I don't think so,' Dilly smilingly assured her. 'I've the constitution of a horse, or so my mother keeps telling me. Nothing keeps me off my food.'

'Good. I'll probably see you at dinner – how long are you staying?'

'Oh, just the one night.' The change in the woman's expression as she went out made Dilly realise that one night had a sleazy ring about it. Wasn't that what pros-titutes did? One night with a client and that was it? But what did she know about prostitutes? Smiling to herself, she tucked in hungrily to the bowl of cornflakes, followed by a large plate of what the menu described as an English breakfast – several slices of bacon, two eggs, mushrooms, black pudding, tomato, accompanied by toast and coffee.

This was the life! No shower to clean, no bed to make, no dishes to wash, just plain wall-to-wall luxury. Debating on whether or not to put the last slice of toast out of its lonely existence, she decided that it would be wiser not to, picked up the small bag with her pyjamas, toothbrush and paste and left a pound coin as a tip to the cheery little waitress. She had never tipped anyone before and hoped that a pound was enough.

It was quite a bright day, she had plenty of time, so she didn't bother to wait for a bus. This part of Great Western Road had lots of 'Bed & Breakfast' signs up, with one or two small hotels, but it soon became a proper city street lined with all kinds of shops to interest her. Holburn Junction, then down Union Street, granite buildings sparkling in the sunshine. This was one of the main routes out of Aberdeen, or into it, depending on which way you were going. She wasn't acquainted with this end of it, but she didn't have far to go now to reach her place of work.

She crossed to the other side, admiring the pillars fronting the Music Hall, into Golden Square, its well-kept grass core ringed by dozens of marked spaces for cars, the inner statue adding to the grandeur of the surrounding offices, all originally houses of wealthy Aberdonians. Every morning, she was glad that the office was in such a beautiful area.

'You look like the cat that's got at the cream.' Aimee

was in the cloakroom when she went in, looking at her with eyebrows raised. 'What were you up to last night?'

Panicking for a second, Dilly realised that her friend was only joking. Aimee knew nothing of what she *had* been up to; not that she had been doing anything wrong anyway.

She was on the verge of admitting that she had been to the theatre when it came to her that Mr Richardson, Neville, might mention that he had seen *Carousel* last night and two and two would be put together to make more than five. 'I was out with a lad I was at school with,' she was saying, when Tracy came in.

'Which lad? Not Malcolm Finnie, surely?'

'God, no! Not him!' Dilly had almost forgotten the episode in the school toilet, and her brain had to work double time to dredge up a name that would be feasible, someone who didn't live in Cruden Bay so that Tracy couldn't ask him about it. 'It was Gary McIvor, actually.'

'You never said anything about meeting him again,' Tracey accused.

'I ran into him in Peterhead on Saturday afternoon with my mum.'

'He asked you out in front of your mum?'

Dilly was struggling now; another tangled web she was weaving, or still part of the same one? 'No, Mum went into a butcher for something.'

Tracey was clearly not satisfied. 'He never struck me as a fast worker.'

'For heaven's sake, Trace! He said his dad gave him two complimentary tickets for His Majesty's Theatre and would I like to go with him. I'd never been to the theatre before, so I jumped at the chance.'

'You never said anything yesterday about it.'

Dilly shook her head as the offended Tracy stamped out, and Aimee said, 'Never mind her. She's likely jealous. Is he good-looking, this Gary?'

'Not bad, but there's nothing going on. Honestly.' She was angry at herself for mentioning the theatre at all. The whole truth could easily come out now.

Her fears gradually lessened as the day passed. Neville Richardson paid no visits to the despatch office, and she felt that in a few days, she could stop worrying.

On the way home with her father that evening, she decided that she shouldn't be worrying at all. Good gracious, she was old enough to please herself what she did, and so was Neville. She could think of him now as Neville, and if he asked her out again, she would tell her parents the truth and anyone else she wanted to. Plus, she would let him know that, as well, and if he wasn't pleased, she would never go out with him again.

Maybe that was going a bit too far, though; cutting off her nose to spite her face. He would be a real catch, had a good job, and he wasn't a sex maniac. Of course, maybe he just wasn't interested in sex, which wasn't really what she wanted. She wasn't in love with him and probably never would be, not in the same way as she loved Roddy, but he was good company and a proper gentleman, and life with him would be pretty easy.

Good grief! What on earth was she doing, letting her imagination run away with her like that? Neville Richardson probably had an 'important other' in his life, as they called it in the glossy magazines, either hidden away somewhere, or already married. He must be in his late thirties, early forties, and there must be somebody.

'You're very quiet tonight. Did something go wrong last night?'

She had nearly forgotten she was sitting beside her father. 'No, it was a great show, Dad. Outstanding. Wonderful. You know, I think I could get addicted to the theatre.'

'I meant, how did things go with Aimee's folk?'

What was wrong with her? Of course that was what he and Mum would want to know first. 'They're really nice. It's quite a big house in Mannofield, and they made me feel really at home.'

'That's good. Your mum'll be pleased about that.'

When she was told, her mother was pleased, but what she said next unsettled Dilly again. 'We'll have to ask Aimee here some time.'

It was two weeks before things for the young woman moved ahead. Neville Richardson sent a memo to her one afternoon, asking for some out-of-date paperwork he needed. In a state of anticipation, it took her some time to find everything, but eventually she tapped at his door, hoping that her face wasn't streaked with dust.

'Ah, thank you, Dyllis.' Leaning back in the large leather chair, he smiled his slightly crooked smile. 'I could have asked anybody to get these, but I wanted to talk to you.'

'Yes, Mr Richardson?'

'What happened to Neville?'

'I thought you said not to call you that in the office.'

'Only if anybody else can hear. However, to be honest, I wouldn't care if they all got to know about our friendship.'

Friendship? It was a start, anyway. 'Why did you want to talk to me, sir – Neville?'

He grinned now, a boyish grin that made his eyes twinkle. 'I am lonely, Dyllis. The night we had at the theatre made me realise just how lonely I am. So I am asking you, begging you, to come out with me again. Please! To the theatre if you wish, or anywhere else you fancy, your wish is my command. Please, Dyllis.'

She couldn't help laughing at him with his hands together as if in prayer. 'You don't need to beg, Neville. I'd love to go out with you again. Anywhere you want.'

'Tomorrow night? I will book the same room for you.'

'All right, thank you. Tomorrow it is, but where . . .?'

'Let me keep it secret? It will be something I am sure you will enjoy.'

She was smiling as she returned to the despatch office, and was so involved in her own thoughts that she didn't notice the knowing looks Aimee and Tracy exchanged.

At dinner that night, she made her announcement. 'I'll be staying out tomorrow night.'

Her mother looked up with a smile. 'Aimee and you going somewhere again?'

Gripping her resolve so that it wouldn't peter out, Dilly said, 'No, not Aimee.'

Roselle's eyebrows shot up. 'Not Aimee? Tracy, then?'

319

'Not Tracy, either.' She took a deep breath. 'It's Mr Richardson.'

'The manager? Oh, but Dilly—'

'That's good,' Brian cut it. 'As long as he isn't sixty years old with a passion for young girls.'

She had to laugh. 'He's in his thirties, I'd say, and quite good-looking. I don't think he's got a passion for young girls.'

'You're a young girl,' Roselle accused.

'I am not. I'm a young lady, and I can tell a fine man from a rotter. He's never asked any of the others out, I know that.'

'You're sure he's not married?'

'Oh, Mum, stop trying to pour cold water all over it. I'm going out with him, I'll be staying overnight in a hotel, and before you say anything, he will not be sharing my bed.'

'That's what you think, but . . .' her mother began, but Brian held up his hand.

'Look, Ros dear, she has to make her own way in life. Let her make her own mistakes. Not that I'm saying you're making a mistake,' he added hastily to his daughter, 'but you never know.'

Unable to tell them that she had proof of Neville's integrity, Dilly wisely said nothing.

The following evening proved a huge success. Neville had opted for truth with no holds barred and took the young woman to his home in Milltimber. He had also invited two other guests to partake of the wonderful meal his housekeeper had prepared. At first, Dilly was disappointed on one hand that they weren't alone, but on the other hand it was strangely something of a relief.

The other two guests were introduced to her as very old friends Mr and Mrs Greig, and she to them as Miss Lewis, a stalwart in the office. It was Mrs Greig who smiled, 'It's Roderick and Lucy, actually, but we're always known as Rod and Luce.'

'I'm Dyllis,' she responded, shyly, adding as an afterthought, 'but I'm usually called Dilly. My twin brother's called Roderick, too, but he's known as Roddy.'

During the meal, it was established that the Greigs had two sons. 'Gordon works for an oil company in Dubai,' Lucy said proudly. 'He's the one with ambitions, and I don't think he'll be satisfied until he's Managing Director of the whole company.'

'My wife loves to boast about our eldest son,' Rod grinned at Dilly. 'She leaves it to me to boast about Freddie.'

Dilly couldn't help noticing the change in Lucy's expression – from outright pride to downright shame. 'What does Freddie do?' she asked and immediately wished that she hadn't been so bold. The woman obviously wished that her husband would say no more.

Rod Grieg, however, was happy to tell their new acquaintance. 'He's an inventor.'

Intrigued, Dilly asked, 'I expect he's very good. What sort of things does he invent?'

'All kinds of excuses not to go out and take a job. He is very good at that.'

'Oh, I'm sorry. I shouldn't have said anything.' She felt really flustered.

'Don't worry, my dear. It doesn't bother me.'

It was blatantly obvious that it did bother his wife, who looked pointedly at her watch and pushed her chair back. 'I nearly forgot, Rod. We promised to go and see how Florrie is, and she needs to go to bed early, so we'll have to hurry.'

It was also plain that this was news to her husband, that it was probably an excuse made up on the spur of the moment, but he got to his feet. 'Sorry, folks. Florrie's her sister, so we'll have to love you and leave you.'

Despite the light-hearted words, Dilly could see that he was livid, and sure enough, Neville had barely closed the door after seeing them out, when the quarrel broke out. From what she could hear, Rod Greig was berating his wife, calling her a selfish bitch as they walked away and then they were too far away for her to hear any more. She had never dreamt that people of their class would behave like that, and she wondered now if she had been foolish to get involved with Neville Richardson.

'Well,' he said, as he re-entered the room, 'I can see by your face that you are trying to figure out what was going on. Let me tell you that, although Lucy thinks she is the boss, she is sadly mistaken. Rod's first wife could tell her a few home truths about him. She wouldn't admit it at first, but explained away any bruises by saying she had accidentally walked into a door, or some other lame excuse. Their marriage hardly lasted two years, and I give this one only another few months or so. He is a bully, a liar, and I wouldn't trust him as far as I could throw him.'

Dilly could scarcely believe this. 'If he's as bad as you say, why do you have anything to do with him? If it was me, I'd never let him darken my door.'

Neville gave a roar of laughter. 'I quite agree with you, my dear, but unfortunately, he is my cousin, my mother's only sister's son, and just before my aunt died, she made me promise to look out for him. She knew what kind of person he was, but blood is thicker than water. I'll tell you this, though – if he doesn't pull up his socks shortly and stop shaming me in front of guests, I'll kick him out. Now, if you think you can bear it, why don't we go through to the lounge and have a drink?'

She could see by the clock that she was too late to catch the last bus home, and she didn't like the idea of him seeing her to her hotel room in case he turned on her at some point like Rod had turned on Lucy.

'I promise I have no intention of getting you tipsy. Just the one drink and then I shall drive you to the hotel. Please? I am nothing like my cousin, I swear.'

Realising that she had no other means of getting there, and that she hadn't the faintest idea of how to walk it, she said, 'Right. One drink and that's the finish.'

The housekeeper came in at that moment to clear the table, so Dilly followed him through to a lovely big room, where, surprisingly, the large Chesterfield suite looked in sad need of attention. The house and its contents had likely belonged to his mother, she thought, which, strangely, made her feel more comfortable about being there.

When he asked what she wanted to drink, she replied honestly that she didn't know. She had never taken any drinks before except the glass of wine at the table.

'My mother liked Bailey's Irish Cream. It's not intoxicating unless you have more than a few, so one won't touch you.'

She was surprised at how thick and smooth the Irish Cream was, and sipped it slowly, enjoying every drop, and when she was finished she laid the glass on the small table beside her. She wished she could ask for a spoon to get at what was still sticking to the sides, but that would most likely be frowned on.

Neville smiled at her knowingly over his chunky glass of Laphroaig – she could see the label on the bottle. 'I think I had better tell you, Dyllis, that my mother always licked out the glass so that she didn't miss anything. Please feel free to do the same.'

She couldn't help smiling – she would have got on fine with his mother – and lifted the glass to her lips.

'Of course,' he cautioned, 'she never did it if anyone else was present.'

She recognised this as a warning for future use, but said nothing. She wasn't entirely sure that they would have a future after tonight.

At a quarter to eleven, he said, 'It is time to go now. It would not be seemly for you to roll in about midnight.'

Once again, he saw her to the door of her hotel room, waited until she had unlocked it and then, after the kiss on the back of her hand, he left. In bed, she went over the events of the unusual evening, fluctuating from being sure that she would never go out with him again, to deciding, a few seconds later, that he had done nothing wrong, so why should she finish with him? It wasn't his fault that his cousin was an absolute rotter.

Brian's first question when they were going home in the car the following night was 'Well, Dilly, where did your boyfriend take you? Somewhere special?'

During the day, she had planned exactly what to say, enough to satisfy her parents, but nothing that would start them worrying about the kind of people she was meeting. 'He took me to his house in Milltimber. He had invited some friends to dinner and he needed a hostess, really. His housekeeper had done all the cooking, and it was a wonderful meal.'

Her father's face had stiffened at the mention of her being at Neville's home. 'And when the visitors left, what happened?'

She had prepared for this. 'I went with them, of course. You surely didn't think he took me to his room and seduced me?'

'It did cross my mind.'

'I told you, Dad, he's a gentleman. He had arranged with two of his friends to drop me off at my hotel on their way home. A husband and wife,' she added with a smile, in case he jumped to the wrong conclusion.

That appeared to satisfy him, but her mother, of course, wanted to hear everything, down to the last little detail. Describing the meal was straightforward enough, and the layout of the room, but Dilly had to delve deep into her imagination to give a description of the dresses worn by the other three women – two of whom were non-existent.

At last her ordeal came to an end. 'So will you be going out with him again?' Roselle asked. 'Or has he got you down as some sort of stand-in hostess?'

'I honestly don't know, Mum, but to be honest, I wouldn't mind doing it again.'

'How much did he pay you?'

This was something the young woman had not fore-seen. Of course, her mother was right. To be hired for a whole evening was a job, not a date. 'He paid for the hotel,' she defended herself, then felt obliged to defend the man. 'He had likely been concentrating on seeing that everything was going well and had forgotten to pay me.'

'Make sure he does, then,' Brian laughed. 'Some of these toffs would conveniently keep on forgetting, if they got away with it.'

Dilly didn't bother to answer this. Neville Richardson wasn't the kind of man to cheat anybody out of anything. He had never mentioned paying her, but she had had a lovely five-course meal, plus another night in a luxurious bed, and an 'English breakfast'. She had no complaints about that. He was wooing her, to use an outdated expression, not employing her, and she was quite happy about that.

Chapter Eleven

His wife was still asleep when Frank Milne slipped out of bed. He always rose at seven on the dot and gave her a cup of tea in bed before he made the breakfast. She had done the same for him for over fifty years, so he was only repaying her, and she deserved every minute of the attention he gave her. Poor lass, she had taken badly after the stroke with not being able to do the things she had always done, but once she'd mastered the laptop, she had regained her old cheerful spirit. It did his heart good to see her tapping away with one good and one useless set of fingers. At least there was nothing wrong with her brain.

He only used the one teabag for the two-cup teapot, and filled the kettle again ready for their breakfast. Lifting the morning newspaper which had just been delivered and tucking it under his arm, he carried the cup through to the lounge, converted to a bedroom because she couldn't climb stairs and he wasn't fit to carry her.

'Shake a leg,' he said, cheerfully, his usual jocular greeting as he pushed open the door, because they were both aware that this was an impossibility.

There was no response, not even a sleepy grunt, and,

panic ripping at his innards, he laid down the cup and hurried over to the bed. 'Helen, lass, come on. I've brought your cup of tea.' He shook her shoulder gently, but there was still nothing. He knew the worst even before he touched her face. It was so peaceful, so unlined, but oh so cold.

His own face crumpled as he took her hand and rubbed it to bring some life back, although he knew that it was far too late. She must have died in her sleep, even before he got up, and he had known nothing about it. Had she known she was dying? Had she longed for him to hold her, while he'd been lying beside her snoring? Had she drawn her last breath thinking he didn't care?

'Oh, God, Helen lass,' he murmured through his tears, 'you aye wanted to do things for yourself, but surely you could have let me share your last few moments?'

The concept of her being absolutely alone at such a time overpowered him then, and it was almost thirty minutes later before he pulled his senses together, drew the curtains and went through to phone the doctor.

It was only in the evening, the undertakers having taken his wife to the funeral home, that it struck Frank how alone he was now. The young couple next door had only been here a week or two, so he hardly knew them – there had been a steady stream of tenants over the years, the Lewises being the ones who had stayed longest.

The Lewises, he thought, a lump coming into his

throat. If only Roselle had been there she'd have helped him through this. But there was nobody – no, that was wrong. He had a son, hadn't he? A son who must be told that his mother was dead. Glad of something to keep his mind occupied, he went over to Helen's desk to find Andrew's address.

Roselle had been feeling out of sorts all the day before, but put it down to worrying about her daughter. Dilly was going to spend the weekend with that Neville Richardson; that meant Friday night, Saturday and Sunday, actually two whole days and three nights. In his house. Alone with him, for she'd said the housekeeper had been given the weekend off. What decent man would do that if he'd no designs on his guest?

Roselle's sigh was long and shuddery. Brian had laughed at her, told her she was making mountains out of mole-hills and that Dilly was well able to look after herself, but that was a man for you – no understanding of morals. Just because he would never take advantage of a young girl, it didn't mean that all men were the same.

But this morning, as well as her problem with Dilly, there was something else troubling her. As soon as Brian and Dilly had left for work, she began to puzzle over what it could be, and one face kept turning up in her mind. Helen Milne! She should have kept in touch with Helen. She shouldn't have let Brian tell her what to do. She would be quite glad of a friend like Helen at the present moment. But something was telling her things were not as they should be. Something was wrong with Helen – that's what her heart was trying to tell her. Should she just say to hell with Brian and write to her old friend, or would it be best to leave things as they were? After more than fifteen years, Helen would likely not want to have anything to do with her, anyway.

She couldn't say anything to the members of the Club, that was for sure. They always laughed at her for being so old-fashioned. She couldn't get over how they joked about their daughters having sex as soon as they left school; even before they left school! What was the world coming to?

Tracy and Aimee were intrigued to see the weekend bag that Dilly brought to work on Friday morning, but she refused to tell them where she was going. Curiosity almost choked them all day, but it was not to be satisfied until they were making ready to go home and the manager came into their office, a most unusual procedure.

'All set, Dyllis?' he asked.

The surprise on the other girls' faces made him add, with a wide smile. 'To save you having to speculate any longer, Dyllis and I are to be spending the weekend together.'

Jaws dropped, eyes widened dangerously. 'You . . . and Dilly?' Tracy asked, incredulously. 'The whole weekend?'

He nodded. 'If she can put up with me for that length of time.'

Dilly had been left as speechless as Aimee. She had never expected him to come out with it openly like that, and she wasn't sure that she liked it. It had been the secrecy of the whole thing that made it all the more exciting. Now that it was common knowledge, the edge had been taken off the gingerbread – if that was the right expression. It just sounded like any other sordid, sleazy, dirty weekend, which was not how she had seen it before. Definitely not! She wasn't going to be given the label 'boss's totty', as they spoke about, or 'Richardson's bit on the side'. No way!

'I've changed my mind,' she burst out. 'I'm sorry, Neville, but sleeping with the boss was never my idea. Sleeping with a man who loved me, a man I loved, that would have been different, but this . . .' She shrugged as she walked to the door. 'I'd better hurry or my Dad'll have gone home without me.'

There was dead silence until they heard her leaving the cloakroom, with, presumably, her weekend bag, and then Mr Richardson, chalk-white, said, 'I'm sorry, girls, that you had to witness that. I should have been more sensitive, and I certainly had not planned to seduce Dyllis, but there you go.' He whipped round and left.

'Jesus!' Tracy exclaimed, immediately covering her mouth at the swearing.

Aimee nodded. 'I hadn't a clue. Had you?'

'Not a sausage. I wonder how long they've been seeing each other?'

'You think they've been seeing each other for a while, then?'

'He wouldn't ask her to spend a weekend with him on

a first date, surely?' Tracy was suddenly struck by another thought. 'She'll get the sack.'

'You think so?'

'Or she'll leave. She can't work here now.'

While they discussed her, Dilly had run to where her father usually picked her up, and to her relief, he spotted her and stopped. 'Change of plans?'

'Don't ask,' she told him.

From the set of her chin, he could tell that she was extremely upset, and wisely made no further awkward remarks.

Dilly ran straight upstairs as soon as she went into the house, and Brian was able to warn Roselle not to say anything to upset the girl. 'There must have been a row, or something, and we'll just have to wait till she gets over it before she tells us anything'

The weekend passed as if they were in mourning, the only conversations being centred on events on the television news broadcasts, and even then, Dilly only appeared for one meal a day, although her mother took her up a cup of tea in the afternoons.

Monday morning brought another surprise, when the young woman said she wasn't going to go to work. 'I think you were right, Dad,' she said, making a face. 'Neville was only after a dirty weekend, and he even came into our office to boast about it.'

'But why —' Roselle began, but stopped when Brian's foot gently tapped her shins under the table.

Well aware that both she and Neville would find it impossible to work with the same firm, in the same building, Dilly spent most of the forenoon typing a letter of resignation on her computer, glad that she didn't have to waste paper even if she changed her mind a dozen times about the wording, but at last she was more or less satisfied and printed it. She asked that the three weeks she was due as holidays should be taken as her notice, so that she would not have to go back and face the man.

On her walk to the tiny sub-Post Office, she wondered if she had over-reacted to Neville's announcement. Maybe he hadn't been boasting that he was going to seduce her. Maybe he had just meant to be open about their relationship. Maybe she had shit in her own backyard, as she had heard Frank Milne saying once, long ago. She had only been five, but it was such a weird expression that it must have implanted itself in her mind.

Fancy remembering Frank Milne, though. She wondered what had become of him and his wife after fifteen years. Helen had been such a kind woman, like a grandmother to her and Roddy, really. She stopped walking abruptly as something occurred to her. At the moment, she was in dire need of someone to advise her on what to do with her life, and who better than Helen? Her spirits lifting, she posted the letter and almost skipped home.

Roselle had seen for herself how upset her daughter was, and had decided not to ask where she had been, but she looked brighter now. 'OK?' she said, hoping this would encourage her to open up.

Dilly took the bait. 'I've just posted a letter of resignation. But I was thinking, I know I'll have to find another job, but I need to talk to somebody about – things.'

'You can talk to me. I'm always willing to listen.'

'Thanks Mum, but it has to be an outsider. I was thinking of going down to see Helen Milne. You used to say she was always giving people advice. What d'you think?'

Roselle took no time to think. 'It's a marvellous idea. I'll come with you.'

'But I know Dad didn't want you to have anything to do with her, so what'll he say?'

'We won't tell him. I'll say I'm taking you away to help you to get over . . .'

'Are you sure, Mum? I don't want to come between you and Dad.'

'I'll be very diplomatic, Dilly. I've been thinking about Helen a lot lately, and I'd love to see her and Frank again.'

When the concocted story was put to him, Brian was quite supportive. 'It'll do you both good to get away for a couple of days. If I wasn't so busy at work, I'd come with you. Have you decided where you're going?'

It was Roselle who came up with the impromptu untruth. 'To Glasgow, to do some shopping. We've never been there, either of us.' Her brain added silently, 'I don't think I have, anyway.' She had given up all hope, some years ago, of regaining her memory.

Her husband almost scuppered their plan by saying that he'd take them right to the station to make sure that they got on to the right train, but realising their true destination would be revealed if he did, Roselle succeeded in talking him out of it. 'Don't make yourself late for work, Bri. We'll easily manage.'

Within half an hour, both women were on their way to Grangemouth, looking forward excitedly to seeing their old friends again.

Andrew Milne had, to his father's great relief, flown over from Belfast as soon as he received the letter about his mother's death. 'You should have let me know as soon as Mum took ill,' he scolded Frank. 'How long was it?'

'Apart from the effects of the stroke, she wasn't ill at all. I rose to make her a cup of tea, and when I went back with it, she was dead.'

A great surge of guilt swamped the younger man. He had never seen his father so upset, and he wished with all his heart that he had come to see his parents at least once a year, instead of letting Peggy talk him into going to Spain, Greece, Germany, Italy or wherever her fancy took them. She was a selfish woman, but he had been stupid to let her rule the roost like that. He had a duty to the old folk, they brought him up, they gave him a good education, and they'd had not a penny of benefit from it. Not that he supposed they had wanted that, but it would have been the proper thing to do.

Now, his mother was dead and his father was a frail old man, having looked after her for years. He wouldn't have minded that, of course. He'd have been happy to do it for his beloved wife, for there was never any doubt about how much they loved each other.

The funeral was taking place the following day, and his father did not feel like going out at all, so they were sitting silently, one on each side of the fire, when someone rang the doorbell. He jumped up. 'I'll go, Dad.'

There had been a steady stream of people coming to tender their condolences – his mother had been well liked – so he was not at all surprised to see two smartly dressed ladies, one perhaps forty-something and the other looked to be her daughter, early twenties, probably. Both seemed very surprised to see him, but he said, graciously, 'You'd better come in.'

To his amazement, his father jumped up and embraced the older lady as if she had been a long-lost daughter. 'Oh, Roselle, if only you'd come a week ago.' Tears coursed down his wrinkled face

Seeing her puzzlement, Andrew stepped in. 'My mother died a few days ago. Her funeral's tomorrow, if you'd like to come.'

His father turned outraged eyes on him. 'Of course they'll come. As long as Roselle has turned up, Helen wouldn't care a docken who else was there.'

Over the next hour or so, Andrew learned what had happened, why the Lewises had moved away, why Roselle had only sent Christmas cards without giving her address. It was so similar to his own behaviour that he could empathise with her guilty sorrow, share her regret for neglecting a woman she loved. Frank, of course, was getting to know the girl, the grown-up Dilly who had also flung her arms around him and wept tears for the missing years.

When evening came – after they had consumed the fish and chips that Andrew had insisted on going out for although they had all said they weren't hungry – they sat quietly by the fire, Andrew and Dyllis mostly listening to Frank and Roselle reliving many happy memories, not forgetting the harrowing time they had shared when Dilly had contracted meningitis.

At last, Roselle glanced at the Westminster clock on the mantelpiece. 'Oh, I'm sorry, Frank, it's nearly midnight. You must be absolutely shattered.'

He shook his silver head. 'I'm OK, lass. It's well past my usual bedtime, but I'm still as bright as a button.'

His grey, lined face, however, told a different story, so she turned to her daughter. 'We'd better go, Dilly. We'll find a bed and breakfast somewhere for the night.'

'Indeed, you will not!' the old man declared, indignantly. 'Helen would give me a right tongueing if I turned you out.'

'I'll sleep on the settee so you can have my bed,' Andrew offered, thinking that it would be no hardship to him. He slept on the settee often enough at home when Peggy locked him out of their room.

Only Frank's insistence that they stay made Roselle agree to this arrangement, but the hands of the Westminster clock on the mantelpiece had gone round a full hour before they were all housed up and, too tired to do anything else, each one fell asleep within minutes.

The next morning was bright and clear, but because this was the day of the funeral, spirits were much lower than they had been the night before. Andrew had breakfast ready when the two women came downstairs, but he felt somewhat awkward with them. 'You must think I've been a terrible son. Never looking near the old folk for years.'

'You're no worse than I was,' Roselle said, sadly. 'Frank and Helen were like parents to me, yet I dropped them when Brian was promoted and we moved away.'

'That was Dad's fault,' Dilly reminded her, but the remark was really intended for Andrew's benefit. 'He wouldn't let Mum give Helen our new address.'

He frowned in puzzlement. 'Why was that?'

Roselle shook her head impatiently. 'He had the idea that Helen was nosey.'

'Mum always wanted to know everything about everybody,' he grinned.

'That's just because she was interested,' Frank said, coming in at that moment. 'She never meant to be nosey, but that's how some people looked at it.'

'That kind of people weren't worth bothering about,' Roselle said, angrily defending the woman who had been like a mother to her. 'Brian included,' she added.

They sorted out an order for using the bathroom, and eventually they were all washed and dressed – Frank and Andrew in smart parson-grey suits, and Roselle wishing that she had something darker than a beige coat to wear over her pink dress, but she hadn't known she would need any mourning clothes. Dilly's tailored grey trouser suit didn't look so out of place, but, really, what did clothes matter in the long run? She was so glad that she was having the opportunity to say a proper farewell to this fine woman, whom she had treated so badly, and she could only hope that Helen would be aware that she was there.

Roselle flatly refused to go back to the house after the funeral. 'We have to go home, Frank, but I'm so glad I got here in time. I only wish . . .'

He slid his arm round her back. 'No, lass, let bygones be bygones. We can't change the past, however much we'd like to. But now you've got back in touch, you'll not forget me, will you?'

She turned to hug him fondly. 'I never did forget you, either of you, it was . . .'

'Aye. Well.'

Andrew, waiting to drive them to the railway station, had settled Dilly into one of the rear seats and was holding the front passenger door open for her. They waved to Frank until the car turned the corner, and then Andrew said, 'He's bearing up quite well.'

'It must have been a terrible shock for him, though, and he'll feel even worse when you go home.'

'Yes, that's why I've made up my mind – maybe you'll think I'm silly—' He stopped, as if still undecided, and then continued, 'I'm going to take him home with me.'

'What a good idea!' Dilly exclaimed.

It was a moment or so before Roselle said, 'I don't know. He's been in that house since he and Helen were married. He won't want to leave it – all the memories.'

'But he's always getting older,' Andrew pointed out. 'There'll come a time when he won't be able to look after himself.'

'Yes, I see what you're getting at, but how would you like to be yanked out of the only home you've known for fifty years?'

His eyes never leaving the road in front of them, he gave her hand a light pat. 'You're a very caring woman, Roselle. Do you know that?'

'I care very much what happens to your father, I know that.'

'I know that too, and I can't thank you enough for it, but I have to look to the future. What does that hold for him? It's a bugger, really.'

A deep silence followed, until, by tacit consent, they started to speak about other things, their own likes and dislikes, including Dilly in the conversation until, before they knew it, they were drawing up in the station car park.

'You don't have to wait,' Roselle said, as they got out. 'Get back to your dad and spend as much time with him as you can. When were you intending going home?'

'I had three weeks' vacation to come, so I took them all. There's still sixteen days to go, so, hopefully, I'll manage to persuade him to come with me.'

'What'll your wife say about having him living with you?'

'I neither know, nor care,' he said, turning away. 'Goodbye, Roselle, Dilly. Hope to see you again some time.'

'He's nice,' the girl observed, as they made their way to the correct platform.

'Mmmm.' But Roselle's mind had suddenly jumped ahead. How was she to explain all this to Brian?

*   *   *

Frank was very glad of his son's company, but he was not at all enamoured of the idea of going to live with him. He'd only met Frank's wife once, at their wedding, and she'd seemed a right madam. A woman who liked her own way and damn the consequences.

No, he didn't think he could be happy there. In any case, as he told Andrew, he was quite happy here in his own house. It would be lonely without Helen, of course, but he'd get used to that, and he'd always have his memories. He'd been doing all the cooking and housework for years, anyway, so that would be nothing new.

The two men were sitting by the fire this rainy day, and having exhausted all topics of conversation that they could think of, were awkwardly silent.

'Dad,' Andrew said, suddenly, 'what are those big books sitting along the sideboard?'

So used to flicking them with the feathery duster every other day, Frank had more or less forgotten what they were, but suddenly realising that this was something that should interest his son, he said, 'Take one down and have a look.'

Removing the volume nearest to him, Andrew was, indeed, eager to see the contents of *Album No. 1,* and settled down to follow the lives of his parents, starting with their wedding portrait – an upright young man in a dark suit beaming proudly as he stood behind the very beautiful girl in the chair, who was smiling shyly at the camera.

'I didn't realise Mum was so pretty,' he exclaimed. 'No wonder you married her.'

'She's always been lovely to me,' Frank murmured. 'And she'll carry on being lovely for as long as I live.'

'You're an old romantic, aren't you? But you were quite handsome yourself.'

'Get away with you.'

Number One having divulged all its secrets, the two men recalling all the events of Andrew's childhood, he replaced it and took down *Album No.2*. He couldn't help chuckling at all the different hairstyles he had adopted during his teens, and the number of different girls he had dallied with. One, in particular, held his attention for some time.

Mandy Troup had been his steady for about two years, and, came the awful truth, she was the one he should have married. Even-tempered, but not a mouse, she could stand her ground about anything she felt strongly about, but, unlike Peggy, she could be rational.

'Would you have any idea what happened to Mandy, Dad?' he asked, casually.

'She's married with five kids,' Frank smiled, then sobered as he recalled how Helen had felt about that. 'They should have been our grandchildren,' she had said once. But there was no need to tell the lad that.

So the afternoon went on, but it was *Album No.5* that seemed to interest Andrew most – dozens of snaps of two charming children, following their growth from babies to toddlers to sturdy, possibly five-year-olds. Even the typed captions at the foot of each page gave him no hint as to their identities. 'Who are Dyllis and Roderick, Dad?' he asked, because something told him that they had once meant a lot to him.

Frank shook his head at this ignorance. 'Dilly and Roddy, of course.'

'The Dilly who was here?'

'Aye, Roselle's twins, but she told me Roddy's in New York now. They were real close twins, you know, hardly ever separate.'

'So it's Roselle with them in these snaps? I didn't recognise her.'

'Ah, well, she's changed a good bit. From some of the things she said, I think she's had her troubles.'

'You mean with her husband?'

'No, not Brian, they're still OK, it's Dilly. She's had some problem with a man, that's why Roselle took her away for a few days, but I think she looked a lot better by the time she went home. Both of them did, in fact.'

'You've no snaps of Brian, then? I'd be interested to see what he looks like.'

'He was usually away working all day, but there should be one or two of him. He was a nice lad, though your mother thought he didn't like her.'

It was only two pages later that Andrew gasped, 'Is this him?'

Frank glanced over. 'Aye, that's him.' Seeing his son's concerned face, he said, 'Hey, are you all right?'

'I think so. Listen, I'm sure this man's face is on a wanted poster I see every day.'

'No, no, it couldn't be Brian. He's not a criminal.'

'The man I'm speaking about *is* a criminal. I can't say any more than that, but would you mind if I take this snap with me? I'll give it back as soon as I can.'

'Help yourself, lad, but I'm sure you're barking up the wrong tree.'

Andrew felt equally as sure that he wasn't, but said nothing further. Unfortunately, the damage had been done. The easy camaraderie that had sprung up between them again was lost, and he could hardly wait for the next morning, to get back into harness.

First up, Andrew looked up his mother's address book where Roselle had written in her address in Cruden Bay before she went home. Mr & Mrs Brian Lewis. Well, that certainly wasn't the name on the poster, but a change was only to be expected for a crime of that magnitude. Of course, he was only a suspect, but, from the information given at the time, he was also the only suspect, so his guilt was practically a certainty.

Roselle couldn't get over how well Brian had accepted the fact that she and Dilly had gone to see Helen. In fact, he even seemed to be pleased about it. 'Frank must really have been devastated by her death,' he had said. 'I'm sure he was glad to see you.'

'He was,' she admitted, 'and I'm really glad I went. I didn't know she had died, of course, and I felt bad about all the troubles she had suffered, but Frank never criticised me at all. His son was there as well, and he's just as nice as his father.'

For a second, it did look as if Brian was feeling angry, or apprehensive, or something not very nice, then he smiled, a sad little smile. 'How did Frank behave towards him? Was he annoyed that his son had never gone to see them?'

'Not while we were there, but to be honest, I don't think there was any ill feeling.'

'Well, it's good that you went just at that time. What's Frank going to do now?'

'Andrew was speaking about taking him to live with them, but I don't think his father would want that. As far as I could make out, he doesn't have a very good opinion of his daughter-in-law.'

'Well it's up to him. He shouldn't be bulldozed into something he doesn't want. Um – how was Dilly while you were there?'

'She was fine. Like me, she was quite emotional at seeing Frank again, especially at such a sad time, but she cheered up. I think she's got over whatever happened to her.'

'Thank heaven for that. She seemed to be quite happy when she was studying the "Situations Vacant" column in the paper last night, and she's speaking about going to the Job Centre in Aberdeen, or whatever they call it nowadays.'

On his way to work, Brian heaved a huge sigh of relief. Helen's death had put an end to the fear that had hung over him like the Sword of Damocles ever since he'd learned that her son was a policeman in Northern Ireland. Having thought that he'd got away with what he had done, it was as if God was playing cat and mouse with him, and although it had got slightly easier since they'd moved to Cruden Bay, there had still been moments when blind terror had gripped him like a vice.

But, God be praised, he had nothing whatsoever to worry about now. It was over! After all, it was more than twenty years ago.

Chapter Twelve

Roderick Lewis liked the work he was doing, he quite liked the people he worked with, but he didn't like New York much – especially in summer. It was so hot, he felt like ripping off every stitch of his clothing, but modesty prevailed. It might have been fun, though. Imagine the reaction he'd get from the painted, over-self-conscious females he generally came in contact with. Instead of the usual supercilious sneers they bestowed on him, they would be fighting to get the attention of this man with the manly physique, and he would take great pleasure in brushing them off – one by one.

Ah, well, there was no harm in dreaming, was there? Nor was there any point in it. He would have to face up to the fact that he didn't fit in here, that making friends wasn't as easy as it had been in Aberdeen, even in Cruden Bay. In other words – he was just plain homesick. He longed to see his mother again, to exchange banter with his father, to spend time with Dilly. No, no, don't go down that road again!

The hand he slid into his back pocket found nothing, zippo, zilch! His first thought was what had he done with his wallet? Then it dawned on him – he had been robbed.

He'd been sitting here daydreaming instead of keeping alert to that possibility. Only now it wasn't just a possibility, it was a godawful certainty. He couldn't pay for his coffee and burger. The police would be sent for, he'd be arrested and bundled into their van, he'd be charged with theft and nobody would believe that he was the victim, not the thief.

He cast his eyes round wildly, but of course the person responsible wouldn't have hung around. He didn't come in here often, but he had been a few times before, so maybe one of the seemingly dozens of girls and boys would remember him and vouch for him? Probably not.

He caught the eyes of the elderly lady sitting in the corner. She looked respectably approachable, but, on the other hand, she could be the kind that would yell for help if anyone did approach her. The only others diners were very young, sixteen or seventeen at most, who were totally absorbed in deep conversation – about boyfriends, no doubt. He couldn't appeal to them. They would either spit in his eye or kick his private parts.

'Excuse me, but can I be of any help?'

He looked up into bright blue eyes twinkling with – surely not? – amusement. 'Sorry?'

'I recognised your panic, and I knew exactly what had happened. You must be more careful, you know. You shouldn't keep your money in your hip pocket. Just asking for trouble. Now, if you'll allow me to settle your bill, I . . .'

'Oh, no, I can't let you . . . you don't know me.'

'I know you better than I did a few moments ago.' She giggled at his perplexed expression. 'I know you're

348

Scottish, and you're not altogether happy working in New York. You've proved you're a perfect gentleman, unable to ask anyone for help, not even those young girls over there, which also tells me you are as honest as the day is long.'

Flabbergasted by her shrewd appraisal of his character he mumbled, 'But I can't . . .'

'You can. There's no shame in letting someone get you out of a hole. I've had to depend on other people many times in my life, and I'm none the worse for it.'

Yielding, he let her pay his bill as well as her own and followed her out of the diner.

'I can't thank you enough, Mrs, um, Miss . . .'

'It's Mrs Rayner, but just call me Philly, everybody does. Short for Phyllis.'

'That's funny. My sister's name is Dyllis, but she's always called Dilly.'

'You see, we're meant to be friends. What's your name?'

'Full name Roderick Lewis, known as Roddy. Look, I don't live far from here. If you walk round with me, I can write you a cheque for what I owe.'

'I don't want to be paid back, but something tells me you need someone to talk to. A problem shared is a problem halved, you know. I promise not to judge you, whatever you tell me. I'm a good listener.'

He pushed aside all thoughts of returning to work, and in his Spartan room on the second floor, he told her exactly why he had left Cruden Bay in the first place, and why the friendship he had made in Liverpool had gone belly-up. As she had said, she was a good listener, nodding here and there but not saying one word until his relationship with the nanny had also been exposed.

'I can understand why you feel the world's against you, Roddy, especially after having your wallet stolen as well, but you have your whole life ahead of you. Look for another job, if you think that would help, or—' She broke off and regarded him searchingly. 'I do realise that you can't tell your parents how you feel abut Dilly, but is there nobody in Scotland who would understand and advise you? An older person, a woman preferably, who knows your family and can see a way out for you?'

Roddy couldn't explain why the only person to come into his mind was Helen Milne. 'There is a woman,' he murmured, slowly, 'though I haven't seen her for years. We used to call her Auntie Helen, but she was more like a grandmother than an aunt. We lived next door to her, so she knew the family well, and I'm sure I could talk to her . . . like I've been talking to you.'

'Yes, but sadly, not knowing your parents, I can't really advise you. The only thing I *can* say is – go back to Scotland. See this Auntie Helen. Be brutally honest about Dilly, lay your heart absolutely bare to her, let her question you as much as she wants, discuss it with her, give careful consideration to any advice she gives you. Go ahead only when you are absolutely convinced of what you should do.' She held out her hand. 'That's my considered opinion. Goodbye, Roderick Lewis and good luck.'

He was so involved in absorbing everything she had said, that she was probably out on the sidewalk before he realised she had gone. She had given him much to think about, however, and, sure that she was right, he wrote a letter of resignation there and then – explaining that family problems prevented him from working the stipulated four weeks' notice – and went out to post it. It didn't take him long to pack, his possessions still fitted easily into the travelling bag he'd arrived with, and then, remembering that there was one more thing he should do, he went downstairs to settle up with Mrs Flynn.

'This is sudden, isn't it?' she asked.

'I got a phone call at work today, asking me to go home as soon as I could. I don't know what's wrong, exactly, but . . .'

His landlady was very sympathetic. 'You poor thing, you must be worried out of your mind. Well, I should really charge you till the end of the month, but it's not your fault.'

'I'd rather pay the full amount. It's not your fault, either. It'll have to be a cheque, though. Somebody stole my wallet this afternoon.'

'A cheque'll do nicely, but things do seem to be going against you. You'll be leaving in the morning? What time would you like breakfast?'

'I meant to say. I won't need any breakfast. I'll get something to eat at the airport.'

'I can give you an earlier breakfast, it's no bother.'

'No, no. I'll have time to shove in. The check-in's a couple of hours before the actual flight.'

Surprisingly, he slept like a log, and wakened even before his alarm went off at five. To save any awkward goodbyes, he washed and dressed quietly, picked up his

bag and crept down the stairs. On the way to the air
terminal, he wondered if there was enough in his bank
account to cover the fare to Edinburgh. If not, he'd have
to go by sea, and he couldn't waste that much time. He
needed help now! Today!

Chapter Thirteen

Frank Milne had cleared up after his evening meal and was checking the television listings in his morning paper to see if there was anything on worth watching. Too many nights lately it had been rubbish on each of the five channels. Maybe Andrew had been right and he should get connected to one of those satellite companies he'd read about. Oh, good! One of David Attenborough's programmes. He couldn't see whether it was a repeat or not, the print was too small, so he had likely seen it before, but they were worth watching twice. Maybe he'd better go to the toilet first, though. He never got much warning nowadays and he didn't want to miss anything.

He had just sat down again when someone rang his front doorbell. It never failed, did it? Every time he was looking forward to watching something decent, somebody rang the bell. He levered himself up gradually, frowning when the bell rang again. Cheeky beggar! One of them door-to-door salesmen, likely, young lads that couldn't wait. His stiff fingers fumbled at the lock, awkward Yale thing, but he didn't unfasten the chain; safer to wait to see who was there. He edged the door open, another young lad. 'Yes?'

'It's me, Uncle Frank. Roddy Lewis.'

'Roddy? No, it can't be. Your mother said you were in America.'

'I was, but I've given up my job. Can I come in? I want to speak to Auntie Helen.'

The old man shook his head as he slid back the chain. 'Come in, lad, but you're too late. My Helen died a couple of weeks ago.'

'Oh, no! I'm really sorry, Frank.'

Closing the door quietly behind him, Roddy turned round and, emotion overwhelming him, flung his arms around the frail figure, shorter and thinner than he remembered, and they wept together for the woman they had both loved.

They drew apart at last, rather self-conscious about showing their feelings, and sat down as if their legs had given way. After a few moments of awkward silence, Frank said, 'Was it something important you wanted to speak to Helen about? Maybe I could help?'

Having almost given up all hope of any solution to his problem, Roddy's story came out in a rush, then in fits and starts, in long silences that the other man did not interrupt, until at last, he said, 'I know there's nothing you can say, Frank. I know I should keep away from Dilly, but, oh, I wish I could see her again.'

'She's grown up into a lovely young woman, I can tell you that.'

'You've seen her?'

So now it was Frank's turn to talk, to tell how Roselle had also been too late to see Helen. 'She'd wanted to ask her to sort Dilly's problems out, but I think the lass went home after the funeral in an easier frame of mind anyway. Just being away from what's troubling you can make a difference, you know.'

Another silence fell, and then Frank said, 'Helen always knew there was something going on between you and Dilly. She said you loved each other too much, and that was when you were just toddlers. It was even more noticeable once you started school – at least, after Dilly started. She'd been at death's door with meningitis, if you remember, and ever after that, you were scared to let her out of your sight in case something bad happened to her.'

'I still feel like that. You know, she once said we should just run away together and get married and have babies.'

'That had been when she was still just a wee lass, though?'

'We had left school by that time, and I had to fight myself really hard not to do it. We could have gone far enough away so nobody would know us, and we could have been happy.'

'But your conscience wouldn't have let you stay happy, lad. You knew it was wrong.'

'But Dilly didn't care that it was wrong, and maybe we *would* have been happy.'

Frank just shook his head, then changed the subject. 'I've just realised. You must be hungry. Will I make something for you?'

'I don't feel like eating. Maybe a cup of tea and a slice of toast?'

Five minutes later, munching quite happily, he said, 'That's what I missed most over there. A decent cup of tea.'

'I've heard other folk saying that. But I was thinking – what are you intending doing?'

Roddy lifted his shoulders. 'I hadn't thought about it.'

'Well, what about stopping here with me? You'll find a job easily enough, and we'd be company for each other in the evenings. If you don't want your mother to know, I'll not tell her, but I'd advise you to tell her yourself. She'll be worried sick if she stops getting letters from America.'

'What if she comes here to see me? She might take Dilly with her. What'll I do?'

'You'll have to be the gentleman. You'll surely manage to cope if you just see her for an hour or two once or twice a year?'

'I'll try.'

Roselle had been late in getting home from her friend's house and was feverishly trying to think of something quick to make for the evening meal. She had just settled on cheese pudding with vegetables when she heard the car drawing up outside. It couldn't be Brian home already? But it wasn't Brian. The man who rang the bell turned out to be an absolute stranger. 'Mrs – um – Pritchard?'

'No, I'm sorry. You've got the wrong house. My name is Lewis. What number are you looking for?'

'Thirty-one, which is what it says on your door, Mrs Lewis. It's your – um – husband I came to talk to.'

Mystified, she said, 'Brian should be home in about half an hour, but are you sure it's him you want? His name's not Pritchard, either.'

'I am quite sure. It *is* your husband I have come to see. I'll wait in the car.'

She waited until he had walked down the path before she closed the door. She didn't feel at all happy about it. Why would he ask for Pritchard first then say it was Lewis he wanted? She put the cheese pudding into the oven then prepared the vegetables, all the while worrying about the man waiting outside. She had a shivery feeling in the pit of her stomach that he was trouble, that she should have closed the door in his face and said nothing, but it was too late to do anything now.

When Dilly walked in some thirty-five minutes later, she said, 'You're late, and where's your father?'

Her daughter looked surprised at her tone. 'We were held up on the road, and Dad's gone off with a man who was waiting for him.'

'Did you hear what the man said to him?'

'He showed Dad an identity card, or something like that, probably to show he was who he said he was.'

'And that was all?'

'Dad went off with him in his car. The man's, I mean.'

'I hope he's not long. Our meal will be spoiled.'

'I'm not waiting, and neither should you.'

Roselle obediently dished up for two, but only her daughter enjoyed the cheese pudding. Roselle was too worried to eat anything. Maybe she was being over-sensitive, but her fears grew with every passing minute. What on earth was going on?

As soon as he saw the man jumping out of his car and striding towards him, Brian's mind jumped to the correct conclusion – a conclusion he had expected for many years but it had been so long in happening that he had come to believe that it never would.

'Look,' he had said, as steadily as he could, 'I'd rather you didn't come into the house. You can say whatever you want to me, but I don't want my wife to know. There's a place we can get peace, it's not far, just a few miles along the road. I'll show you.'

His first thought had been Slains Castle, the old ruin quite near the edge of the cliff, but then he remembered the Bullers of Buchan, that slim path between two fearsome inlets of the sea. It was farther along, but it was better.

After the car had been parked, Brian ushered him along the dangerously narrow path, pointing down to the seething waters far below on both sides. 'It's some sight, isn't it? Doesn't it make you wonder how it happened?'

'I haven't time to be wondering about anything; I've more important things to attend to. I suppose you know why I've come?'

'Not really. May I see your ID again?' After glancing at the card, he went on, 'So you're a Detective Inspector? From Peterhead? I think you have come on a short wild goose chase.'

'I think not. We have been alerted by the constabulary in Belfast that you are on their Wanted list.'

'My name is Brian Lewis and you won't find that on any wanted poster.'

'Possibly not, but Brian Lewis is not your real name, is it? You needn't try to pull the wool over my eyes, a photograph of you as Brian Lewis has been verified as being Robin Pritchard, wanted for embezzlement and murder.'

Brian made a reasonably good attempt at a scornful laugh. 'You can't possibly think that I'm capable of murder? Look at me – an ordinary, straightforward man with a wife and twins to my name.'

Jed Logan's red face deepened in intensity. 'Twins? The records say one son only.'

'I have a daughter and a son. Yes, Detective Inspector, you've got the wrong man.'

'I am still obliged to take you in for questioning.'

The time had come for Brian to carry out the plan he had hastily made when he suggested this dangerous spot for their discussion, but something held him back. It would be so easy to give this lump of a bobby a sharp push and send him to his doom, but . . . he wasn't finding it easy – second time around. He wasn't really a killer. He'd done it once out of sheer desperation, and although he was going to lose everything that he had saved then, he couldn't bring himself to do it. Twenty years of dreading this very moment had taken their toll on him.

He gave a sigh of defeat. 'All right, Inspector, you win, but will you please let me say goodbye to my wife first?'

Roselle had been trying all night to contact her son despite Dilly's stream of orders for her to take a rest. 'We need to stay together as a family to support your dad,' she wailed now. 'Are you sure that horrible 'tec didn't tell you anything?'

Dilly shook her head sadly. 'I told you. All he said was

Dad had committed a crime about twenty years ago, and he was being taken in for questioning.'

'He told me years ago what he'd done, but it was only about a hundred pounds or so he stole. They surely wouldn't wait twenty years to arrest him for that.'

'There must have been more to it than that, Mum.' The detective had said something about a body being found, but she couldn't believe that they suspected her father of being a murderer, and she was definitely not going to tell her mother about it.

'I can't cope with this, Dilly. I don't know what to do. I need a man to be there for me. I need Roddy.'

Her daughter agreed wholeheartedly with this. She, too, desperately needed Roddy. Then she remembered a man who would be more than delighted to give them support. 'Why don't we go to back to see Frank? I'm sure he'd know what to do.'

'But I don't want to bother him. It's not long since he lost Helen, and we can't saddle him with our troubles as well.'

'I'm sure he'd be glad to help, Mum. Go and pack a weekend bag for us and I'll let the police know we'll be down there if they need us.'

'You'd better phone Frank, as well, to let him know we're coming.'

'No, he'll worry about us till he knows what's what. We'll just go, he won't mind.'

After their evening meal, Frank Milne and Roddy were taking it easy by the fireside. They had spent the whole afternoon working in the garden, Roddy mowing the patch of lawn and trimming the edges, and Frank hoeing the paths and weeding the little rockery.

'I'm glad that's done,' Frank observed suddenly into the comfortable silence that had fallen. 'The longer I keep putting it off, the worse it gets. Helen always used to keep me up to the mark.'

'With two of us now, though, we'll manage fine.'

'Once you've got a job, you won't have time. Have you written to your mother yet?'

'I will when I'm back on my feet properly. I don't want her worrying.'

'Roddy, lad, she'll worry more about not hearing from you.' The older man had been on the verge of calling her several times, but had thought better of it. If he alienated the boy, he'd most likely up tail and off.

He closed his eyes again, thinking about the strange coincidences that had happened to him recently. First, though it had been in response to a letter, his son had turned up after years of more or less ignoring his mother and father; second, Roselle had appeared with Dilly out of the blue; third, Roddy had popped in and it was like having a son again. He was a lucky man, a very lucky man, especially having had a woman like Helen for a wife for almost fifty years.

The doorbell rang, breaking into his pleasant thoughts, and even before Roddy was halfway to answer it, it rang sharply again. He couldn't hear who it was, his hearing wasn't good nowadays, but he was not left long to wonder. In came an avalanche of bodies, tangled through each other and making for his chair. It took him only a split second to recognise the older woman, and he struggled valiantly to get to his feet.

'Don't get up, Frank,' the older woman laughed. 'It's just Dilly and me, and I see Roddy's here already.'

There was much hugging and kissing, and it didn't escape the old man that Roddy, although obviously trying to fend his twin off at first, eventually gave an affectionate, if very brief, greeting.

When the emotions had subsided a little, the explanations began, and by the time the young man went out to get fish and chips for four, he and Frank were acquainted with the stark facts of Brian's arrest and, like the women, they could not believe it.

'I knew he'd embezzled some money,' Roselle remarked sadly, 'But he swore it was only a hundred pounds or so, and it was over twenty years ago. I wouldn't have thought the police would still have been looking for him for that.'

Dilly had not taken much part in the discussion – the other three mentally excusing her for three different reasons – but now she said, 'It wasn't just the money Mum. That 'tec said Dad was wanted for . . . murder.'

'Murder?' The word was ejaculated on three levels – contralto, baritone and bass – as the others voiced their horror.

She nodded. 'Yes, that's what he said. And he said Dad's name wasn't really Brian Lewis. It was Robin Pritchard.'

The worry disappeared from Frank's face. 'That's it, then,' he declared, positively. 'They've got the wrong man. I knew there had to be some mistake. This Pritchard must look a bit like Brian, and some stupid bobby's got it into his head that Brian is guilty.'

Four very relieved people went to bed then, Roddy opting for the old bed-settee to give his mother and Dilly the bed he had been using. Not one of them, however, had a decent night's sleep, each going over the events of the day as he or she knew them, and coming to the conclusion that the trauma could be put behind them now, although a tiny niggle of doubt refused to be ignored.

The following forenoon brought a telephone call from Peterhead to tell Roselle that her husband had been taken to Belfast, to be charged with, and eventually to stand trial for, embezzlement and murder. At that point, the receiver fell from her lifeless hands, to be picked up by Frank, who more or less took over the role of a defence lawyer.

'There has definitely been a grave mistake,' he said, authoritatively. 'I have known Brian Lewis for over twenty years, and I know him to be an honest, hardworking, loving husband and father. Perhaps he did embezzle a small amount of money when he was much younger, but there is not the slightest doubt in my mind that he has never, ever, committed a murder. What?' His face chalk-white, he listened for several minutes before replacing the receiver and almost collapsing into his chair.

'What did they say?' Roddy demanded. 'What's wrong, Frank?'

Casting an apologetic glance at Roselle, the old man said, 'It's all true, I'm afraid. He's admitted everything. Oh, God, I can't tell you how sorry I am.'

His arms round his mother and his sister, Roddy said,

'I can't understand. Why did he have to embezzle any money, for a start? And who did he murder? And why?' He looked round at Roselle accusingly. 'Did you know anything about it?'

She plumped into the other armchair, face drawn, eyes displaying a deep emotion. 'I knew about the money. He told me . . . I heard him praying when we were in the hospital waiting to hear what was wrong with Dilly when she had meningitis, remember? He was asking God not to punish Dilly for the crimes he had committed. It didn't really mean much at the time, I was so worried, but I thought about it later and asked him. He said he'd stolen money, but he'd done it for me and you two, so we could have a better life.'

'He never said anything about a murder, though?'

'If he had, I'd have told the police.' She shook her head as if to clear her thoughts, and added, 'Maybe I wouldn't have, though – I loved him too much.'

A brooding silence fell, Frank wishing that he could do something to help Roselle, Dilly praying that it was all just a nightmare, Roddy wondering how any man could have lived a normal family life for so long after having killed somebody. Roselle herself was hardly capable of any rational thought, until a tiny flash of memory suddenly made sense.

'Whatever happened,' she murmured, 'that was what made me forget everything that had happened before it. What Brian wanted me to forget.' Her eyes glazed for a moment, as if she were trying to recall it. 'He took us away from here after Helen told me Andrew was a policeman in

364

Northern Ireland. It's all fitting now. He'd been scared Andrew would recognise him if he ever came to see you, Frank.'

Frank's eyes widened in surprise. 'Andrew did recognise him. When he was here, Roselle. He was looking through Helen's photo albums, and he asked if I'd mind if he took the snap. He sent it back very quickly, though.'

'He'd likely taken a copy,' Roddy pointed out.

'But I never gave him your address, Roselle, so he couldn't have . . .'

'I wrote it in Helen's address book.'

'So my son's responsible for breaking up your family. Oh, Roselle, you don't know how sorry I am.'

'It wasn't your fault, Frank.' She leaned across and patted his hand. 'It was Fate, and you know this? I'm glad. The murder must have had something to do with the money, and if he stole because of me and the twins – well, he wasn't really to be trusted, was he?'

Roddy stepped in now. 'I think we'd better stop playing guessing games. We'll likely find out soon enough what happened.'

Chapter Fifteen

Brian Lewis – real name Robin Pritchard – was subjected to several days of questioning, over and over again, getting at the truth from a dozen different angles, until the police were in no doubt that he was guilty of all charges. On one point, however, he was adamant. 'I refuse to give Roselle's real name. She knew nothing about it.'

Written Statement of Robin Pritchard

It all started when I met Roselle waiting for a bus in a deluge of rain. I heard someone saying there had been an accident and all traffic had been held up. I asked if she would like to come for a coffee with me to pass the time and that was it. We made a date, even though we had both said we were married. She had a three-month-old daughter and I had a baby son, less than a week older.

We fell madly in love, and kept seeing each other, though she always said she felt guilty. Another factor that drove us together was the fact that her husband was often away on business, and my wife was involved with so many charities that she was hardly ever at home.

366

I began to dream of taking Roselle away, of buying a house somewhere and bringing up the children together. The trouble was, of course, that I couldn't afford this, so I began to fiddle with my clients' moneys. The old ladies, who trusted me implicitly, never knew that I was cheating them, and the hundreds of pounds soon grew into thousands, until I had enough to buy a new home for us somewhere else.

Unfortunately, my boss had discovered that the books did not tally, and suspecting that I was the culprit, he came to confront me. Young and hot-blooded, I let fly with my fist and knocked him to the ground, but he hit his head on the corner of the dining-room table and never got up again.

First making sure that he had definitely stopped breathing, I dragged him to the kitchen, lifted the trapdoor to the cellar and tipped him in. I was lucky. He had told nobody of his suspicions and when the auditors discovered the discrepancies, they thought he was the thief and had run away to avoid being caught. He was a bachelor, so no one else suffered.

I might never have had the courage to carry out the plan I had made if it had not been for Fate. A gang, who pretended to be IRA, had been experimenting with explosives, and one night they decided to try them out on Roselle's street. Her husband was away at the time, and I had just left her when the noise began. Realising what was happening, I ran back just as the house next door got it, and I managed to get her and the baby away a few seconds before her house was flattened.

My wife had gone on a week's holiday with an old friend, so I got my son and told the babysitter to let my wife know when she came home that I had taken him. I also took all the false identity papers I'd had made in readiness and, under our new names, my family left Belfast for good – a man and his wife with twin babies.

Luckily for me, Roselle had been so traumatised by the bombing that her previous life was blotted from her mind, and the children, of course, were too young to remember anything. I have lived an exemplary life ever since, and the only thing I have ever regretted was the accidental killing of an innocent man, although I did toy with the idea of finishing off the detective who arrested me, but only because he was putting an end to my idyll.

Signed Brian Lewis

which I will remain till the end of my life, but if you insist –

Signed Robin Pritchard

The statement read, agreed upon and signed, he had two questions to ask. The first was, 'I can't understand how you found the body', to which he was told that workmen had found it after his wife reported a vile smell coming up from the cellar, something that had never crossed his mind.

His second question was, 'How did you manage to find me, after all this time?'

A detective he had never seen before stepped forward now. 'I saw a snap of you in a photograph album.'

'Where? Not in Cruden Bay I'm sure.'

'In my father's house.'

'How did he come to have a snap of me? Do I know him?'

'You knew him very well at one time – and my mother.'

'The only person who ever took photos of me and my family was . . .'

'My mother, Helen Milne.' Andrew was taken aback by the half-strangled laugh that escaped the prisoner.

'Helen Milne? Even after her death she's causing trouble for me.' He stopped, looking sheepishly at the other man. 'That was unforgivable, and I'm truly sorry.'

'My mother never knew about you.'

'I'm truly sorry. But what about Frank?'

'He is very well, thank you.' After a brief hesitation, clearly wondering whether or not to say it, Andrew went on, 'As a matter of fact, he is doing what you should be doing – looking after your family.'

'What do you mean?'

After being told all that had happened, and why and when it had happened, Brian said, seriously, 'I'm glad he's looking after them.'

'And they're looking after him,' Andrew pointed out.

'How is Roselle bearing up?'

'I believe she has decided to stay there and be Father's housekeeper. He's getting a bit doddery in his old age.'

'I'm glad she'll be with him. He and your mother were very good to us when our Dilly was so ill.' Brian stopped momentarily, recalling events he had forgotten for many years, and then pulled a wry face. 'What about them? Dilly and Roddy, I mean. How are they dealing with this?'

'Much better than you'd imagine, I think. Knowing they're not twins has made a big difference to them. Dad says they're—' He broke off, embarrassed.

'It's OK,' Brian assured him. 'I knew they loved each other, have done since they were kids, and that love grew deeper as they grew older. That's another thing I regret, now I come to think about it. I should have told them the truth long ago, but at least they can get together properly now. I'm pleased for them.'

'So am I. They make a lovely couple.'

At that precise moment, Dilly and Roddy were in Cruden Bay packing all the personal items they were being allowed to keep, before the house was sold. With the proceeds from the sale of the contents of the rented house, plus what was left in his London bank account and which had been gaining interest every year, most of the money he had embezzled would be made up.

'I can't really believe this,' Dilly said now. 'It seems too good to be true, and we can be married and live happily ever after, just as I always knew we would.'

'It's not all happiness, though,' Roddy reminded her, 'but thank goodness a murderer doesn't get hanged nowadays.'

'But Dad's not a real murderer. It was an accident.'

She looked so woebegone that he was sorry for pricking her balloon. 'Of course it was, and the court will take that into account. Now, have we got everything, do you think? We'd better be going if we're going to catch that train.'

While he turned the key in the lock, however, he couldn't help thinking that their future wouldn't be as rosy as Dilly believed. No matter how innocent they were – it was their father who had told the world that they were twins – public opinion would probably be against them. People would believe that they had been lovers for years, and they'd have to be really strong to withstand all the knowing looks and whispered scandal.

'You're awful quiet, Roddy,' Dilly said, as they walked away from what had been their home. 'Is something wrong?'

Looking at her, his heart swelled with love and he cast aside all his doubts. 'Nothing's wrong, Dil,' he smiled. 'In fact, I've never been so happy in all my life.'

Roselle was engrossed in the book she was reading, and as Frank Milne looked across at her bent head, some silver hairs already showing in the brown, he thanked God for his good luck in having such a woman, nearly as industrious as his Helen had been in her younger days, willing to look after him and his house, as well as her twins. He shook his head at his stupidity. They weren't real twins, and it was a blessing things had turned out so well for them, too. By the look of things, it wouldn't be long before they were getting married and setting up house on their own, and he wished them all the luck in the world.

It was poor Roselle that was getting the rough end of the stick. The man she'd thought was her husband wasn't her husband at all, and was going to be locked up for who knew how long. The man who had been her real husband had declared her dead after seven years and married somebody else. That didn't seem to bother her, though.

Of course, Brian had come off worst of all, but it was his own fault, wasn't it? Stealing was a crime, and punching a man hard enough to knock him down wasn't much better. He'd be punished for that, as he should be, but it was more than likely that Roselle would be there for him when he came out of prison.

Not that *he* would live to see that, Frank thought, smiling a little. He didn't care, he'd had a good life and he wasn't done yet. Roselle, the daughter he had never had, had told him he should take up bowling, and by Jove, he might just do that. He wasn't seventy yet, and it would be something to look forward to.